Praise for Michael Connelly

'*The Late Show* introduces a terrific female character . . . The pacing is breathless . . . Connelly expertly hides a trail of bread crumbs that leads straight to the denouement, with so much else going on that it's impossible to see where he's heading'   *New York Times*

'A master of the genre'   Stephen King

'Crime thriller writing of the highest order'   *Guardian*

'Superb storytelling, with a feisty new character of whom we will hear far more, this cements Connelly's place at the very top of the crime-writing tree'   *Daily Mail*

'The new novel from America's greatest living crime writer is a gripping thrill ride that will entrance you and keep you reading until the small hours'   *Daily Express*

'Fast-paced, gripping and stamped all over with Connelly's trademark stunning police procedural and authentic forensic detail, this is as close up to the real-life work of a detective you can get'   *Lancashire Evening Post*

'Classy and clever, with a tenacious heroine' *Sunday Mirror*

'Connelly is a crime writing genius' *Independent on Sunday*

Also by Michael Connelly

A former police reporter for the Los Angeles Times, Michael Connelly is the internationally bestselling author of the Harry Bosch thriller series. The TV tie-in series – *Bosch* – is one of the most watched original series on Amazon Prime and is now in its third season. He is also the author of several bestsellers, including the highly acclaimed legal thriller, *The Lincoln Lawyer*, which was selected for the Richard & Judy Book Club in 2006, and has been President of the Mystery Writers of America. His books have been translated into thirty-nine languages and have won awards all over the world, including the Edgar and Anthony Awards. He spends his time in California and Florida.

To find out more, visit Michael's website or follow him on Twitter or Facebook.

www.michaelconnelly.com
f /MichaelConnellyBooks
y @Connellybooks

MICHAEL CONNELLY

THE LATE SHOW

ORION

An Orion paperback

First published in Great Britain in 2017
by Orion Books
This paperback edition published in 2018
by Orion Books,
an imprint of The Orion Publishing Group Ltd,
Carmelite House, 50 Victoria Embankment
London EC4Y ODZ

An Hachette UK company

1 3 5 7 9 10 8 6 4 2

A CIP catalogue record for this book
is available from the British Library.

ISBN 978 1 4091 4754 1

Typeset by Input Data Services Ltd, Somerset

Printed and bound in Great Britain by Clays Ltd, St Ives plc

MIX
Paper from
responsible sources
FSC® C104740

www.orionbooks.co.uk

In Honor of Sgt. Steve Owen
Los Angeles County Sheriff's Department
Executed, shot through the badge, October 5, 2016

1

Ballard and Jenkins rolled up on the house on El Centro shortly before midnight. It was the first call of the shift. There was already a patrol cruiser at the curb out front and Ballard recognized the two blue suiters standing on the front porch of the bungalow with a gray-haired woman in a bathrobe. John Stanley was the shift's senior lead officer—the street boss—and his partner was Jacob Ross.

"I think this one's yours," Jenkins said.

They had found in their two-year partnership that Ballard was the better of the two at working with female victims. It wasn't that Jenkins was an ogre but Ballard was more understanding of the emotions of female victims. The opposite was true when they rolled up on a case with a male victim.

"Roger that," Ballard said.

They got out of the car and headed toward the lighted porch. Ballard carried her rover in her hand. As they went up the three steps, Stanley introduced them to the woman. Her name was Leslie Anne Lantana and she was seventy-seven years old. Ballard didn't think there was going to be much for them to do here. Most burglaries amounted to a report, maybe a call for the fingerprint car to come by if they got lucky and saw some indication that the thief had touched surfaces from which latent prints were likely to be pulled.

"Mrs. Lantana got a fraud alert e-mail tonight saying someone attempted to charge a purchase on Amazon to her credit card," Stanley said.

"But it wasn't you," Ballard said to Mrs. Lantana, stating the obvious.

"No, it was on the card I keep for emergencies and I never use it online," Lantana said. "That's why the purchase was flagged. I use a different card for Amazon."

"Okay," Ballard said. "Did you call the credit-card company?"

"First I went to check on the card to see if I'd lost it, and I found my wallet was missing from my purse. It's been stolen."

"Any idea where or when it was stolen?"

"I went to Ralphs for my groceries yesterday, so I know I had my wallet then. After that I came home and I haven't gone out."

"Did you use a credit card to pay?"

"No, cash. I always pay cash at Ralphs. But I did pull out my Ralphs card to get the savings."

"Do you think you could've left your wallet at Ralphs? Maybe at the cash register when you pulled out the card?"

"No, I don't think so. I'm very careful about my things. My wallet and my purse. And I'm not senile."

"I didn't mean to suggest that, ma'am. I'm just asking questions."

Ballard moved in another direction, even though she wasn't convinced that Lantana had not left her wallet behind at Ralphs, where it could have been snatched by anybody.

"Who lives here with you, ma'am?" she asked.

"No one," Lantana said. "I live alone. Except for Cosmo. He's my dog."

"Since you got back from Ralphs yesterday, has anyone knocked on your door or been in the house?"

"No, nobody."

"And no friends or relatives visited?"

"No, but they wouldn't have taken my wallet if they had come by."

"Of course, and I don't mean to imply otherwise. I'm just trying to get an idea of comings and goings. So you're saying you have been home the whole time since Ralphs?"

"Yes, I've been home."

"What about Cosmo? Do you walk Cosmo?"

"Sure, twice a day. But I lock the house when I go out and I don't go far. He's an old dog and I'm not getting any younger myself."

Ballard smiled sympathetically.

"Do you take these walks at the same time every day?"

"Yes, we keep a schedule. It's better for the dog."

"About how long are your walks?"

"Thirty minutes in the morning and usually a little longer in the afternoon. Depending on how we feel."

Ballard nodded. She knew that all it would have taken for a thief cruising the area south of Santa Monica was to spot the woman walking her dog and follow her home. He'd keep watch to determine if she lived alone and then come back the next day at the same time when she took the dog out again. Most people didn't realize that their simplest routines made them vulnerable to predators. A practiced thief would be in and out of the house in ten minutes tops.

"Have you looked around to see if anything else is missing, ma'am?" Ballard asked.

"Not yet," Lantana said. "I called the police as soon as I knew my wallet was gone."

"Well, let's go in and take a quick look around and see if you notice anything else missing," Ballard said.

While Ballard escorted Lantana through the house, Jenkins went to check whether the lock on the back door had been tampered with. In Lantana's bedroom, there was a dog on a sleeping cushion. He was a boxer mix and his face was white with age. His shining eyes tracked Ballard but he did not get up. He was too old. He emitted a deep-chested growl.

"Everything's all right, Cosmo," Lantana assured him.

"What is he, boxer and what?" Ballard asked.

"Ridgeback," Lantana said. "We think."

Ballard wasn't sure whether the "we" referred to Lantana and the dog or somebody else. Maybe Lantana and her veterinarian.

The old woman finished her survey of the house with a look through her jewelry drawer and reported that nothing other than the wallet seemed to be missing. It made Ballard think about Ralphs again, or that the burglar possibly thought he had less time than he actually had to go through the house.

Jenkins rejoined them and said there were no indications that the lock on the front or back door had been picked, jimmied, or in any other way tampered with.

"When you walked the dog, did you see anything unusual on the street?" Ballard asked the old woman. "Anybody out of place?"

"No, nothing unusual," Lantana said.

"Is there any construction on the street? Workers hanging around?"

"No, not around here."

Ballard asked Lantana to show her the e-mail notice she had received from the credit-card company. They went to a small nook in the kitchen, where Lantana had a laptop computer, a printer, and filing trays stacked with envelopes. It was obviously the home station, where she took care of paying bills and online ordering. Lantana sat down and pulled up the e-mail alert on her computer screen. Ballard leaned over her shoulder to read it. She then asked Lantana to call the credit-card company again.

Lantana made the call on a wall phone with a long cord that stretched to the nook. Eventually the phone was handed to Ballard and she stepped into the hallway with Jenkins, pulling the cord to its full extension. She was talking to a fraud alert specialist with an English-Indian accent. Ballard identified herself as a detective with the Los Angeles Police Department and asked for the shipping address that had been entered for the credit-card purchase before it was rejected as possibly fraudulent. The fraud alert specialist said he could not provide that information without court approval.

"What do you mean?" Ballard asked. "You are the fraud alert specialist, right? This was fraud, and if you give me the address, I might be able to do something about it."

"I am sorry," the specialist said. "I cannot do this. Our legal office must tell me to do so and they have not."

"Let me talk to the legal office."

"They are closed now. It is lunchtime and they close."

"Then let me talk to your supervisor."

Ballard looked at Jenkins and shook her head in frustration.

"Look, it's all going to the burglary table in the morning," Jenkins said. "Why don't you let them deal with it?"

"Because they won't deal with it," Ballard said. "It will get lost in the stack. They won't follow up and that's not fair to her."

She nodded toward the kitchen, where the crime victim was sitting and looking forlorn.

"Nobody said anything about anything being fair," Jenkins said. "It is what it is."

After five minutes the supervisor came on the line. Ballard explained that they had a fluid situation and needed to move quickly to catch the person who stole Mrs. Lantana's credit card. The supervisor explained that the attempted use of the credit card did not go through, so the fraud alert system had worked.

"There is no need for this 'fluid situation,' as you say," he said.

"The system only works if we catch the guy," Ballard said. "Don't you see? Stopping the card from being used is only part of it. That protects your corporate client. It doesn't protect Mrs. Lantana, who had someone inside her house."

"I am sorry," the supervisor said. "I cannot help

you without documentation from the courts. It is our protocol."

"What is your name?"

"My name is Irfan."

"Where are you, Irfan?"

"How do you mean?"

"Are you in Mumbai? Delhi? Where?"

"I am in Mumbai, yes."

"And that's why you don't give a shit. Because this guy's never going to come into your house and steal your wallet in Mumbai. Thanks very much."

She stepped back into the kitchen and hung up the phone before the useless supervisor could respond. She turned back to her partner.

"Okay, we go back to the barn, write it up, give it to the burglary table," she said. "Let's go."

2

Ballard and Jenkins didn't make it back to the station to begin writing the report on the Lantana burglary. They were diverted to Hollywood Presbyterian Medical Center by the watch commander to check out an assault. Ballard parked in an ambulance slot by the ER entrance, left the grille lights on, and then she and Jenkins entered through the automatic doors. Ballard noted the time for the report she would write later. It was 12:41 a.m. according to the clock over the reception window in the ER waiting room.

There was a P-1 standing there, his skin as white as a vampire's. Ballard gave him the nod and he came over to brief them. He was a slick sleeve and maybe even a boot and too new in the division for her to know his name.

"We found her in a lot on Santa Monica by Highland," the officer stated. "Looked like she had been dumped there. Whoever did it probably thought she was dead. But she was alive and she sort of woke up and was semiconscious for a couple minutes. Somebody had worked her over really good. One of the paramedics said she might have a skull fracture. They have her in the back. My TO's back there too."

The assault may have now been elevated to an abduction, and that increased Ballard's level of interest. She checked the patrolman's plate and saw his name was Taylor.

"Taylor, I'm Ballard," she said, "and this is Detective Jenkins, fellow denizen of the dark. When did you get to Super Six?"

"First deployment actually," Taylor said.

"Right from the academy? Well, welcome. You'll have more fun in the Six than you'll have anywhere else. Who's your training officer?"

"Officer Smith, ma'am."

"I'm not your mother. Don't call me ma'am."

"Sorry, ma'am. I mean—"

"You're in good hands with Smitty. He's cool. You guys get an ID on the vic?"

"No, there was no purse or anything but we were trying to talk to her while we were waiting on the paramedics. She was in and out, not making a lot of sense. Sounded like she said her name was Ramona."

"She say anything else?"

"Yeah, she said 'the upside-down house.'"

"'The upside-down house'?"

"That's what she said. Officer Smith asked if she knew her attacker and she said no. He asked where she was attacked and she said 'the upside-down house.' Like I said, she wasn't making a lot of sense."

Ballard nodded and thought about what that could mean.

"Okay," she said. "We'll go back and check things out."

Ballard nodded to Jenkins and headed toward the door that led to the ER's treatment bays. She was wearing a charcoal-gray Van Heusen suit with a chalk

9

pinstripe. She always thought the formality of the suit went well with her light brown skin and sun-streaked hair. And it had an authority that helped overcome her slight stature. She pulled her jacket back enough for the receptionist behind the glass window to see the badge on her belt and open the automatic door.

The intake center consisted of six patient assessment and treatment bays behind closed curtains. Doctors, nurses, and technicians were moving about a command station in the center of the room. There was organized chaos, everybody with a job to do and some unseen hand choreographing it all. It was a busy night, but every night was at Hollywood Pres.

Another patrol officer was standing in front of the curtain for treatment bay 4 and Ballard and Jenkins proceeded directly toward him. He had three hash marks on his sleeves— fifteen years on the department—and Ballard knew him well.

"Smitty, the doc in there?" Ballard asked.

Officer Melvin Smith looked up from his phone, where he had been composing a text.

"Ballard, Jenkins, how's it hanging?" Smith said. Then: "Nah, she's alone. They're about to take her up to the OR. Fractured skull, brain swelling. They said they need to open her head up to relieve the pressure."

"I know the feeling," Jenkins said.

"So she's not talking?" Ballard asked.

"Not anymore," Smith said. "They sedated her and I overheard them talking about inducing a coma till the swelling goes down. Hey, how's Lola, Ballard? Haven't seen her in a while."

"Lola's good," Ballard said. "Did you guys find her, or was it a call?"

"It was a hot shot," Smith said. "Somebody must've called it in but they were GOA when we got there. The vic was just lying there alone in the parking lot. We thought she was dead when we first rolled up."

"Did you call anybody out to hold the crime scene?" Ballard asked.

"Nah, there's nothing there but blood on the asphalt, Ballard," Smith said. "This was a body dump."

"Come on, Smitty, that's bullshit. We have to run a scene. Why don't you guys clear here and go hold the lot until we can get a team there. You can sit in the car and do your paperwork or something."

Smith looked to Jenkins as the senior detective for approval.

"She's right," Jenkins said. "We have to set up a crime scene."

"Roger that," Smith said, his tone revealing he thought the assignment was a waste of time.

Ballard went through the curtain into bay 4. The victim was on her back on a bed, a light green hospital smock over her damaged body. She was tubed in both arms and nose. Ballard had seen plenty of victims of violence over her fourteen years with the department, but this was one of the worst cases she had seen where the victim was still alive. The woman was small and looked to be no more than 120 pounds. Both of her eyes were swollen tightly shut, the orbit of the right eye clearly broken under the skin. The shape of her face was further distorted by swelling down the entire right side, where the skin was abraded. It was clear she had been

beaten viciously and dragged across rough terrain—
probably the parking lot—on her face. Ballard leaned in
close over the bed to study the wound on the lower lip.
She saw that it was a deep bite mark that had savagely
split the lip. The torn tissue was being held together by
two temporary stitches. It would need the attention of a
plastic surgeon. If the victim survived.

"Jesus Christ," Ballard said.

She pulled her phone off her belt and opened the
camera app. She started taking photos, beginning with
a full-face shot of the victim, then moving into close-
ups of the individual facial wounds. Jenkins watched
without comment. He knew how she worked.

Ballard unbuttoned the top of the smock to examine
the chest for injuries. Her eyes were drawn to the left
side of the torso, where several deep bruises were delineated and straight and appeared to have come from an
object rather than someone's fists.

"Look at this," Ballard said. "Brass knuckles?"

Jenkins leaned in.

"Looks like it," he said. "Maybe."

He pulled back, disgusted by what he saw. John Jenkins had twenty-five years in and Ballard knew he had
been running on empty for a long time when it came to
empathy. He was a good detective—when he wanted to
be. But he was like a lot of guys who had been around
for so long. He just wanted a place to be left alone to do
his job. The police headquarters downtown was called
the PAB, for Police Administration Building. Guys like
Jenkins believed that PAB stood for Politics and Bureaucracy, or Politics and Bullshit, take your pick.

The night-shift assignment was usually awarded to

those who had run afoul of the politics and bureaucracy of the department. But Jenkins was a rare volunteer for the eleven-to-seven shift. His wife had cancer and he liked to work during her sleeping hours so he could be home every day when she was awake and needed him.

Ballard took more photos. The victim's breasts were also damaged and bruised, the nipple on the right side torn, like the lip, by gnashing teeth. The left breast was round and full, the right smaller and flat. Implants, one of which had burst inside the body. Ballard knew it took a hell of an impact to do that. She had seen it only once previously, and that victim was dead.

She gently closed the smock over the victim and checked the hands for defensive wounds. The fingernails were broken and bloody. Deep purple marks and abrasions circled the wrists, indicating that the victim had been bound and held captive long enough to produce chafing wounds. Ballard guessed hours, not minutes. Maybe even days.

She took more photos and it was then that she noticed the length of the victim's fingers and the wide spread of the knuckles. Santa Monica and Highland—she should have understood. She reached down to the hemline of the gown and raised it. She confirmed that the victim was biologically a man.

"Shit, I didn't need to see that," Jenkins said.

"If Smitty knew this and didn't tell us, then he's a fucking asshole," Ballard said. "It changes things."

She shoved the flare of anger aside and got back on track.

"Before we left the barn, did you see if anybody was working in vice tonight?" she asked.

"Uh, yeah, they have something going on," Jenkins said. "I don't know what. I saw Pistol Pete in the break room, brewing a pot."

Ballard stepped back from the bed and swiped through the photos on her phone screen until she came to the shot of the victim's face. She then forwarded the photo in a text to Pete Mendez in the Hollywood vice unit. She included the message:

Recognize him? Ramona? Santa Monica stroll?

Mendez was legendary in the Six, but not for all the right reasons. He had spent most of his career as a UC in vice and as a younger officer was often put out on the stroll posing as a male prostitute. During these decoy operations he was wired for sound because the recording was what made the case and usually caused the suspect to plead guilty to the subsequent charges. A wire recording from one of Mendez's en-counters was still played at retirement parties and unit get-togethers. Mendez had been standing on Santa Monica Boulevard when a would-be customer rolled up. Before agreeing to pay for services, the john asked Mendez a series of questions, including how large his penis was when erect, though he did not use such polite terms.

"About six inches," Mendez responded.

The john was unimpressed and drove on without another word. A few moments later a vice sergeant left his cover location and drove up to Mendez on the street. Their exchange was also recorded.

"Mendez, we're out here to make busts," the sergeant

chided. "Next time a guy asks how long your dick is, *exaggerate*, for crying out loud."

"I did," Mendez said—to his everlasting embarrassment.

Ballard pulled the curtain back to see if Smith was still hanging around but he and Taylor were gone. She walked to the command station to address one of the nurses behind the counter. Jenkins followed.

"Ballard, Jenkins, LAPD," she said. "I need to speak to the doctor who handled the victim in bay four."

"He's in two right now," the nurse said. "As soon as he's out."

"When does the patient go up for surgery?"

"As soon as space opens."

"Did they do a rape kit? Anal swabs? We also need to get fingernail clippings. Who can help us with that?"

"They were trying to save his life—that was the priority. You'll have to talk to the doctor about the rest."

"That's what I'm asking. I want to speak to—"

Ballard felt her phone vibrate in her hand and turned away from the nurse. She saw a return text from Mendez. She read his answer out loud to Jenkins.

"'Ramona Ramone, dragon. Real name Ramón Gutierrez. Had him in here a couple weeks back. Priors longer than his pre-op dick.' Nice way of putting it."

"Considering his own dimensions," Jenkins said.

Drag queens, cross-dressers, and transgenders were all generally referred to as dragons in vice. No distinctions were made. It wasn't nice but it was accepted. Ballard had spent two years on a decoy team in the unit herself. She knew the turf and she knew the slang. It

15

would never go away, no matter how many hours of sensitivity training cops were subjected to.

She looked at Jenkins. Before she could speak, he did.

"No," he said.

"No, what?" she said.

"I know what you're going to say. You're going to say you want to keep this one."

"It's a vampire case—has to be worked at night. We turn this over to the sex table, and it will be just like that burglary—it will end up in a stack. They'll work it nine to five and nothing will get done."

"Still no. It's not the job."

It was the main point of contention in their partnership. They worked the midnight shift, the late show, moving from case to case, called to any scene where a detective was needed to take initial reports or sign off on suicides. But they kept no cases. They wrote up the initial reports and turned the cases over to the appropriate investigative units in the morning. Robbery, sexual assault, burglary, auto theft, and so on down the line. Sometimes Ballard wanted to work a case from beginning to end. But it wasn't the job and Jenkins was never inclined to stray one inch from its definition. He was a nine-to-fiver in a midnight-shift job. He had a sick wife at home and he wanted to get home every morning by the time she woke up. He didn't care about overtime—money- or workwise.

"Come on, what else are we going to do?" Ballard implored.

"We're going to check out the crime scene and see if there really is a crime scene," Jenkins said. "Then we go back to the barn and write up reports on this and the old lady's burglary. If we're lucky, there will be no more callouts and we'll ride the paperwork till dawn. Let's go."

He made a move to leave but Ballard didn't follow. He spun and came back to her.

"What?" he demanded.

"Whoever did this is big evil, Jenks," she said. "You know that."

"Don't go down that road again, because I'm not going with you. We've seen this a hundred times before. Some guy's cruising along, doesn't know the territory, sees a chick on the stroll and pulls over. He makes the deal, takes her into the parking lot, and gets buyer's remorse when he finds a Dodger dog under the miniskirt. He beats the living shit out of the guy and drives on."

Ballard was shaking her head before he was finished with his summation of the case.

"Not with those bite marks," she said. "Not if he had brass knuckles. That shows a plan, shows something deep. She was tied up for a long time. This is big evil out there and I want to keep the case and do something for a change."

Technically he was the senior partner. He made the call on such things. Back at the station Ballard could appeal to command staff if she wanted to, but this was where the decision had to be made for partnership unity.

"I'm going to swing by the crime scene and then go back to start writing," Jenkins said. "The break-in goes to the burglary table, and this—this goes to CAPs. Maybe even homicide, because that kid isn't looking too good in there. End of story."

Decision made, he again turned toward the doors.

He had been so long in the job that he still called the individual crime units *tables*. Back in the '90s that's what they were—desks pushed together to create long tables. The burglary table, the crimes against persons table, and so on.

Ballard was about to follow him out, when she remembered something. She went back to the nurse behind the counter.

"Where are the victim's clothes?" she asked.

"We bagged them," the nurse said. "Hold on."

Jenkins stayed by the door and looked back at her. Ballard held up a finger, telling him to wait. From a drawer at the station the nurse produced a clear plastic bag with whatever belongings were found with the victim. It wasn't much. Some cheap jewelry and sequined clothing. There was a small mace dispenser on a key chain with two keys. No wallet, no cash, no phone. She handed the bag to Ballard.

Ballard gave the nurse a business card and asked to have the doctor call her. She then joined her partner and they were walking through the automatic doors to the sally port when her phone buzzed. She checked the screen. It was the watch commander, Lieutenant Munroe.

"L-T."

"Ballard, you and Jenkins still at Hollywood Pres?"

She noted the urgent tone in his voice. Something was happening. She stopped walking and signaled Jenkins closer.

"Just leaving. Why?"

"Put it on speaker."

She did.

"Okay, go ahead," she said.

"We've got four on the floor in a club on Sunset," Munroe said. "Some guy in a booth started shooting the people he was with. An RA is heading your way with a fifth victim that at last report was circling the drain. Ballard, I want you to stay there and see what you can get. Jenkins, I'm sending Smitty and his boot back to grab you. RHD will no doubt be taking this over but they will need some time to mobilize. I've got patrol securing the scene, setting up a command post, and trying to hold witnesses, but most of them scattered when the bullets started flying."

"What's the location?" Jenkins said.

"The Dancers over by the Hollywood Athletic Club," Munroe said. "You know it?"

"Roger that," Ballard said.

"Good. Then, Jenkins, get over there. Ballard, you come as soon as you finish up with the fifth victim."

"L-T, we need to set up a crime scene on this assault case," Ballard said. "We sent Smitty and—"

"Not tonight," Munroe said. "The Dancers is an all-hands investigation. Every forensic team available is going there."

"So we just let this crime scene go?" Ballard asked.

"Turn it over to day shift, Ballard, and let them worry about it tomorrow," Munroe said. "I need to go now. You have your assignments."

Munroe hung up without another word. Jenkins gave Ballard a told-you-so look about the crime scene. And as if on cue, the sound of an approaching siren flared in the night. Ballard knew the difference between the siren from a rescue ambulance and from a cop car. This was Smitty and Taylor coming back for Jenkins.

"I'll see you over there," Jenkins said.

"Right," Ballard said.

The siren died as the patrol SUV came down the chute to the sally port. Jenkins squeezed into the back and it took off, leaving Ballard standing there with the plastic bag in her hand.

She could now hear the distant sound of a second siren heading her way. An ambulance bringing the fifth victim. Ballard looked back in through the glass doors and noted the time on the ER clock. It was 1:17 a.m. and her shift was barely two hours old.

3

The siren died as the ambulance came down the chute into the sally port. Ballard waited and watched. The double doors at the back of the ambulance opened and the paramedics brought out the fifth victim on the gurney. She was already hooked to a breathing bag.

Ballard heard the team communicate to the waiting ER team that the victim had coded in the ambulance and that they had brought her back and stabilized her, only to have her flat-line once again as they were arriving. The ER team came out and took control of the gurney, then moved swiftly through the ER and directly into an elevator that would take them up to the OR. Ballard tagged along behind and was the last one on before the doors closed. She stood in the corner as the team of four medical workers in pale blue surgical garb attempted to keep the woman on the gurney alive.

Ballard studied the victim as the elevator jolted and slowly started to rise. The woman wore cutoff jeans, high-top Converses, and a black tank that was soaked in blood. Ballard noticed the tops of four pens clipped to one of the jeans pockets. She guessed that this meant the victim was a waitress at the club where the shooting took place.

She had been shot dead center in the chest. Her face was obscured by the breathing mask but Ballard put her at mid-twenties. She checked the hands but saw no rings or bracelets. There was a small black-ink tattoo depicting a unicorn on the woman's inside left wrist.

"Who are you?"

Ballard looked up from the patient but could not tell who had addressed her, because everyone was wearing masks. It had been a male voice but three of the four people in front of her were men.

"Ballard, LAPD," she said.

She pulled the badge off her belt and held it up.

"Put on a mask. We're going into the OR."

The woman pulled a mask out of a dispenser on the wall of the elevator and handed it to her. Ballard immediately put it on.

"And stay back and out of the way."

The door finally opened and Ballard quickly exited and stepped to the side. The gurney came rushing out and went directly into an operating room with a glass observation window. Ballard stayed out and watched through the glass. The medical team made a valiant attempt to bring the young woman back from the dead and prepare her for surgery, but fifteen minutes into the effort they called it and pronounced her dead. It was 1:34 a.m. and Ballard wrote it down.

After the medical personnel cleared the room and went on to other cases, Ballard was left alone with the dead woman. The body would soon be moved out of the operating room and taken to a holding room until a coroner's van and team arrived to collect it, but that gave Ballard some time. She entered the room and studied the woman. Her shirt had been cut open and her chest was exposed.

Ballard took out her phone and snapped a photo of the bullet wound on the sternum. She noted that there was no gunpowder stippling, and that told her that the shot came from a distance of more than four feet. It seemed to have been a skilled shot, the work of a marksman who had hit the ten ring while most likely on the move and in an adrenalized situation. It was something to consider should she ever come face-to-face with the killer, as unlikely as that seemed at the moment.

Ballard noticed a length of string around the dead woman's neck. It wasn't a chain or any kind of jewelry. It was twine. If there was a pendant, she couldn't see it because the string disappeared behind a tangle of blood-matted hair. Ballard checked the door and then looked back at the victim. She pulled the string free of the hair and saw that there was a small key tied to it. Seeing a scalpel on a tray of surgical instruments, she grabbed it and cut the string, then pulled it free. She took a latex glove from her coat pocket and placed the key and string inside it in lieu of an evidence bag.

After pocketing the glove, Ballard studied the victim's face. Her eyes were slightly open and there was still a rubber airway device in her mouth. That bothered Ballard. It distended the woman's face and she thought it would have embarrassed her in life. Ballard wanted to remove it but knew it was against protocol. The coroner was supposed to receive the body as it was in death. She had already crossed the line by taking the key but the indignity of the rubber airway got to her. She was reaching for it when a voice interrupted from behind.

"Detective?"

Ballard turned and saw that it was one of the

paramedics who had brought the victim in. He held up a plastic bag.

"This is her apron," he said. "It has her tips."

"Thank you," Ballard said. "I'll take it."

He brought the bag to her and she held it up to eye level.

"Did you guys get any ID?" she asked.

"I don't think so," the paramedic said. "She was a cocktail waitress, so she probably kept all of that in her car or a locker or something."

"Right."

"But her name's Cindy."

"Cindy?"

"Yeah, we asked back at the club. You know, so we could talk to her. Didn't matter, though. She coded."

He looked down at the body. Ballard thought she saw sadness in his eyes.

"Wish we had gotten there a few minutes earlier," he said. "Maybe we could have done something. Hard to tell."

"I'm sure you guys did your best," Ballard said. "She would thank you if she could."

He looked back at Ballard.

"Now you'll do your best, right?" he said.

"We will," she said, knowing that it would not be her case to investigate once RHD took over.

Shortly after the paramedic left the room, two hospital orderlies entered to move the body so that the operating room could be sterilized and put back into rotation—it was a busy night down in the ER. They covered the body with a plastic sheet and rolled the gurney out. The victim's left arm was exposed and

24

Ballard saw the unicorn tattoo again on her wrist. She followed the gurney out, clutching the bag containing the victim's apron.

She walked along the hallway, looking through the windows into the other operating rooms. She noticed that Ramón Gutierrez had been brought up and was undergoing surgery to relieve pressure from the swelling of his brain. She watched for a few moments, until her phone buzzed, and she checked the text. It was from Lieutenant Munroe, asking the status of the fifth victim. Ballard typed out an answer as she walked toward the elevator.

KMA—I'm heading to scene.

KMA was an old LAPD designation used at the end of a radio call. Some said it stood for *Keep Me Apprised* but in use it was the equivalent of *over and out*. Over time it had evolved to mean end of watch or, in this case, the victim's death.

While riding down on the slow-moving elevator, Ballard put on a latex glove and opened the plastic bag the paramedic had given her. She then looked through the pockets of the waitress's apron. She could see a fold of currency in one pocket and a pack of cigarettes, a lighter, and a small notepad in the other. Ballard had been in the Dancers and knew the club got its name from a club in the great L.A. novel *The Long Goodbye*. She also knew it had a whole menu of specialty drinks with L.A. literary titles, like the Black Dahlia, Blonde Lightning, and Indigo Slam. A notebook would be a requirement for a waitress.

Back at the car Ballard popped the trunk and placed the bag in one of the cardboard boxes she and Jenkins used for storing evidence. On any given shift they might collect evidence from multiple cases, so they divided the trunk space with cardboard boxes. She had earlier placed Ramón Gutierrez's belongings in one of the boxes. She put the bag containing the apron in another, sealed it with red evidence tape, and closed the trunk.

By the time Ballard got over to the Dancers, the crime scene was a three-ring circus. Not the Barnum & Bailey kind, but the police kind, with three concentric rings denoting the size, complexity, and media draw of the case. The center ring was the actual crime scene, where investigators and evidence technicians worked. This was the red zone. It was circled by a second ring, and this was where the command staff, uniformed presence, and crowd and media control command posts were located. The third and outer ring was where the reporters, cameras, and the attendant onlookers gathered.

Already all eastbound lanes of Sunset Boulevard had been closed off to make room for the massive glut of police and news vehicles. The westbound lanes were moving at a crawl, a long ribbon of brake lights, as drivers slowed to grab a view of the police activity. Ballard found a parking spot at the curb a block away and walked it in. She took her badge off her belt, pulled out the cord wound around the rear clip, and looped it over her head so the badge would hang visibly from her neck.

Once she'd covered the block, she had to search for the officer with the crime scene attendance log so she could sign in. The first two rings were cordoned off by yellow crime scene tape. Ballard lifted the first line and went under, then saw an officer holding a clipboard and standing post at the second. His name was Dunwoody and she knew him.

"Woody, put me down," she said.

"Detective Ballard," he said as he started writing on the clipboard. "I thought this was RHD all the way."

"It is, but I was at Hollywood Pres with the fifth victim. Who's heading it up?"

"Lieutenant Olivas—with everybody from Hollywood and West Bureau command staff to the C-O-P sticking their nose in."

Ballard almost groaned. Robert Olivas headed up one of the Homicide Special teams at RHD. Ballard had a bad history with him, stemming from her assignment to his team four years earlier when he was promoted to the unit from Major Narcotics. That history was what landed her on the late show at Hollywood Division.

"You seen Jenkins around?" she asked.

Her mind was immediately moving toward a plan that would allow her to avoid reporting on the fifth victim directly to Olivas.

"As a matter of fact, I did," Dunwoody said. "Where was that? Oh, yeah, they're bringing a bus in for the witnesses. Taking them all downtown. I think Jenkins was watching over that. You know, making sure none of them try to split. Apparently it was like rats on a sinking ship when the shooting started. What I heard, at least."

Ballard moved a step closer to Dunwoody to speak confidentially. Her eyes raked across the sea of police vehicles, all of them with roof lights blazing.

"What else did you hear, Woody?" she asked. "What happened inside? Was this like Orlando last year?"

"No, no, it's not terrorism," Dunwoody answered. "What I hear is that it was four guys in a booth and something went wrong. One starts shooting and takes out the others. He then took out a waitress and a bouncer on his way out."

Ballard nodded. It was a start toward understanding what had happened.

"So, where is Jenkins holding the wits?"

"They're over in the garden next door. Where the Cat and Fiddle used to be."

"Got it. Thanks."

The Dancers was next to an old Spanish-style building with a center courtyard and garden. It had been an outdoor seating area for the Cat and Fiddle, an English pub and major hangout for off duty and sometimes not-off-duty officers from the nearby Hollywood Station. But it went out of business at least two years earlier—a victim of rising lease rates in Hollywood—and was vacant. It had now been commandeered as a witness corral.

There was another patrol officer posted outside the gated archway entrance to the old beer garden. He nodded his approval to Ballard and she pushed through the wrought-iron gate. She found Jenkins sitting at an old stone table, writing in a notebook.

"Jenks," Ballard said.

"Yo, partner," Jenkins said. "I heard your girl didn't make it."

"Coded in the RA. They never got a pulse after that. And I never got to talk to her. You getting anything here?"

"Not much. The smart people hit the ground when the shooting started. The smarter people got the hell out and aren't sitting in here. As far as I can tell, we can clear as soon as they get a bus for these poor folks. It's RHD's show."

"I have to talk to someone about my victim."

"Well, that will be Olivas or one of his guys, and I'm not sure you want to do that."

"Do I have a choice? You're stuck here."

"Not like I planned it this way."

"Did anybody in here tell you they saw the waitress get hit?"

Jenkins scanned the tables, where about twenty people were sitting and waiting. It was a variety of Hollywood hipsters and clubbers. A lot of tattoos and piercings.

"No, but from what I hear, she was waiting on the table where the shooting started," Jenkins said. "Four men in a booth. One pulls out a hand cannon and shoots the others right where they're sitting. People start scattering, including the shooter. He shot your waitress when he was going for the door. Took out a bouncer too."

"And nobody knows what it was about?"

"Nobody here, at least."

He waved a hand toward the witnesses. The gesture apparently looked to one of the patrons sitting at another stone table like an invitation. He got up and approached, the wallet chain draped from a front belt loop to the back pocket of his black jeans jangling with each step.

"Look, man, when are we going to be done here?" he said to Jenkins. "I didn't see anything and I don't know anything."

"I told you," Jenkins said. "Nobody leaves until the detectives take formal statements. Go sit back down, sir."

Jenkins said it with a tone of threat and authority that totally undermined the use of the word sir. The patron stared at Jenkins a moment and then went back to his table.

"They don't know they're getting on a bus?" Ballard said in a low voice.

"Not yet," Jenkins said.

Before Ballard could respond further, she felt her phone buzz and she pulled it out to check the screen. It was an unknown caller but she took it, knowing it was most likely a call from a fellow cop.

"Ballard."

"Detective, this is Lieutenant Olivas. I was told you were with my fifth victim at Presbyterian. It would not have been my choice but I understand you were already there."

Ballard paused before answering, a feeling of dread building in her chest.

"That's right," she finally said. "She coded and the body is waiting for a coroner's pickup team."

"Were you able to get a statement from her?" he asked.

"No, she was DOA. They tried to bring her back but it didn't happen."

"I see."

He said it in a tone that suggested it was some failing

on her part that the victim had died before she could be interviewed. Ballard didn't respond.

"Write your reports and get them down to me in the morning," Olivas said. "That's all."

"Uh, I'm here at the scene," Ballard said before he disconnected. "Next door with the witnesses. With my partner."

"And?"

"And there was no ID on the victim. She was a waitress. She probably had a locker somewhere inside that would have her wallet and her phone. I'd like to—"

"Cynthia Haddel—the bar manager gave it to me."

"You want me to confirm it and gather her property or have your people take it?"

Now Olivas paused before responding. It was like he was weighing something unrelated to the case.

"I have a key that I think is to a locker," Ballard said. "The paramedics turned it over to me."

It was a significant stretch of the truth but Ballard did not want the lieutenant to know how she got the key.

"Okay, you handle it," he finally said. "My people are fully involved elsewhere. But don't get charged up, Ballard. She was a peripheral victim. Collateral damage—wrong place at the wrong time. You could also make next-of-kin notification and save my guys that time. Just don't get in my way."

"Got it."

"And I still want your report on my desk in the morning."

Olivas disconnected before Ballard could respond.

She kept the phone to her ear a moment, thinking about his saying that Cindy Haddel was collateral damage and in the wrong place at the wrong time. Ballard knew what that was like.

She put the phone away.

"So?" Jenkins asked.

"I need to go next door, check her locker, and find her ID," she said. "Olivas also gave us next-of-kin."

"Ah, fuck."

"Don't worry, I'll handle it."

"No, it doesn't work that way. You volunteer yourself, you volunteer me."

"I didn't volunteer for next-of-kin notification. You heard the call."

"You volunteered to get involved. Of course he was going to give you the shit work."

Ballard didn't want to start an argument. She turned away, checked out the people sitting at the stone tables, and saw two young women wearing cutoff jeans and tank tops, one shirt white and one black. She walked over to them and showed her badge. The white tank top spoke before Ballard could.

"We didn't see anything," she said.

"I heard," Ballard said. "I want to ask about Cindy Haddel. Did either of you know her?"

The white top shrugged her shoulders.

"Well, yeah, to work with," said the black top. "She was nice. Did she make it?"

Ballard shook her head and both of the waitresses brought their hands to their mouths at the same time, as if receiving impulses from the same brain.

"Oh god," said the white top.

"Does either of you know anything about her?" Ballard asked. "Married? Boyfriend? Roommate? Anything like that?"

Neither did.

"Is there an employee locker room over at the club? Someplace she would have kept her wallet and her phone, maybe?" Ballard asked.

"There are lockers in the kitchen," the white top said. "We put our stuff in those."

"Okay," she said. "Thank you. Did the three of you have any conversation tonight before the shooting?"

"Just waitress stuff," the black top said. "You know, like who was tipping and who wasn't. Who was grabby—the usual stuff."

"Anybody in particular tonight?" Ballard asked.

"Not really," the black top said.

"She was all bragging because she got a fifty from somebody," the white top said. "I actually think it was somebody in that booth where the shooting started."

"Why do you think that?" Ballard asked.

"Because that table was hers and they looked like players."

"You mean show-offs? Guys with money?"

"Yeah, players."

"Okay. Anything else?"

The two waitresses looked at each other first, then back at Ballard. They shook their heads.

Ballard left them there and went back to her partner.

"I'm going next door."

"Don't get lost," he said. "As soon as I'm done babysitting, I want to go get next-of-kin over with and start writing. We're done."

33

Meaning the rest of the shift would be dedicated to paperwork.

"Roger that," she said.

She left him sitting on the stone bench. As she made her way to the entrance of the Dancers she wondered if she would be able to get to the kitchen without drawing the attention of Lieutenant Olivas.

4

The interior of the Dancers was crowded with detectives, technicians, photographers, and videographers. Ballard saw a woman from the LAPD's architectural unit setting up a 360-degree camera that would provide a high-density 3-D recording of the entire crime scene after all evidence was marked and investigators and technicians momentarily backed out. From it she could also build a model of the crime scene to use as an exhibit in court during an eventual prosecution. It was an expensive move and the first time Ballard had ever seen it employed in the field outside of an officer-involved-shooting investigation. There was no doubt that at this point, at least, nothing was being spared on the case.

Ballard counted nine detectives from the Homicide Special Section in the club, all of whom she knew and even a few she liked. Each of them had a specific piece of the crime scene investigation to handle and they moved about the club under the watchful eye and direction of Lieutenant Olivas. Yellow evidence placards were everywhere on the floor, marking shell casings, broken martini glasses, and other debris.

The victims, all except Cynthia Haddel, had been left in place to be photographed, videoed, and examined by the coroner's team before being removed for autopsy. The coroner herself, Jayalalithaa Panneerselvam, was on scene. That was a rarity in itself and underlined the importance that the investigation of the mass killing had taken on. Dr. J., as she was known, stood behind her photographer, directing the shots she wanted him to take.

The club was a massive space with black walls and two levels. The bar ran along the back wall on the lower level, which also had a small dance floor surrounded by palm trees and black leather booths. The palm trees, hung with white lights, rose all the way to a glass atrium two floors up. To the right and left of the bar were two wings six steps up from the main floor and lined with more booths and served by smaller bars.

There were three bodies in a booth on the main level. It was located in a cloverleaf of four booths. Two of the dead men were still seated. The one on the left was a black man with his head tilted all the way back. The white man next to him was slightly leaning against him as though he had drunkenly fallen asleep. The third man had tilted all the way to his side and his head and shoulders dangled outside the confines of the booth into the aisle. He was white and had a graying ponytail that hung down and dipped into a pool of blood on the floor.

A fourth body was on the floor twenty feet away in a separate aisle created by the cloverleaf booths. He was a very large black man who was facedown on the floor, hands at his sides and his knuckles on the tile. On his belt on the right hip was an empty Taser holster. Ballard could see the yellow plastic stunning device under a nearby table.

Another ten feet past the fourth body was a smear of blood surrounded by evidence markers and some of the debris left by the paramedics who had tried to save Cynthia Haddel's life. Among the items on the floor was a round stainless-steel cocktail tray.

Ballard walked up the steps to the second level and then turned around to look down and get a better view of the crime scene. Lieutenant McAdams had said the shooting erupted in a booth. With that as a starting point, it was easy to figure out what had happened in basic terms. Three men were shot where they sat. The shooter had them pinned in and pivoted efficiently from one to the other with the aim of his weapon. He then moved from the booth and down the lane separating the pods. This put him on a collision course with the bouncer, who had drawn his Taser and was moving toward the problem. The bouncer was shot, most likely killed instantly, and dropped face-first to the floor.

Behind him stood waitress Cynthia Haddel.

Ballard imagined her standing frozen, unable to move as the killer came toward her. Maybe she was raising her cocktail tray up like a shield. The killer was moving but still able to put the one shot dead center in her chest. Ballard wondered if the gunman had shot her simply because she was in the way or because she might have been able to identify him. Either way it was a cold choice. It said something about the man who had done this. Ballard thought about what she had said earlier to Jenkins about the person who had assaulted Ramona Ramone. Big evil. There was no doubt that the same callous malignancy moved through the blood of the shooter here.

Detective Ken Chastain came into Ballard's view. He had his leather folder with the legal pad on one arm, pen in the other hand, the way he always did at a crime scene. He stooped down to look at the dead man who was half hanging out of the booth and started to take notes without noticing Ballard on the upper level, looking down at him. He looked haggard to Ballard and she hoped that was because guilt was eating at him from the inside. For nearly five years they had been partners in the Homicide Special Section, until Chastain had chosen not to back Ballard in the complaint she had filed against Olivas. Without his confirmation of the lieutenant's behavior—which he had directly witnessed—there was no case. Internal Affairs concluded that the complaint was unfounded. Olivas kept his job and Ballard was transferred to Hollywood Division. The captain at Hollywood, an academy classmate of Olivas's, put her on the night shift with Jenkins. The late show. End of story.

Ballard turned away from her old partner and looked at the ceiling and the upper corners of the club. She was curious about cameras and whether the shooting was caught on video. Pulling video from within the club and the streets outside would be a priority in the investigation. But she saw no obvious cameras and knew that many Hollywood clubs did not use cameras, because their clientele, especially the celebrities, did not care to have their nocturnal behavior recorded. Video ending up on the TMZ gossip site or elsewhere on the Internet was a prescription for bankruptcy for the high-end clubs. They needed celebrities because they drew the paying customers, the people who lined up at the velvet ropes outside. If celebrities started staying away, the paying customers eventually would as well.

Feeling conspicuous on the steps, Ballard returned to the lower level and looked for the forensic unit's equipment table. It was out of the way and over by the other set of stairs. She went over and took a couple of plastic evidence bags out of a dispenser and then headed toward the main bar. A set of double doors to the right presumably led to the kitchen.

The kitchen was small and empty, and Ballard noticed that some of the gas burners on the stove were still on. The Dancers was not known for its culinary attributes. It was basic bar food that came off a grill or out of a deep fryer. Ballard walked behind the polished stainless-steel prep line and turned off the burners. She then came back around and almost slipped on a grease spot in the paper booties she had put on over her shoes before entering the club.

In the back corner of the kitchen she found an alcove with a freestanding rack of small lockers against one wall and a break table with two chairs against the other. There was an ashtray brimming with cigarette butts on the table just below a no smoking sign. Ballard was in luck. Pieces of tape with each locker holder's name were affixed to the lockers. There was no cindy but she found a locker marked CINDERS and assumed it belonged to Cynthia Haddel, and that was confirmed when the key she had taken from the body of the fifth victim opened the padlock.

The locker contained a small Kate Spade purse, a light jacket, a pack of cigarettes, and a manila envelope. Ballard gloved up before removing anything from the locker and examining it. She knew the contents of the locker were more than likely going to be booked as property as opposed to evidence, but it was a good practice, just in case she stumbled across something that might affect the direction of the investigation.

The purse contained a wallet that produced a driver's license confirming the name Cynthia Haddel and her age at twenty-three. The address on the DL was an apartment or condo on La Brea. She lived within a twenty-minute walk of the club. There was $383 in cash in the wallet, which seemed on the high side to Ballard, plus a Wells Fargo debit card and a Visa credit card. There was a ring with two keys that did not appear to belong to a vehicle. Most likely apartment keys. There was also a cell phone in the purse. It was powered on but its contents were protected by Touch ID. Ballard needed Haddel's thumbprint to access the phone.

Ballard opened the manila envelope and saw that it contained a stack of 8 × 10 head-shot photos of Haddel giving a smiling come-hither look. The name at the bottom of the photo was Cinders Haden. Ballard turned the top photo over and saw a short résumé and list of appearances Haddel/Haden had made in film and television productions. It was all minor stuff, with most of her characters not even having names. "Girl at the Bar" appeared to be her most frequent role. She had played the part in an episode of a television show called *Bosch*, which Ballard knew was based on the exploits of a now-retired LAPD detective who had formerly worked at RHD and the Hollywood detective bureau. The production occasionally filmed at the station and had underwritten the division's last Christmas party at the W Hotel.

The résumé section said that Haddel/Haden was born

and raised in Modesto, which was up in the Central Valley. It listed her local theater credits, acting teachers, and various skills that might make her attractive to a production. These included Rollerblading, yoga, gymnastics, horseback riding, surfing, fluency in French, bartending, and waitressing. It also said roles involving partial nudity were acceptable.

Ballard flipped the photo back around and studied Haddel's face. It was obvious that her job at the Dancers was not where her ambitions were focused. She kept the head shots in the locker in case she encountered a customer who might inquire if she was "in the business" and offer to help. It was one of the oldest come-ons in Hollywood, but it always worked when you were a young woman with big dreams.

"Modesto," Ballard said out loud.

The last thing she pulled from the locker was the Marlboro Lights box and she immediately knew it was too heavy to hold cigarettes only. She opened the top and saw cigarettes stacked on one side and a small glass vial on the other. She pulled out the vial and found it half-filled with yellow-white pills with small hearts stamped into them. Ballard guessed that it was Molly, a synthetic drug that had replaced Ecstasy as the clubbers' drug of choice in recent years. It looked to Ballard like Haddel might have been supplementing her income by selling Molly at the club, with or without management's knowledge and permission. Ballard would put it into her report and it would be up to Olivas and his crew to decide whether it had anything to do with the massacre that had occurred that night. It was always possible that the peripheral could become pertinent.

Ballard put the contents of the locker, except for the key ring, into one of the evidence bags and relocked the padlock. She then put the key from the padlock into the bag as well and sealed and signed it. Finally, she left the kitchen and returned to the main floor of the club.

Chastain was still squatting in front of the body hanging halfway out of the booth. But now he was joined by Dr. J., who was bending over his right shoulder to get a better view of the dead man, while Olivas was observing from over his left. Ballard could tell that Chastain had found or noticed something worth pointing out. Despite his betrayal of Ballard, she knew Chastain was a good detective. They had closed several cases in the years she had worked with him at RHD. He was the son of an LAPD detective killed in the line of duty and his badge always had a black mourning band around it. He was a closer, no doubt, and was deservedly the lieutenant's go-to guy on the squad. The only problem was that outside of his cases his moral compass didn't always point true north. He made choices based on political and bureaucratic expediency, not right and wrong. Ballard had learned that the hard way.

Dr. J. patted Chastain on the shoulder so that he would move out of the way and allow her closer access to the body. When they shifted positions, Ballard got a good look at the dead man hanging out of the booth. He had one clean bullet wound between his eyebrows. He had died instantly and then fallen to his left. His shirt was open, exposing a hairless chest. There was no sign of a second wound that Ballard could see but the coroner was closely examining the area, using a gloved hand to open the shirt wide.

"Renée."

Chastain had noticed Ballard standing outside the immediate investigative circle.

"Ken."

"What are you doing here?"

It was said in a tone of surprise, not accusation.

"I caught the fifth victim at the hospital," Ballard said. "I was already there."

Chastain looked at his pad.

"Cynthia Haddel, the waitress," he said. "DOA."

Ballard held up the evidence bag containing Haddel's things.

"Right," she said. "I cleared her locker. I know you're thinking she's peripheral to this, but—"

"Yes, thank you, Detective."

It was Olivas, who had turned from the booth. His words shut Chastain down.

He moved toward Ballard and she looked at him without flinching as he stepped close to her. This was the first time she had stood face-to-face with Olivas since she had filed the complaint against him two years before. She felt a mix of dread and anger as she looked at his angular features.

Chastain, perhaps knowing what was coming, stepped back from them, turned, and went about his work.

"Lieutenant," she said.

"How's the late show treating you?" Olivas said.

"It's good."

"And how is Jerkins?"

"Jenkins is fine."

"You know why he's called that, right? Jerkins?"

43

"I . . ."

She didn't finish. Olivas lowered his chin and moved an inch closer to her. To Ballard it felt like a foot. He spoke in a low voice only she could hear.

"The late show," he said. "That's where they put the jerkoffs."

Olivas stepped back from her.

"You have your assignment, don't you, Detective?" he asked, his voice returning to normal.

"Yes," Ballard said. "I'll inform the family."

"Then go do it. Now. I don't want you messing up my crime scene."

Over his shoulder, Ballard could see Dr. J. watching her dismissal but then she turned away. Ballard glanced at Chastain, hoping for some kind of sympathetic reaction, but he was back to work, squatting on the floor, using gloved hands to put what looked like a black button into a small plastic evidence bag.

Ballard turned from Olivas and headed toward the exit, her cheeks burning with humiliation.

5

Jenkins was still next door with the witnesses. As Ballard approached him, he had his hands up, fingers spread as if trying to push them back. One of the club patrons had the high-pitched tone of frustration in his voice.

"Man, I have to work in the morning," he said. "I can't sit here all night, especially when I didn't see a fucking thing!"

"I understand that, sir," Jenkins said, his own voice a notch or two above its usual measured tone. "We will get statements from all of you just as soon as possible. Five people are dead. Think about that."

The frustrated man made a dismissive hand gesture and turned back to a bench. Someone else cursed and yelled, "You can't just keep us here!"

Jenkins did not respond but the truth on a technical level was that they could hold all patrons from the club until the investigators sorted out who was a potential witness and who might be a suspect. It was flimsy because common sense dictated that none of these people were suspects, but it was valid.

"You okay?" Ballard asked.

Jenkins turned around like he thought he was about to be jumped, then saw it was his partner.

"Barely," he said. "I don't blame them. They're in for

45

a long night. They're sending a jail bus for them. Wait till they see the bars on the windows. They'll really go apeshit then."

"Glad I won't be here to see it."

"Where are you going?"

Ballard held up the evidence bag containing Cynthia Haddel's property.

"I have to run by the hospital. They found more of her stuff. I'll be back in twenty, we'll do the notification, and then it will be all over except for the paperwork."

"Next-of-kin will be a breeze compared to dealing with these animals. I think half of them are coming off highs. It's going to get uglier once they're all downtown."

"And not our problem. I'll be back."

Ballard hadn't told her partner the real reason she was returning to the hospital, because she knew he would not approve of her true plan. She turned to go back to the car but Jenkins stopped her.

"Hey, partner."

"What?"

"You can lose the gloves now."

He had noticed she still had crime scene gloves on. She held one hand up as if noticing the gloves for the first time.

"Right," she said. "As soon as I see a trash can."

At the car, Ballard kept the gloves on while she secured Cynthia Haddel's property in the same cardboard box that contained her tip apron. But first she removed Haddel's cell phone and slipped it into her pocket.

It was ten minutes back to Hollywood Presbyterian. She was banking on the fact that the shooting and mass casualties at the Dancers had slowed the operations of the coroner's office and that Haddel's body would still be waiting for pickup. She confirmed that was so when she got back to the ER and was led to a room where there were actually two covered bodies awaiting transport to the coroner. She asked the attendant to see if the doctor who had attempted to resuscitate Haddel was available.

Ballard had kept her gloves on. She now pulled back the sheet on one of the bodies and saw the face of a young man who had wasted to no more than a hundred pounds. She quickly re-covered the face and went to the other gurney. She confirmed it was Haddel and then moved down the gurney to the victim's right hand. She pulled out the cell phone and pressed the pad of the dead woman's right thumb to the home button on the screen.

The phone remained locked. Ballard tried the index finger and that failed to open the phone as well. She moved around the gurney and went through the process again with the left thumb. This time the phone unlocked, and Ballard had access.

She had to take one of her gloves off to manipulate the screen. She wasn't concerned with leaving fingerprints because the phone was property, not evidence, and likely would never be analyzed for latent prints.

Having an iPhone herself, she knew the phone would re-lock soon if the screen didn't remain active. She went into the GPS app and scrolled through previous

47

destinations. There was a Pasadena address and Ballard clicked on it and set up a route there. It would keep the screen activated even as Ballard ignored the directions and went her own way. The phone would remain unlocked and she'd have access to its contents after leaving the hospital. She checked the battery level and saw that it was at 60 percent, which would give her more than enough time to go through the phone. She muted the phone so the GPS app would not be audibly correcting her when she did not follow its directions to Pasadena.

She was pulling the sheet back over the body when the door opened and one of the ER doctors looked in.

"I heard you asked for me," he said. "What are you doing in here?"

Ballard remembered his voice from the elevator ride up to the OR.

"I needed to get a fingerprint," Ballard said, holding up the phone in further explanation. "But I wanted to ask you about another patient. I saw that you also worked on Gutierrez—the assault victim with the skull fracture? How is the patient?"

She was careful not to speak in terms of gender. The surgeon wasn't. He went with anatomy.

"We did the surgery and he's still in recovery," he said. "We are inducing coma and it will be a waiting game. The sooner the swelling goes down, the better chance he has."

Ballard nodded.

"Okay, thanks," she said. "I'll check back tomorrow. Did you happen to take any swabs for a rape kit?"

"Detective, our priority was keeping the victim alive," the doctor said. "That can all come later."

48

"Not really. But I understand."

The doctor was about to leave the doorway, when Ballard pointed to the other gurney in the room.

"What's the story there?" she asked. "Cancer?"

"Everything," the doctor said. "Cancer, HIV, complete organ shutdown."

"Why's he going downtown?"

"It's a suicide. He pulled his tubes, disconnected the machines. I guess they have to be sure."

"Right."

"I need to go."

The doctor disappeared from the doorway and Ballard looked at the other gurney and thought about the man using his last ounces of strength to pull the tubes. She thought there was something heroic in that.

In the car she moved off the GPS screen on Cynthia Haddel's phone and opened the list of favorite contacts. The first one was labeled "Home" and Ballard checked the number. It was a 209 area code and she expected that it was the number of the home where Haddel had grown up, in Modesto. There were four other favorite contacts, all listed by first name only: Jill, Cara, Leon, and John, all with L.A. area codes. Ballard figured she had enough to get to Haddel's parents if the number marked "Home" didn't work.

She next pulled up the texting app and checked that. There were two recent communications. One was to Cara.

Cindy: Guess who just scored a 50 on a round of martinis?
Cara: You go girl.

Haddel responded with an emoji showing a happy face. The text before that began with a question from someone who wasn't on her favorites list.

DP: How are you fixed?
Cindy: I think I'm good. Maybe tomorrow.
DP: Let me know.

There were no previous messages, indicating it was either a new acquaintance or the earlier exchanges had been deleted. There were several other text conversations on the app but none of the others were active in the hours since Haddel had come to work. Ballard pegged Cara as most likely Haddel's best friend and DP as her drug supplier. She moved on to the e-mail file and found that the incoming messages were largely generic notifications and spam. Haddel apparently didn't do much in the way of e-mailing. Haddel's Twitter feed was as expected. She followed a number of entertainers, primarily in the music business, the Dancers' own account, the LAPD's Hollywood Station feed regarding crime alerts, and the former presidential candidate Bernie Sanders.

The last app Ballard opened was the phone's photo archive. It said there were 662 photos. Ballard thumbed through the most recent and saw many photos of Haddel involved in activities with friends, working out, at the beach, and with cast and crew members on sets where she had found work as an actress.

Ballard's own phone buzzed and a photo of Jenkins came up on the screen. She answered the call with a question.

"The bus get there?"

"Just left. Get me out of here."

"On my way."

Ballard re-engaged the GPS route to Pasadena so the phone's screen would remain active and headed back to the Dancers. After she picked up Jenkins, they drove to the La Brea address on Cynthia Haddel's driver's license. The first step of the notification process was to go to the victim's home to see if there might be a husband or other relative sharing the premises.

It was a recently built apartment building a half block north of Melrose in an area of shops and restaurants popular with the younger crowd. There were ramen noodle and build-your-own-pizza restaurants fronting the first floor, with the building's entrance in the middle.

Haddel's license listed her in unit 4B. Ballard used one of the keys on the ring taken from the locker to gain entrance through a security door to the elevator lobby. She and Jenkins rode to the fourth floor and found 4B at the end of the hallway leading to the back of the building.

Ballard knocked twice but no one answered. It did not mean there was no other occupant. Ballard knew from experience that someone could still be sleeping inside. She used the second key to open the door. By law they should have had a search warrant but both detectives knew they could cite exigent circumstances if a problem developed later. They had five people dead and no suspects and no motive. They needed to check on the safety of any possible roommates of their victim, no matter how peripheral to the case she might be.

"LAPD! Anyone home?" Ballard called out as they entered.

"Police!" Jenkins added. "We're coming in."

Ballard kept her hand on her hip holster as she entered but she did not draw her gun. There was a single light on in the living room, which opened off a short entrance hallway. She visually checked a galley kitchen to the right and then moved toward another hallway leading to the back of the apartment. It led to a bathroom and a single bedroom. The doors to these rooms were open and Ballard quickly hit light switches and scanned them.

"Clear," she called out when she confirmed there were no other occupants.

She stepped back into the living room, where Jenkins was waiting.

"Looks like she lived alone," she said.

"Yep," Jenkins said. "Doesn't help us any."

Ballard started looking around, paying attention to the personal details of the small apartment: knick-knacks, photos on shelves, a stack of bills left on the coffee table.

"Pretty nice place for a cocktail waitress," Jenkins said. "The building is less than a year old."

"She was slinging dope at the club," Ballard said. "I found her stash in her locker. There may be more here someplace."

"That explains a lot."

"Sorry, I forgot to tell you."

Ballard moved into the kitchen and saw a variety of photos on the refrigerator. Most of them were like the ones on Cynthia's phone—outings with friends.

Several were of a trip to Hawaii that showed Haddel surfing on a training board and riding on a horseback trail through a volcano crater. Ballard recognized the outline of Haleakalā in the background and knew it was Maui. She had spent many years growing up on the island and the shape of the volcano on the horizon had been part of her daily existence. She knew it the way people in L.A. knew the crooked line of the Hollywood sign.

There was a photo partially obscured by newer additions to the refrigerator but Ballard saw a woman of about fifty who shared the same jawline as Haddel. She carefully pulled it off and found that it showed Cynthia Haddel between a man and woman at a Thanksgiving table, the cooked turkey on full display. It was most likely a shot of Haddel and her parents, the lines of heredity clear in both their faces.

Jenkins came into the kitchen and looked at the photo in Ballard's hand.

"You want to do it now?" he asked. "Get it over with?"

"Might as well," she said.

"Which way you want to go with it?"

"I'll just do it."

Jenkins had been referring to the choice they had here. It is a harsh thing to learn by a telephone call that a loved one has been murdered. Ballard could have called the Modesto Police Department and asked them to make the notification in person. But going that way would remove Ballard from the process and she would lose the opportunity to get immediate information about the victim and any possible suspects. More

53

than once in her career when she had made next-of-kin notification, she had come up with credible leads to follow in the investigation. That seemed unlikely with Cynthia Haddel, since she was probably not at the center of motivation for the mass shooting. As Olivas had said, she was collateral damage, a fringe player in what had happened. So it was a valid question from Jenkins, but Ballard knew that she would feel guilty later if she didn't make the call. She would feel like she had skirted a sacred responsibility of the homicide detective.

Ballard pulled out Haddel's phone. The GPS program had kept the screen active. She pulled up the contacts list to get the number for home and then called it from her own phone. It rang through to a voice-mail greeting confirming that it was the Haddel family home. Ballard left a message identifying herself and asking for a call back to her cell number, saying it was urgent.

It was not unusual for people not to answer a blocked call in the middle of the night, but Ballard hoped that her message would bring a quick return call. She stepped over to the refrigerator and looked at the photos once again while waiting. She wondered about Cynthia growing up in Modesto and then journeying south to the big city, where roles with partial nudity were okay and selling dope to Hollywood scenesters supplemented her income.

After five minutes, there was no call back. Jenkins was pacing and Ballard knew he wanted to keep moving.

"Call the cops up there?" he asked.

"No, that could take all night," Ballard said.

Then a phone started buzzing, but it wasn't Ballard's. Cynthia's phone showed an incoming call from the home number. Ballard guessed that her parents had gotten the message she just left and had chosen to call their daughter first to see if she was all right.

"It's them," she said to Jenkins.

She answered the phone.

"This is Detective Ballard with the Los Angeles Police Department. Who am I speaking with?"

"No, I called Cindy. What is going on there?"

It was a woman's voice, already choked with desperation and fear.

"Mrs. Haddel?"

"Yes, who is this? Where is Cindy?"

"Mrs. Haddel, is your husband with you?"

"Just tell me, is she all right?"

Ballard looked over at Jenkins. She hated this.

"Mrs. Haddel," she said. "I'm very sorry to tell you that your daughter has been killed in a shooting at the club where she worked in Los Angeles."

There was a loud scream over the line, followed by another, and then the sound of the phone clattering to the floor.

"Mrs. Haddel?"

Ballard turned toward Jenkins and covered the phone.

"Call Modesto, see if they can send somebody," she said.

"Where?" Jenkins asked.

Then it hit Ballard. She didn't have an address to go with the phone number. She could now hear moaning and crying on the line, but it was distant from the phone, which was apparently still on the floor somewhere in Modesto.

Suddenly a gruff male voice was on the line.

"Who is this?"

"Mr. Haddel? I am a detective with the LAPD. Is your wife all right?"

"No, she's not all right. What is going on? Why do you have our daughter's phone? What happened?"

"She's been shot, Mr. Haddel. I am so sorry to do this by phone. Cynthia has been shot and killed at the club where she worked. I'm calling to—"

"Oh, Jesus . . . Jesus Christ. Is this some kind of a joke? You don't do this to people, you hear me?"

"It's not a joke, sir. I am very sorry. Your daughter was hit by a bullet when someone started firing a weapon in the club. She fought hard. They got her to the hospital but they were unable to save her. I am so sorry for your loss."

The father didn't respond. Ballard could hear the mother's crying growing louder and she knew that the husband had gone to his wife while still clutching the phone. They were now together. Ballard looked at the photo in her hand and pictured the couple holding on to each other as they grappled with the worst news in the world. She herself grappled with how far to push things at the moment, whether to intrude further into their agony with questions that might be meaningless in terms of the investigation.

And then:

"This is all because of that bastard boyfriend of hers," the father said. "He's the one who should be dead. He put her to work in there."

Ballard made a decision.

"Mr. Haddel, I need to ask you some questions," she said. "It could be important to the case."

6

Back at Hollywood Station, they divvied up the report writing. Jenkins took the Lantana burglary their shift had started with and Ballard agreed to take the paper on Ramona Ramone and Cynthia Haddel. It was an uneven split but it guaranteed that Jenkins would walk out the door at dawn and be home when his wife woke up.

It was still called the paperwork but it was all done digitally. Ballard went to work on Haddel first so that she could be sure to get the reports in before Olivas could ask for them. She also had plans to stall the Ramone case. She wanted to keep it for herself, and the longer she took doing the paperwork, the better chance she had of making that happen.

The two partners did not have assigned desks in the detective bureau but each had a favorite spot at which to work in the vast room that was usually left abandoned at night. These choices were primarily dictated by the comfort of the desk chair and the level of obsolescence of the computer terminal. Ballard preferred a desk in the Burglary-Auto Theft pod, while Jenkins posted himself at the opposite end of the room in the Crimes Against Persons unit. There was a daytime detective who had brought in his own chair from the Relax the Back store and Jenkins treasured it. It was locked by a long bike cable to the desk in the CAPs module, so that anchored him there.

Ballard was a quick writer. She had a degree in journalism from the University of Hawaii and while she had not lasted long as a reporter, the training and experience had given her skills that helped immeasurably with this side of police work. She reacted well to deadline pressure and she could clearly conceptualize her crime reports and case summaries before writing them. She wrote short, clear sentences that gave momentum to the narrative of the investigation. This skill also paid dividends when Ballard was called into court to testify about her investigations. Juries liked her because she was a good storyteller.

It was in a courtroom that the direction of Ballard's life had changed dramatically fifteen years earlier. Her first job out of the University of Hawaii had been as one of a phalanx of crime reporters for the *Los Angeles Times*. She was assigned to a cubbyhole office in the Van Nuys courthouse, from which she covered criminal cases as well as the six LAPD divisions that comprised the north end of the city. One particular case had caught her attention: the murder of a fourteen-year-old runaway who had been snatched off the beach one night in Venice. She had been taken to a drug house in Van Nuys, where she was repeatedly raped over several days, and then eventually strangled and dropped in a construction site trash hauler.

The police made a case and took two men to trial for the murder. Ballard covered the preliminary hearing of the case against the accused. The lead detective testified about the investigation and in doing so recounted the many tortures and indignities the victim endured before her eventual death. The detective started crying on the stand. It wasn't a show. There was no jury, just a judge to decide whether the case should go to trial. But the detective cried, and in that moment Ballard realized she didn't want to just write about crime and investigations anymore. The next day she applied to enter the LAPD training academy. She wanted to be a detective.

It was 4:28 a.m. when Ballard began to write. Though Cynthia Haddel would need to be formally identified by the Coroner's Office, there was little doubt that she was the victim. Ballard put her name on the reports and listed her address on La Brea. She first wrote the death report that listed Haddel as a victim of a homicide by gunshot wound and included the basic details of the crime. She then wrote a chronology, a step-by-step accounting of the moves she and Jenkins had made once they received the call from Lieutenant Munroe while at Hollywood Presbyterian.

After the chrono was completed, she used it as an outline for her Officer's Statement, which was a more detailed summary of where the case had taken her and Jenkins through the night. After that, she moved on to documenting and filing the property she had collected from the hospital and the employee locker at the Dancers.

Before starting the process, she counted how many individual pieces she would be filing and then called the forensics lab and spoke to the duty officer, Winchester.

"Have they started booking evidence from the four on the floor in Hollywood?" she asked. "I need a DR number."

Every piece of booked evidence required its own Division of Records number.

"That place is a mess," Winchester said. "They're still on scene and will probably be collecting all night and into the day. I don't expect they'll start booking evidence till noon. It's up to five now, by the way. Five on the floor."

"I know. Okay, I'll get my own numbers. Thanks, Winchester."

She got up and made her way over to Jenkins.

"I'm going to buy DRs out of the manual. You need any?"

"Yeah, get me one."

"Be right back."

She took the rear hallway to the property room. She knew there would be no clerk on duty. There never was at this hour. The property room was left as empty as the detective bureau at night. But there was a Division of Records ledger on the counter and it contained an up-to-date listing of DR numbers for booking property and evidence. Everything went to the FSD—the Forensic Sciences Division—for analysis as potential evidence. Since the lab could not provide a sequence of numbers for the RHD case, the property that Ballard and Jenkins had collected in their cases would be booked under Hollywood Division numbers instead and shipped to the FSD for sorting.

Ballard grabbed a scratch pad from the counter and wrote down a number from the ledger for Jenkins and then a seven-number sequence for herself. The numbers all started with the year and the o6 designation for Hollywood Division. As she walked back down the empty hallway to the detective bureau, she heard a sudden echo of laughter from the watch office, which was in the opposite direction. Among the chortles, she identified the infectious sound of Lieutenant Munroe's laugh and smiled to herself. Cops were not humorless people. Even in the depths of the midnight shift on a night of massive violence they could always find something to laugh about.

She gave Jenkins his DR number but didn't bother to ask how far along he was. She could see he was typing with two fingers and still on an incident report. He was slow to the point of frustration. Ballard usually volunteered to do all the paperwork so she didn't have to wait for him to finish.

Back at her borrowed desk, Ballard gloved up and went to work. It took her thirty minutes to process everything. This included the contents of the locker, the key the victim wore around her neck, and the money she had been carrying in her wallet and tip apron. It had to be counted out and documented. For her own protection Ballard called Jenkins over so he could witness the money count and she took cell-phone photos of each evidence bag after sealing it.

She took all of the plastic bags and placed them in one large brown paper sack that she marked with the DR number and sealed with red evidence tape. She then carried it back down the hallway to the property room and placed it in one of the lockers, where it would remain until someone working the case in RHD picked it up or it was carried by courier to the lab for forensic analysis.

When Ballard returned to the bureau, she saw that

it was 6:11 on the clock over the television screens. Her shift was supposed to end at seven a.m. and overtime was only a slim possibility because it was the middle of the month's deployment period and money in the OT bucket was probably already gone. She didn't want overtime, however. She just wanted to push the Ramona Ramone case into her next shift.

On the Dancers case, she still had summaries to write regarding her interviews with Haddel's parents and fellow waitresses. She knew it would take her to the end of shift. She settled back into the workstation, opened up a new file on the computer screen, and was about to start the summary of her talk with Nelson Haddel, when her cell buzzed and she saw it was Lieutenant Munroe.

"L-T."

"Ballard, what's your location?"

"I'm in detectives. Filing paper. Heard you guys laughing it up a little while ago."

"Oh, yeah, we're having a ball up here. I need you to take a statement."

"From who? I'm in the middle of this and still have the assault I haven't even touched yet."

"A guy just walked in, said he was in the Dancers when the shooting started. He says he has photos."

"You sure? It's a no-photo place."

"He snuck a couple selfies."

"Anything in them?"

"They're dark but he's got something. Looks like muzzle flash. Maybe they can enhance at the lab. That's why I need you to take this guy and see what he has and what he knows. He's sitting on a chair in the lobby.

Grab him before he decides he doesn't want to wait any longer."

"On my way. But hey, L-T, I'm out of here in sixty. You signing any greenies tonight? I still haven't touched the assault and now I have this witness."

She was referring to the green voucher cards a shift supervisor had to sign to authorize overtime.

"I'll give you an hour, that's it," Munroe said. "I can't blow the bank in one night. That should give you enough time to talk to this guy and finish up the paper on the Dancers. The assault you can push till tomorrow—as long as the vic is still kickin'. I can't stall a homicide."

"Last I checked, she came through surgery."

"Okay, then come take this guy off my hands."

"Roger that."

Ballard clicked off. She was pleased that she would not be turning the Ramona Ramone case over to the CAPs unit at the end of shift. That was more important to her than the overtime. On her way to the front lobby she cruised by Jenkins's desk and saw that he was still typing with two fingers. She told him about the witness and added that they'd scored an hour of overtime, if he wanted it. He said no thanks, he had to get home.

7

The witness was a twenty-three-year-old clubber named Zander Speights. Ballard took him back to the detective bureau and put him in a small interview room. He was a slightly built man wearing a dark blue hoodie over gray sweatpants. He kept his hands in the pockets of the hoodie, even when he sat down.

"Zander—is that your real name?" Ballard began.

"Short for Alexander," Speights said. "I like Zander better."

"Okay. What do you do for a living, Zander?"

"Oh, a little bit of this and a little bit of that. I'm sellin' shoes at the moment."

"Where?"

"On Melrose. A place called Slick Kicks."

Ballard was not taking notes. When they entered the room, she had adjusted the thermostat, which actually turned on the room's recording devices. It was wired for sight and sound.

"So you were in the Dancers earlier this morning when the shooting started?" she asked.

"That's right," Speights said. "I was there."

"Were you alone?"

"No, I was with my boy Metro."

"What's Metro's real name?"

"I don't rightly know. He's just Metro to me."

"Where'd you meet him?"

"He works at Kicks. Met him there."

"So when did you get to the Dancers?"

"Last night, 'round midnight."

"And you saw the shooting?"

"No, it was like behind me. Two booths away, so I had my back to it. But just when it went down, I was taking selfies and I got the first shot. It's crazy."

"Show me."

Speights took his iPhone out of his hoodie's pocket and opened up the photo archive.

"I took three on Live Photos," he said. "You can swipe through."

He put the phone down on the table between them and slid it to Ballard. She looked at the photo on the screen. Front and center was Speights himself but over his right shoulder Ballard could see the dark outlines of the other crowded booths. No one was identifiable. It would be up to the video unit in the lab to try to enhance.

"Keep going," Speights urged. "I got the shot."

The second photo Ballard swiped to was similar to the first, but the third grabbed her interest. The camera had captured a flash of light in the second booth over Speights's shoulder. He had indeed taken the photo just as the shooting started. He got the muzzle flash. Because the phone's camera had the Live Photos feature, it captured a second of action leading to the actual freeze-frame. Ballard tapped it several times to replay and saw that within that single second she could see the killer's arm raise the weapon and then the shot.

Ballard used her fingers to expand the photo and

center the screen on the flash of light. It was very blurry but she could tell that the shooter's back was to the camera. She could see the indistinct lines of the back of his head and his right shoulder. His right arm was up, holding the weapon and pointing it directly across the booth at the man who would moments later slump to his left and hang out of the booth. The victim's face was blurred as he recoiled at the sight of the weapon.

"I bet they can enhance that," Speights said. "Is there a reward or something?"

Ballard looked over the top of the phone at Speights as his motives for coming into the station became clear.

"A reward?" she asked.

"Yeah, you know, like for helping solve the case," Speights said.

"I don't know anything about a reward."

"Well, there should be. I was in danger."

"We'll have to see about that later. Tell me what happened when the shooting started. What did you do?"

"Me and Metro got under the table and hid out," Speights said. "Then the shooter ran by our table and shot some more people. We waited until he was gone and then got the fuck out of there."

Ballard texted the photo showing the muzzle flash to her own phone.

"Mr. Speights, do you know where Metro lives?" she asked.

"Nah, I don't know," Speights said. "This was the first time we hung out and we both had our own wheels."

"Okay, we'll find him through Slick Kicks if we need to."

"He'll be there."

"And I'm sorry but we're going to have to keep your phone for a while."

"Ah, fuck, man, you just texted the photo to yourself, right? You got the photo."

He pointed to his phone.

"I understand," Ballard said. "But your phone has the Live Photos feature and the lab may be able to pull stills from each moment of the shot you took. It looks like the gun is clearer before the recoil from the shot. It could be very useful, and I think they'll want the camera it was taken on, not just a copy of the photo. They need to look at your phone."

"Fuck me. How long?"

"I'm not sure but hopefully just a few days."

She knew that was a lie. He would probably never get the phone back, as it would be held as evidence. But she decided to leave that for someone in RHD to explain.

"What do I use for a phone in the meantime?" Speights demanded.

"Maybe you can borrow one or get a burner," Ballard offered.

"Fuck me."

"I want you to stay here while I print a property-received receipt."

"Goddamn. There better be a reward or something."

Ballard stood up.

"I'll look into that. And I'll be back as soon as I print the receipt."

Ballard left the room with the phone and walked over to Jenkins, who was still typing.

She held the phone up in front of him and tapped the photo, setting the one-second video into motion.

"Holy shit," Jenkins said.

"Yeah," Ballard said. "Million-to-one shot."

"Can you see anybody?"

"Not the shooter—his back's to the camera. But I think the lab might be able to identify the gun off it."

"Nice. You tell Olivas?"

"About to."

Back at her borrowed workstation she realized she had left her rover in the car and did not have a phone contact for Lieutenant Olivas. His number had been blocked when he called her earlier. She could send him an e-mail but that wasn't expedient. Opening her phone, she scrolled through the contacts until she came to the name Ken Chastain. She had kept his number, even after he betrayed their partnership and she had been transferred out of RHD. She sent him a text.

> Tell Olivas: walk-in witness at 6 was in nearby booth. Has cell photo of shooting. Lab may be able to enhance.

After sending it, she printed a property receipt for Speights. She went to grab it out of the printer and then drop by the break room to get a coffee. She allowed herself one cup a night, and it was time. It would give her enough of a boost to finish the shift and then an hour's paddle on the bay. After that, she would crash and recuperate. On her way she called across the room to Jenkins but he passed on the caffeine.

In the break room she was putting a coffee pod into the brewer when her phone dinged with a return text from Chastain.

Who's this?

He had not even kept her number in his phone. She answered with her old radio designation from RHD—King65—and also forwarded the muzzle-flash photo. If Chastain had a newer iPhone, he would be able to see the split-second video image and realize its value.

By the time she got back to her workstation her phone was buzzing with a blocked call. She expected it to be Chastain but it was Olivas.

"Detective, do you still have the witness there?"

"Yes, he's in an interview room. Probably wondering where I've been for twenty minutes."

"Hold him. Chastain is en route and will be there in five minutes. Does he have any other photos?"

"Not like the one I sent Chastain."

"And you have the phone?"

"On my desk and about to get the guy to sign a receipt."

"Good. Chastain will be taking the phone too."

"Got it."

"Have you filed your reports, Detective?"

"About to. I booked the victim's property here and just have a couple interview summaries to finish."

"Finish and file, Detective."

Again, Olivas disconnected before she could respond. She looked up and saw that Jenkins had sauntered over.

"What's happening?"

"Chastain is coming for the phone and the witness. We're still out of it."

"Good. I'm almost done with the burglary."

He started to turn back toward his corner of the room.

"Don't you ever want to see something through?" Ballard asked.

Jenkins didn't turn around.

"Not anymore," he said.

He kept going. Ballard then heard pounding on the door of the interview room. Zander Speights had just found out he had been locked in. Ballard went to the room with the receipt and opened the door.

"What the fuck? You lock me in here like I'm a prisoner or somethin'?"

"You're not a prisoner, Mr. Speights. It's department policy. We can't have civilians roaming around the station."

"Well, what's going on? Where's my phone?"

"I have your phone and another detective is coming to talk to you. It's his case and he thinks you may be quite an important witness. In fact, you should talk to him about the reward. I'm sure he can help with that."

"Really?"

"Yes, really. So I need you to step back and have a seat and calm down. Here is the receipt for your phone. I need you to sign one copy and keep the second. Detective Chastain should be here in a few minutes."

She pointed to his seat at the table and he started moving back from the door. He sat down and signed the receipt with a pen she handed him. She then took the signed copy and retreated, closing the door and locking it again.

Chastain got there five minutes later, walking in from the back hallway. He came directly to Ballard at her workstation.

"Where's my witness?"

"Room two. His name is Zander Speights. And here's the phone."

She had already put it in a clear plastic evidence bag. She held it up to him and he took it.

"Okay, I'm going to take him."

"Good luck."

He turned and headed toward the interview room. Ballard stopped him.

"Oh, I also booked the waitress's property, if you want it," she said. "When I talked to the parents a little while ago, her father said her boyfriend was a drug pimp. Made her sell in the club."

Chastain nodded.

"Interesting but probably not related," he said.

"I didn't think so," Ballard said. "But the stuff's there in property. If you don't take it, it'll get sent down with the next courier pickup."

Chastain did another one-eighty to head toward the interview room but then once again walked back to her.

"How's Lola doing?"

"She's good."

"Good."

Then nothing. But Chastain didn't move. Ballard finally looked up at him.

"Something else?" she asked.

"Uh, yeah," he said. "You know, Renée, I'm really sorry about how everything worked out back then."

Ballard looked at him for a moment before answering.

"It took you two years to say that?" she finally said.

He shrugged.

"I guess so. Yeah."

"You're totally forgetting something you told me back then."

"What are you talking about?"

"I'm talking about when you told me to back off the complaint. About how you said Olivas was going through a bad divorce and losing half his pension and not acting right and all of that bullshit—as if it made what he did to me okay."

"I don't understand what that has to do with—"

"You didn't even keep my number in your phone, Kenny. You washed your hands of the whole thing. You're not sorry about anything. You saw an opportunity back then and you took it. You had to throw me under the bus but you didn't hesitate."

"No, you're wrong."

"No, I'm right. If anything, you feel guilty, not sorry."

She stood up at her desk to get on equal footing with him.

"Why the hell did I ever think you would do the right thing and back your own partner?" she said. "I was stupid to trust you, and here I am. But you know what? I'd rather be working the late show with Jenkins than be with you at RHD. At least I know what to expect from him."

Chastain stared at her for a moment, color rising in his cheeks. Ballard remembered that he had an easy tell when people got to him. And she had gotten to him. Next came the awkward smile and the mouth wipe. She had hit the trifecta.

"Okay, then," he finally said. "Thanks for the witness."

He turned toward the interview room.

"Anytime," Ballard called after him.

She grabbed the empty coffee cup off the desk and headed toward the squad room exit. She didn't want to be anywhere near Chastain.

8

The hour of overtime she had worked pushed Ballard into the heavy morning traffic moving west toward the beaches. The army of service industry workers advanced from the east side to their minimum-wage-and-under jobs in hotels, restaurants, and neighborhoods where they could not afford to live. It took Ballard almost an hour to get to Venice. Her first stop was to pick up Lola from the overnight caretaker and then they headed to the beach.

The only good thing about the slog across the city was that the marine layer was already burning off by the time she got to the sand, and she could see that the bay was cobalt blue and as flat as glass. She parked in one of the lots by the north end of the boardwalk and went to the back of her van. She let Lola out, grabbed one of her tennis balls out of the basket by the wheel well, and threw it across the empty parking lot. The dog took off after it and had it in her mouth in three seconds. She dutifully brought it back to Ballard, who threw it a few more times before putting it back in the basket. The dog whined at having such a short game.

"We'll play later," Ballard promised.

She wanted to get out on the water before the wind kicked up.

Ballard's van was a white Ford Transit Connect that she'd bought used from a window washer who was retiring and closing his business. It had eighty thousand miles on it but the previous owner had taken good care of it. Ballard kept the ladder racks on the roof for carrying her board, and as in the work car she shared with Jenkins, the rear storage area of the van was compartmentalized with cardboard boxes.

Before exiting Hollywood Station, Ballard had changed into faded jeans and a red hoodie over a tank suit, leaving her work suit in a locker. She now stripped down to the tank and put the other clothes in a backpack along with underwear, socks, and a pair of New Balance trainers. She next grabbed one of the wet suits off a hanger hooked on the inside wall of the van. She squeezed into it and pulled the rear zipper up her back with a short tether. She took a big beach towel out of one of the boxes and stuffed that into the backpack last. She clipped her tent bag to the side of the backpack and put it on over both shoulders.

Lastly, she grabbed a multigrain-and-chocolate energy bar out of an insulated cooler she kept food in and was ready. She closed and locked the van, then pulled her board off the roof racks. It was an eight-foot One World board with the paddle attached to clips on the deck. It was a bear to bring down off the van's roof and she was careful not to bounce the tail fin on the asphalt. She put her fingers into the center grip hole and carried the board under her right arm while using her left to feed herself. She trudged toward the water barefoot and walking gingerly until she was off the parking lot and into the sand. Lola followed dutifully.

She set up the tent twenty-five yards off the water's edge. Its assembly was an easy, five-minute routine. She placed her backpack inside to stabilize the tent against any wind and then zipped the entrance closed. She buried the key to the van in the sand by the front-right corner of the tent and then pointed at the spot until the dog took her place there.

"Keep watch," she said.

The dog bowed her head once. Ballard hefted the thirty-pound board again and carried it to the water. She wrapped the leash around her right ankle and secured it with the Velcro strap, then pushed the board out ahead of her.

Ballard only weighed 125 pounds and could step up onto the board without tipping the balance. She powered through four right-hand strokes with the paddle to get out past the low rollers and then at last was smoothly gliding through what was left of the morning mist. She looked back once at her dog, even though she knew she didn't have to. Lola sat at attention at the right-front corner of the tent. She would do so until Ballard got back.

Ballard had started a paddling routine soon after her transfer to the late show. She had grown up surfing on the West Maui beaches between Wailea and Lahaina and had traveled to surf with her father in Fiji, Australia, and elsewhere, but she left surfing behind when she moved to the forty-eight to pursue a career in law enforcement. Then one night she and Jenkins were called to a residential burglary in the bird streets in the hills off Doheny Drive. A couple had come home from dinner at Spago and found the door to their $5 million home ajar and the interior ransacked. Patrol officers arrived first and then Ballard and Jenkins were called out because the victims were deemed HVC—high-value constituents—by the station commander. He wanted detectives to roll along with a crime scene team right away.

Shortly after arriving, Jenkins was supervising the crime scene techs at the point of entry while Ballard surveyed the home with the lady of the house, trying to determine exactly what had been taken. In the master bedroom they entered a massive walk-in closet. It was hidden behind floor-to-ceiling mirrors and not seen when the first patrol officers to arrive had checked the house. On the floor of the closet a fur coat was spread open. Piled in the center of the coat's silk lining were a mound of jewelry and three pairs of high-heeled shoes with red soles that Ballard knew cost more than a thousand dollars apiece.

At that moment, Ballard realized that the burglar might still be in the home. At the exact same moment, the intruder jumped from behind a row of clothes on hangers and tackled her to the ground. The lady of the house backed up against a mirrored wall in the closet and stood there frozen and mute as Ballard struggled with a man who had almost a hundred pounds on her.

The intruder grabbed one of the red-soled shoes and was attempting to drive the spiked heel into Ballard's eye. She held his arm back but knew he was too strong to hold off for long. She managed to call out for Jenkins as the spike came closer to her face. She turned her face at the last moment and the spike dragged across her cheek, drawing a line of blood. The intruder pulled it back to start another go at her eye, when he was suddenly hit from behind by Jenkins wielding a small bronze sculpture he had picked up on his way through the bedroom. Ballard's attacker collapsed unconscious on top of her. The sculpture broke in two.

The intruder turned out to be the couple's schizophrenic son, who had disappeared from the home years earlier and was presumed to be living on the streets in Santa Monica. Ballard ended up with four butterfly stitches applied to her cheek at Cedars-Sinai, and Jenkins and the department got sued by the couple and their son for using excessive force and for damaging an expensive work of art. The city settled the lawsuit for a quarter million dollars and Ballard took up paddleboarding to increase her upper-body strength and clear her mind of the memory of the spiked heel inching toward her eye.

The sky turned gray as the sun slipped behind the clouds, and the water turned a dark, impenetrable blue. Ballard liked turning the paddle blade sideways and watching it slice a thin line down through the water until the white tip on it disappeared in darkness. She would then turn the blade and power through a full stroke, the board and paddle making barely a mark on the surface as she moved. She called it stealth paddling.

She made a wide loop that took her at least three hundred yards offshore. She checked her tent every few minutes and saw no one approaching or disturbing it or the dog. Even from a distance she could identify the lifeguard in the station seventy-five yards down the beach. Aaron Hayes was one of her favorites. He was her backup to Lola. She knew he would be watching over her things and would probably visit her later.

Her mind wandered as she worked and she thought of the confrontation earlier with Chastain in the detective bureau. She wasn't happy with herself. She had waited two years to say what she had said to him but it had been the wrong time and place. Ballard had been too consumed with his betrayal to remember what was important in the present—the murder of five people, including Cynthia Haddel.

She turned the board and paddled further out. She felt guilty. It didn't matter that Haddel was a peripheral victim—Ballard felt that she had let her down by putting her own agenda with Chastain first. It went to the sacred bond that existed between homicide victims and the detectives who speak for them. It wasn't Ballard's case but Haddel was her victim and the bond was there.

Ballard bent her knees sharply and took several deep digging strokes as she tried to move on from the Chastain loop she kept playing in her head. She tried to think about Ramona Ramone instead and about Officer Taylor saying that she had been at the upside-down house. Ballard wondered what that meant, and it worked on her, becoming the new loop that played in her head.

After an hour on the water, Ballard had a layer of sweat building between her skin and the wet suit. It kept her warm but she could feel her muscles tightening. Her shoulders, thighs, and hamstrings ached and it felt like the point of a pencil had been pushed into a spot between her shoulder blades. She turned back toward the shore and finished with a sprint of deep, long pulls on the paddle. She came out of the water so thoroughly exhausted that she tore the leash off her ankle and dragged the tail of the board in the sand all the way back to the tent. Even as she did it she knew she was violating the first thing her father ever taught her: "Don't drag the board. Bad for the glass."

Lola had not moved from her position as sentry at the front of the tent.

"Good girl, Lola," Ballard said. "Good girl."

She put the board down next to the tent and patted her dog. She unzipped the entrance and grabbed a treat for Lola out of a pocket on the inside flap. She also pulled her backpack out. After feeding the dog the treat, she told her to stay and walked across the sand to the row of public showers behind the paddle-tennis courts. She stripped off the wet suit and showered in her bathing suit, keeping a wary eye out for the homeless men who had started to wake and move about the nearby boardwalk. Her late start put her on their schedule. She was usually finished paddling and showering before any life even stirred on the boardwalk.

When she was sure she had all the salt out of her hair, she cut the water and dried off with the large beach towel she removed from the backpack. She pulled the straps of her bathing suit down over her shoulders, then wrapped the towel around her body from armpits to knees. She dropped the wet bathing suit to the concrete and brought her underwear up her legs and under the towel. She had been dressing on beaches this way ever since she used to surf before classes at Lahainaluna

High School. By the time she dropped the towel, she was dressed again in her jeans and hoodie. Using the towel to dry her hair, she went back across the sand to the tent, patted Lola on the head again, and crawled into the nylon shelter.

"Easy, girl," she said.

Lola dropped down into a resting pose but maintained her spot on top of where the key was buried. Ballard got another dog treat out of the pocket on the tent flap and tossed it to her. The dog ripped it out of the air with her teeth and then quickly returned to her stoic pose. Ballard smiled. She had bought Lola off a homeless man on the boardwalk two years earlier. The animal was emaciated and chained to a shopping cart. She had open wounds that looked like they had come from fighting other dogs. Ballard had simply wanted to rescue her but a bond quickly formed and the dog stayed with her. They took training classes together and soon it seemed as though the dog had a sense that Renée had saved her. She was unfailingly loyal to Ballard, and Ballard felt the same way.

Ready to sleep, Ballard pulled the zipper on the tent flap down. It was eleven a.m. Normally she would sleep until it was almost sunset but this time Ballard set her phone to wake her at two p.m. She had plans for the day before starting her official shift at eleven.

She hoped for three hours of sleep but barely got two. Shortly after one o'clock she was awakened by the low growl Lola projected when someone invaded her no-fly zone. Ballard opened her eyes but didn't move.

"Come on, Lola. You don't love me anymore?"

Still coming out of interrupted sleep, Ballard recognized the voice. It was Aaron Hayes.

"Lola," she said. "It's okay. What's up, Aaron? I was sleeping."

"Sorry. You want some company in there? I got my lunch break."

"Not today, Aaron. I've gotta get up soon and go in."

"Okay. Sorry I woke you up. By the way, you looked good out there today. Like you were walking on water. Good, long strokes."

"Tired myself out, but thanks, Aaron. Good night."

"Uh, yeah, good night."

She heard him chuckle as he walked away in the sand.

"Good girl, Lola," she said.

Ballard rolled onto her back and looked up at the roof of the tent. The sun was high and so bright she could see it through the nylon. She closed her eyes and tried to remember if she had been dreaming before Aaron woke her. She couldn't remember anything but thought there was something there in the gray tendrils of her sleep. There had been a dream. She just couldn't remember what it was. She tried to retrieve it, to slip back in, but she knew that a standard sleep cycle was about ninety minutes. To go back to sleep and get a full cycle would take longer than she had. Her alarm was going off in less than an hour and she wanted to stick to her plan of getting up and going in to work on finding out who had used brass knuckles to assault Ramona Ramone in the upside-down house—and then left her for dead in a Hollywood parking lot.

She got out of the tent, packed and folded it up, and

then returned to the van. She restowed everything and placed the wet suit on its hanger. The board was harder to put back on the roof racks than it had been to take down. Ballard was five foot seven and had to open the side doors and stand on the sill while she secured the straps. The second strap cut across the One World logo on the underside of the board. It showed the black silhouette of a surfer riding the nose, his hands and arms up over his head and thrown back like he was flying down the steep face of a monster wave. It always reminded Ballard of her father and his last wave. The one that took him and left her running up and down the beach, unsure of what to do or where to go, and howling helplessly at the open sea.

She and Lola walked down the boardwalk to the Poke-Poke window, where Ballard ordered the Aloha bowl with added seaweed for herself and a teriyaki-beef-and-rice bowl for the dog. Lola drank from the dog bowl under the window as they waited and the man behind the counter handed Ballard a treat for Lola as well.

After lunch she took the dog back out on the sand and threw the ball a few more times. But Ballard's mind wasn't on it. The whole time she was thinking about work. She was officially off the Dancers case but couldn't help thinking about Cynthia Haddel. Ballard had the name and digits of the distributor who, according to her parents, had put her into the club to deal drugs. If RHD wasn't interested, then the buy-bust team at Hollywood Division would take the tip and do something with it. She made a mental note to drop by the unit when she got back to the station.

From the beach Ballard drove back to the critter sitter to drop off Lola. She apologized to the dog for the short day but promised to make it up to her. Lola bowed her head once, letting Ballard off the hook.

On the way into Hollywood, Ballard checked the *Los Angeles Times* feed on her phone every time she caught a red light. It had been barely twelve hours since the shooting at the Dancers, so the newspaper had scant reporting on it. Ballard was still ahead of the media curve with the limited information she had gathered on her shift. The *Times* did say, however, that there were no arrests or suspects in the mass killing as of the latest update from the LAPD. The story went out of its way to reassure readers that the police were not looking at this as a possible terrorist attack like those seen in other nightclubs domestically and around the world.

Ballard was disappointed that the newspaper had not by now gotten the names of the three men shot to death in the booth. That was the angle she was wondering about. Who were they? What went wrong in that booth?

After checking the *Times* feed, she also checked her e-mail and saw nothing on return from Lieutenant Olivas about the reports she had submitted. Apparently her paper had been accepted, if not gone unnoticed. Either way the time stamps on the e-mail she had sent would protect her from any complaint from Olivas about her failing to file her reports in a timely fashion.

Using the van's Bluetooth connection, Ballard called Hollywood Presbyterian and asked for the duty nurse in the surgical intensive-care unit. A woman who called herself Nurse Randall answered and Ballard identified herself, right down to her serial number.

85

"An assault victim named Ramona Ramone was brought in last night. I was the responding detective. She underwent brain surgery and I am checking on her status."

Ballard was put on hold, and when Randall came back, she said there was no patient in the hospital named Ramona Ramone and that Ballard must be mistaken.

"You're right," Ballard said. "Can you check a different name? Ramón Gutierrez. I forgot that's the victim's actual name."

Randall put her on hold again but this time came back more quickly.

"Yes, he's here, and he's stable after surgery," she said.

"Do you know if he's conscious yet?" Ballard asked.

"That's information you will need to get from the patient's attending physician."

"Is that physician available?"

"Not at this time. He's on his rounds."

"Nurse Randall, I am investigating this crime and trying to find out who attacked Mr. Gutierrez. If the victim is conscious, I need to drop what I'm doing and come talk to him. If he's not, then I need to proceed with the investigation. There is a very dangerous individual out there responsible for this. Are you sure you can't help me by answering that simple question? Has he regained consciousness?"

There was a long pause as Randall decided whether to break the rules.

"No, he hasn't. He is still in an induced coma."

"Thank you. Can you also tell me, have any family

members or friends come in to check on her? Him, I mean?"

"There is nothing here about that. No family listed. Friends would not be allowed to visit in ICU."

"Thank you, Nurse Randall."

Ballard disconnected. She decided she was going straight into Hollywood Station.

9

Ballard kept all her work suits in her locker at the station and dressed for her shifts after arriving each night. She had four different suits that followed the same cut and style but differed in color and pattern. She dry-cleaned them two at a time so that she always had a suit and a backup available. After arriving nearly eight hours early for her shift, Ballard changed into the gray suit that was her favorite. She accompanied it with a white blouse. She kept four white blouses and one navy in her locker as well.

It was Friday and that meant Ballard was scheduled to work solo. She and Jenkins had to cover seven shifts a week, so Ballard took Tuesday to Saturday and Jenkins covered Sunday to Thursday, giving them three overlap days. When they took vacation time, their slots usually went unfilled. If a detective in the division was needed during the early-morning hours, then someone had to be called in from home.

Working solo suited Ballard because she didn't have to run decisions by her partner. On this day, if he had known what Ballard's plan was, Jenkins would have put the kibosh on it. But because it was Friday, they would not be working together again until the following Tuesday, and she was clear to make her own moves.

After suiting up, Ballard checked herself in the mirror over the locker room sinks. She combed her sun-streaked hair with her fingers. That was all she usually had to do. Constant immersion in salt water and exposure to the sun over years had left her with broken, flyaway hair that she kept no longer than chin length out of necessity. It went well with her tan and gave off a slightly butch look that reduced advances from other officers. Olivas had been an exception.

Ballard squeezed some Visine drops into her eyes, which were red from the salt water. After that she was good to go. She went into the break room to brew a double-shot espresso on the Keurig. She would be operating now and through the night on less than three hours of sleep. She needed to start stacking caffeine. She kept her eye on the wall clock because she wanted to time her arrival in the detective bureau at shortly before four p.m., when she knew the lead detective in the CAPs unit would also be watching the clock, getting ready to split for the weekend.

She had at least fifteen minutes to kill, so she went upstairs to the offices of the buy-bust team next to the vice unit. Major Narcotics was located downtown but each division operated its own street-level drug squad that moved nimbly and was responsive to citizen complaints about drug-dealing hot spots. Ballard had limited connections to the officers assigned to the unit, so she went in cold-calling. The duty sergeant took the information she had on Cynthia Haddel's boyfriend/drug pimp. The name Cynthia's father had given Ballard was someone the sergeant said was already on their radar as a small-time dealer who worked the Hollywood club scene.

What made Ballard feel bad was that he said that the guy had a girlfriend working —and selling for him —in just about every hot spot in the division. She left the office, wondering if Haddel had known that or had believed she was the only one.

At 3:50 p.m. Ballard entered the detective bureau and looked for a spot to use as a work base. She saw that the desk she had used the night before was still empty and she thought maybe the detective who owned it had left early or was on the four-tens schedule and off Fridays. As she took the spot, she scanned the bureau and her eyes settled on the four-desk pod that comprised the CAPs unit. She saw all the desks were empty except for Maxine Rowland's, the unit lead. It looked like she was packing her briefcase for the weekend.

Ballard sauntered over, timing it perfectly.

"Hey, Max," she said.

"Renée," Rowland responded. "You're early. You have court?"

"No, I came in early to clean up some work. I owe you a case from last night but the Dancers thing blew up and everything got pushed sideways."

"I get it. What's the case?"

"An abduction and assault. The victim is a transgender biological male, found circling the drain in a parking lot on the Santa Monica stroll. She's in a coma at Hollywood Pres."

"Shit."

Rowland just saw her exit to the weekend blocked. And that was what Ballard was counting on.

"Was there a sexual assault?" Rowland asked.

Ballard could tell what she was thinking: push this onto the sexual assault unit.

"Most likely but the victim lost consciousness before being interviewed," she said.

"Shit," Rowland said again.

"Look, I just came in to start the paper on it. I was also thinking I'd have time before my shift to make some calls. Why don't you get out of here and let me run with it? I'm on tomorrow, too, so I could take it through the weekend and get back with you next week."

"You sure? If it's a bad beat, I don't want to part-time it."

"I won't. I'll work it. I haven't been able to follow up on anything off the late show in a long while. There are some leads here. You recall anything lately with brass knuckles?"

Rowland thought for a moment and then shook her head.

"Brass knuckles . . . No."

"What about an abduction off the stroll? She was taken somewhere and bound, then taken back. Could've been a couple days."

"It's not ringing any bells but you need to go up to talk to vice."

"I know. It was my next stop if you let me run with it. What about the 'upside-down house'? That mean anything to you?"

"How do you mean?"

"She said it. To the patrol cops. She momentarily regained consciousness while they were waiting for the RA. She said she had been attacked at the upside-down house."

"Sorry. Never heard of it."

"Okay, anything else on your plate like this? Somebody grabbed on the stroll?"

"I'll have to think, but I can't remember anything right now."

"I'll run it through the box, see what comes up."

"So you're sure you'll take it? I can call a couple of my guys back in. They won't be happy but those are the breaks."

"Yes, I've got it. You go home. Don't call anybody in. If you want, I'll send you updates over the weekend."

"Tell you the truth, I can wait till Monday. Going up to Santa Barbara for the weekend with my kids. The less I have to worry about, the better."

"You got it."

"Don't fuck me on this, Renée."

"Hey, I'm telling you I won't."

"Good."

"Have a nice weekend."

Rowland was always blunt and Ballard took no offense. Something about working sex cases had taken subtlety out of her personality.

Ballard left her there to finish packing up and went back to the second floor, this time ducking into the vice unit. Like the buy-bust guys, the vice cops kept odd hours, and there was never a guarantee that anyone would be in the unit. She entered and leaned over the counter to look into the alcove where the sergeants sat. She got lucky. Pistol Pete Mendez was at one of the desks, eating a sandwich. He was the only one there.

"Ballard, what do you want?" he asked. "Come around."

It was his usual gruff greeting. Ballard reached over the half door to where she knew the lock switch was located and let herself in. She went into the alcove and pulled out the chair opposite Mendez's desk.

"Ramón Gutierrez," she said. "I'm working follow-up on that case. You guys hear anything about it last night?"

"Not a peep," Mendez said. "But we were working East Hollywood and that's a whole different kettle of fish from the dragon walk."

"Right. When was the last time you were over there on Santa Monica?"

"Been about a month because things have been pretty tame there. But it's like cockroaches. You can fumigate but they always come back."

"You heard anything about a bad actor picking up pros and hurting them?"

"Not in a long while."

"Ramone was worked over with brass knuckles. The guy was also a biter."

"We get our fair share of biters but nothing comes to mind with brass knuckles. Is your he-she going to make it?"

"That remains to be seen. Still in a coma at Hollywood Pres for now, but they'll be moving her down to County as soon as they realize they don't have a paying customer."

"That's the way it goes. Her?"

"Yeah, her. You have a file on *Ramona* I could borrow?"

"Yeah, I'll get it for you. But it's under *Ramón* Gutierrez, last I checked. What else you got?"

"You ever heard of a place called the upside-down house? Ramona said it to the blue suiters who first responded to the call."

Like Rowland, Mendez thought about it and then shook his head.

"Not that we know about here," he said. "There's an underground bondage club called Vertigo. Moves around to different locations."

"I don't think that's it," Ballard said. "Vertigo means dizzy, not upside-down. Plus I don't think this was a club thing. It's deeper than that. This victim's lucky to be alive."

"Yeah, well, I can't think of anything else. Let me find that file."

He got up from the desk and Ballard remained seated. While he was gone, she studied the schedule on the bulletin board next to his desk. It looked like vice ran operations just about every night in a different part of Hollywood. They put out undercover officers as bait and arrested the johns once they offered cash for sex. Like Mendez said, it was like cockroaches, something that never went away. Even the Internet, with its easy connections for free and paid-for sex, could not kill the stroll. It would always be there.

She could hear Mendez opening and closing file cabinets as he looked for a file on Gutierrez.

"How'd you guys end up doing last night?" she asked.

"Bubkes," Mendez said from the other side of the room. "I think that thing at the club on Sunset scared people away. We had cruisers going up and down the streets all night."

He came back to the desk and dropped a manila file down in front of Ballard.

"That's what we got," he said. "You probably could have pulled the whole thing off the box."

"I'd rather have the hard copy," Ballard said.

She would take a paper file over a computer file any day. There was always a chance that there was more in the hard file, handwritten notes in the margins, phone numbers scribbled on the folder, extra photos of crime scenes. That was never the case with a computer file.

Ballard thanked Mendez and said she would be in touch if anything developed on the case. He said he would keep his eyes and ears open on the streets.

"I hope you catch the guy," he said.

Back on the first floor, Ballard had one more stop before she was in the clear to work the case. The lieutenant in charge of the detective bureau had an office in the far corner of the squad room. The room had three windows that looked out on the squad, and through them Ballard could see Lieutenant Terry McAdams at his desk, working. Ballard often went weeks without seeing her direct supervisor because of the hours of her shift. McAdams usually worked an eight-to-five day because he liked to arrive after his detectives were in and had gotten things going for the day, and then he liked to be the last man out.

She knocked on the open door of the office and McAdams invited her in.

"Long time no see, Ballard," he said. "I heard you had a fun shift last night."

"Depends on what you consider fun," she said. "It was busy, that's for sure."

"Yeah, I saw on the watch log that before the shit hit the fan at the Dancers, you and Jenkins caught an abduction caper. But I didn't see any paper on it."

"Because there isn't any. That's what I want to talk to you about."

She summarized the Ramona Ramone case and told McAdams that she had Maxine Rowland's go-ahead to stick with it for a few days. Technically, Ballard should have started by getting an approval from McAdams, but she knew that as an administrator, McAdams liked to be brought things that were already tied in a bow. It made his job easier. He just had to say yes or no.

McAdams said what Ballard knew he would say.

"Okay, have at it, but don't let it get in the way of your normal duties," he said. "If it does, then we have a problem, and I don't like problems."

"It won't happen, L-T," she said. "I know my priorities."

Leaving the lieutenant's office, Ballard saw a small group of remaining detectives gathered in front of the three television screens mounted on the back wall of the bureau. The screens were usually silent but one of the men had raised the sound on the middle screen to hear the report on the Dancers shooting, which kicked off the five-o'clock news hour.

Ballard sauntered over to watch. On the screen was video from a press conference held earlier in the day. The chief of police was at the podium and he was flanked by Olivas and Captain Larry Gandle, commander of the Robbery-Homicide Division. The chief was reassuring the media and the public that the shooting at the Dancers was not an act of domestic terrorism. While the exact motivation for the mass killing was not known, he said, detectives were zeroing in on the circumstances that caused the extreme violence.

When the report shifted back to the news anchor, she reported that the names of the victims had not yet been released by the Coroner's Office but that sources told channel 9 that three of the victims, all believed to have been the intended targets of the shooter, had criminal records ranging from drug charges to extortion and acts of violence.

The anchor then moved on to the next story, this one about another LAPD press conference, to announce arrests in a human-trafficking investigation at the Port of Los Angeles, where a cargo container that was used to bring in young women abducted from Eastern Europe had been intercepted earlier in the year. There was file video showing the stark interior of the shipping container and aid workers offering water to and wrapping blankets around the victims as they were shepherded to safety. It was then coupled with new video showing a line of men in handcuffs being walked off a jail bus by detectives. But the story wasn't about Hollywood, and the detective with the remote lost interest. He hit the mute button. No one objected and the group around the screens started to dissipate as everybody moved back to their respective pods or headed out of the station for the weekend.

Once she got back to her desk, Ballard looked through the file Mendez had lent her. There were several arrest reports going back three years, as well as booking photos that showed the progression of Ramona Ramone's physical changes as she transitioned. There were more than cosmetic changes, like eyebrow shaping. It was clear from the front and side photos that her lips had gotten fuller and she'd had her Adam's apple shaved.

There were three shake cards clipped to the inside of the file folder. These were 3 × 5 cards with handwritten notes taken while patrol or vice officers stopped Ramone on the stroll to question what she was doing. Officially called field interview or FI cards, they were more often called shake cards because the American Civil Liberties Union had repeatedly complained that the unwarranted interviews of people whom the police were suspicious of were actually shakedowns. The rank and file embraced that description and continued the practice of stopping and interviewing suspicious individuals and writing down details about their description, tattoos, gang affiliation, and hangout locations.

The cards written on Ramona Ramone largely said the same thing and most contained information Ballard already knew. Some of the notes revealed more about the personality of the officer than it did about Ramone. One officer wrote, *Holy shit this is a guy!*

The one piece of useful information Ballard gleaned from the cards was that Gutierrez/Ramone had no driver's license and therefore no verifiable home address. The official reports simply stated the address where the arrest was made, most often on Santa Monica Boulevard. But during the field interviews, she had twice given an address on Heliotrope. The third card said, *Lives in trailer, moves around the 6.* This information was good to have and Ballard was glad she had gone up to see Mendez.

Finished with her review of the file and Ramone's background, Ballard fired up the computer terminal and went to work, looking for the suspect. Her plan was to start small and go big—to look for local cases that were similar to the attack on Ramone. If she found nothing, then she would widen her computer search to look for similar cases in the state of California, then the country, and then even the world.

Working the department's computer archives was an art form. Formally, the system was called DCTS— Detective Case Tracking System. One wrong input in the search parameters could easily result in a "no records found" response, even if there was a closely matching case somewhere in the data. Ballard composed a short list of details that she would enter and subtract from until she got a hit.

Transgender
Bite
Brass Knuckles
Bound Prostitute
Santa Monica Boulevard

She entered them into a search of all cases in the archive and got a quick "no records found." She eliminated Santa Monica Boulevard, searched again, and got the same response. She continued to search, dropping words as she went and then trying different combinations and adding variations, using "bindings" and "tied up" instead of "bound," "escort" instead of "prostitute." But none of the combinations scored a hit in the data.

Frustrated and beginning to feel the effects of less than three hours' sleep, Ballard got up from her station and started walking down the now empty aisles of the bureau, hoping to get her blood moving. She wanted to avoid a caffeine headache, so she held off on going to the break room for another coffee. She stood for a moment in front of the silent TV screens and watched a man in front of a weather map that showed no sign of inclement weather heading toward L.A.

She knew it was time to widen the search outside the city. With that would come a lot of desk work as she tried to chase down far-off cases that might be connected to hers. It would be a slog and the prospect was daunting. She returned to the desk and put another call in to Hollywood Presbyterian to check on her victim on the off chance she had miraculously come to and could be interviewed.

But there was no change. Ramona Ramone was still in an induced coma.

Ballard hung up the phone and looked at the list of case attributes that had failed to draw a hit from the data bank.

"Key words, my ass," she said out loud.

She decided to try one more angle.

California was one of only four states that made possession of brass knuckles—or metal knuckles, as they were referred to in the statutes—illegal. Other states had age minimums and laws against using them in the commission of a crime, but in California they were illegal across the board, and violating the law could be charged as a felony.

Ballard typed in one more search of the LAPD's data

archive, asking for all cases in the last five years involving an arrest for possession of brass knuckles, felony or misdemeanor.

She got fourteen hits on separate cases, which she thought was surprisingly high given that the weapon had so rarely come up in cases she had worked or had even known about in her ten years as a detective.

Ballard checked the wall clock and started the task of pulling up expanded records on the cases to see if anything in the summary reports remotely connected in MO to her case. She was quickly able to move through most of the cases because they involved gang arrests in South Los Angeles, where it appeared to Ballard that brass knuckles were employed in lieu of firearms by gangbangers who probably didn't know they were illegal.

There were other arrests involving pimps and mob enforcers for possession of metal knuckles, with their intended use of the weapons being obvious. And then Ballard came across a three-year-old case that immediately held her attention.

A man named Thomas Trent had been arrested for possession of brass knuckles by the Valley Bureau vice unit. The case had not come up on Ballard's previous key-word search because none of the other words in her combinations was in play. Trent had been charged with the brass knuckles offense only, nothing else.

And yet it was a vice case. That contradiction was what had initially caught Ballard's eye. When she pulled up the digital case file, she learned that Trent, thirty-nine at the time, had been arrested during a sting operation at a motel on Sepulveda Boulevard. The summary report said he had knocked on the door of a room at the Tallyho Lodge near Sherman Way, where the vice unit had been sending men who had connected online with an officer posing as an underage Latino male available for submissive role play. Trent had made no appointment at the motel and the vice officers could not connect him to any of the men who had taken part in the online conversations.

They believed he had probably been one of the online suitors but they did not have evidence of that and could not charge him with solicitation of a minor. But they also did not need to pursue linking him to the online sting once they found brass knuckles in his pockets. He was arrested for felony possession of a dangerous weapon and booked into the Van Nuys jail.

The summary report listed the undercover officer who arrested Trent by serial number only. Ballard sent the report to the bureau's printer, then picked up the desk phone and called the department's personnel unit. She quickly had a name to go with the serial number of the vice officer. He was Jorge Fernandez and he was still assigned to the Valley Bureau's vice squad. Ballard called the Valley vice unit and was told that Fernandez was off duty. She left her cell number and a message for him to call her back, no matter what time.

She next took a deeper dive into online records and pulled up an abstract on Trent's case. She learned that following his arrest, Trent negotiated an agreement with the District Attorney's Office in which he pleaded no contest to a misdemeanor charge of possession of a dangerous weapon, paid a five-hundred-dollar fine, and was placed on three years' probation. The plea was part of a pretrial intervention program that would allow Trent to have his record cleaned if he completed probation without another arrest.

On the court records, Trent's home address was listed on Wrightwood Drive in Studio City. Ballard plugged the address into Google and found a map showing that Wrightwood dropped off of Mulholland Drive on the northern slope of the Santa Monica Mountains. She clicked on the street-view feature and saw what looked like a contemporary ranch house with a double-wide garage. But she knew from the map that the house was on the mountain and that it was most likely that the structure stretched one or two levels down the slope from the street. It was a very typical design of many of the homes in the hills. The top floor contained the common areas—kitchen, dining room, living room, and so on—while the lower levels contained the bedrooms. There would be stairs, or in some cases an elevator, that led down to the lower floors.

Ballard realized that someone unfamiliar with these mountainside designs could view the houses as odd because the bedrooms were on the bottom floors. In that way, Trent's home might be considered an upside-down house.

That realization dumped a jolt of adrenaline into Ballard's blood. She leaned closer to the computer screen to study Trent's booking photo and arrest report. The personal details on the report said Trent was a car salesman who worked at an Acura dealership on Van Nuys Boulevard. The first question that struck her at that point was how a car salesman afforded a home in the hills, where price tags easily started in the seven figures.

She switched over to a different search site that handled public records and put in Trent's name and date of birth. Soon she was looking at records of a marriage dissolution that occurred seven months after his arrest. Beatrice Trent had claimed irreconcilable differences in her divorce petition and it appeared that Trent did not contest the filing. The three-year marriage was dissolved.

There was also a record of a lawsuit from 2011 in which Trent was the plaintiff in a personal injury claim against a company called Island Air and its insurer. The record showed only the filing—for injuries sustained in a helicopter crash in Long Beach—but not the outcome of the case. Ballard assumed that this meant the case had been settled before trial.

Ballard printed all of these reports and then picked up the desk phone and called the dealership where Trent worked. She asked for him by name and the call was transferred.

A voice said, "This is Tom. How can I help you?"

Ballard hesitated and then disconnected. She looked at the clock and saw it was just past six o'clock and in the guts of rush hour. It would be a miserable crawl from Hollywood up into the Valley.

There was no guarantee that Trent would even still be working by the time she got there, but Ballard decided to give it a shot. She wanted to get a look at him.

10

The Acura dealership where Thomas Trent worked was at the end of a long stretch of competing dealerships that stretched north along Van Nuys Boulevard toward the center of the Valley. It took Ballard almost an hour to get there. She had driven her own van because the city-ride assigned to her and Jenkins screamed COP! with its baby-shit-brown paint, no-frills hubcaps, and grille-and-rear-window flashers. Her purpose was only to get a look at Trent and get a read on him, not to alert him to the police interest.

She had downloaded the mug shot from Trent's arrest three years earlier to her phone and she pulled it up on the screen now. Parked at a curb on Van Nuys, she studied it and then scanned the new-and used-car lots for salesmen. There was no match. The interior showroom was still a possibility, but since the sales booths appeared to be lined along the rear wall, she had no angle on their occupants. She called the dealership's main number and asked for Trent again, just to make sure he hadn't left for the day. He once again answered in the same way, but this time Ballard didn't disconnect.

"This is Tom, how can I help you?"

There was a salesman's confidence in his voice.

"I wanted to come in and look at an RDX but with this traffic I may be a while getting there," Ballard said.

She had read the name of the model off the windshield of an SUV that sat on a pedestal near the lot's entrance.

"No worries!" Trent exclaimed. "I'm here till we shut her down tonight. What's your name, hon?"

"Stella."

"Well, Stella, are you looking to buy or lease?"

"Purchase."

"Well, you're in luck. We have a one percent financing deal going on this month. You bringing in a trade for me?"

"Uh, no. I think I'm just looking to buy."

Through the showroom glass Ballard saw a man stand up in one of the booths on the rear wall. He was holding a corded phone to his ear. He put his arm down on top of the booth's partition and spoke into the phone.

"Well, whatever you want, we've got," he said.

Ballard heard the words at the same time the man in the showroom said them. It was Trent, though his appearance had changed some since his bust on Sepulveda Boulevard. He had a shaved head now and eyeglasses. Judging from what she could see of him, he had bulked up as well. His shoulders stretched the fabric of his short-sleeved dress shirt and it looked like his neck was too thick for him to connect the top button behind his tie.

Ballard saw something then and quickly reached into the storage compartment in the center console. She pulled out a compact set of binoculars.

"So, when you think you'll get here?" Trent asked.

"Um . . ." Ballard stalled.

She put the phone on her lap and looked through

the binos. She focused and got her first good look at Trent. The hand that was holding the phone to his ear appeared to be bruised along the knuckles.

She picked the phone back up.

"Twenty minutes," she said. "I'll see you then."

"Good deal," Trent said. "I'll have an RDX ready to go."

She ended the call, started the van, and pulled away from the curb.

Ballard drove up Van Nuys two blocks and took a right into a neighborhood of World War II-era homes. She pulled to a stop in front of one without any lights on and then climbed into the back of the van. She took off her gun, badge, and rover and put them into the lockbox welded to the wheel well. She pulled her wallet out of her shoulder bag and put it in there as well—no matter what happened at the dealership, she was not going to give Trent her driver's license. She had already given a fake name and she would never risk him knowing her real name or address.

She quickly took off her suit next and put on a pair of jeans to go with her blouse. The jeans were loose-fitting so that she could wear her backup pistol in an ankle holster without it being obvious.

After putting on a pair of running shoes, she climbed back into the driver's seat. She returned to the dealership and this time drove in through the entrance and parked in front of the showroom.

Before she even got out, a silver RDX glided up behind her van and stopped—a salesman's trick. It would prevent her from leaving. Trent got out smiling and pointing his finger at Ballard as she stepped out of the van.

"Stella, right?"

Without waiting for confirmation he raised his hand to present the RDX.

"And here she is."

Ballard stepped to the back of the van. She looked at the RDX even though she wanted to look at Trent.

"Nice," she said. "Is that the only color you have?"

"At the moment," he said. "But I can get you any color you want. Two days tops."

Now she looked at Trent and put out her hand.

"Hi, by the way," she said.

He took her hand and she squeezed his firmly as they shook. She studied his face as she made sure to apply pressure to his knuckles. He never lost his salesman's smile but she saw pain pulse in his cheeks. The bruising was fresh. She knew that brass knuckles, if fitted loosely, could easily damage and bruise the hand of the user.

"You want to take a test-drive?" Trent asked.

"Sure," Ballard said.

"Perfect. I just need to make a copy of your driver's license and insurance."

"No problem."

She opened her bag and began looking through it.

"Oh, damn," she exclaimed. "I left my wallet at the office. It was my turn to pay for Starbucks and I must've left it on my desk. Damn it."

"Not a problem," Trent said. "Why don't we take the RDX and drive to your office, then we'll make copies and you drive back here?"

Ballard had considered that he might offer that and she had worked a response into her play.

"No, my office is out in Woodland Hills and I live

in Hollywood," she said. "That will take too long. My wife's already going to be waiting for me for dinner. We go out on Fridays."

"Your—" Trent said before catching himself. "Uh, well . . ."

He glanced through the glass into the showroom as if looking for someone.

"Tell you what," he said. "We'll make an exception to the rules this time if you want to take a short test-drive. Then we'll set everything up for tomorrow and you can come back with ID, insurance . . . and your checkbook. Okay?"

"All right, but I'm not completely sure I want the car," Ballard said. "I also don't like silver. I was hoping for white."

"I can get white here by Sunday, Monday at the latest. Tell you what, let's roll!"

He walked quickly around the car to the passenger side, his arms pumping as though he were running. Ballard got in behind the wheel, drove the car out onto Van Nuys Boulevard, and headed north.

Trent gave her instructions to go up to Sherman Way and then turn west to the 405. She could then take the freeway down to the Burbank Boulevard exit and back over to Van Nuys, completing a driving rectangle that would give her a sense of the vehicle in urban and freeway environments. Ballard knew that the pattern would twice take them across Sepulveda Boulevard, the street where Trent had been arrested three years earlier.

Trent's plan hit a snag when they got on the 405. It was still a virtual parking lot with evening commuters. Ballard said she would get off early at Vanowen. Most of the conversation up until that point had been about the RDX and what Ballard was looking for in a vehicle. She incorporated mention of her wife into a few of the answers to see if she could get a read on whether Trent had an issue with same-sex couples, but he never took the bait.

After exiting on Vanowen, Ballard turned south on Sepulveda. It ran parallel to Van Nuys and would take them right by the Tallyho Lodge without it seeming like she was purposely going out of their way.

The area was lined with cluttered strip malls, gas stations, mini-markets, and cheap hotels. It was prime territory for vice operations. As she drove, Ballard scanned the sidewalks but knew it was too early in the night to catch street prostitutes out and about. After they crossed Victory Boulevard, they caught a light and she used the time to survey the area and comment.

"I didn't realize it was so sketchy over this way," she said.

Trent looked about as if seeing it for the first time himself before commenting.

"Yeah, I hear it gets pretty bad over here at night," he said. "Pimps, drug pushers. Streetwalkers of all kinds."

Ballard faked a laugh.

"Like what?" she asked.

"You'd be surprised," Trent said. "Men who dress up as women, women who used to be men. Every variety of disgusting thing you can imagine."

Ballard was silent and Trent seemed to realize that he might have endangered his sale.

"Not that I make any judgments on anybody," he said. "I say, to each his own, live and let live."

"Me too," Ballard said.

After the test-drive, Ballard told Trent she wanted to think about the purchase and would call him in a day or two. He asked her to come into the showroom and go to his desk so he could fill out a customer information sheet. She declined, saying she was already late for dinner. She offered her hand again and when he shook it, she clinched her thumb and index finger sharply, causing an involuntary flinch from Trent. She turned his wrist slightly and looked down at his hand, acting as if she saw the bruising for the first time.

"Oh, I'm so sorry! I didn't know you were hurt."

"It's okay. Just a bruise."

"What happened?"

"It's a long story and not worth the time. I'd rather talk about how we can get you into a new RDX."

"Well, I'll think about it and give you a call."

"Hey, do you mind, I got a boss who's a stickler for documenting our leads. It goes into the performance evaluations, to tell you the truth. Any chance I can get you to give me your number so I can show I took the car out on a valid lead? Otherwise, he'll ding me for not verifying license and insurance."

"Uh . . ."

Ballard thought about it and decided it would not be an issue. He would not be able to trace the number to her real name.

"Sure."

She gave him the number and he wrote it down on the back of one of his own business cards. He then gave a clean one to her.

"Have a great date night, Stella."

"Thanks, Tom."

As Ballard backed her Ford out of its parking space, Trent stood in the lot and watched her go, sending her off with a friendly wave. She drove up Van Nuys Boulevard and back to the same street and spot where she had parked before. She pulled out a notebook and wrote down as many quotes from her conversation with Trent as she could remember. Extemporaneous notes written just moments after a conversation were given greater weight in court than those written much later. She had no idea if her undercover encounter with Trent would eventually become part of a case but she knew it was the smart thing to do.

After putting her notebook away, she climbed into the rear of the van again to retrieve her gun, badge, and rover. She decided she would change back into her work suit when she got to Hollywood Station. Her phone buzzed as she was climbing into the driver's seat. It was an 818 number and she took the call. It was Trent.

"Just looking at the computer here, Stella," he said. "We can get you a white one. They have them all over the place—Bakersfield, Modesto, Downey, plenty of choices. All of them fully loaded, backup camera, everything."

Ballard guessed that he was only calling to see if she had stiffed him with a phony number. The fact that she had not seemed to energize him.

"All right, well, let me think about it," Ballard said.

"You sure I can't pull the trigger on one of these right now?" Trent asked. "You would qualify for our end-of-the-day discount. That's a five-hundred-dollar credit on your down payment, Stella. You could take that money and order custom door mats or upgrade the headliner, if you want. There's a lot of—"

"No, Tom, not yet," Ballard said decisively. "I told you I was going to think about it and I will call you tomorrow or Sunday."

"Okay, Stella," Trent said. "Then I'll wait to hear from you."

The line went dead. Ballard started the engine and pulled away from the curb. She started heading south toward the mountains. She checked the dashboard clock. If Trent was working at the dealership until the ten p.m. closing, then it would be two hours before he got home. That was plenty of time for what she had planned.

11

Ballard sat in the van at the Mulholland Overlook about two blocks from Wrightwood Drive. It was a clear night and the lights of the Valley spread out to infinity toward the north. She had her rover on and tuned to the North Hollywood Division dispatch frequency. She didn't have to wait long. A radio call went out to all patrol units, reporting a possible prowler and home break-in on Wrightwood. A patrol unit accepted the call and asked where they would meet the person who reported the incident. The dispatcher said the call came from a passing motorist who declined to identify herself.

After another thirty seconds went by, Ballard keyed her rover. She identified herself to dispatch as a Hollywood Division detective who was in the area and would respond to the call as well. Dispatch repeated the information to the responding patrol unit so the officers would know that there was a friendly in the neighborhood. The dispatcher then called for an air unit to fly over the hillside neighborhood with its powerful spotlight.

Ballard pulled away from the overlook and headed to Wrightwood. As she dropped down the steep street and took the first curve, she saw a patrol car—its blue lights engaged—parked a block away. She flashed her beams as she approached and stopped the van alongside the cruiser. Two officers were getting out. Since she was in her personal car, she held her badge out the window so they could confirm she was a cop. They were from North Hollywood Division, so they were strangers to Ballard.

"Hey, guys," she said. "I was passing through and heard the call. Want some help or you've got it handled?"

"Not sure what there is to handle," said one of the officers. "Whoever called it in is GOA and we don't know exactly where this prowler was. Seems like a bull-shit call."

"Maybe," Ballard said. "But I've got a few minutes. I'm going to pull over."

She parked behind the patrol car and got out with a flashlight in one hand and the rover in the other. After introductions were made, Ballard volunteered to head up the street, knocking on doors and checking houses. The two patrol officers would work their way down the street. They had just split up when a helicopter came over the crest of the mountain and put its light down on the street. Ballard waved her own light up at it and proceeded up the street.

Thomas Trent's house was the third house she came to. There were no lights on inside that she could see. She used the butt of the metal flashlight to bang loudly on the door. She waited but no one came. She knocked again and when she was satisfied there was no one home, she stepped back to the street and started sweeping the front of the house with her light as if checking for signs of a break-in.

Ballard turned and looked down the street. She could see the flashlights of the two patrol officers on opposite sides of Wrightwood. They were checking houses and moving further away from her. The chopper had banked out and was following the curve of the hillside, training its light on the back of the homes. Ballard saw an alcove where trash cans were kept and beyond it a gate. She knew it blocked access to a set of steps that led down the side of Trent's house. It was a code requirement that hillside houses have a secondary means of access in case of fire or other emergency. She quickly moved around the trash cans to see if Trent had put a lock on the gate and she found that he had not. She opened it and started moving down the stairs.

Almost immediately her movements engaged a motion-activated light that illuminated the stairway. She brought her hand up and held it out to block the light, pretending to be blinded. She looked up through her spread fingers and checked the exterior of the house for any cameras. She saw nothing and dropped her hand. Satisfied that her image was not being recorded, she proceeded down the stairs.

The stairway had landings at two lower levels of the house, giving access to decks that ran across the rear of the structure. Ballard stepped onto the first level down and saw it was furnished with outdoor furniture and a barbecue grill. There were four sliding doors and she checked these but found them locked. She put her beam on the glass but curtains had been drawn behind the doors and she could not see inside the house.

Ballard quickly returned to the stairs and went down to the lowest level, where the deck was much smaller and there were only two sliding doors. As she approached the glass, she saw the curtain inside was only halfway extended across the door. She pointed her light at the gap and saw that the room beyond was almost empty. There was a straight-backed wooden chair at the center with a small table next to it. There appeared to be nothing else in the room.

As she swept the beam across the room, she was momentarily startled by a flash but then realized the entire wall to the right was a mirror. It was her own light that she had seen.

Ballard tried the door and found it unlocked, but after she started to slide it open, it abruptly stopped moving. She shone her light down into the door track and saw that there was a sawed-off broomstick placed in the inside track to prevent the door from being opened from the outside.

"Shit," Ballard whispered.

She knew she didn't have a lot of time before the patrol officers doubled back to check on her. She swept the flashlight across the room one more time and then moved down the deck to get a better angle on a partially opened door inside the house at the far side of the room. Through the opening she could see a hallway and part of a staircase going up to the next level of the house. She noticed a rectangular shape on the floor in the small alcove next to the stairs. She thought it might be a trapdoor leading to the foundation of the structure.

She walked out to the edge of the deck and pointed the light down over the railing. The beam shone on a lower platform on which the house's air conditioner unit sat. Ballard realized that there must be access to the equipment from beneath the house.

"Find anything?"

Ballard turned quickly from the railing. One of the patrol officers had come down the steps—the older, senior officer with four hash marks on his sleeve. His name was Sasso. He raised his light and pointed it at her.

Ballard raised her hand to block the glare.

"Do you mind?" she said.

He lowered the flashlight.

"Sorry," he said.

"No, nothing," she said. "The gate up top was open, so I thought maybe somebody came down here. But it doesn't look like anybody's even living here."

She flashed her beam on the glass doors, revealing the room that contained only the chair and table. Sasso directed his light through the door as well, then looked back at Ballard. His face was in shadow now.

"So you were just in the neighborhood?" he asked.

"I had a meeting down in the Valley and was heading over the hill," Ballard said. "I work the late show and was going in early. You heard about the club shooting last night on Sunset? I wanted to see what they were putting out in roll call about it."

"And you cross over on Wrightwood to get to Hollywood?"

There was a clear note of suspicion in his voice. Sasso had twenty years in, according to his sleeves. He had probably been party to more than a few radio calls staged by detectives to create reason to case a house. It was called ghosting.

"Things were moving slow on Laurel Canyon, so I hopped over to Vineland and it brought me up here," she said. "I was going to shoot over to Outpost and take that down."

Sasso nodded, but Ballard suspected he wasn't buying it.

"We're going to clear," he said. "We're stacking legit calls and need to get to them."

It was his way of chastising her for wasting their time.

"Sure," she said. "I'm out of here too."

"I'll call off the bird," he said.

Sasso headed back up the stairs. Ballard took one more glimpse over the deck rail before following him. She pointed her light down and saw no exterior access to the platform holding the air conditioning unit below. She was sure that access came from both inside and underneath the house.

At the top she pulled the gate closed and put the trash cans back into place as she had first seen them. She then walked back down the street to her van. The patrol car behind her made a three-point turn and went down the hill. Ballard heard the sound of the helicopter tailing away into the night. She considered returning to Trent's house to make an attempt to get down to the utility platform, but Sasso's suspicions gave her pause. He and his partner might double back to see if she had lingered in the neighborhood.

She started the van and headed up to Mulholland. Just as she had told Sasso, she took it to Outpost, passing intermittent vistas of the lighted city below, and then dropped down into Hollywood. She was on Sunset a few blocks from Wilcox when her phone buzzed. It was the return call from Jorge Fernandez of the Valley Bureau vice unit. Ballard thanked him for calling back and briefly described the case she was working with an assault victim she was unable to speak to.

"So how can I help you?" Fernandez asked.

Ballard noticed as she passed the Dancers that an FSD van was parked out front, and through the open front doors she could see bright lights inside—the kind used at crime scenes. She wondered what could be going on there twenty hours after the crime.

"Hey, Ballard, you there?" Fernandez prompted.

"Oh, yeah, sorry," she said. "So I have this guy. I wouldn't call him a suspect yet. Let's say he's more on the level of a person of interest."

"Okay, and what's it got to do with me?"

"You arrested him three years ago on a vice sting up on Sepulveda Boulevard."

"I've arrested a lot of people up there. What's his name?"

Ballard turned down Wilcox toward the station.

"Thomas Trent," she said.

There was a pause before Fernandez responded.

"Nothing," he said. "Rings no bells."

Ballard gave him the date of the arrest, said it was at the Tallyho and that Trent was the guy who had brass knuckles in his pockets.

"Oh, yeah, that guy," Fernandez said. "I remember the brass knuckles. They had words on them."

"What words?" Ballard asked. "What do you mean?"

"Shit, I can't remember. But each one had a word on it so that it would leave a mark or a bruise that said the word."

"There wasn't a description in the arrest report. It just said brass knuckles."

"I'm thinking . . ."

"Were you with a partner? You think he would know? It could be important."

"It was a task force. The whole unit was out there. I can ask around, see who remembers."

"Well, tell me about the arrest if you can. This guy brought brass knuckles to a motel room where he thought there would be an underage prostitute, and he ends up on probation. How does that happen?"

"Good lawyer, I guess."

"Seriously? You can't give me anything else?"

"Well, we were setting up in the room because we had one of these creeps coming at ten, but then there's a knock on the door at nine and it's your guy—Brass-Knuckles. We were like, what the fuck is this? So we jammed him and found the brass knuckles in the pocket of his jacket. I remember he had an excuse—he said he was like a used-car salesman or something and went on test-drives with sketchy people and needed something to protect himself."

"Brass knuckles?"

"I'm only telling you what he said."

"Okay, okay—what happened next?"

"Well, it was a wobbler. We thought he was probably our ten-o'clock guy but we couldn't connect him to the script we had running, so we—"

"What script?"

"That's what we called the conversations we were working on the Internet. So we didn't have intent. We called our filing D.A. and told him what we had and how we weren't sure he was the one from the script. The D.A. said to arrest him for the knuckles and if we connected him later, we could add it on. So we booked him as instructed and that was it."

"Was there ever any further work on connecting him to the script?"

"Look—it's Ballard, right?"

"Yeah, Ballard."

"You have any idea how time-consuming it is to do a computer-to-computer verification? And this guy worked in a car dealership where he had access to computers on every fricking desk. We had him on the knuckles and we booked it as a felony. That was it. We had other fish to fry."

Ballard nodded to herself. She knew how the system worked. There were too many cases, too many variables, too many legal rules. They got Trent on a felony and that was one more dirtbag off the street. It was time to move on and get the next one.

"Okay, thanks for the call back," she said. "This helps. Do me a favor—if anybody in the unit remembers what was on the knuckles or anybody happened to take pictures, let me know. It could help the case."

"You got it, Ballard."

Ballard pulled into the gated entrance to the station's rear parking lot and held her ID out the window to the electronic reader. The steel wall rolled away and she entered and started cruising the lot, looking for a spot to park. The lot was often more crowded at night because there were fewer cars in the field.

She entered the station through the back door and saw two drunks cuffed to the lockup bench. Both had vomited on the floor between their feet. Ballard was carrying her suit. She went down the rear hallway and upstairs to the locker room to change.

The detective bureau was deserted as usual when she got there. Because she had no assigned desk, she had to check the receptionist's desk to see if there were any messages for her. There was one pink slip: a call had come in at four p.m. from an 888 area code. The name scribbled on the caller line looked like Nerf Cohen, a name she didn't recognize. Ballard took it back to her regular workstation and sat down.

Before checking out the message, she opened the photo archive on her cell phone and swiped back through her pictures until she came to the close-up shots she had taken of the bruising on Ramona Ramone's torso. She used her thumb and finger to enlarge each photograph to look for any indications of a pattern in the bruising that she had deduced had come from brass knuckles. She wasn't sure if it was the power of suggestion coming from Fernandez's information, but she now thought she could see what she had not noticed before in the hospital. She thought she saw distinctive patterns in the bruises on the right and left sides of the torso. Not enough to make out words but she believed she could see the letter *C* or *O* on the left side and either an *N* or a *V* on the right side. She realized that the markings she was looking at, if they were words, would likely appear backward in bruising if they read the right way on the attacker's fists.

Still, the bruising patterns were significant. What Ballard was looking at wasn't scientific or remotely conclusive but it was a little piece of the puzzle that seemed to fit with Trent, and therefore it gave her a nice jolt of momentum. She decided it was time to start committing her investigative moves—the legal ones, at least—to a digital record. She checked the clock over the television screens on the far wall and saw that it was an hour till the late show roll call. She could get a lot done in that time. She went to work, starting an Investigator's Chronology, even though it would not be the first document in the file. She knew from long experience that the chrono was the written centerpiece of a case.

She was a half hour into her work when her phone buzzed with a call from a blocked number. She answered.

"This is Ballard."

"Good and evil."

She recognized the voice of Jorge Fernandez. Her voice jumped up a notch with excitement.

"That was on the knuckles?"

"Yep. I asked the guys and somebody remembered. Good and evil, the constant battle within man. You get it?"

"I get it."

"Does it help?"

"I think so. Can you give me the name of the officer who remembered? I might need it."

"That would be Dapper Dave Allmand. We call him that 'cause he's got a certain sartorial style. This is vice but he thinks it's a fucking fashion show."

"Got it. And thanks, Fernandez. I owe you one."

"Happy hunting, Ballard."

After disconnecting, Ballard pulled up the photos of Ramona Ramone's bruises on her phone again. Now she could see it: the double O in GOOD and the V in EVIL. They read the same backward or forward.

Ballard knew that it was highly unlikely that Trent would have gotten back the brass knuckles he had been arrested with. After three years, they would have been destroyed by the property unit. But if the weapons were part of a paraphilia—in this case, a sadomasochistic fantasy—it was not a stretch to believe he would go back to wherever he got the original set and buy a duplicate pair.

The adrenaline jolt Ballard had felt earlier now turned into a locomotive charging through her veins. To her mind, Trent was no longer just a person of interest. The train had gone by that stop. She believed he was her man, and there was nothing quite like that moment of knowing. It was the Holy Grail of detective work. It had nothing to do with evidence or legal procedure or probable cause. It was just knowing it in your gut. Nothing in her life beat it. It had been a long time coming to her on the late show but now she felt it and she knew deep down it was the reason she would never quit, no matter where they put her or what they said about her.

12

Ballard went upstairs to the roll-call room early. It was always a good time to socialize, hear station gossip, and pick up street intel. There were already seven uniformed officers seated, including Smith and Taylor, when she walked in. Two of the others were a female team Ballard knew well from crossing paths in the locker room. As would be expected, the conversation under way was about the quintuple murder of the night before. One of the officers was saying that RHD had put a tight seal on internal news about the case, not even releasing the names of the victims as of twenty-four hours after the crime.

"You were inside, Renée," said Herrera, one of the women. "What's the scoop on the victims? Who were they?"

Ballard shrugged.

"No scoop," she said. "I just handled one of the peripheral victims, the cocktail waitress. They didn't bring me into the inner circle. I saw three dead guys in a booth but I don't know who they were."

"I guess they weren't going to bring you in with Olivas in charge," Herrera said.

It was a reminder that in a police station, there were few secrets. Within a month of her transfer to Holly-wood, everyone in the station knew about her losing her complaint against Olivas, even though personnel matters were supposed to be kept secret by law.

Ballard tried to change the subject.

"So coming in, I saw FSD was inside there tonight," she said. "They miss something last night?"

"I heard they never left," Smith said. "They've been at it almost twenty-four hours."

"That's got to be a record or something," Herrera added.

"The record is the Phil Spector case—forty-one hours on scene with forensics," Smith said. "And that was for one body."

Spector was a famous music producer who had killed a woman he brought home from a bar. It was a sheriff's case but Ballard decided not to make that distinction.

More officers soon entered the room, followed by Lieutenant Munroe. He took a position behind the podium at the head of the room and convened roll call. It was uneventful and dry, with the usual reporting of area crimes, including the credit-card theft Ballard had handled the night before. Munroe had no news on the Dancers case, not even an artist's drawing of a suspect. His report lasted less than ten minutes. He concluded by throwing it to Ballard.

"Renée, anything you want to talk about?"

"Not much. We had the assault last night. The victim is still hanging in. Happened on the he-she stroll and anything anybody picks up on that would be welcome. Note that the suspect used brass knuckles. Ask around about that. Other than that and five people murdered in the Dancers, quiet times."

People laughed.

"Okay," Munroe said.

The lieutenant moved on to housekeeping announcements about scheduling and body-camera training. Ballard wanted to leave but knew it would be rude, so she pulled her phone to surreptitiously check messages down by her thigh. She saw that she had received a text from Jenkins a few minutes before. He was just checking in with her, as was their custom on the shifts they worked alone.

> Jenkins: Howzit going?
> Ballard: I think I found the upside-down house.
> Jenkins: How?
> Ballard: Prior with brass knuckles.
> Jenkins: Cool. Are you making a move tonight?
> Ballard: No, still gathering string. I'll let you know.
> Jenkins: Good.

Roll call ended as she was finishing the text exchange. Ballard put her phone away and headed toward the stairs. Munroe called to her from behind as she was making the turn on the first landing.

"Ballard, you're not going over to the Dancers, are you?" he asked.

Ballard stopped and waited for him to catch up.

"No, why?" she said.

"Just wanted to know what my people are doing," Munroe said.

Technically, Ballard was not one of Munroe's people but she let the remark slide. He ran patrol in the division during the late show, but Ballard was a detective and reported to Lieutenant McAdams, the dayside D bureau commander.

"Like I said in roll call, I'm working the assault from last night," she said. "McAdams gave it to me."

"Yeah, I didn't get the memo on that," Munroe said.

"Did you get a memo telling you to keep me away from the Dancers?"

"No, I told you, just want to know where everybody on the shift is."

"Yeah, well, now you know what I'm working on. I have to go by the hospital for a minute but I'm around if you need me."

She turned and went down the last flight of steps and moved directly into the detective bureau. She wondered if Munroe was hiding something. She usually worked autonomously, without the patrol lieutenant keeping tabs on her. Had Olivas or someone else from downtown told him to keep her clear of the club and the investigation?

The exchange with Munroe unnerved her but she put the thoughts aside so she could focus on the case she had at hand. She got keys for the late show city-ride out of the drawer of the receptionist's desk, then grabbed a fresh battery for her rover out of the charging station. She went back to her desk for her handbag and the radio and then headed out. Once she was in the car, she could immediately tell someone had used it during the day—someone who had ignored the rule prohibiting smoking in all city vehicles. She opened up all the windows as she pulled through the lot gate and turned north on Wilcox toward Sunset.

At Hollywood Presbyterian, she badged her way past a security guard and two nursing stations in order to get to the room where Ramona Ramone was lying comatose in a bed. Ballard had asked a nurse named Natasha to accompany her in case there came a time when she needed backup testimony at a trial.

The victim actually looked worse a night later. Her head had been partially shaved and the surgery to repair the skull fracture and limit the impact of brain swelling had left her face puffy and unrecognizable. She lay at the center of a nest of tubes, drips, and monitors.

"I need you to open her smock so I can photograph the bruises on her torso," Ballard said.

"Wasn't it done last night?" Natasha asked.

"It was. But the bruises will look different today."

"I don't understand."

"You don't have to, Natasha. Just open the smock."

Ballard knew that bruising occurred when blood vessels beneath the skin were damaged by impact and red blood cells leaked into the surrounding tissues. The bruise sometimes grew larger and darker in the twenty-four hours after an injury because blood continued to seep from the damaged vessels. Ballard was hoping that Ramona Ramone's bruises would now be more defined and possibly even legible.

The nurse moved some tubing out of the way, then pulled down a thermal blanket that covered the patient. She unbuttoned the pale blue smock to expose the victim's naked body. There was a catheter attached to the penis and the urine in the clear tube had a reddish hue from internal bleeding. The nurse pulled the blanket back up slightly and Ballard didn't know if that was a show of modesty or revulsion.

Ballard noted that the right and left sides of the upper torso were fully covered in deep purple bruising. The delineated edges of the red impact marks she had seen the night before were now blurred as the blood continued to spread beneath the skin. If the damage were being seen for the first time now, it would be impossible to deduce that it had been inflicted with brass knuckles. Ballard leaned down over the bed from the left side to study the purple blossoms closely. Before long she identified two side-by-side rings of deep purple against a lighter shade of bruising. She believed it was the double O in the word GOOD.

"Natasha, will you look at this?"

Ballard straightened up and stepped to her left so the nurse could move in. She pointed to the pattern.

"What is that?" Ballard asked.

"You mean the bruising?" Natasha said.

"There's a pattern there. Do you see it?"

"I see . . . well, maybe. You mean the circles?"

"Exactly. Let me photograph it."

Ballard pulled out her phone and moved in close again when Natasha stepped back. As she took photos, she thought about the billboards she had seen all over the city that showed stunning, professional-grade shots taken on the new iPhone camera. Ballard guessed that these kinds of photos would never be put on billboards.

"Is that from the weapon?" Natasha asked. "Like maybe he had two big rings on his fingers when he punched this man."

Ballard continued to shoot, with and then without the flash.

"Something like that," she said.

She moved around to the other side of the bed and studied the bruising on the left side of Ramona Ramone's torso. Here the purple blossoms were an even deeper color and Ballard could find no pattern indicative of the word *EVIL*. She did know that the deeper color meant deeper injury, and the imbalance between the two sides of the torso indicated that the attacker's power hand was his right. She tried to recall if Thomas Trent had done anything during their inter-action and test-drive earlier to reveal whether he was right-handed. It had been evident that the knuckles on his right hand were painfully bruised. She then remem-bered him writing down her phone number with his right hand.

Ballard took photos of the left side just so she could document the extent of the injuries.

"You can cover her up, Natasha," she said. "I'm fin-ished for now."

Natasha started rebuttoning the smock.

"You saw that he's a man, right?" the nurse asked.

"Biologically, yes," Ballard said. "But she chose to live as a woman. That's what I go with."

"Oh," Natasha said.

"Do you know if she has had any visitors? Any family?"

"Not that I know of."

"Are they going to transfer her?"

"I don't know. Probably."

Hollywood Presbyterian was a private hospital. If

family or insurance was not found for Ramone, she would be transferred to a county hospital, where she wouldn't get the same level of care she was getting here.

Ballard thanked Natasha for her help and left the room.

After clearing the hospital, Ballard drove to a neighborhood in the shadow of an elevated section of the 101 freeway. Ramona Ramone had no driver's license under her current or birth name and the only address Ballard had found for her was on Heliotrope Drive. It was the address on two shake cards in her vice file and the one given when she was last arrested.

Ballard had thought it was most likely a phony, not because there wasn't a street in Hollywood called Heliotrope but because she knew something about plants and flowers from growing up in Hawaii. She had often worked with her family on tomato farms and plant nurseries on the dense mountainsides of Maui. A heliotrope was a plant that blossomed with fragrant purple and blue flowers and was known for turning its petals toward the sun. It seemed to Ballard like a metaphor of some kind, that maybe Ramona Ramone had chosen the name of the street because it fit with her desire to change and turn her petals to the sun.

Now, as she followed the road to the freeway, she saw that the address corresponded to a row of old RVs and house trailers parked stem to stern under the overpass. It was one of L.A.'s many homeless encampments, and beyond the row of beat-up vehicles on the street, she could see pitched tents and shelters made of blue tarp

13

Ballard knew something about the social structure of the city's teeming homeless encampments. Both the city and the department had been attacked and sued by civil rights groups for ill-advised handling of encounters with homeless people and their communities. It had resulted in problem-specific sensitivity training and what amounted to a hands-off policy. She had learned from those sessions that a homeless encampment evolves much like a city, with a need for a social and government hierarchy that provided services like security, decision-making, and waste management. Many had individuals who served as mayors, sheriffs, and judges. As Ballard moved into the Heliotrope encampment, she was looking for the sheriff.

Other than the constant sound of traffic on the freeway overhead, it was all quiet in the camp. It was after midnight, the temperature was dropping into the fifties, and the inhabitants were mostly hunkered down and bracing for another night facing the elements, with walls made of plastic tarp or, if they were lucky, the aluminum shell of a camper.

Ballard noticed one man moving through what looked like a debris field where the people who lived off the trash of others threw their own trash. He was buckling his belt and his zipper was down. When he looked up from the operation and saw Ballard, he startled.

"Who the fuck are you?"

"LAPD. Who the fuck are you?"

"Well, I live here."

"Are you the sheriff? I'm looking for somebody in charge."

"I'm not the sheriff but I got the night shift."

"Really? You're security?"

"That's me."

Ballard pulled her badge off her belt and held it up.

"Ballard, LAPD."

"Uh, Denver. People call me Denver."

"Okay, Denver. I don't want to hassle anybody. I just need your help."

"Okay."

Denver stepped forward and put out his hand. Ballard held back from openly cringing. Luckily she was holding her rover in her right hand and avoided the outstretched hand.

"Elbow bump, Denver," she said.

She offered her elbow but Denver didn't know what to do with it.

"Okay, never mind that," she said. "Let's just talk. The reason I'm here is I think one of your citizens is in the hospital, hurt really bad. I want to find her place here. Can you help me?"

"Who is it? We have people come and go. Sometimes they just leave their stuff."

"Her name's Ramona Ramone. Kinda short Spanish girl? She said she lived here."

"Yeah, I know Ramona. But one thing you should know—she's a man."

"Yes, I know that. She was born a man but identifies as a woman."

That seemed to confuse Denver so Ballard moved on.

"So she lives here?"

"Well, she did. She was gone like a week and we didn't think she was coming back. Like I said, people come and go, just leave their shit behind. So somebody took her spot, you know what I mean? That's how it works around here. You snooze, you lose."

"Which spot was it?"

"She was in the 'seventy-four Midas at the front of the wagon train."

He pointed toward the ragtag line of RVs parked along the curb in front of the open encampment area. The first RV was a dirty white camper with a Dodge van cab. There was a faded-orange accent stripe down the side and a plastic American flag draped over the back edge of the roof as a leak stopper. From the outside, the vehicle showed every bit of its forty years.

"I heard she bought it from the previous guy for four hundred bucks and then he moved into the jungle."

Denver now pointed toward the encampment. It was clear that the RVs, no matter how decrepit and despairing, were the choice habitats in the community. A cottage industry had recently arisen in which old inoperable campers were pulled out of junkyards and backyards, towed to street parking locations under freeways or in industrial areas, and sold cheap or even rented to homeless people. They were passed from hand to hand and were often the subject of ownership fights and unlawful evictions. The department was in the process of putting together a task force to deal with this and the many other issues of the city's growing homeless population—the largest west of New York City.

"How long was she there?" Ballard asked.

"A year or thereabouts," Denver said.

"Is somebody in there now?"

"Yeah, a guy. Stormy Monday took it."

"That's the name he uses?"

"Yeah. People 'round here use a lot of different names, you know? They've left their other names behind."

"Got it. Let's go talk to Stormy. I've got to look inside."

"He's not a happy guy when you wake him up. They call him Stormy Monday but he's kind of a dick every single day."

"I know the type. We'll deal with that, Denver."

As she started toward the front of the train of RVs, she brought her rover up and called in a request for a backup. She was given an ETA of four minutes.

"You know, when police come around here, it makes people upset," Denver said after she lowered the radio.

"I understand," Ballard said. "We don't want to cause any problems. But it will be up to Stormy Monday."

Ballard had a small tactical light in her pocket that she had gotten out of the glove box of her car. The butt end was a heavy steel point. She used it to rap on the door of the Dodge Midas. She then stepped a comfortable four feet back and two to the left. She noticed that there was no handle on the door, just two holes through which were threaded the links of a steel chain. It was a way to lock the vehicle when you were inside it as well as out.

There was no answer and no movement from the RV.

"It looks like somebody's locked in," Ballard said.

"Yeah, he's in there," Denver said.

Ballard rapped harder on the door this time. The sound echoed off the concrete overhead and could be heard well above the din of the freeway.

"Hey, Stormy!" Denver called out. "Come on out here a minute."

A patrol car cruised slowly down Heliotrope, and Ballard flicked her light at it. The car pulled to a stop in the street beside the Midas. The two female blue suiters from roll call got out. Herrera was the lead and her partner was Dyson.

"Ballard, what've we got?" Herrera asked.

"Gotta roust a guy in here," Ballard said. "Denver here says he's not going to be happy."

The RV's springs were shot after so many decades of use. The vehicle started to creak and move as soon as there was movement inside. Then, from the other side of the door came a voice.

"Yeah, what do you want?"

Denver stepped in unbidden.

"Hey, Stormy, you got the police out here. They want to see inside the crib on account of Ramona used to live here."

"Yeah, she ain't livin' here now," Stormy replied. "I'm sleeping."

"Open the door, sir," Ballard said loudly.

"You have a warrant or something? I know my rights."

"We don't need a warrant. We need you to open the door, or what we'll do is tow this vehicle with you in it to the police yard, where the door will be forcibly opened and you'll be arrested for obstructing an investigation. You'll be in county jail and this prime spot will go to somebody else. Is that what you want, sir?"

Ballard thought she had covered everything. She waited. Herrera stepped away to listen to a call on her shoulder mic. Dyson stayed with Ballard. Thirty seconds went by and then Ballard heard the rattle of the chain inside the door. Stormy Monday was opening up.

Based on the moniker and the prep that he was an angry guy, Ballard was expecting a big man to come out of the trailer, ready for confrontation. Instead, a small man with glasses and a gray beard stepped out with his hands up. Ballard told him to put his hands down and walked him over to Dyson and Herrera, who had returned to the group. Ballard questioned him about the ownership of the RV and its contents. The man, who identified himself as Cecil Beatty, said he had moved in only two days earlier, and that was after the RV had been picked through by others. He said that he didn't think there were any belongings left that had been Ramona Ramone's.

Ballard told the patrol officers to watch Beatty while she took a look inside the RV. She put on latex gloves and went up the two steps and in. She swept her light across a small two-room space that was littered with junk and smelled as sour as the Hollywood Station drunk tank on a Sunday morning. Ballard put her mouth and nose into the crook of her elbow as she moved through the debris that littered every surface and the floor. She saw nothing that stood out as possibly belonging to Ramona

Ramone. She moved through the first room and into the back room, which essentially consisted of a queen-size bed piled with darkly stained sheets and blankets. She nearly lost it when the sheets suddenly moved and she realized there was someone in the bed.

"Dyson, come here," Ballard called. "Now!"

Behind her, Ballard heard the officer enter the RV. She kept her light on the face of the woman in the bed. She was bedraggled, her hair in unkempt dreadlocks. There were scabs on her face and neck. A person at the dead end of addiction.

"Take her out of here," Ballard said.

Dyson moved in, yanked back the sheets, and pulled the woman, who was fully clothed in multiple layers of sweaters and jackets, off the bed. She walked her out and Ballard continued to search.

Seeing nothing that was of value to her investigation, she backed out of the bedroom area. There was a kitchenette section opposite what once was a tiny bathroom but had long since gone unused. The two-burner grill was probably now used mostly to cook spoons of heroin or crystal meth. Ballard started opening the overhead cabinets, half expecting to find rats skittering in the back shadows. Instead, she found a small empty box that had once held a disposable phone. The box looked fairly new, unlike the rest of the junk in the RV.

Ballard stepped out of the RV and over to where Beatty and the woman were standing, heads down, next to the two unies. She held the box up to Beatty.

"Is this yours?" she asked.

Beatty looked at it and then looked away.

"Nope, not mine," he said. "That was there."

"Was it Ramona's?"

"Maybe. I don't know. I never saw it before."

Ballard assumed that the box had belonged to Ramona. If there was anything on or in the box that revealed a serial or product number, then she had a shot at running down calls made on the phone even though the phone itself was missing and supposedly untraceable. If there were calls that linked Ramona to Trent, then that evidence would be usable at trial, and the whole roust, and her breathing in the putrid air of the RV, would not be for naught.

"Okay, thank you for your cooperation," she said.

She gave Herrera and Dyson the nod to release the two inhabitants of the RV and they immediately scurried back inside. She then turned to Denver and signaled him over for a private discussion.

"Thank you for your help on this, Denver. I appreciate it."

"No problem. That's my job here."

"When we first talked about Ramona, you said she had been gone a week."

"Yeah, we have a rule. Nobody squats in another guy's spot unless they haven't been around for four days. 'Cause you know, people get arrested, and that can take you out for seventy-two hours. So we wait four days before a spot is up for grabs."

"So you're sure she was gone four days before Stormy moved in two days ago?"

"I'm sure. Yeah."

Ballard nodded. It was an indication that Ramona might have been held captive by her attacker for as long as five days of pain and torture before being dumped in the parking lot the previous night and left for dead. It was a grim thought to consider.

Ballard thanked Denver again and this time she shook his hand. She wasn't sure if he noticed that she still had the latex gloves on.

Back at the Hollywood Station by 1:30 a.m., Ballard wandered through the watch office before heading back to the D bureau. Munroe was at his desk and another officer was at the report-writing desk at the far end of the room.

"Anything happening?" she asked.

"Quiet," Munroe said. "After last night, I'll take it."

"The crims are still at the Dancers?"

"I wouldn't know. The forensic unit doesn't answer to me."

"Well, maybe since it's so slow, I'll go over and see if they need some help."

"Not ours, Ballard. You need to stay here just in case."

"Just in case of what?"

"In case we need you."

Ballard had no intention of going by the Dancers. She had just wanted to see how Munroe would react, and his agitation and quick response confirmed that he had gotten word to keep Ballard and possibly all Hollywood Division personnel away from that crime scene.

Munroe tried to change the subject.

"How's your victim?" he asked.

"Hanging in there," Ballard said. "That's what I wanted to talk to you about. Looks like she's going to make it. I'm worried the suspect might get wind and try to finish the job."

"What, he's going to sneak into the hospital? Smother the vic with a pillow?"

"I don't know, maybe. There hasn't been any press on the case but—"

"You've watched *The Godfather* too many times. If this is about me putting somebody on this whore's door, it's not going to happen, Ballard. Not from my end. I've got no people for that. I'm not going to leave myself short on the street to have a guy twiddling his thumbs or making time at the nurses' station. You can shoot a request down to Metro Division, but if you ask me, they'll evaluate this and take a pass too."

"Okay. Got it."

When she returned to her borrowed desk in the detective bureau, Ballard put down the phone box she had collected from the RV and was prepared to spend the rest of her shift attempting to trace the phone it had once contained. But then she saw the pink message slip she had picked up earlier. She sat down and lifted the desk phone. Calling the number in the middle of the night did not give her pause. It was a toll-free number, which meant it most likely connected to a business. It would be either open or closed, so she would not be waking anybody up in the middle of the night.

While she waited for the call to go through, she once again tried to decipher the name written on the slip of paper. It was impossible. But as soon as her call was answered, she realized who had called and left the message.

"Cardholder services. How can I help you?"

She heard an English-Indian accent—like from the

men from Mumbai that she had spoken to on Mrs. Lantana's phone the night before.

"May I speak to Irfan?"

"Which one? We have three."

Ballard looked at the pink slip. It looked like it said Cohen. She turned the C to a K and thought she had it.

"Khan. Irfan Khan."

"Hold the line, please."

Thirty seconds later, a new voice came on the line and Ballard thought she recognized it.

"This is Detective Ballard, Los Angeles Police Department. You left a message for me."

"Yes, Detective. We spoke on the phone a little over twenty-four hours ago. I tracked you down."

"Yes, you did. Why?"

"Because I have received permission to share with you the intended delivery address of the attempted fraudulent purchase on the credit card that was stolen."

"You got court approval?"

"No, my department head gave me approval. I went to him and said we should do this because you were very insistent, you see."

"To be honest, I am surprised. Thank you for following up."

"Not a problem. Happy to help."

"What is the address, then?"

Khan gave her an apartment number and address on Santa Monica Boulevard and Ballard could tell it was not far from El Centro Avenue and the home of Leslie Anne Lantana. It was probably walking distance.

Ballard checked the urge to tell Khan that the chances of her being able to make an arrest on the case were hampered by the twenty-four-hour delay in getting the address. Instead, she thanked him for pursuing the matter with the department head and ended the call.

She then grabbed her rover and the key to the plain wrap and headed for the door.

14

The address that came from Mumbai corresponded to a run-down motel called the Siesta Village. It was a two-story U-shaped complex with parking inside the U, as well as a small pool and an office. A sign out front said FREE WIFI AND HBO. Ballard pulled in and cruised the lot. Each room had a large plate-glass window that looked out on the center of the complex. It was the kind of place that would still have box TVs in each room, locked to the bureau with a metal frame.

Ballard located room 18 and saw no lights on behind its curtained window. She noted the beat-up Ford pickup parked in front of its door. Eighteen was the last room before a well-lit alcove that contained an ice dispenser and Coke machine housed in a steel cage with cutouts for depositing money and removing drinks. She kept moving and parked the city-ride on the other side of the office so that it would not be seen should someone in room 18 split the curtain and look out the window. The car could be identified as a police car a mile away.

Before getting out, she used the rover to request a wants-and-warrants check on the pickup. It came back clean and registered to a Judith Nettles of Poway, a small town Ballard knew was down in San Diego County. Nettles had no record and no warrants on the computer.

Ballard proceeded on foot to the motel office, where

she had to push a button on the glass door and wait until a man came out from a back room located behind the counter. Ballard had her badge up already and he buzzed her in.

"Hey there," Ballard said as she entered. "I'm Detective Ballard from the Hollywood Station. I was wondering if I could ask you a few questions."

"Evening," said the counterman. "Ask away, I guess."

He stifled a yawn as he sat down. Behind him on the wall were several clocks showing the time in cities all over the world, as if the place catered to the international traveler who had to keep tabs on business around the globe. Ballard could hear the sound of a TV coming from the back room. It was the audience laughter of a late-night talk show.

"Do you have a guest in room eighteen tonight?" Ballard asked.

"Uh, yes, eighteen is occupied," the man said.

"What's that guest's name?"

"Don't you need a warrant to ask that?"

Ballard put her hands on the counter and leaned toward the man.

"You watch too much TV in that back room, sir. I don't need a warrant to ask questions and you don't need to be presented with a warrant to answer them. You just need to choose right now to either help the LAPD with an investigation or hinder the LAPD."

He stared at her for a moment and then turned the seat clockwise until he was facing a computer screen to his right. He hit the space bar and the screen came to life. He then pulled up the motel's occupancy chart and clicked on room 18.

"His name is Christopher Nettles," he said.

"He alone in there?" Ballard asked.

"Supposed to be. Registered as a single."

"How long has he been here?"

The man referred to his screen again.

"Nine days."

"Spell the first and last name for me."

After getting the spellings, Ballard told the clerk she would be right back. She grabbed a couple of pamphlets for a Homes of the Stars bus tour off a stack on the counter and used them to keep the door from latching. She stepped into the parking lot to be out of the counterman's earshot and used the rover to call communications and check Christopher Nettles for wants and warrants. He came up clean but Ballard was smart enough to know not to leave it there. She pulled her phone and called the Hollywood Station watch office and asked a desk uni to run the name through the national crime index database.

She paced on the asphalt while waiting for the results and noticed that there was no water in the motel pool. She walked around to the corner of the office so she could get another visual on room 18. It was still dark behind the curtain. She checked the pickup truck and pegged it as at least twenty years old. It likely didn't have an alarm and would not be useful in drawing Nettles out of the room.

The desk officer came back on the line and reported that there was a Christopher Nettles in the system with a 2014 conviction on multiple theft charges, including burglary of an occupied dwelling. This Christopher Nettles was white, twenty-four years old, and on parole after serving two years in state prison for the convictions.

Ballard asked the officer to put Lieutenant Munroe on the line.

"L-T, it's Ballard. I'm at Siesta Village and I have a line on a suspect in the four-five-nine on El Centro last night. Can you send me a unit?"

"I can do that. I had all hands on a domestic but it's calm now and I'll pull a car off and send them your way. They're ten out."

"Okay, have them hold a block back and go to Tact four and I'll call them in. I want to try to caper this guy out of the room."

"Roger that, Ballard. You got a name I can write down?"

He was asking for the suspect's name in case things went sideways and they had to go hunting for him without Ballard's help. She gave him the details she had on Nettles and then disconnected. She switched her rover to the Tactical 4 frequency and went back into the office, where the counterman was waiting.

"How has Mr. Nettles been paying for his room?" she asked.

"He pays with cash," he said. "Every three days he pays for three days in advance. He's good till Monday."

"Has he been getting deliveries here?"

"Deliveries?"

"You know, boxes, mail. Have people been sending him stuff?"

"I wouldn't really know. I work during the night. The only deliveries are pizza deliveries. Matter of fact, I think Nettles got a pizza a couple hours ago."

"So you've seen him? You know what he looks like?"

"Yeah, he's come in and paid for the room a couple times at night."

"How old is he?"

"I don't know. Twenties, I'd say. Young. I'm not good at that stuff."

"Big or small?"

"I'd say on the big side. Looks like he works out."

"Tell me about the free Wi-Fi."

"What can I tell you? It's free. That's it."

"Does every room have a router, or is there a main router for the whole place?"

"We got the setup in the back here."

He hooked a thumb over his shoulder toward the room behind him. Ballard knew that the router's history could be examined for proof that Nettles had attempted to make purchases online with Leslie Anne Lantana's credit card, but that would require a warrant and a commitment of time and money from the department's Commercial Crimes Division that outweighed the importance of the case. It would never happen unless Ballard or someone working the daytime burglary unit did it.

"What about phones? Are there phone lines in the rooms?"

"Yes, we have phones. Except for a couple rooms where they got stolen. We haven't replaced them."

"But eighteen has a phone?"

"Yes, there's a phone."

Ballard nodded as she considered a plan for getting Nettles out of his room so she could question and possibly arrest him.

"Can you turn the light off in that alcove with the Coke machine?"

"Uh, yeah. I have a switch here. But it turns out the light on the second floor alcove too."

"That's okay, turn them both off. Then I need you to call his room and get him to come to the office."

"How do I do that? It's almost three o'clock in the morning."

He pointed over his shoulder toward the wall of clocks to underline that it was too late for him to call Nettles's room. As if on cue, her rover squawked and she heard her call code. She brought the rover up to respond.

"Six-William-twenty-six, you guys in position?"

"That's a roger."

She recognized the voice. It was Smith. She knew she had a solid cop and a gung-ho boot as backup.

"Okay, hold there. When I call you in, drive in the main entrance and don't let anyone out. Suspect has a 1990s Ford one-fifty, silver in color."

"Roger that. Weapons?"

"No known weapons."

Smith clicked twice on the radio to acknowledge.

"Okay, five minutes," Ballard said. "I'll give you a standby pop, followed by a go sign."

The counterman was looking wide-eyed at her when Ballard turned her attention back to him.

"Okay, so now I need you to call room eighteen and tell Nettles that the police were just here asking about him," she said.

"Why would I do that?" the clerk said.

"Because it's what just happened. And because you

want to continue to cooperate with the LAPD."

The counterman didn't say anything. He looked very concerned about being pulled into something.

"Look," Ballard said. "You're not lying to the guy. You are telling him exactly what just happened. Keep it simple. Say something like 'Sorry to wake you up but a police detective was just here asking about you.' He'll then ask you if the police are still here and you say you think they left. That's it. If he asks anything else, tell him you've got another call and have to go. Short and simple."

"But how come you want him to know you were here?" the clerk asked.

"I'm just trying to spook him and get him to come out of that room and make it safer to approach him. Now give me three minutes and make the call. You good?"

"I guess so."

"Good. Your cooperation is greatly appreciated by your police department."

Ballard left the office and followed the walkway in front of the rooms until she got to room 18. She walked by and entered the alcove to the right of its window. The overhead light in the alcove was now off but the plastic front of the Coke machine was brightly lit, and Ballard needed cover, not illumination. She reached behind the machine and pulled the plug, plunging the recessed area into full darkness. She stood back in the shadow and waited, checking her watch to see when three minutes had passed.

Just as she did so, she heard the ringing of a phone through the wall between the alcove and room 18. Four rings went by before it was answered with a muffled but gruff response. She keyed the mic on her rover twice, sending the standby alert to the backup team waiting in the street.

She continued to hear a muffled voice through the wall as she assumed Nettles was asking questions of the counterman. She moved up to the edge of the alcove so she had an angle on the pickup. Just as she did so, she heard the door to the room open. Before looking, she shrank back into the shadow for a moment, opened the mic on the rover, and whispered, "Go. We are go."

When Ballard edged back to the corner of the alcove, she saw a man wearing blue jeans and nothing else pushing a cardboard box into the rear of the truck's crew cab. His back was to her and she could see the grip of a black handgun tucked into the rear belt line of the jeans.

That changed things. She quickly pulled her weapon out of her hip holster and stepped out of the alcove. The man, who was struggling with the heavy box, did not see her as she approached from behind. She held her weapon up and brought the rover to her mouth.

"Suspect is armed, suspect is armed."

She then dropped the rover to the ground and moved into a combat stance with both hands on her weapon, pointing it at the suspect. In that moment she realized her tactical mistake. She could not cover the man at the door of the pickup and the door to room 18 at the same time. If there was someone else in the room, they had the drop on her. She started moving sideways to close the angle between the two possible danger points.

"Police!" she yelled. "Let me see your hands!"

The man froze but did not comply. His hands remained on the box.

"Put your hands on the roof of the truck!" Ballard yelled.

"I can't," the man yelled back. "If I do, the box will drop. I have to—"

A patrol car came rushing into the lot off the street. Ballard kept her eyes on the man at the truck but had the cruiser in her peripheral vision. A flood of relief started moving through her. But she knew she wasn't clear yet.

She waited for the car to stop, the officers to get out, and there to be three guns on the suspect.

"Get down!" Smith yelled.

"On the ground," yelled Taylor.

"Which is it?" the man at the truck yelled. "She said hands on top. You say get on the ground."

"Get on the fucking ground, asshole, or we'll put you there," Smith yelled.

There was enough tension in Smith's voice to make it clear that his patience had run out, and the man at the truck was smart enough to read it.

"Okay, okay, I'm getting down," he yelled. "Easy now, easy. I'm getting down."

The man took a step back from the truck and let the box fall to the ground. Something made of glass inside it broke. The man turned toward Ballard with his hands up. She lost sight of the gun but held her eyes on his hands.

"You assholes," he said. "You made me break my stuff."

"On your knees," Smith yelled. "Now."

The suspect went down one knee at a time and then

pitched forward to lie flat on the asphalt. He locked his hands behind his head. He knew the routine.

"Ballard, take him," Smith yelled.

Ballard moved in, holstering her weapon and pulling her cuffs free. She put one hand on the man's back to hold him down and yanked the gun out of his belt line with the other. She slid the weapon across the asphalt in the direction of the unies. She then moved up, put one knee on the small of the man's back, and pulled his hands down one at a time to cuff them behind him. The moment the second cuff clicked, she yelled to the other officers.

"Code four! We're good!"

15

The man Ballard cuffed was identified as Christopher Nettles. But that came from the wallet in his back pocket, not from him. The moment the cuffs were closed on his wrists, he announced that he wanted a lawyer and refused to say anything else. Ballard turned him over to Smith and Taylor and then went toward the open door of room 18. Pulling her gun free again, she had to clear the room and make sure there was not another suspect hiding. She had already been surprised once this night, by Stormy Monday's roommate. She wasn't going to let it happen again.

She entered to find the room stacked with boxes and items ordered from online retailers. Nettles had quite an operation, taking stolen plastic and turning it into merchandise he could pawn or sell. She quickly determined that there were no other occupants in the room and backed out.

Because Nettles was on parole for a felony conviction, Ballard did not need to jump through most of the constitutional hoops that protected citizens from unlawful search and seizure. By legal definition, being on parole from prison meant Nettles was still in the custody of the state. By accepting parole he had given up his protections. His parole agent was allowed to access his home, vehicle, and workplace without so much as a nod from a judge.

Ballard pulled her phone and called the cell number she had for Rob Compton, the state parole officer assigned to Hollywood Division. She woke him up. She had done so in the past on numerous occasions and knew how he would react.

"Robby, wake up," she said. "One of your customers has run wild in Hollywood."

"Renée?" he said, his voice slurred with sleep. "Ballard, fuck, it's a frickin' Friday night! What time is it anyway?"

"It's time to earn your keep."

He cursed again and Ballard gave him a few seconds to come to.

"You awake now? Christopher Nettles, you know him?"

"No, he's not mine."

"Because he's up here out of San Diego County. I'm sure they know him down there but he's in Hollywood, so that makes him your problem."

"Who is he?"

"He's got a two-year tail on a hot prowl plus conviction and it looks like he's been up here plying his mad skills for a couple weeks. I've got a motel room full of Amazon and Target boxes and I need you to violate him so I can get in there and go through all this stuff."

"What motel?"

"The Siesta Village on Santa Monica. I'm sure you know the place."

"Been there a few times, yeah."

"So how about coming out tonight and helping me with this guy?"

"Ballard, no. I was dead asleep and I'm supposed to go fishing tomorrow with my boys."

Ballard knew Compton was divorced and had three sons he saw only on weekends. She had learned that one morning when she went home with him after working a case through the night.

"Come on, Robby, this place looks like the back room of a Best Buy. And I forgot, he had a firearm. I will really owe you one if you can help me out."

It was one of the times Ballard unabashedly used her sexuality. If it could help persuade male officers to do what they were supposed to do, then she wasn't above using it. Compton was good at what he did but he was always reluctant to come out at night. He still had to keep regular office hours, no matter what extra-curricular work he did. On top of that, Ballard liked his company off duty. He was attractive and neat, his breath was usually fresh, and he had a sense of humor that most of the cops she worked with had lost a long time ago.

"I need a half hour," he finally said.

"Deal," Ballard said quickly. "It will take me that long to get him squared away. Thanks, Robby."

"Like you said, you're gonna owe me, Renée."

"Big time."

She knew that last line would shave ten minutes off his half hour. She was happy to know he was coming. Bringing the department of parole in would streamline things considerably. Compton had the authority to revoke Nettles's parole, which would also suspend his legal protections. There would be no need to deal with the District Attorney's Office or the grumpy on-call judge to get a search warrant for the motel room. They could just enter both the room and pickup truck to conduct full-scale searches.

They would also be able to hold the suspect on a no-bail booking. Nettles would be out of circulation and heading back to prison before charges in the new cases were even filed—if they were ever filed. Sometimes the return to prison and the clearing of cases was enough for the system to just move on. Ballard knew that with prison overcrowding forcing lighter sentences for non-violent crimes, Nettles returning for a year or two in prison on a parole violation would probably net him more time than he would get if they mounted a prosecution on the burglaries he had committed. The reality was that the gun charge would be the only add-on that would likely get consideration from the D.A.'s Office.

After finishing the call with Compton, she walked over to Smith and Taylor and told them they could take Nettles to the station and book him on a charge of ex-convict in possession of a firearm. She said she would stay on scene and wait for the parole officer to arrive before going through the property in the motel room.

Smith didn't respond. He just moved slowly after receiving the orders, and Ballard couldn't tell what was bugging him.

"Something wrong, Smitty?" she asked.

He kept moving toward her car to collect Nettles, who had been placed in the backseat.

"Smitty?" she asked.

"Tactics," he said without looking back.

"What are you talking about?" she demanded.

He didn't respond, so she followed him. She knew better than to leave something unsaid out there with a male officer—especially a training officer. They carried weight. She wondered if this was about the bad angle she had taken when she stepped out of the alcove, but she didn't think the patrol officers had arrived in time to see that.

"Talk to me, Smitty. What about tactics?"

Smith held his hands up like he wanted to stop the discussion he had started.

"No, man, you brought it up," Ballard insisted. "The guy's in the back of the car, nobody's hurt, no shots fired, what about my tactics?"

Smith wheeled around on her. Taylor stopped, too, but it was clear he was at sea as far as what his partner's complaint was.

"Where's your raid jacket?" Smith said. "And I can tell you're not wearing a vest. Number one, you should've had them on, Ballard. Number two, we should have been right here and in on the bust, not driving up to save your ass."

Ballard nodded as she took it all in.

"That's all bullshit," she threw back. "You're going to beef me for a raid jacket and a vest?"

"Who said anything about beefing you?" Smith said. "I'm just saying, that's all. You didn't do this right."

"We got the guy, that's what matters."

"Officer safety is what matters. I'm trying to teach this boot the street and you don't set the example."

"Were you setting the example last night when you

decided not to tape off a crime scene on Santa Monica Boulevard?"

"What, with that dragon? Ballard, you're the one slinging bullshit now."

"All I'm saying is we just took down a felon with a firearm and nobody got hurt. I think the kid learned something, but if you want to fill his ears with bullshit, go ahead."

Smith opened the back door of Ballard's plain wrap and that ended the argument. They knew better than to continue it in front of the suspect. Ballard waved off Smith and turned back toward room 18.

Compton arrived fifteen minutes after Smith and Taylor left the motel with Nettles. By then Ballard had walked off her anger, pacing in front of the open door of the room. Though she had cooled down considerably, she knew that Smith's complaint would stick with her for several days and would taint her feelings about what had been accomplished by the Nettles arrest.

Compton was a well-built man who usually wore tight shirts to accentuate his muscles and impress or intimidate the parolees he was charged with monitoring. But tonight he was wearing a loose-fitting and long-sleeved flannel shirt that understated his physical attributes.

"You okay?" he asked.

"Yeah, fine," she said. "Why?"

"Your face is red. So where's my guy?"

"We had a little excitement taking him down. My patrol team took him to be booked. I can hook you up with the watch commander if you want to no-bail him. I told them you would."

162

"That's fine. How do you want to do this?"

"There's a lot of stuff in the room. I think we start there. The truck is empty except for the box he was loading when we took him down. It's a flat-screen, and it's broken."

"Then let's do it."

"I called the watch commander and somebody's going to bring over the surveillance van we've got at the station. Hopefully we can fit all of this stuff in."

"Sounds like a plan."

They worked through the rest of the night, taking an inventory of room 18 and loading the boxes and other property into the van. They had an easy rapport from working together previously. Along the way, they found a cache of credit cards with eight different names on them, including the card taken from Leslie Anne Lantana's purse. They also found two other firearms, which had been stashed under the room's mattress.

Once back at the station, Ballard was able to connect five of the other names from the credit cards to burglaries reported in Hollywood Division in the prior seven days. Meantime, Compton borrowed a desk and computer and started a trace of the three guns with the federal Bureau of Alcohol, Tobacco, Firearms, and Explosives. None of the firearms had shown up on the burglary reports Ballard had found but Compton learned that the Glock—the weapon Nettles had in his belt line—had been reported stolen in Texas two years before. Details of the theft were not available on the computer. Compton then made a request for further information from the ATF but both he and Ballard knew that the return on that would be measured in days if not weeks.

By six a.m., all the merchandise recovered from the motel room had been placed in a storage trailer outside the back door of the station, the pickup truck had been impounded and towed, and an inventory and full report on the Nettles arrest had been placed on the desk of the burglary unit supervisor. Although he would not return to work until Monday morning, there was no hurry, because Nettles was going nowhere. Compton had formally placed a no-bail hold on him.

The three recovered pistols were the last items to be taken care of. All firearms were stored in gun boxes before being placed in lockers for firearms in the property unit office. Ballard left Compton in the detective bureau and took the weapons back. Her banging the door of the gun locker drew the attention of Lieutenant Munroe, who came down the hallway and stuck his head into the property room.

"Ballard, nice work tonight."

"Thanks, L-T."

"How many you think he's good for?"

"I have eight different names on credit cards that connect to six cases so far. My guess is they're all going to be victims."

"And the guns?"

"One was reported stolen out of Dallas two years ago. We've asked ATF for the details. We'll hopefully know more next week."

"A one-man crime wave, huh? Sweet bust. The captain will like it."

"The captain doesn't like me, so it doesn't matter."

"He likes anybody who clears cases and gets dirtbags off the street. Funny thing is, this guy Nettles said no on the withdrawal room."

Munroe was telling her that Nettles had denied being a drug addict and turned down a padded jail cell for detainees who were going through withdrawal. This was unusual. Most burglaries were motivated by the need for money to buy drugs and feed addictions. Nettles might be different. Ballard had seen no physical indications of drug addiction in the short time she was handling him during the arrest.

"He was building a bankroll for something," she said. "He had twenty-six hundred in cash in his pocket. I found another thousand in the truck along with a bunch of pawn slips. He was stealing the plastic, ordering stuff online before the accounts were shut down, and then pawning it for cash."

"Which pawn shop?"

"A few different ones. He spread it out to fly under the radar. The mystery is that there was no laptop in the room or the truck."

"He must've been going to office centers and using rental computers."

"Maybe. Or maybe he had a partner. Burglary can figure that out Monday."

Munroe nodded, and there was an awkward pause. Ballard knew he had something else to say and she had a good idea what it was.

"So," she said. "Did Smitty beef me?"

"He said something about tactics, yeah," Munroe said. "But I'm not worried about him. On my watch, if you get results, you get a pass."

"Thanks, L-T."

"Doesn't mean I'm not worried about you, though."

"Look, Lieutenant, it was the best way to take the guy down. Even now, if I had it to do again, I would do the exact same thing—draw him out of the room. Only I'd put on a vest and a raid jacket just so Smitty wouldn't get so fucking confused."

"Take it easy, Ballard. Sometimes you're like a feral fucking cat. Smitty wasn't confused, okay? He just wanted his boot to know how it should be done."

"Whatever. You said you weren't writing me up."

"And I'm not. I told Smitty I'd talk to you, and I have. That's it. Learn from it, Ballard."

She paused before responding. She could tell he wanted some kind of acknowledgment from her in order to put this to rest, but it was hard for her to give it up when she knew she wasn't wrong.

"Okay, I will," she finally said.

"Good," Munroe said.

He disappeared back into the watch office and Ballard headed back to the detective bureau. Her shift was over and she regretted that she had been pulled away from the Ramona Ramone case for most of the night. She felt fatigue weighing in her bones and knew she needed sleep before thinking about next steps regarding Thomas Trent.

When she got to the bureau, Compton was still there waiting for her.

"Let's go," she said.

"Where?" he said.

"Your place."

16

Ballard was deep in a blue dream. Her father's long hair and reckless beard were floating free all around his head. His eyes were open. The water felt warm. A bubble formed in his mouth and then rose toward the murky light far above them.

She opened her eyes.

Compton was sitting on the side of the bed with his hand on her shoulder. He was gently rocking her awake. His hair was wet from the shower and he was fully dressed.

"Renée, I gotta go," he said.

"What?" she said. "What time is it?"

She tried to shake off the dream and the grip of sleep.

"It's twenty to eleven," Compton said. "You're okay to stay and sleep. I just wanted to tell you I was leaving. I gotta pick up my boys."

"Okay," she said.

She turned onto her back and looked up at the ceiling. She was trying to get her bearings. She rubbed her eyes with both hands. She remembered they had come home in his car. Her van was still at the station.

"What were you dreaming about?" Compton asked.

"Why, was I talking?" she asked.

"No, you were just . . . it looked really intense."

"I think I was dreaming about my father."

"Where is he?"

"He's dead. He drowned."

"Oh, I'm sorry."

"It was a long time ago—more than twenty years."

A fleeting resonance of the dream came back. She remembered the bubble going to the surface like a call for help.

"You want to come fishing with us?" Compton asked.

"Uh, no, I'm going to go paddle and then do some work," Ballard said. "But thanks. Someday I'd like to meet your sons."

Compton got up off the bed and went over to the dresser. He started putting his wallet and cash into the pockets of his blue jeans. Ballard watched him. He had a broad, muscular back, and the tips from a couple of the flames from his sun tattoo poked above the collar of his T-shirt.

"Where are you taking them?" she asked.

"Just down to the rocks by the entrance to the marina," he said.

"Is fishing legal there?"

He held up his badge to her, then clipped it to his belt. The implication was clear. If a lifeguard or someone else tried to tell him fishing was illegal on the rock jetty at the mouth of Marina del Rey, then he would employ the law enforcement exclusion rule.

"I might go down that way when I'm paddling," she said. "I'll look for you guys."

"Yeah, come on by," he said. "We'll try not to snag you with a hook."

He turned from the dresser, smiling and ready to leave.

"There's OJ in the fridge," he said. "Sorry, no coffee."

"That's okay," she said. "I'll hit Starbucks."

He came over and sat down on the bed again.

"So you were just a kid when your dad drowned."

"Fourteen."

"What happened?"

"He was surfing and went under a wave and just never came up."

"Were you there?"

"Yeah, but there was nothing I could do. I was running up and down the beach, screaming like a crazy person."

"That's rough. What about your mother?"

"She wasn't there. She wasn't really a part of my life. Then or now."

"What did you do after he was gone?"

"Well, I lived the way we had been living. On the beach, on friends' couches when it got cold. Then, after about a year, my grandmother came over and found me, brought me back here when I was sixteen. Ventura, where my dad was from."

Compton nodded. They had been as intimate physically as you could get, but neither had shared the innermost details of their lives before. Ballard had never met his sons and didn't even know their names. She had never asked him about his divorce. She knew this moment might bring them closer or could serve to push them apart.

She sat up on the bed and they hugged.

"So I'll see you around, okay?" he said. "Call me—and not just about work."

"Okay," she said. "But thanks for last night."

"Anytime for you, Renée."

He moved in for a kiss but she turned her face to his shoulder.

"You've brushed your teeth. I haven't," she said.

She kissed his shoulder.

"I hope they're biting today," she said.

"I'll text you a photo if we get anything," he said.

He got up and left the room. Ballard heard the front door close, then the sound of his car starting out front. She thought about things for a few minutes and then got up for the shower. She felt a bit sore. End-of-shift sex was never good sex. It was quick, perfunctory, often rough in the service of a primal drive to somehow reaffirm life through carnal satisfaction. Ballard and Compton had not made love. They had simply gotten what they needed from each other.

When she got out of the shower, she had no choice but to dress in the same clothes as the night before. She noted the scent of adrenalized perspiration left in her blouse from that moment when Nettles left the room and she saw he had a gun. She paused for a moment to relive that thrill. The feeling was addictive and dangerous, and she wondered whether there might be something wrong with her for craving it.

She continued dressing, knowing she would switch to a fresh suit before starting work. Her goal for the day was to track down and get a look at Thomas Trent's ex-wife, the woman who left him a few months after his arrest on Sepulveda Boulevard and probably knew a lot of his secrets. Ballard knew she had to make a decision about whether to go straight at her for an interview or to finesse a conversation without revealing she was a cop.

As she checked herself in the mirror and ran her fingers through her hair, she felt a text vibration from her phone. Surprised the battery still had some juice, she pulled it out of her suit pocket and checked the screen. She saw she had a missed call from Jenkins that had come in while she was in the shower and a text from Sarah, her critter sitter, asking if Ballard planned on picking up Lola anytime soon.

Ballard first texted Sarah, apologized about the late pickup, and said she would be getting Lola within the hour. She next called Jenkins back, thinking he had just been checking in on how things went the night before.

"Partner, what's up?" she said.

"I was just calling with condolences," Jenkins said. "That was bad news."

"What are you talking about?"

"Chastain. You didn't get the RACER?"

He was referring to a digital alert from the Real-time Analysis and Critical Emergency Response unit, which put out e-mails to all personnel in detective services when a major crime or civic activity was occurring. Ballard had not yet checked her e-mail that morning.

"No, I haven't looked," she said. "What happened to Chastain?"

She had a bad feeling growing in the pit of her stomach.

"Uh, he's dead," Jenkins said. "His wife found him in their garage this morning."

Ballard walked over and sat down on the bed. She leaned forward, bringing her chest down to her knees.

"Oh god," she managed to say.

She flashed on the confrontation they'd had in the

detective bureau two nights earlier. The one-sided confrontation. Her mind leaped to the idea that she had kicked off some sort of cascade of guilt that had led Chastain to take his own life. Then she remembered that they didn't send out RACER alerts for cop suicides.

"Wait a minute," she said. "How was he killed? He didn't do it himself, did he?"

"No, he was hit," Jenkins said. "Somebody got him in the garage when he was getting out of his car. The RACER alert says execution-style hit."

"Oh my god."

Ballard was beside herself. Chastain had betrayed her, yes, but her mind skipped over all that to the five solid years of their partnership before it. Chastain was a skilled and determined investigator. He had five years in RHD before Ballard came in, and he'd taught her a lot. Now he was gone and soon his badge and name would join his father's on the memorial to fallen officers outside the PAB.

"Renée, you okay?" Jenkins asked.

"I'm okay," she said. "But I gotta go. I'm going to go up there."

"That's probably not a good idea, Renée."

"I don't really care. I'll talk to you later."

She disconnected and flipped over to her Uber app to summon a ride back to Hollywood Division.

Chastain had lived with his wife and teenage son up in Chatsworth in the far-northwest corner of the city. It was about as far as you could get from downtown and the PAB and still live within the borders of the city. Most cops escaped the city at the end of their shifts and lived outside its boundaries but Chastain had been ambitious and he always thought it would pay off to tell promotional boards that he had always lived in the city he policed.

Once back at the station, Ballard quickly changed into a fresh suit, then grabbed the plain wrap assigned to the late show and headed north, taking a series of three different freeways to get to Chatsworth. An hour after she had gotten the call from Jenkins, she pulled to the curb behind a long line of police cruisers and plain wraps clogging the cul-de-sac at the end of Trigger Street. Passing by the street sign reminded Ballard that Chastain used to joke about being a cop who lived on Trigger Street.

Now it seemed sadly ironic.

The first thing Ballard noticed as she got out of her car was that there appeared to be no media on the perimeter of the scene. Somehow, no one in the legion of reporters who covered L.A. had tumbled to or been tipped to the story. It was probably because it was a Saturday morning and the local media machinery was getting a late start.

She hung her badge around her neck as she approached the yellow tape at the driveway. Save for the media, she saw all the other routine participants in a crime scene: detectives, patrol officers, and forensic and coroner's techs. The house was a midcentury ranch house built when Chatsworth was the utter boondocks of the city. The double-wide garage door was open onto the center of activity.

A patrol officer from Devonshire Division was running the clipboard at the yellow tape. Ballard gave her name and badge number and then ducked under as he wrote it down. As she walked up the driveway toward the garage, a detective she had once worked with at RHD stepped out and walked toward her with his hands up to stop her. His name was Corey Steadman, and Ballard had never had a problem with him.

"Renée, wait," he said. "What are you doing here?"

Ballard stopped in front of him.

"He was my partner," Ballard said. "Why do you think I'm here?"

"The lieutenant will shit a brick if he sees you," Steadman said. "I can't let you in."

"Olivas? Why is his team handling this? Isn't it a conflict of interest?"

"Because it's related to the Dancers thing. We're folding it in."

Ballard made a move to go around Steadman but he sidestepped quickly and blocked her. He held his hand up again in front of her.

"Renée, I can't," he said.

"Okay, then just tell me what happened," Ballard said. "Why's he in the garage?"

"We think he got hit last night when he came in. The shooter was either waiting inside or, more likely, waiting outside and came in behind him in the blind spot when he drove in."

"What time was this?"

"The wife went to bed at eleven. She had gotten a text from Kenny saying he'd be working until at least midnight. She gets up this morning and sees that he never got home. She texts, he doesn't answer. She takes some trash out to the cans in the garage and finds him. That was about nine."

"Where was he hit?"

"Sitting in the driver's seat, one in the left temple. Hopefully he never saw it coming."

Ballard paused for a moment as feelings of anger and sorrow combined in her chest.

"And Shelby didn't hear the shot? What about Tyler?"

"Tyler was staying the weekend with a friend from the volleyball team. Shelby didn't hear anything, we think because there was an improvised suppressor. We've got some paper fibers and a liquid residue on the car seat and body. Sticky. We're thinking orange soda but that's up to the lab."

Ballard nodded. She knew that Steadman was talking about the method of taping a plastic liter bottle of soda to the muzzle of a gun. Empty out the liquid and stuff in cotton, paper towels, anything. The setup considerably dampened the sound of the muzzle blast but also expelled some of the material in the bottle.

And it was good for one shot only. The shooter must have been confident that it would get the job done.

"Where was he last night?" Ballard asked. "What was he doing?"

"The lieutenant actually sent him home at six," Steadman said. "He'd been running eighteen hours straight by then and L-T told him to take a break. But he didn't go home. Shelby said he texted that he had to go wrangle a witness and would be home late."

"That was the word he used in the text? 'Wrangle'?"

"That's what I heard, yeah."

Ballard had heard Chastain use the word on multiple occasions when they had been partners. She knew that to him, *wrangling a witness* meant dealing with a complicated situation. It could be complicated for numerous reasons but most often it meant going out and looking for a reluctant witness, one that needed to be controlled and herded into court or into giving a statement.

"Who was the wit?"

"I don't know. Somebody he heard about or had a line on."

"And he was working by himself?"

"He's been the squad whip. You know, since you . . . transferred out."

The whip was a detective elevated to a role secondary to the lieutenant. Most often it was someone being groomed for promotion and without an assigned partner. It explained why Chastain might have gone out on his own.

"How is Shelby?" Ballard asked.

"I don't know," Steadman said. "I haven't talked to her. The L-T was dealing with her inside."

Mentioning Olivas seemed to conjure him. Looking over Steadman's shoulder, Ballard saw the lieutenant step out of the garage and head toward them. He had his suit jacket off, the sleeves of his white shirt rolled up, and his shoulder holster exposed—counterbalanced with gun on the left and two bullet clips on the right. In a low voice she warned Steadman.

"Here he comes," she whispered. "Tell me to get out of here again. Make it loud."

It took Steadman a moment to understand the warning.

"I told you," he said forcefully. "You can't be here. You need to go back to your—"

"Corey!" Olivas barked from behind. "I'll handle this."

Steadman turned as if just realizing Olivas was behind him.

"She's leaving, L-T," he said. "Don't worry about it."

"No, go back in," Olivas said. "I need to speak to Ballard."

Olivas waited for Steadman to head back to the garage. Ballard stared at him, ready for what she knew would be a verbal assault.

"Ballard, did you have any contact with Chastain yesterday?" he asked.

"Not since I turned a witness over to him on the morning after the shooting," Ballard said. "That was it."

"Okay, then you need to leave. You're not welcome here."

"He was my partner."

"Once. Until you tried to co-opt him with your lies. Don't think for one minute you can make up for it now."

Ballard held her hands wide and looked around like she was asking who could possibly hear them where they stood on the driveway.

"Why are you lying? There's nobody else here. Don't tell me you've told it to yourself so often, you actually believe it."

"Ballard, you—"

"We both know exactly what happened. You made it clear on more than one occasion that my trajectory in the department relied upon you and that I had to put out or I'd get pushed out. Then at the Christmas party I get pushed up against a wall and you try to put your tongue down my throat. You think lying to my face about it will help convince me it didn't happen?"

Olivas seemed taken aback by the intensity of her voice.

"Just leave. Or I'll have you escorted off the property."

"What about Shelby?"

"What about her?"

"Did you just leave her alone in there? She needs somebody to be with her."

"*You*? Not in a million fucking years."

"We were tight. I was her husband's partner and she trusted me not to sleep with him. I could be of use to you here."

Olivas seemed to take a moment to consider the option.

"We take care of our own here, and you're not one of us. Show some integrity, Ballard. Show some respect. You have thirty seconds before I ask the patrol officers to remove you from the property."

With that, Olivas turned and headed back toward the open garage. Ballard looked past him and saw that several of the people in the garage had been surreptitiously watching their confrontation. She could also see her ex-partner's take-home plain wrap parked in the right-side bay. The trunk was open and she wondered if that was for processing or to help shield the view of his body slumped in the driver's seat.

Chastain had betrayed their partnership in the worst way a partner could. It was unacceptable and unforgivable but Ballard understood it, considering Chastain's ambitions. Still, she always thought there would be a personal reckoning and that he would eventually do the right thing, that he would back her and tell the world what he saw Olivas do. Now there would never be a chance for that. Ballard felt the loss for both Chastain and herself.

She turned and headed down the driveway to the street. She passed a black SUV pulling up that she knew was carrying the chief of police. Her eyes were stinging with tears before she made it to her car.

17

Ballard picked up Lola with profuse apologies to Sarah and went to the beach. At first she just sat cross-legged on the sand with her dog and watched the sun drop toward the horizon. She decided not to paddle. She knew that sharks cruised the shoreline at dusk, looking for food.

She thought about the time Chastain had told her the real story of his father, of how he had been an Internal Affairs hack who was pulled out of a car and murdered by a mob during an explosion of racial tensions that he had helped touch off through his own actions. Chastain didn't know the truth until after he became a cop and earned the juice it took to pull the sealed records on his father's death. He confided in Ballard that the thing that had made him so proud growing up had ultimately made him deeply and privately humiliated as a man with a badge. It had fired his ambition to climb through the ranks and redeem his father and himself in some way.

The only problem was, he had trampled over Ballard on the climb.

"Renée?"

Ballard looked up. Aaron the lifeguard stood there.

"Are you okay?" he asked.

"I'm fine, yeah," she said.

She wiped tears off her cheeks.

"Somebody who totally fucked me over died today," she said.

"Then why are you sad?" he asked. "I mean, fuck him. If it was a him."

"I don't know. I guess because it means what he did can never be changed. His death makes it permanent."

"I think I get that."

"It's complicated."

He was wearing a red nylon jacket with the word rescue on it. The temperature was dropping with the sun, which was just about to dip into the ocean. The sky was turning neon pink.

"You're not going to try to sleep out here tonight, are you?" Aaron asked. "Night patrol is out here in force on a Saturday night."

"No," Ballard said. "I'm going in to work. Just wanted to see the sunset."

Aaron said good night and moved on down the beach toward the lifeguard tower, where he was posted until dark. Ballard watched the sun sink into the black water and then got up. She once again bought takeout for herself and Lola on the boardwalk and ate sitting on a nearby bench. She could not generate much enthusiasm for food and ended up giving half her order of black beans, yellow rice, and plantains to a homeless man she knew named Nate. He was a street artist who until January had done decent business selling portraits of the former president. He reported to Ballard that images of the new president went unsold because his kind of people didn't come to Venice Beach.

She returned Lola to Sarah's house with more apologies to both dog and sitter, and then headed east back into the city and the cases. She got to Hollywood Station three hours before her shift was scheduled to start. In the locker room, after changing into her suit, she pulled the black elastic mourning band from behind her badge and stretched it across the front of the shield.

Once she was in the detective bureau, she set up in her usual spot and went right to work on the computer, starting with opening the *Los Angeles Times* website. She knew she could use the department's own data network—most investigations resulted in basic information being put online for internal access—but that would leave a signature trail. She wanted the names of the three men murdered in the booth at the Dancers and believed the city's main media standard-bearer would have acquired them by now, nearly forty-eight hours since the massacre.

She was correct and quickly found a story that credited the Medical Examiner's Office with releasing the names of the dead after next-of-kin notifications and autopsies had been completed. The story identified Cynthia Haddel and Marcus Wilbanks as the Dancers employees killed by the unknown gunman, and Cordell Abbott, Gordon Fabian, and Gino Santangelo as the three customers who were murdered in the booth where they sat.

Names in hand, Ballard proceeded to background the three men in the booth by signing into the crime index and DMV computers. This, too, would leave a trail of her searches but these would not be as easily detected as her simply using her department access to open the online files of the case. Going that way could leave a flag, immediately alerting the case investigators of her activities.

She went through the three names one by one and built data profiles of each. As had been reported the night before on the television news, all three men had criminal records. What raised Ballard's intrigue level was that they appeared to come from different parts of the criminal underworld, and that made their meeting in that booth unusual.

Cordell Abbott was a thirty-nine-year-old black man who had four convictions on his record for gambling offenses. In each of these cases, he was accused of banking illegal games. In layman's terms, he was a bookie. He took bets on sports ranging from horse races to Dodgers games. It appeared that, despite four convictions, he had never served time in a state prison. At most, his crimes cost him county jail time measured in weeks and months, not years.

Similarly, Gordon Fabian had escaped prison time, despite a long history of convictions for various drug-related crimes. Fabian was white and, at fifty-two years old, the oldest victim of the massacre. Ballard counted nineteen arrests on his record dating back to the 1980s. These all related to the personal use or small-time sale of drugs. He received probation and time-served sentences in most cases. In some others, charges were dropped. However, at the time of his murder, Fabian had finally made it to the big leagues and was awaiting an upcoming trial in federal court for possession of a kilo of cocaine. He was out on bail but facing a long prison sentence if convicted.

The third victim, Gino Santangelo, was a forty-three-year-old white man and the only one of the three with a record of violence. He had been charged with assault three times over a fifteen-year period. One case involved a firearm in which he shot but did not kill the victim and the other two times the charges included a GBI—great bodily injury—add-on by the D.A.'s Office. In each of the cases, Santangelo pleaded guilty to lesser charges and received lesser penalties. His first conviction involved the use of the firearm, and that cost him three years in a state prison. After that, he apparently got smart and dropped the use of a gun from his repertoire because it would add years to the penalty spectrum. In subsequent arrests, he used his hands and feet to assault the victims and was allowed to plead out to lesser charges, like battery and disturbing the peace, leading to sentences of under a year in the county jail. Ballard's read on Santangelo, without having the details of each case in front of her, was that he was an enforcer for the mob. She keyed on the third case, in which he was charged with assault with GBI. It was pleaded down to misdemeanor battery. For a case to drop like that, Ballard knew there had to be a witness or victim issue. Santangelo had a history of violence but the victim, or maybe a witness, was afraid or refused to testify. The result was a thirty-day sentence reduced to a week in the county jail.

There was much Ballard could deduce by reading between the lines of the case extracts, but she did not have access to detailed case summaries that put the crimes and the individuals in context. For that, she would need to pull actual files, and that wasn't going to happen on a Saturday night. She did look at booking photos of the three men, which allowed her to recall their positions in the booth where they were murdered.

Cordell Abbott was easy to place because he was the only black victim. Ballard remembered seeing his body to the immediate left of the open space in the booth. That put Abbott right next to the shooter.

Gordon Fabian's side-view mug shot showed a man with a gray ponytail, and that easily put him in the seat across from the shooter. He was the victim who had fallen halfway out of the booth, the end of his ponytail dipping into his own blood like a paintbrush.

And that put Gino Santangelo in the middle.

Ballard leaned back in her desk chair and thought about what she knew and what she could assume. Four men slide into a booth. Did they just randomly take their positions, or was there a choreography based on the relationships between the men? There was a bookie, an enforcer, a drug dealer, and, for lack of better information, a shooter.

Added to this was a question about shooting sequence. Ballard did not have access to the crime and property reports, but if she had to name one person in the booth besides the shooter who was armed, she would go with Santangelo. He had previously been convicted of a gun crime, and even though he appeared to shrug off the use of firearms in his strong-arm tactics, it was unlikely that he would stop carrying. His record showed him to be a career criminal and the gun would be one of the tools of the trade.

This led to the next question. The split-second selfie video provided by the witness Alexander Speights clearly showed the shooter firing first on Fabian, the drug dealer. Why would he do that if he had knowledge of who Santangelo was and that he was most likely armed?

Ballard drew several conclusions from her admittedly incomplete information. The first was that the men in the booth didn't all know each other. It was likely that the shooter knew Abbott, the bookie, if he knew any of the men, because he sat next to him. And she figured he fired first on the drug dealer because of malice or momentum. Malice if he held the drug dealer accountable for whatever went wrong during the meeting. Momentum if he simply chose to shoot the other men in a one-two-three pattern. It would have been the fastest and safest way to shoot, provided he didn't know that Santangelo was armed.

Ballard knew her assumptions got her nowhere. There were myriad other possibilities and factors at work. The shooter might have checked the others for weapons before joining the meeting, and the seating arrangement could have been dictated simply by the separate arrivals of the men. There was no way of knowing anything for sure and her final conclusion was that she was just spinning her wheels on a case that was not hers and that she had been clearly ordered to stay away from.

But still, she couldn't drop it. It pulled at her because of Chastain. And she now considered a move that would surely get her fired if discovered by the department.

Ballard and Chastain had been partners for nearly five years before the falling-out over her complaint about Olivas. During that time they worked closely on high-priority and often dangerous investigations. It drew them close and in many ways their partnership was like a marriage, although there was never any crossing or even blurring of the professional line. But still, they shared all things work-related, and Ballard even knew

Chastain's password into the department's computer system. She had sat next to him too many times while he logged in not to notice and remember it. It was true that the department required detectives to change their passwords every month, but investigators were creatures of habit and most simply updated the last three digits of a steady password, using the month and year.

She believed it was unlikely that he had switched his main password after the dissolution of their partnership. Ballard had not changed her own, because it was easy to remember—her father's name spelled backward—and she didn't want to be bothered memorizing a combination of letters and numbers that might have no significance to her. She knew that Chastain's password was the date of his marriage followed by his and his wife's initials and the current month and year.

Ballard doubted Chastain's account would already have been deleted following his death. In a bureaucracy like the LAPD, it might take months before the digital access unit wiped the system of his user access. But she knew that if she logged in as Chastain now, the breach could be traced back to the exact computer used. It didn't matter that it wasn't technically Ballard's computer or desk. She would become the primary suspect and it would result in her dismissal from the force, if not criminal prosecution for hacking.

She logged her own user account off the computer and pulled up the entry prompt. She drummed her fingers on the desk for a few moments, waiting for an inner voice to caution her against taking the next step. But it never came. She typed in Chastain's user name and password, then waited.

She was in. She was now able to follow her old partner's ghost in the system and she quickly used his approved access to open files on the Dancers case. She opened numerous crime scene and evidence reports, as well as witness summaries and the chronological logs kept by the investigators on the case. Ballard scanned the reports to identify what they were and then sent them to the detective bureau's printer for a more thorough review later. She felt like she had broken into someone's house and needed to get out before being discovered.

Fifteen minutes later, she logged out and was clear. She went to the printer room and pulled out a sheaf of copies nearly two inches thick.

For the next hour, she took her time and reviewed the documents. Most of it was routine paperwork but some of the reports offered a fuller glimpse of the crime and the parts individuals played. Most notable were the fuller background reports on the three victims in the booth. The bio on Santangelo stated that he was a known loan shark and debt collector connected with an organized-crime family based in Las Vegas. Additionally, the crime scene report noted that a .45 caliber handgun was indeed found tucked into the waistband of his suit pants. The gun was traced back to a 2013 home burglary in Summerland, Nevada.

One document that was surprising for its lack of content was the video survey report. It stated that a review of footage from cameras at the entrance of the Dancers as well as from nearby businesses on Sunset Boulevard and the vicinity revealed no images of the suspected shooter or his vehicle. The video unit could not provide even the barest minimum description of a getaway vehicle or direction of travel—east or west—the killer had taken. To Ballard it was almost as if the shooter knew there were no cameras or had chosen the location of the meeting based on the video cracks he could slip through.

Disappointed, Ballard moved on and finished with the investigative chronologies. There were five detectives assigned full-time to the case, plus Lieutenant Olivas. This produced three chronos from the two pairs of detectives and Chastain, the task force whip. There was no chronological report yet from Olivas.

From these documents Ballard was able to see the moves being made and discern that the primary focus of the investigation was Santangelo. It was believed that the mass killing might have been a hit on the mob figure, with the four other victims being collateral damage. One of the detective teams had been dispatched to Las Vegas to pursue this angle.

Ballard knew that all of this would likely change with the murder of Chastain. Investigative priorities would be recalibrated. If the detective's murder and the Dancers massacre were linked forensically or by other evidence, then it would obviously mean the killer was still in Los Angeles.

Ballard read through Chastain's chrono last. She saw that he had dutifully logged his visit to the Hollywood Division to consult with her and to pick up the witness Alexander Speights. It also showed that he later identified Metro, the friend and coworker Speights had been with at the club, as Matthew Robison, twenty-five, who lived on La Jolla Avenue in West Hollywood. Chastain interviewed Robison Friday morning at his apartment after getting the information from the manager of the Slick Kicks store. A note in the chrono after the entry said *DSS*, which Ballard remembered was Chastain's shorthand for a witness who supposedly didn't see shit.

Neither Speights nor Robison was a probative witness but the split-second video that Speights came up with was still of high value. If charges and a trial ever emerged out of the investigation, Speights would be a witness, if only to introduce the selfie in which he had captured the first shot. If he was challenged in some way by the defense, his pal Robison could be brought in to testify and back up his story.

Chastain's chrono contained two phone-call entries that intrigued Ballard. The first was at 1:10 p.m. Friday. It was an outgoing call that Chastain had placed to someone named Dean Towson. And the second was the last entry in the chrono, an incoming call at 5:10 p.m. from Matthew Robison, the witness who supposedly hadn't seen shit. No further explanation of either of the calls was registered in the log. Chastain had probably intended to fill out the details later. But Ballard noted that the call had come in and Chastain had logged it shortly before he got the word from Olivas that he was off duty for the evening.

The name Dean Towson was familiar to Ballard but she couldn't place it. She Googled it on the computer and soon was looking at the website for a criminal defense attorney specializing in federal court cases.

"Fabian," Ballard said out loud.

It clicked. Fabian was facing federal drug charges. Towson specialized in federal cases. It was likely that he was Fabian's attorney on the kilo case and that Chastain had reached out to him to see if he might know why his client was in that booth at the Dancers when the shooting started.

Ballard checked the clock over the TV screens and saw it was almost ten. She knew she could run Towson's home address down through the DMV and go knock on his door, but it was late on a Saturday and she decided her approach to the lawyer would probably be better received in daylight hours. She put the idea aside and instead called the phone number Robison had called Chastain from. The chrono listed it as a 213 area code. Her call went unanswered and direct to a beep without an outgoing greeting. She left a message.

"Mr. Robison, this is Detective Ballard with the LAPD. I am following up on the phone conversation you had Friday with Detective Chastain. Could you give me a call back as soon as possible?"

She was leaving her number on the message when she saw on one of the TV screens video footage from outside Ken Chastain's house. The media had finally been alerted to the story. The sound was down on the screen but on the video Ballard saw the chief of police addressing several reporters while Olivas stood just behind him and to his left. The chief looked ashen, as though he knew that whatever had started in that booth at the Dancers had now reached deep into his department and done irreparable damage.

Ballard didn't need to hear his statement to know it.

The last set of documents Ballard looked through were Chastain's own rough notes on the autopsies. He had transferred them to a digital file in preparation for writing reports to be submitted to the overall case file.

He was dead before he got the chance to accomplish that.

Because the case was of highest priority—high enough to draw Dr. J., the coroner herself, out to the crime scene—the examinations of the bodies were conducted late Friday morning at the Medical Examiner's Office, with Dr. J. supervising several deputy coroners assigned to each of the bodies. While there was little doubt as to cause of death of the victims, recovery of bullets from the bodies was an important step in the investigation and thus gave the individual cases priority status. Usually autopsies weren't even scheduled for twenty-four to forty-eight hours. These were conducted less than twelve hours after the deaths.

Dr. J. conducted the Fabian autopsy herself. The actual autopsy report would take several days to produce but in the meantime Chastain took notes as the attending investigator. It was in those notes that Ballard came across a sentence and a question that turned her thoughts on the case in a new direction.

According to Chastain's notes, Dr. J. had labeled a wound on Fabian's chest as a first-degree burn that had occurred at the time of death but was not caused by a firearm. Chastain had added a second notation to this conclusion: "Battery burn?"

Ballard froze as she remembered seeing Chastain, Dr. J., and Lieutenant Olivas gathered around Fabian's body at the crime scene and studying his chest.

Now she knew why. Fabian had a burn on his chest that may have come from a battery.

Ballard quickly moved back to the property report on Fabian and saw nothing listed as recovered with the body that could explain the burn. Whatever was burning him at the time of the shooting was taken from the scene—apparently by the shooter.

It all tumbled together for Ballard. She believed that Fabian was wearing a listening device. He was wired at the Dancers meeting, and the battery of the device had started to burn him. It was a well-known hazard in undercover work. Compact listening devices overheat and oils and sweat from the body can create an arcing connection with the battery. Professional UCs take measures to insulate themselves from what they call bug burn, wrapping the devices in rubber sheathing to place the devices away from the body's sweat glands.

There was nothing in the background material on Fabian that Ballard had reviewed that showed he had ever worked as an undercover operative. But there was a burn on his chest that indicated otherwise in the Dancers massacre.

Ballard believed that Chastain was onto something and it might have been what got him killed.

18

Ballard waited until nine a.m. Sunday to knock on Dean Towson's door. She had just come from breakfast at the Du-par's in Studio City after a relatively slow night on the late shift. She'd had only two callouts, first to sign off on a suicide, and second to aid in the search for a missing old man with Alzheimer's. He was found in a neighbor's carport before she even got to the call location.

It had taken all of her will and patience to hold back from attempting to make contact with Towson in the middle of the night. The more she considered Ken Chastain's autopsy notes, the more she believed that Towson might hold a key to solving the mystery of what had happened in the booth at the Dancers.

But she managed to exercise restraint and used the time between the callouts to take a deeper dive into all law enforcement databases available in a search for details about the three men murdered in the booth at the Dancers. The effort paid off just before dawn. By collating the criminal histories of the three men along with their incarceration locations she was able to find the crossing point—the place where all three of them could have previously met and interacted. Five years earlier, all three men from the booth were housed at the Peter J. Pitchess Detention Center in Castaic.

Pitchess was part of Los Angeles County's vast jail system. Decades earlier it was a minimum-security drunk farm, where hapless miscreants dried out and served their sentences for drunk driving and public intoxication. Now it was the biggest facility in the county system and operated under heavy security. Almost eight thousand male inmates were housed there while awaiting trial or serving sentences of less than a year. In May 2012, Santangelo was in Pitchess in the middle of a ninety-day sentence for battery while Fabian was there for a thirty-day stint for a drug-possession rap and Abbott was finishing a six-month term for an illegal gaming conviction. As far as Ballard could determine, the three men had overlapped at Pitchess for three weeks.

Ballard knew Pitchess was a big place. She had been there numerous times to conduct interviews with inmates. But she knew there were ways of cutting down the population pool that would have included the three men from the booth. Gangs were segregated according to race and affiliation, and the dorms dedicated to gangs at Pitchess accounted for half of the facility's capacity. Ballard had found no record of any of the three booth men having street gang affiliation.

The remaining half of the facility was further segregated into dorms for inmates awaiting trials and hearings, and for those already convicted and serving out sentences. Santangelo, Fabian, and Abbott were in this latter group—they were already sentenced. That put the pool that they were swimming in at approximately two thousand inmates. It was a small enough number that Ballard believed it was possible that the three men interacted. All three were involved in crimes of vice—gambling, loan-sharking, and drugs—and they may have engaged in their businesses even behind the steel fences of the jail. The bottom line was that Ballard had good reason to believe that Santangelo, Fabian, and Abbott had known each other for as long as five years before their fateful and final meeting at the Dancers.

There was nothing in the case reports Ballard had reviewed to indicate that the official investigation of the Dancers massacre had reached the same conclusion about the victims in the booth. Ballard now faced the dilemma of whether she should find a way to share her information with the investigation, even though it was headed by the man who had done his level best to drive her from the police department.

Additionally, her conclusions about the three men could reflect on the fourth unknown man in the booth—the shooter. Had he also been at Pitchess with the other three? Was he also a trafficker in vice operations? Or was he someone whose connection to the other men came from a completely different angle?

As she checked out at the end of shift and headed for breakfast, Ballard decided that she would continue her investigation and would find a conduit for feeding her findings to the official inquiry. She somehow felt she owed that to Chastain.

Fed and full, she now wanted to brace Towson before he could leave home for the day. Eight o'clock would have been her preferred time but she gave him an extra hour of sleep because it was a Sunday. She was counting on his cooperation, and that extra hour of sleep could pay off.

She also hoped to catch him before he'd had time to read the *Times*, because she knew there was a story in it about Chastain's murder. If Towson was aware of the murder, he might refuse to talk to her out of fear that whoever had targeted Chastain might go after him next.

Ballard knew that all of Chastain's moves over the last two days would be retraced by the detectives investigating his murder. The *Times* story, which she had read at Du-par's, said that the murder was being folded into the Dancers investigation but that the team working the case would be bolstered by detectives from the Major Crimes Unit.

Ballard had pulled Towson's home address off the DMV computer and proceeded to Sherman Oaks after breakfast, carrying with her two cups of coffee in a cardboard tray.

The defense lawyer lived in a town house on Dickens, just a block south of Ventura Boulevard. The place had underground parking and a security entrance on the street. Ballard waited on the sidewalk and went in when someone stepped through the gate to walk a dog.

"Forgot my keys," she mumbled.

She located Towson's door and knocked. She pulled her badge off her belt and had it up and ready. He answered the door in what she assumed were his sleep clothes: workout pants and a T-shirt with a Nike Swoosh on it. He was about fifty and short with a potbelly, glasses, and a gray beard.

"Mr. Towson, LAPD. I need to ask you a few questions."

"How'd you get in the building?"

"The security door was ajar. I just came in."

"It has a spring. It should have automatically closed. Anyway, I already talked to the LAPD and it's a Sunday morning. Can't this wait until tomorrow? I have no court. I'll be in the office all day."

"No, sir, it can't wait. As you know, we have a critical investigation under way and we're cross-matching our interviews."

"What the hell is cross-matching?"

"Different detectives covering the same ground. Sometimes one picks up something the other missed. Witnesses remember new details."

"I'm not a witness to anything."

"But you have information that is important."

"You know what cross-matching sounds like? It sounds like what you do when you don't have jack shit."

Ballard didn't respond. She wanted him to think that. It would make him feel important and he would be more open. It seemed clear that he didn't know that Chastain was dead. She proffered the cardboard tray.

"I brought you a coffee," she said.

"That's okay," he said. "I brew my own."

He stepped back so she could enter. She was in.

Towson offered Ballard a seat in the kitchen so they could talk while he brewed. Ballard drank her Du-par's coffee. She had been running for almost twenty-four hours straight and needed it.

"Do you live alone here?" she asked.

"Yep," he said. "I'm as single as they come. You?"

It was an odd question to throw back to her. She had been establishing the lay of the land: who was in the house and how she might conduct the interview. His question to her wasn't an appropriate response but she

198

saw in it the opportunity to foster cooperation and to get what she needed from him.

"Nothing serious," she said. "I work odd hours and it's hard to keep anything going."

There, she had shown him the possibility. It was now time to get down to business.

"You were handling Gordon Fabian's defense in the federal drug case," she said.

"That's right," Towson said. "And I know it sounds cynical but his getting killed saved my having to put a goose egg on my scorecard, if you know what I mean."

"You mean you were going to lose the case?"

"That's right. He was going to go down."

"Did Fabian know it?"

"I told him. They caught him fair and square with a kilo in the glove compartment of a car he was driving, was alone in, and that was registered to him. There really was no way out of that box. Their probable cause to stop him was down-the-line legit as well. I had nothing to work with. We were going to trial and it was going to be a very quick ride to a guilty verdict."

"He wasn't interested in a plea agreement?"

"None was offered. The kilo had cartel markings on it. The prosecutor would only talk about a plea if Fabian gave up his connection. And Fabian wasn't going to do that, because he said he'd rather go to prison for five years—that's the mandatory minimum—than have the Sinaloa Cartel put a hit on him for flipping."

"He was out on bail. A hundred K. How'd he come up with money for that and money for you? You are one of the better, more expensive attorneys in town."

"If there is a compliment in there, thank you. Fabian

liquidated his mother's home as well as some other valuables. It was enough to cover my fee and a ten percent bond."

Ballard nodded and took a long drink of tepid coffee. She saw Towson surreptitiously check his reflection in the glass of an overhead cabinet door and smooth his hair. She had him saying more than he should about the case. Maybe it was because the client was dead and it didn't matter. Maybe it was because he was interested in her and he knew the best way to a detective's heart was through cooperation. She knew that she now had to get to the purpose of her visit.

"My colleague Detective Chastain called you Friday," she said.

"That's right," Towson said. "And I told him pretty much what I'm telling you. I know nothing about what happened."

"You don't have any idea why Fabian was at the Dancers on Thursday night?"

"Not really. All I know is he was a desperate man. They do desperate things."

"Like what?"

"Like I don't know."

"Had he ever mentioned the name Cordell Abbott or Gino Santangelo to you before?"

"We are straying into areas of attorney-client privilege, which happens to stay solidly in place after death. But I'll tell you this: the answer is no, he never mentioned them to me, though it is obvious that he knew them. He was, after all, murdered with them."

Ballard decided to get to the point. Towson was either willing to cross the privilege line or he was not.

"Why was Fabian wearing a wire to that meeting at the Dancers?" she asked.

Towson stared at her for a moment before answering. Ballard could tell the question had struck a chord. It meant something.

"That's interesting," Towson said.

"Really?" Ballard said. "Why is it interesting?"

"Because as we have already established, he was fucked. And at some point in our relationship, I told him that if he wasn't willing to give up the cartel, his only way out might be to give up somebody else."

"And how did he respond to that?"

Towson breathed out heavily.

"You know what, I think I need to wave the attorney-client confidentiality flag here. We are getting too far into private communications between—"

"Please, six people are dead. If you know something, I need to know it."

"I thought it was five."

Ballard realized that she had slipped and included Chastain in the count.

"I mean five. What did Fabian say when you asked if he could give somebody else up?"

Towson finally began to pour himself a cup of coffee. Ballard watched him and waited.

"Do you know that I worked for the District Attorney's Office as a baby lawyer?" he asked.

"No, I didn't know that," Ballard said.

Ballard silently rebuked herself for not backgrounding Towson when she was backgrounding his client.

Towson got a half gallon container of skim milk out of the refrigerator and topped off his cup.

"Yes, I was eight years there as a deputy D.A.," he said. "The last four, I was in J-SID. You know what that is, right?"

He pronounced it Jay-Sid. Everybody called it that and everybody knew what it meant. The Justice System Integrity Division was the D.A.'s own watchdog unit.

"You investigated cops," Ballard said.

Towson nodded, then leaned back against the counter and stayed standing as he sipped from the cup. Ballard thought it was some kind of a male thing. Stay standing and you have the higher ground in the conversation.

"That's right," he said. "And we ran a lot of wires, you know? Best way to bring a dirty cop to ground was to get them on tape. They always folded if they knew their own words were going to be played in open court. Their own guilty words."

He paused there and Ballard said nothing. She knew he was trying to give her something and still not tread all the way across the line of his dead client's confidentiality. She waited and Towson took another drink of coffee before continuing.

"So let me preface this by saying again that I do not know why Fabian was in that club Thursday night and that I have no idea who he was meeting with or what it was about. But I explained to him that if he was going to give somebody up in exchange for a plea agreement, it had to be a bigger fish than himself. I mean, obviously that's how it works. He had to give up somebody the US Attorney's Office would want more than it wanted him."

"Okay. And what did he say to that?"

"He said, 'How about a cop?'"

Towson made a gesture with his coffee cup of sweeping his arm away from his body like he was saying, you can take the story from there.

Ballard composed herself and her thoughts. What Towson was saying matched the theory she had been considering through the night: that Fabian had worn a wire to the meeting at the Dancers and that the fourth man in the booth was a police officer. It was the only explanation for Chastain's behavior—his continuing to work the case Friday night after being told to go home.

"Let's back up a second," she said. "When was your conversation about bigger fish with Fabian?"

"About a month ago," Towson said. "It was the last time I spoke to him."

"And what did you say when he said, 'How about a cop'?"

"I said I knew from my J-SID days that the feds always liked to trade for cops. Sorry, but it's a fact. More headlines, more political cachet. Single-key drug dealers are a dime a dozen. Prosecuting a cop gets a D.A. salivating."

"So you told him all that. Did you tell him to wear a wire?"

"No, I never said that. I cautioned him. I said crooked cops are very dangerous because they have so much to lose."

"Did you ask who the cop was?"

"No, I didn't. You have to understand that this was a very general conversation. It was not a planning meeting. He didn't say, 'I know a bent cop.' He said, 'What if I could deliver a cop?' And in very general terms I said,

'Yeah, a cop would be good.' And that was it. I didn't tell him to wear a wire but I may have said something along the lines of making sure that he had something solid. That was it and that was the last time we spoke. I never saw him again."

Ballard now believed she knew the motive for the massacre and the reason the shooter took out Fabian first—because he was the traitor. The shooter eliminated everyone in the booth, then reached into Fabian's shirt and pulled the recorder.

The question was, how did the shooter know about the wire? To Ballard it seemed obvious. The recorder had started to burn Fabian's chest and he revealed himself either by flinching or by attempting to pull the wire off his skin. There was some kind of tell that the cop in the booth picked up on. And he acted quickly and decisively when he realized the meeting was a setup.

Ballard looked at Towson and wondered how much she should reveal now.

"Did Detective Chastain ask you any questions along these lines Friday?"

"No. He didn't. He never mentioned any of this."

"Good."

"Good? Why is that good?"

"Did you watch or read the news last night or this morning, Mr. Towson?"

"I just got up. I haven't seen anything."

"There actually are six victims now. Detective Chastain was murdered late Friday night."

Towson's eyes widened as he computed the news and went straight to Ballard's intended conclusion.

"Am I in danger?" he asked.

"I don't know," Ballard said. "But you should take all possible precautions."

"Are you kidding me?"

"I wish I was."

"Don't put me in the middle of this thing. I made a suggestion to a client, that's it."

"I understand that, and as far as I'm concerned, this conversation was private. It won't go into any report or record. I promise you that."

"Jesus Christ. You should have told me that Chastain got clipped."

"I did."

"Yeah, after you got what you wanted from me."

Five minutes later, after assuring Towson she would not put him in harm's way, Ballard was putting on sunglasses as she was headed back to her van. At its door she pretended to fumble with her keys as she surreptitiously checked her surroundings.

She had spooked Towson and in doing so had spooked herself. It was time for her to follow her own advice and take all possible precautions.

19

Ballard needed to sleep but she kept pushing herself. After leaving Towson she drove back over the hill and down into West Hollywood. Her next stop was Matthew "Metro" Robison's home. She had left three messages through the night for him and he had not returned the calls.

Robison's DMV address led Ballard to an apartment complex on La Jolla south of Santa Monica. As she cruised by, she saw an obvious city-ride parked at the curb out front. She kept going and pulled over a half block away. Steadman had told Ballard that Chastain texted his wife about wrangling a witness. Identifying and finding that witness would be priority one, and since Chastain had documented a call from Robison as the last investigative move on his chrono, it looked like the shoe salesman was of high interest to the task force.

Ballard adjusted her side-view mirror so she could keep an eye on the city-ride. After twenty minutes, she saw two detectives leave Robison's building and get in. She identified them as Corey Steadman and his partner, Jerry Rudolph. They did not have anyone with them, which meant either Robison had not been home or he was home and had answered questions to their satisfaction. Judging by the lack of response from Robison the night before, Ballard was thinking that the most likely scenario was that he had not been there.

Ballard waited until Steadman and Rudolph drove off before she got out of her car and walked back to the apartment building. There was no security gate. She got to Robison's door and was surprised when her knock was answered. A small woman who looked like she was about nineteen peered out at her from behind a security chain. Ballard showed her badge.

"Are you Metro's girlfriend?" she asked.

She was hoping her gender and seeming familiarity would get her further than the two white male detectives who had just been here.

"What about it?" the young woman said.

"Like those two men who were just here, I'm looking for him," Ballard said. "But for different reasons."

"What's your reason?"

"I'm worried about him. He reached out to my partner on Friday. And now my partner's dead. I don't want Metro to get hurt."

"You know Metro?"

"Not really. I was just trying to keep him and his friend Zander out of this as much as I could. Do you know where he is?"

The girl tightened her lips and Ballard saw her holding back tears.

"No," she said in a strangled voice.

"When was the last time he was home?" Ballard asked.

"Friday. I had work, and when I got off at ten, he wasn't here, and he didn't answer his texts. He's gone and I've been waiting."

"Was he supposed to work at Kicks yesterday?"

"Yes, and he didn't show. I went there and I talked to Zander and he said he never came in. They said he's fired if he doesn't show up today. I'm freaking out."

"My name is Renée," Ballard asked. "What's yours?"

"Alicia," the girl said.

"Did you tell all of this to those two detectives who were just here, Alicia?"

"No. They scared me. I just said he hasn't been here. They came last night, too, and asked the same questions."

"Okay, let's go back to Friday. Metro called my partner at about five o'clock. Were you with him then?"

"No, I go in at four."

"And where is that?"

"Starbucks on Santa Monica."

"Where was Metro when you last saw him?"

"Here. He was off Friday and he was here when I left for work."

"What was he doing?"

"Nothing. Just watching TV on the couch."

She turned away from the door opening as if to check the couch in the room behind her. She then turned back to Ballard.

"What should I do?" she asked, a tone of desperation clearly in her voice.

"You're in West Hollywood here," Ballard said. "Have you reported him missing to the Sheriff's Department?"

"No, not yet."

"Then I think what you should do is report him missing. It's been two nights and he hasn't come home and he hasn't reported for work. Call the West Hollywood substation and make the report."

"They won't do anything."

"They will do what they can, Alicia. But if Metro is hiding because he's scared, that will make it hard to find him."

"But if he is hiding, why doesn't he text me?"

Ballard had no answer for that and was afraid her face revealed her true theory about Metro's fate.

"I'm not sure," she said. "Maybe he will. Maybe he's keeping his phone off because he's afraid people can track him through it."

That provided no comfort.

"I have to go," Alicia said.

Slowly she closed the door. Ballard reached out her hand and stopped it.

"Let me give you a card," she said. "If you hear from Metro, tell him the safest thing for him to do is call me. Tell him Detective Chastain and I used to be partners, and he trusted me."

She pulled out a business card and passed it through the opening. Alicia took it without a word and then closed the door.

Ballard got back into the car and folded her arms on the steering wheel. She leaned her forehead down against them and closed her eyes. She was beyond tired but her mind couldn't let go of the case. Matthew Robison had at first been a witness classified as DSS—didn't see shit. And then at 5:10 p.m. Friday, he called Chastain. Within hours one would be dead and one would be missing. What had happened? What did Metro know?

Ballard startled as her phone rang. She pulled her

head up and checked the screen. It was her grandmother.

"Tutu?"

"Hello, Renée."

"Is everything okay, Tutu?"

"Everything is fine. But a man was here. He said he was police and he was looking for you. I thought you should know."

"Sure. Did he tell you his name and show you a badge?"

She tried to keep the urgency and concern out of her voice. Her grandmother was eighty-two years old.

"He had a badge and he gave me a business card. He said you have to call him."

"Okay, I will. Can you read me his name and give me the number?"

"Yes, it's Rogers—with the *s* at the end—Carr, spelled with two *r*'s."

"Rogers Carr. What about a number so I can call him?"

Ballard grabbed a pen out of the center console and wrote a 213 number on an old parking receipt. She didn't recognize the name or number.

"Tutu, does it say under his name where he works? Like what unit?"

"Yes, it says Major Crimes Unit."

Now Ballard understood what was happening.

"Perfect, Tutu. I'll give him a call. Was he by himself when he came to the door?"

"Yeah, by himself. Are you coming up tonight?"

"Uh, no, I don't think so this week. I'm working a case, Tutu."

"Renée, it's your weekend."

"I know, I know, but they've got me working. Maybe I'll get an extra day next week if we wrap this up. Have you been out to check the break lately?"

"Every day I walk on the beach. A lot of boys on the water. It must be good."

Ballard's grandmother lived in Ventura not far from Solimar Beach and Mussel Shoals, the places where her son—Renée's father—had grown up surfing.

"Well," Ballard said. "I hope it's still good next week. I'm going to call this guy now, Tutu, and see what he wants. I'll let you know next week when I'm heading up."

"Okay, Renée. Be careful."

"I know, Tutu."

Ballard disconnected and looked at the clock on the screen. It was 11:11, and that meant the stores on Melrose Avenue were open. According to Alicia, Zander Speights wasn't missing. She had spoken to him on Saturday at Kicks when she went in looking for Metro.

Ballard started the engine and dropped the car into drive. She headed down La Jolla toward Melrose. Despite what she had said to her grandmother, she had no intention of calling Rogers Carr. She knew what he was up to and what he wanted. Major Crimes had been folded into the Dancers/Chastain investigation and, like Steadman and Rudolph, Carr was most likely involved in tracing Chastain's last steps. That would include his visit to Hollywood Station to pick up Zander Speights and his cell phone. It would also include the final conversation she had with Chastain. That was personal and private and she didn't want to share it.

Ballard listed her grandmother's address as her permanent address on all departmental personnel records. She had a bedroom in the little bungalow and spent most of her days off up there, drawn by Tutu's home cooking and conversation, the nearby surf breaks, and the washer and dryer in the garage. But nobody besides her partner, Jenkins, knew exactly where she went on days off the job. The fact that Carr had made the ninety-minute drive up to the house in Ventura told Ballard that he had gotten access to her personnel jacket, and that bothered her. She decided that if Carr wanted to talk to her, then he could come find her.

Kicks was like a lot of shops that lined Melrose between Fairfax and La Brea. Minimalist chic and expensive. It was essentially a custom-athletic-shoe store. Shoes by recognizable brands like Nike, Adidas, and New Balance were modified with dyes, pins, zippers, and sewn-on sequins, crosses, and rosaries and then sold for hundreds of dollars over the original retail price. And by the looks of things when Ballard entered, nobody seemed to mind. There was a sign behind the cash register station that said THE SHOE IS ART.

Ballard felt about as with-it as a chaperone at a high school dance. She scanned the already crowded store and saw Speights opening a shoe box for a customer interested in a pair of Nikes with pink lipstick kisses emblazoned on them. He was extolling the cool factor of the shoes when he saw Ballard hovering nearby.

"I'll be right with you, Detective," he said.

He said it loud enough to draw everyone in the store's attention to Ballard. She ignored the stares and picked up a shoe off one of the clear plastic pedestals used to display the store's wares. It was a red Converse high-top that had somehow been mounted on a three-inch platform heel.

"You would look great in those, Detective."

Ballard turned. It was Speights. He had broken away from his customer, who was pacing in front of a mirror and considering the Nikes with kisses that she had tried on.

"I'm not sure they would hold up on a fast break," she said.

His face betrayed that Speights didn't get the joke. Ballard moved on.

"Zander, I need to talk to you for a few minutes. Do you have an office in the back where we can have some privacy?"

Speights gestured toward his customer.

"I'm working, and this is a commission shop," he said. "We have a sale today and I have to sell. I can't just—"

"Okay, I get it," Ballard said. "Just tell me about Metro. Where is he?"

"I don't know where Metro is, man. He's supposed to be here. He didn't show yesterday either, and when I called him, he didn't pick up."

"If he was hiding, where would he go?"

"What? I don't know. I mean, who goes into hiding? This is so weird."

"When was the last time you saw him?"

"That night when we left the club. Look, my customer is waiting."

"Let her look at herself for a couple more minutes. What about Friday? You didn't see him Friday?"

"No, we're both off Fridays. That's why we went out Thursday night."

"So you don't know what he was doing Friday? You never called him to tell him about coming to the station and the police taking your phone? You didn't warn him that we might want to talk to him?"

"No, because he didn't see anything that night. Neither of us did. And besides, I couldn't call him, because you and that detective took my phone."

"So why did he call the police on Friday at five? What did he know?"

"I have no idea why he called or what he knew, and I'm about to lose a sale. I gotta go."

Speights walked away from Ballard and over to his customer, who was now sitting down and taking off the Nikes. It looked to Ballard like a no-sale. She realized that she was still holding the Converse with the three-inch heel. She checked the underside of the shoe and saw a price tag of $395. She then carefully put it back on its pedestal, leaving it there like a work of art.

Ballard headed out to Venice and sleep after that. She picked up Lola and pitched her tent fifty yards north of the Rose Avenue lifeguard stand. She was so tired that she decided to sleep first and paddle afterward.

Her sleep was repeatedly interrupted by a series of calls to her phone from a 213 number that matched digit for digit the number her grandmother had read off the business card given to her by Rogers Carr. She didn't answer and he kept calling, popping her out of sleep every thirty or forty minutes. He never left a message. After the third interruption, Ballard put the phone on mute.

After that, she slept a solid three hours, waking with her arm draped around Lola's neck. She checked her phone and saw that Carr had called two more times and finally, after the last call, had left a message:

"Detective Ballard, this is Detective Rogers Carr with Major Crimes. Listen, we need to talk. I'm on the team investigating the murder of fellow officer Ken Chastain. Can you call me back so we can set up a face-to-face?"

He left two numbers: his cell—which Ballard already had—and his landline at the PAB. Ballard was always annoyed by people who prefaced what they said with the word *listen*.

Listen, we need to talk.

Listen, no we don't.

She decided not to call him back yet. It was supposedly her day off, and she was losing the light. Through the tent's zippered slot she checked the water and saw that the afternoon wind had kicked up a light chop. She looked up at the sun and estimated she could get in an hour's paddle before dusk, when the sharks came out.

Fifteen minutes later Ballard was on the water with a passenger. Lola sat on her haunches, weighting down the front of the board as it nosed through the chop. Ballard paddled north against the wind so she could count on it to be at her back when she was spent and returning to the beach.

She dug deep into the water with long, smooth strokes. As she worked, she let the details of the Dancers case flow through her mind. She tried to delineate what she knew, what she could assume, and what she didn't know. If she assumed that the fourth man in the booth was a cop, that made it a meeting of individuals with expertise in several areas of vice and law enforcement—gambling, loan-sharking, and drugs. Fabian, the drug dealer, had asked his attorney about delivering a cop to trade for help on his case. That indicated that he knew of a cop who was involved in illegal activities. Perhaps a cop who had taken bribes or had run interference on cases. Perhaps a cop who owed money.

Ballard could see a scenario where a cop who owed money to a bookie would be introduced to a loan shark with perhaps the drug dealer as the go-between. Another scenario she paddled through had the cop already owing the bookie and loan shark and being introduced to the drug dealer to set up a deal that would pay off his debts.

There were many plausible possibilities and she could not narrow anything down without more facts. She changed the direction of the board and shifted her focus to Chastain. His actions indicated that he had been on the same path that Ballard was on now but that he had somehow drawn attention to it, and it had gotten him killed. The question was, how did he get there so fast? He did not have the information Ballard had gotten from Towson, yet something had told him it was a cop who had been in that booth.

She went back to the start, to the callout on the case. She quickly went through her own steps in the investigation, beginning at Hollywood Presbyterian and carrying it through to her dismissal by Olivas at the crime scene. She examined each moment as though it were a film and she was interested in everything in its frame.

Eventually she saw something that didn't fit. It was that last moment at the crime scene, Olivas in her face, insulting her and telling her to leave. She had looked over his shoulder for a sympathetic eye. First it was to the coroner and then it was to her old partner. But Dr. J. had looked away and Chastain had been busying himself bagging evidence. He never even looked her way.

She now realized that that was the moment. Chastain was bagging something—it had looked like a black button to Ballard—while Olivas had his back turned and was looking at her. Chastain also had his back turned to Dr. J. so she would not have a view of what he was doing either.

Detectives didn't bag evidence at crime scenes. The criminalists did. On top of that, it had been too early for anyone to be picking up and bagging evidence. The crime scene was fresh, bodies were still in place, and the 3-D crime scene camera had not even been set up. What was Chastain doing? Why was he breaking protocol and removing something from the crime scene before it was properly noted, recorded, and cataloged?

Ballard was exhausted but she picked up her pace, pushing herself harder with each dig of the paddle. Her shoulders, arms, and thighs were vibrating with the strain. She needed to get back. She needed to return to Chastain's case files to figure out what she had missed.

As she cut into the shore, she forgot about the pain and her plans when she saw a man waiting next to her tent. He was in jeans and a black bomber jacket and wearing black aviators. She knew he was a cop before she could make out the badge on his belt.

Ballard came out of the water and quickly removed the board's leash. She then wrapped the Velcro ankle strap around the ring on Lola's collar. She knew Lola could easily break it if she lunged but Ballard was hoping that she would feel the tug of the strap and know she was under Ballard's control.

"Be easy, girl," Ballard said.

With the board under her left arm and her fingers in the grip hole, she walked slowly toward the man in the aviators. He looked familiar but she couldn't place him. Maybe it was just the sunglasses. They were standard with most cops.

He spoke before Ballard had to.

"Renée Ballard? I've been trying to reach you. Rogers Carr, Major Crimes."

"How'd you find me?"

"Well, I'm a detective. Some people, believe it or not, say a pretty good one."

"Don't joke with me. Tell me how you found me or you can go fuck off."

Carr held his hands up in surrender.

"Whoa, sorry. I didn't mean to piss anybody off. I put out a broadcast on your van and a couple of bicycle cops saw it in the lot. I came, I asked around. I'm here."

Ballard put her board down next to her tent. She heard a low rumbling, like distant thunder, coming from Lola's chest. The dog had picked up her vibe.

"You put out a broadcast on my van?" she asked. "It's not even registered in my name."

"I know that," Carr said. "But I met Julia Ballard today. I believe she is your grandmother? I ran her name for registered vehicles and came up with the van. I heard you like surfing and put two and two together."

He gestured toward the ocean as if it confirmed his investigative logic.

"I was paddleboarding," Ballard said. "It's not surfing. What do you want?"

"I just want to talk," Carr said. "Did you get my message on your cell?"

"Nope."

"Well, I left you a message."

"I'm off today. My phone's off too."

"I'm on the Chastain case and we are retracing his moves in the last forty-eight hours. You had some interaction with him and I need to ask you about it. That's it. Nothing sinister, strictly routine. But I have to get it done."

Ballard reached down and patted Lola on the shoulder, letting her know everything was all right.

"There's a place down there on Dudley called the Candle," she said. "It's on the boardwalk. I'll meet you there in fifteen minutes."

"Why can't we go now?" Carr asked.

"Because I need to get a shower and to wash the salt off my dog's legs. Twenty minutes tops. You can trust me, Carr. I'll be there."

"Do I have a choice?"

"Not if this is as routine as you claim it is. Try the mahimahi tacos, they're good."

"Meet you there."

"Get an outside table. I'm bringing the dog."

20

Carr was dutifully sitting at a table along the outer railing of the restaurant's side porch when Ballard showed up. She hooked the leash to the railing so Lola could be next to their table but on the sidewalk outside the restaurant. She then walked around to the porch entrance—crossing behind Carr's back—and sat down across from the Major Crimes detective. She put her phone on the table. As she passed his back, she had turned on the recording app she used for documenting her own interviews.

Carr didn't seem to suspect anything. Putting a phone on a table was a routine, though rude, habit with many people. He smiled as Ballard sat down. He looked over the railing at her dog lying on the sidewalk.

"Is that a pit bull?" he asked.

"Boxer mix," she said. "First things first, Carr. Am I a suspect in any criminal investigation or internal investigation? If so, I want a defense rep."

Carr shook his head.

"No, not at all," he said. "If you were a suspect, we'd be having this conversation in the box at Pacific Division. It's like I told you. I'm on the Chastain thing and I'm part of a team retracing his steps in the last forty-eight hours of his life."

"So I guess that means you guys don't have shit," she said.

"That's a fair assessment. No suspects in the Dancers shooting, so no suspects on Chastain."

"And you're sure they are connected?"

"Seem to be, but I don't think we're sure about anything. On top of that, it's not my call. I'm a gofer on this. Yesterday morning I was booking a bunch of Eastern European bastards for human trafficking. I got yanked off that and put on this."

Ballard realized where she recognized him from. He was on the video that had followed the report on the Dancers shooting on the newscast she had watched in the station on Friday. She was just about to ask a question about the case, when a waitress came over and asked if Ballard wanted something to drink. She ordered an iced tea. When offered a menu, she said she wasn't eating and the waitress went away.

"You sure?" Carr asked. "I ordered the fish tacos."

"I'm not hungry," Ballard said.

"Well, I've been running all day and need the fuel. Besides, you told me to get them."

"This isn't a date, Carr. Get to your questions. What do you want?"

Carr raised his hands in surrender again and Ballard noted it as a habit.

"I want to know about that last interaction between you and Chastain," he said. "But first I need background. You two were former partners, correct?"

"Correct," Ballard said.

Carr waited for more but soon realized that Ballard

was not going to give more than one-word answers—unless he found a way to change that.

"How long did you two work together?" he asked.

"Almost five years," Ballard said.

"And that ended twenty-six months ago."

"That's right."

"You're the one who beefed Olivas, aren't you?"

Once again the blue pipeline had betrayed Ballard. What had transpired between Olivas and Ballard was a personnel matter that was supposed to be confidential. But just as the blue suiters in Hollywood Division roll call knew the story, so, obviously, did the detectives in Major Crimes.

"What's that have to do with this?" Ballard asked.

"Probably nothing," Carr said. "But you're a detective. You know it's good to know all the facts. The word I got is that when Chastain came to see you at Hollywood Station early Friday morning, things got tense."

"And that's based on what? He filed a report?"

"It's based on a conversation he had afterward with a third party."

"Let me guess. Olivas."

"I can't discuss that. But never mind what Chastain said. How would you characterize the meeting at Hollywood Division?"

"I wouldn't even characterize it as a meeting. He came to pick up a witness who had come in and I had interviewed. His name was Alexander Speights. He took a photo on his phone that captured the exact moment of the first shot at the Dancers. Kenny came to collect both."

"Kenny?"

"Yeah, we were partners once, remember? I called him Kenny. We were very familiar with each other, but we didn't fuck, if that was going to be your next question."

"It wasn't."

"Well, good for you."

"What was the confrontation about? His quote to a third party afterward was 'She's still pretty mad about things.'"

Ballard shook her head, annoyed. She could feel anger boiling up. She instinctively looked over the railing next to the table and down at her dog. Lola was lying on the concrete, tongue out, watching the procession of people going by on the boardwalk. The crowd was filtering out and off the beach post-sunset.

Lola had been through a lot before Ballard had rescued her. Abuse, starvation, fear—but she persevered and always maintained her calm—until there was a legitimate threat to herself or her owner.

Ballard composed herself.

"Am I okay discussing personnel matters since you believe they are somehow significant to your investigation?" she asked.

"I think yes," Carr said.

"Okay, then the so-called confrontation occurred when Ken Chastain offered a half-assed apology for totally fucking me over in my harassment complaint two years before. Put that in your report."

"He said he was sorry. For what?"

"For not doing the right thing. He didn't back me and he knew he should have. So here we are two years later and I'm out of RHD and working the late show in

Hollywood, and he apologizes. Let's just say the apology wasn't accepted."

"So this was just an aside. Nothing to do with the witness or the Dancers investigation."

"I told you that at the beginning."

Ballard leaned back as the waitress brought her iced tea and Carr's tacos. She then squeezed the lemon into her glass as he began to eat.

"You want one of these?" Carr offered.

"I told you, not hungry," Ballard said.

His starting to eat gave her time to think. She realized that she had dropped her own agenda for the conversation. She had been put on the defensive, largely through her own anger, and had lost sight of what she needed to accomplish with this interview—that is, get more information than she gave up. She suspected that Carr had pushed things in this direction purposely, knocking her off stride at the top of the interview with questions even he knew weren't germane. It made her vulnerable to the questions that were. She looked at Carr crunching down on a taco and knew she had to be extra cautious now.

"So," Carr said, his mouth full of food. "Why'd you call Matthew Robison?"

There it was. Now Carr was getting down to business. Ballard realized that he was here to deliver a message.

"How do you know I called Matthew Robison?" she asked.

"We've got a task force of eight investigators and two supervisors on this," Carr said. "I don't know how every piece of intelligence or evidence is procured. All I know is that you called him last night—several times—and I want to know why. If you don't want to answer, then maybe we will book that room over at Pacific Division and have a sit-down there."

He dropped a half-eaten taco to his plate. Things had suddenly gotten very serious.

"I called Robison to check on him," Ballard said. "I felt responsible. I gave Speights to Chastain, and Speights gave him Robison. Now Chastain is dead. I went to Kenny's house. They wouldn't let me get close but I picked up some intel, that the last thing they knew about Kenny was that he was out Friday night, trying to wrangle a witness. I know what 'wrangle a witness' means and I thought about Robison. I figured he was the guy Kenny—sorry, Chastain—was trying to wrangle. So I called and left messages and he hasn't called me back. That's it."

She had chosen her words very carefully so as not to reveal her extracurricular activities, including hacking her dead former partner's computer files. For all she knew, Carr was taping her while she was taping him. She needed to make sure she said nothing that would bring Internal Affairs down on her.

Carr used a napkin to wipe guacamole off the corner of his mouth and then looked at her.

"Are you homeless, Detective Ballard?" he asked.

"What are you talking about?" she asked indignantly.

"You list that place two hours up the freeway as your home on personnel records. And it's on your driver's license too. But I don't think you're there that much. That lady up there didn't seem to know when you were coming back."

"That 'lady' doesn't give up information to strangers, badge or no badge. Look, I work the late show. My day begins when your day ends. What's it matter where I sleep or when I sleep? I do my job. The department requires me to have a permanent residence and I have one. And it's not two hours up the coast when I drive it. Do you have any real questions?"

"Yes, I do."

Carr picked up his plate and handed it to a busboy who was walking by their table.

"Okay," he said. "For the record, let's go over your activities Friday night."

"You want my alibi now?" she asked.

"If you have one. But like I said at the top, you are not a suspect, Detective Ballard. We have the trajectory of the shot that killed Chastain. You would've had to be standing on a step stool to make the shot."

"And do you have time of death yet?"

"Between eleven and one."

"That's easy. I was on shift. I went to roll call at eleven, then I went to work."

"You leave the station?"

Ballard tried to remember her movements. So much had happened in the past seventy-two hours that it was hard to recall what happened when. But once she got a bead on things, it all fell into place.

"Yes, I left," she said. "Right after roll call, I left and went to Hollywood Presbyterian to check on a victim from an attempted murder I'm working. I took photos, and a nurse over there named Natasha helped me. Sorry, I didn't get her last name. I never thought I'd need it to confirm an alibi."

"That's okay," Carr said. "When did you clear the hospital?"

"A little after midnight. I then went to look for my victim's crib. I had an address on Heliotrope and it turned out to be a homeless camp. She lived in an RV there but somebody had taken it over and was squatting in it, so I called for backup so I could take a look around inside. Officers Herrera and Dyson got the call."

"Okay. And after that?"

"I returned to the station by one-thirty. I remember driving by the Dancers and seeing the crime scene vans still out there. So when I got back, I went into the watch office to see what the lieutenant knew about it. I remember seeing the clock in there and it was one-thirty."

Carr nodded.

"And you were tucked in for the rest of the night?" he asked.

"Hardly," Ballard said. "I got a line from a credit-card security office in India on a motel room being used as a drop for stolen credit-card purchases. I went over there and busted a guy. This time it was Officers Taylor and Smith backing me up and then the suspect's parole agent came in as well. His name is Compton, if you need it. Inventorying all the shit in the motel room and booking the suspect carried me through to dawn and end of shift."

"Great, and all easily checked."

"Yeah, for someone who isn't even a suspect, I'm glad I wasn't home sleeping all night. I'd be in big trouble."

"Listen, Detective, I know you're all pissed off but this had to be done. If we end up taking a guy down for Chastain, the first thing his lawyer will look at is whether we ran a full field investigation and checked out other possibles. You and Chastain had a falling-out.

227

A good defense lawyer could make hay with that at trial, and all I'm doing here is getting us into a position to head that off. I'm not the bad guy. I'm helping to make sure that we get a guilty verdict on whoever did do this."

His explanation seemed plausible on the surface but Ballard couldn't buy in. She had to remember he was part of an investigation headed up by Lieutenant Olivas, a man who wouldn't mind her being completely banished from the department.

"Oh, good to know," she said.

"Thanks for the sarcasm," Carr said. "And for what it's worth, I think you got royally screwed on your beef with Olivas. I know it, everybody knows it, just like everybody knows he's the kind of guy who would do what you said he did."

He did the surrendering hands thing again.

"Now, would I say that if I was a bad guy?" he said. "Especially when I know you're recording every word I say?"

He nodded toward her phone on the table.

Ballard picked up her phone, opened the screen, and closed the recording. She shoved the phone halfway into one of the back pockets of her jeans.

"Happy now?" she asked.

"I don't care if you recorded me or not," he said.

She looked at him a moment.

"What's your story, Carr?" she asked.

He shrugged.

"No story," he said. "I'm a cop. And funny, but I don't like it when cops get murdered. I want to contribute but they put me off on you, and I know it's bullshit, but it's my part in this, so I am going to do my part."

"They?"

"Olivas and my lieutenant."

"Other than spinning their wheels with me, do they have anything at all to go on?"

"Near as I can tell, nothing. They don't know who the fuck they're looking for."

Ballard nodded and thought about how much she could or should trust Carr. What he had said about her complaint against Olivas went a long way with her. But she knew he had either been shut out of some of the case information or was holding back. If it was the former, that would be par for the course. Task force investigations were often compartmentalized. If it was the latter, then she was talking to a man she couldn't trust.

She decided to move forward and see how he reacted.

"Has there been any mention of the possibility of it being a cop?" she asked. "In the booth. And with Chastain."

"Seriously?" Carr asked. "No, nothing. Not that I've heard. But I arrived late to the party and there is a clear separation between the Homicide Special guys and us Major Crimes folk. We're riding in coach on this."

Ballard nodded.

"Why, what have you got?" Carr asked.

"The burn on Fabian's chest," Ballard said. "There was a theory that he was wearing a wire."

"What, for Internal Affairs?" he asked.

"For himself. He was looking at five years in the federal pen unless he could come up with something to trade."

"And you know this how?"

229

Ballard had a problem here. She didn't want to give up Towson but they were going to come to him anyway because one of Chastain's last calls had been to the defense attorney. If they came to him and he mentioned Ballard's visit, then she would face the wrath of Lieutenant Olivas.

"You have to protect me on this," she said. "What I know will help you."

"Shit, Ballard, I don't know," Carr said. "Don't put me in the middle of something where I get jammed up."

"You said you're retracing Chastain's steps, right?"

"Me and others, yeah."

"Well, somebody drew Fabian's lawyer. Chastain talked to him Friday. Call whoever drew the assignment and say you'll take it."

"Well, first of all, I already drew that assignment. Dean Towson is on my to-do list. But more importantly, how do you know Chastain talked to him, and how do you know about any of this stuff? The burn on the chest, the wire, the lawyer—what have you been doing, Ballard?"

"I was at the crime scene Thursday night. I was there when they found the burn. When Chastain got killed, I made a couple calls. He was my partner and taught me a lot. I owed it to him."

Carr shook his head, not seeing the validity of her moves.

"Look," he said. "I'm working the Chastain side of this. I don't know anything about a burn mark or a wire. But even if Fabian was wired, it doesn't mean he was taping a cop. He could've been taping one of the other mutts in the booth. They were all criminals."

Ballard shrugged.

"They weren't high enough value for the feds," she said. "Talk to Towson. It was a cop."

Carr frowned. Ballard pushed on.

"Speaking of the other mutts in the booth, how do they connect them?" she asked.

"I'm not sure," Carr said. "I'm on Chastain."

"They weren't strangers. They were all in Pitchess together five years ago. Same month."

"That doesn't mean anything. Pitchess is a big place."

"If someone looked into it, I think they'd find they were in the same dorm. That cuts it down to size."

Carr stared at her eye to eye.

"Ballard, really, what the fuck have you been doing?"

"My job. I get a lot of downtime on the late show. And I guess you could say I'm like you. Nobody should put a cop down and walk away from it. I had my problems with Kenny but he was my partner for almost five years and he was a closer. I learned a lot with him. But look, I'm outside the case. You're in. I can feed you whatever I get. You just have to protect me on it."

"I don't know. If they find out you're sniffing around on it, then it comes back to me. I think you just need to steer clear, Ballard. I'll go with what you just gave me but you need to stand down. That's the message I was supposed to deliver."

Ballard stood up.

"Fine. Whatever. Message received. I've got other cases to work."

"Look, don't go off mad."

She stepped away from the table and went through the opening in the railing. She came back around to unhook the dog's leash. She looked at Carr one more time.

"You need me, you know where to find me."

"Sure."

She walked off with her dog. It was almost dark now on the beach and the wind off the water was getting cold.

21

Ballard's first stop was at the critter sitter's off Abbot Kinney. Sarah was reluctant to take the dog in, even though she was paid extra when Lola spent more than the night at her home.

"She's getting depressed," she said. "She misses you all the time."

Sarah was a longtime resident of Venice who sold sunglasses on the boardwalk. She had offered to help when Ballard rescued Lola from her homeless and abusive owner. That had amounted to a place to stay while Ballard worked the midnight shift, but the schedule had gone out the window in recent days.

"I know," Ballard said. "It's not fair but I keep thinking that things will return to normal soon. I just got a bunch of cases all at once."

"If it keeps up, maybe you should take her up to your grandmother's to stay," Sarah suggested. "So she has some continuity with someone."

"That's a good idea," Ballard said. "But I hope soon it will all slow down and go back to normal."

Ballard drove east toward Hollywood, trying to bury her frustrations from the conversations with both Sarah and Carr. With Carr she was particularly stressed because she had put herself on the line with her revelations and had not gotten a clear signal from him that he would push forward on the case in return. His final message was to stand down, but she didn't know if that was because he was going to take it from there or if nothing would happen at all.

At the station she put the Chastain investigation aside for the time being and went back to work on the Ramona Ramone case. Her first move was to call Hollywood Presbyterian to check on the victim's medical status. After a runaround that included several minutes of being on hold, she started to worry that Ramone had taken a bad turn and succumbed to her injuries. But finally Ballard was talking to an evening supervisor, who reported that earlier in the day the patient had been transferred to the Los Angeles County–USC Medical Center in downtown. Ballard asked if the transfer meant that Ramone had come out of the coma, but the supervisor refused to share details of her medical condition, citing privacy laws. Nevertheless, Ballard knew there were laws regulating patient dumping, and she didn't think that moving a patient in a coma was allowed. This gave her hope that Ramona Ramone might finally be able to take part in the investigation.

Ballard decided that she would go down to County-USC to check on Ramone's medical status, security, and availability as a witness as soon as possible. But for the moment her focus was still squarely on Thomas Trent, and it was time to get back on the case and keep pushing.

Ballard still wanted to talk to Trent's ex-wife. Her ending the marriage following his arrest and her apparent decision not to fight for a share of the house in the hills indicated that this was a woman who just wanted to get away from a bad guy and a bad mistake. Ballard thought his ex-wife might talk about Trent without turning around and tipping him off to the police's interest in him. There were other precautions that could be taken to guard against this, but overall Ballard felt confident in her decision to go directly to the ex-Mrs. Trent.

Tracing Beatrice Trent on the DMV database, Ballard was able to follow her through three addresses and a name change since the divorce. She was now Beatrice Beaupre, and by going back in time with the search, Ballard learned that that was her name when she received her first California driver's license two decades earlier. She was now forty-four years old and currently listed on DMV records as living in Canoga Park.

Before leaving the station, she put together a six-pack of mug shots that included the photo taken of Thomas Trent after his arrest for the brass knuckles. She hoped that before the night was through, she would be showing the lineup to Ramona Ramone.

Sunday-evening traffic was a breeze and Ballard got to Canoga Park before nine. It was late to be calling on the unsuspecting Beatrice Beaupre, but not that late. Whether at nine in the morning or evening, Ballard always liked to employ the cold call at the odd hour. It put people back on their heels a bit, made them easier to talk to.

But it was Ballard who was knocked back on her heels when she got to the address on Owensmouth Avenue listed with the DMV as Beaupre's home address. She was in the middle of a deserted warehouse district where small businesses and manufacturers operated by day but shut down tight at night. She pulled to a stop in front of an aluminum-sided building with a door that was marked only with an address number. There were five other cars and a van parked near the door and a flashing-red strobe located above it. Ballard knew enough about the Valley's most prosperous industries to figure out that inside the warehouse, there was a porno shoot under way. The flashing light meant do not enter until the scene was completed.

Ballard sat in her car and watched the strobe. It stayed on for the next twelve minutes and she wondered if that meant people inside were having sex for that long. As soon as it went off, she got out and reached the door before it started flashing again. The handle was locked and she knocked. She was ready with her badge when the door opened, and a man wearing a wool beanie looked out.

"What's up?" he said. "You checking condoms?"

"No, I don't care about condoms," Ballard said. "I need to talk to Beatrice Beaupre. Can you get her, please?"

He shook his head.

"Nobody named that here," he said.

He started to pull the door closed but Ballard grabbed it and recited the description she remembered from Beaupre's DMV records.

"Black female, five foot ten, forty-four years old. She might not be using the name Beatrice."

"That sort of sounds like Sadie. Hold on."

This time Ballard let him close the door. She clipped her badge to her belt and turned her back to the door as she waited. She noticed that two of the warehouses across the street had no outside signage either. One of them had a strobe light over the door as well. Ballard was at ground zero for the billion-dollar-plus industry that some said kept the Los Angeles economy rolling.

The door finally opened and a woman fitting the description in the DMV records stood there. She wore no makeup, her hair was pulled back in a haphazard knot, and she wore a T-shirt and baggy workout pants. She was not what Ballard expected a porn star to look like.

"What can I do for you, Officer?"

"It's Detective. Are you Beatrice Beaupre?"

"I am, and I'm working. You need to state your business or be gone."

"I need to talk to you about Thomas Trent."

That hit Beaupre like a swinging door.

"I don't know anything about him anymore," she said. "And I gotta go."

She started backing inside and pulling the door closed. Ballard knew that she had one shot and that it might risk the whole investigation if she took it.

"I think he hurt someone," she said. "Badly."

Beaupre paused, her hand on the knob.

"And he'll do it again," Ballard said.

That said it all. Ballard waited.

"Fuck," Beaupre finally said. "Come in."

Ballard followed her into a dimly lit entry with hallways that went right and left. A sign with an arrow said the stages were to the left and offices and craft services to the right. They went right and along the way passed the man who had originally opened the door to Ballard.

"Billy, tell them we're taking a fifteen-minute break,"

Beaupre said. "And I mean fifteen. Don't let anybody leave the stage. In ten minutes, start Danielle fluffing. We shoot as soon as I get back."

They next passed an alcove set up with a kitchen counter covered with baskets of snacks and candy bars as well as a coffeemaker. A long cooler was open on the floor and filled with water bottles and cans of soda. They went into an office with the name Shady Sadie on the door. The walls were lined with posters from adult film features that showed nearly nude performers in provocative poses. It looked to Ballard from the titles, costumes—what little there was of them—and poses that the videos slanted toward bondage and sadomasochistic fetishes. A lot of female domination.

"Have a seat," Beaupre said. "I can give you fifteen minutes and then I have to shoot. Otherwise it will be like herding cats out there."

Beaupre sat behind a desk and Ballard took the chair opposite her.

"You're the director?" Ballard asked.

"Director, writer, producer, cinematographer—you name it," Beaupre said. "I'd do the whipping and fucking, too, but I'm too old. Who did Thomas hurt?"

"At the moment he's a person of interest. The victim was a transgender prostitute that I believe was abducted, raped, and tortured over a four-day period and then left for dead."

"Fuck. I knew he would do it one day."

"Do what?"

"Act out his fantasies. That's why I left him. I didn't want him acting them out on me."

"Ms. Beaupre, before we go on, I need you to promise

238

that what we talk about here will be kept confidential. Especially from him."

"Are you kidding? I don't talk to that man. He's the last person on earth I would talk to."

Ballard studied her for signs of deception. She saw nothing that dissuaded her from proceeding. She just wasn't sure where to start. She pulled out her phone.

"Do you mind if I record this?" she asked.

"Yes, I do," Beaupre said. "I don't want to be involved in this and I don't want a recording floating around out there that he might one day hear."

Ballard put the phone away. She had expected Beaupre's response. She proceeded without recording.

"I'm trying to get a bead on your ex-husband," she began. "What kind of guy he is. What would make him do something like this crime. If he did it."

"He's fucked up," Beaupre said. "Simple as that. I make S and M videos. The action is fake. The pain is not real. A lot of the audience knows that and a lot don't want to know that. They want it to be real. He's one of them."

"Did you meet because he was interested in your videos?"

"No, we met because I wanted to buy a car."

"He was the salesman?"

"That's right. I think he recognized me but he always claimed he didn't."

"From directing?"

"No, I was still a performer back then. I think he'd seen me on video and came running across the showroom, you know, wanting to help put me into something sweet. He always denied it but I think he'd seen my work."

Ballard pointed a thumb toward the door.

"Shady Sadie, that's your porno name?"

"One of many. I've had a long line of names and looks. I sort of reboot every few years, like the audience does. Right now I'm Shady Sadie the director. Let's see, I've been Ebony Nights, Shaquilla Shackles, B. B. Black, Stormy Monday, a few others. What, you seen me?"

She had noted Ballard's smile.

"No, it's just a weird coincidence," Ballard said. "Two nights ago I met a man who called himself Stormy Monday."

"In porn?" Beaupre asked.

"No, something else entirely. So you said Trent had fantasies."

"He was all fucked up. He was into pain. He wanted to give pain, see it in their eyes."

"Their eyes? Who are we talking about?"

"I'm talking about his fantasies. What he liked in my videos, what he wanted to do in real life."

"You're saying he never acted out?"

"Not with me. I don't know about with others. But he got arrested and he had metal knuckles on him. That was crossing the line."

"That's why you left?"

"That whole thing. Not only was he going there to hurt someone but the police were saying it was a boy. When I heard that, I had to go. It was too fucked up, even for me."

"What's your take on the psychology of this?"

"What the fuck does that mean?"

"My victim's Latina. With the brass knuckles thing, he was going to see a Latino male. His ex-wife is

African-American but light-skinned. There's a victim type here and—"

"I was no fucking victim."

"Sorry, I misspoke. But he's got a type. It's part of what is called a paraphilia. Part of his sexual program, for lack of a better word."

"It's part of the subjugation and control thing he has. In my films, I was the top, the dominatrix. In our marriage, he wanted to control me, keep me under his thumb. Like I was a challenge to him."

"But he wasn't abusive?"

"He wasn't. Not to me, at least, because I would have been out the door. But that doesn't mean he didn't use intimidation and his physical size to control things. You can use your size without being physically abusive."

"How much porno did he watch?"

"Look, don't go down that road. The whole porno-made-him-do-it thing. We provide a service. People watch these films and that *keeps* them in check, *keeps* it in fantasy."

Ballard was not sure Beaupre believed the words as she said them. Ballard could easily take the side that pornography was a gateway to aberrant behavior, but she knew now was not the time. She needed this woman as a source and eventually a potential witness. Calling her on her lifestyle and occupation was not the way to do it.

"I need to get back to the stage," Beaupre said abruptly. "There's no tomorrow on this. I lose one of my performers at midnight. She has school tomorrow."

Ballard spoke urgently.

"Please, just a few more minutes," she said. "You

241

lived with him in the house on Wrightwood Drive?"

"Yes, he had that when I met him," Beaupre said. "I moved in."

"How'd he get a place like that selling cars?"

"He didn't get it selling cars. He exaggerated his injuries from when he was in a helicopter crash coming back from Catalina. Got a hack doctor to back him on it and sued. He ended up getting like eight hundred thousand and bought the upside-down house."

Ballard leaned forward in her chair. She wanted to proceed cautiously and not feed any answers to Beaupre.

"You mean like it was in foreclosure?" she asked. "They were upside down on their mortgage?"

"No, no, it was literally upside down," Beaupre said. "The bedrooms were downstairs instead of up. Tom always called it the upside-down house."

"Is that how he would describe it to others? To visitors? The upside-down house?"

"Pretty much, yeah. He thought it was funny. He said it was 'an upside-down house for an upside-down world.'"

It was a key piece of information, and the fact that Beaupre had volunteered it made it all the more convincing. Ballard kept moving.

"Let's talk about the brass knuckles," she said. "What do you know about them?"

"I mean, I knew he had them," Beaupre said. "But I didn't think he'd ever use them. He had all kinds of weapons—stick knives, throwing stars, metal knuckles. He called them metal knuckles because technically not all of them were brass."

"So he had multiple pairs?"

"Oh, yeah. He had a collection."

"Did he have duplicates? The pair that were seized during his arrest said *good* and *evil* on them. Did he have another pair like that?"

"He had a bunch of them, and most said that. That was his thing. He said he would've had that tattooed on his knuckles—*good* and *evil*—except that he'd probably lose his job."

Ballard knew it was a big get. Beatrice was giving her the building blocks of a case.

"He kept his weapons in the house?"

"Yeah, in the house."

"Guns?"

"No guns. He didn't like guns for some reason. He said he liked 'weapons with edges.'"

"What else is in the house?"

"I don't know. I haven't been there in a long time. I know this, though—he put all his money into buying the house because he said real estate was better than putting money in the bank, but that meant he didn't have much left over to furnish the place. A couple of those bedrooms were completely empty, at least when I lived there."

Ballard thought about the room she saw off the lower deck. Beaupre stood up.

"Look, we wrap at midnight," she said. "You want to hang and watch or come back then, we can talk more. But I need to go. Time is money in this business."

"Right," Ballard said. "Okay."

She decided to take a shot in the dark.

"Did you keep a key?" she asked.

"What?" Beaupre said.

243

"When you got divorced, did you keep a key to the house? A lot of people who go through a divorce keep a key."

Beaupre looked at Ballard with indignation.

"I told you, I wanted nothing to do with that man. Back then or now. I didn't keep a key, because I never wanted to go near that place again."

"Okay, because if you did, I might be able to use it. You know, in an emergency. The guy who did the damage to my victim, it wasn't the kind of thing he'll do only once. If he thinks he got away with it? He'll do it again."

"That's too bad."

Beaupre stood next to the door to usher Ballard out. They moved down the hallway, and when they passed by the alcove where the snacks were, Ballard saw a woman who was naked except for thigh-high boots, pausing over a choice of candy bar.

"Bella, we are shooting," Beaupre said. "I'm going back now."

Bella didn't respond. Beaupre led Ballard to the front door and ushered her out, offering her good luck in her investigation. Ballard handed her a business card with the usual request to call if anything else came to mind.

"The DMV lists this as your home address," Ballard said. "Is that true?"

"Isn't a home the place where you eat and fuck and sleep?" Beaupre said.

"Maybe. So no other place?"

"I don't need another place, Detective."

Beaupre closed the door.

Ballard started her car but then opened her notebook

and started writing down as much as she could remember from the interview. Head down and writing, she was startled by a sharp rap on the car window. She looked up to see Billy, the doorman in the beanie. She lowered the window.

"Detective, Shady said you forgot this," he said.

He held out a key. It was not on a ring. It was just a key.

"Oh," Ballard said. "Right. Thank you."

She took the key and then put the window back up.

22

Ballard made her way to the 101 freeway and headed south toward downtown. She drove with internal momentum. She still didn't have a shred of direct evidence but the interview with Beatrice Beaupre pushed Thomas Trent further across the line that separated person of interest and suspect. He was now Ballard's one and only focus and her thoughts were exclusively on how to build a prosecutable case.

She was just taking the curve into the Cahuenga Pass when her phone buzzed, and she saw it was Jenkins. She connected her earbuds and took the call.

"Hey, partner, just checking in before heading in. I got any holdovers from you?"

Jenkins was on shift by himself for the next two nights. It was supposed to be Ballard's weekend.

"Not really," she said. "Hopefully you'll have a quiet watch."

"I wouldn't mind sitting in the bureau all night," Jenkins said.

"Well, at least for the first hour or so. I have the car."

"What? You're supposed to be up in Ventura, surfing. What's going on?"

"I just came from an interview with the ex-wife of the suspect on the Ramona Ramone case. It's him, no doubt. He's our guy. Calls his crib the upside-down

246

house, just like the victim said to Taylor and Smith."

"All right."

She could tell by his tone and the way he drew out the words that he was not as convinced.

"He also collects sets of brass knuckles," she added. "With *good* and *evil* on them. You can see the letters in the bruising on Ramona. I went back to check and take pictures."

Jenkins was silent at first. This was new information to him and it also was an indication of her obsession with the case. Finally, he spoke.

"You have enough for a search warrant?"

"I'm not there yet. But the victim was transferred to County, which I don't think they could do if she was still in the coma. So I'm headed there, and if she's awake, I'm going to have her look at a six-pack. If she makes the ID, then I'll bring the package to McAdams in the morning and come up with a plan."

There was only silence from Jenkins as he apparently dealt with having been left on the platform as the train sped by without stopping.

"Okay," he finally said. "You want me to divert and meet you at County?"

"No, I think I've got it covered," Ballard said. "You get in and take roll call, see what's going on. I'll let you know when I'm on my way back with the car."

County-USC used to be a dire place but in recent years it had gotten a face-lift and a paint job and it was no longer as cheerless as it had once been. Its medical staff were no doubt as dedicated and skilled as the crew at any private hospital in the city but, like with most giant bureaucracies, everything always came down to budget. Ballard's first stop was at the security office, where she showed her badge and attempted to persuade a nighttime supervisor named Roosevelt to put extra eyes on Ramona Ramone. Roosevelt, a tall, thin man nearing retirement age was more interested in whatever was on his computer screen than in what Ballard was selling.

"No can do," he said bluntly. "I put someone on that room, I gotta take him off the ER door, and no way those nurses down there will let me do that. They'd skin me alive if I left them unprotected like that."

"You're telling me you got one guy in the ER and that's it?" Ballard said.

"No, I got two. One inside, one out. But ninety-nine percent of our violence happens in the ER. So we have two-step protection: one guy on the walk-ins, another to handle those that come in the back of an ambulance. I can't lose either one."

"So meantime my victim is up there naked—no protection at all."

"We have security in the elevator lobbies, and I float. If you want extra protection up on that room, then I would invite you to ask the LAPD to provide it."

"That's not going to happen."

"Then I'm sorry."

"I got your name, Roosevelt. If anything happens, it'll go in the report."

"Make sure you spell it right. Just like the president."

Ballard next went up to the acute-care ward, where Ramone was being treated. She was disappointed to learn that, while the patient had been conscious and semi-alert when transported from Hollywood

Presbyterian, she had since been sedated and intubated after a setback in her condition. Choosing to find and interview Beaupre as the day's priority had cost Ballard a chance to communicate with her victim. She nevertheless visited Ramone and took cell-phone photos as part of the continuing documentation of the depth of her injuries and treatment. She hoped someday to show them to a jury.

Afterward Ballard made a stop at the nursing desk on the ward and handed the duty nurse a stack of her business cards.

"Can you pass these around and keep one there by your phone?" she asked. "If anybody comes in to see the patient in three-oh-seven, I need to know. If you get any phone calls inquiring about her status, I need to know. Take a name and number and say you'll get back to them. Then call me."

"Is the patient in danger?"

"She was the subject of a vicious attack and left for dead. I checked with your security officer and got turned down on extra security. So all I'm saying is be vigilant."

Ballard left then, hoping that putting the word in the duty nurse's ear might get some results. Hospital security would find it harder to resist internal safety concerns than those from the LAPD.

Back at the station by midnight, Ballard was walking down the rear hallway toward the D bureau as Jenkins came down the stairs from the roll-call room. They walked into the bureau side by side.

"Anything going on?" Ballard asked.

"All quiet on the western front," Jenkins said.

He held up his hand and she put the city-ride's keys in his palm.

"Ramona look at a six-pack?" Jenkins asked.

"Nope," Ballard said. "Missed my chance. I'm pissed at myself. I should've been there when she was awake."

"Don't beat yourself up. Brain injury like that—chances are, she's not going to remember a thing. And if she did, a defense attorney would go to town on the ID."

"Maybe."

"So you going to go up the coast now?"

"Not yet. I want to write up a summary on my witness from tonight."

"Man, you act like this place still pays overtime or something."

"I wish."

"Well, get it done and get out of here."

"I will. What about you?"

"Munroe says I have to write up a report about the witness bus from the other night. Somebody filed a notice of intent to sue, said they suffered pain and humiliation because they were locked up in a jail bus. I have to say they were never locked up."

"You gotta be kidding me."

"I wish."

They went off to their respective corners of the room. Ballard got right to work on a witness statement drawn from the interview with Beatrice Beaupre, putting special emphasis on the revelation that Thomas Trent often referred to his home as the upside-down house. It would be ready to go into a charging package if Ramona Ramone ever IDed Trent.

Thirty minutes later, she completed the report. She was also finished for the night but then remembered she wanted to check the property report on the Dancers case. She went to her filing cabinet and looked through the thick ream of documents she had printed while going through Chastain's files. She located the preliminary evidence report and took it back to her desk. The evidence list was seven pages long. It wasn't the official evidence report from forensics but the ledger that an RHD detective would keep while at the crime scene. It served as a reference for the investigators on any evidence that had been collected while they awaited the official report. Ballard went through it twice but saw nothing listed that resembled the small black button she had seen Chastain scoop into an evidence bag. She became convinced that her former partner had taken evidence from the scene without documenting it. It was something small and something that sent him off the reservation, conducting his own investigation. An investigation that got him killed.

Ballard sat there motionless as she ran the image of Chastain at the crime scene through her mind. Her attention was then drawn to the other side of the room when she noticed Lieutenant Munroe enter the bureau from the front hallway and head toward where Jenkins was sitting.

Ballard thought Munroe was probably going to send her partner out on a call. She grabbed the evidence report and got up to go listen, in case it was a situation in which Jenkins would need a backup. She grabbed her rover as well and headed their way.

Though the desks Jenkins and Ballard used were in

diagonally opposite corners of the squad room, there wasn't a direct pathway between them. Ballard had to walk down an aisle along the front of the room and then down a second aisle to come up behind Munroe. As she approached, she saw an uncomfortable look on her partner's face as he looked up at the watch commander, and she realized that Munroe wasn't handing out an assignment.

". . . all I'm saying is, you're the lead, you call the shots, put her on the leash and—"

The rover in Ballard's hand started broadcasting a call. Munroe stopped and turned to see Ballard standing there.

"And what, L-T?" she said.

Munroe's face momentarily showed his shock and then he threw a glance back at Jenkins, registering his betrayal at not being warned of her approach.

"Look, Ballard . . ." he said.

"So you want me on the leash?" Ballard asked. "Or are you just the messenger?"

Munroe held up both hands, as if trying to stop a physical rush from her.

"Ballard, listen to me, you . . . I . . . I didn't know you were here," he stammered. "You're supposed to be off. I mean, if I knew you were here, I would've said the same thing to you as I said to Jenks."

"Which was what?" she asked.

"Look, there are people who are afraid you're going to fuck things up, Ballard, afraid you're going to cross a line on this Chastain thing. It's not your case, and you need to stand the fuck down."

"What people, L-T? Olivas? Is he worried about me or himself?"

"Look, I'm not naming names. I'm just—"

"You're naming me. You just went to my partner and said, 'Put Ballard on a leash.'"

"Like you just said, I'm only the messenger here, Detective. And the message is delivered. That's it."

He turned and headed toward the rear hallway, taking the long way to the watch office rather than having to pass by Ballard.

Ballard looked at Jenkins when they were alone.

"Asshole," she said.

"Fucking coward," Jenkins said. "Took the long way back."

"What would you have said to him if I hadn't walked up?"

"I don't know. Maybe I would have said, 'You got something to say to Ballard, tell her yourself.' Maybe I would have said, 'Fuck off.'"

"I hope so, partner."

"So what exactly have you been doing that's got their balls twisted?"

"That's the thing. I'm not sure. But that's the second so-called message I've gotten today. Some guy from Majors went up to Ventura and then down to the beach to find me and tell me the same thing. And I don't even know what I did."

Jenkins scrunched his face up in suspicion and worry. He wasn't buying that she didn't know what she had done. He was worried she would keep doing it.

"Watch yourself, kid. These people don't fuck around."

"I already know that."

He nodded. Ballard stepped up to his desk and put down the rover for him to use.

"I think I'm going up to the suite," she said. "Come get me if you need me. Otherwise, I'll probably catch you before you leave."

"Don't bother," Jenkins said. "Sleep late if you can. You need it."

"Just pisses me off that he comes in here to you because he thinks I'm out."

"Look, I've been reading about Japan to Marcie, and they have this saying over there: The—"

"I'm talking about these men and you're telling me about Japan?"

"Would you listen to me? I'm not one of 'these men,' okay? I read her books about places we never got to. She's interested in Japanese history right now, so that's what I'm reading to her. And there's this saying they have about conformist society: The nail that sticks out gets pounded down."

"Okay, so what are you saying?"

"I'm saying there's a lot of guys in this department with hammers. Watch yourself."

"You don't have to tell me that."

"I don't know—sometimes I think I do."

"Whatever. I'm going. I'm suddenly so tired of all this."

"Get some sleep."

Jenkins solemnly held up a fist, and Ballard bumped it with her own. It was a way of saying they were okay.

Ballard put the evidence report back in her file drawer and locked it, then left the bureau. She went up the stairs in the back hall to the station's second floor, where, across the hall from the roll-call room, there was a room known as the Honeymoon Suite. It was a bunk room with three-tier bunks running along opposite walls. It was first-come, first-served, and on a counter at one end of the room were stacks of plastic-wrapped bunk packs: two sheets, a pillow, and a thin jail blanket.

The slide sign on the door was moved to OCCUPIED. Ballard took out her phone, turned on the light, and quietly opened the door and moved into the room. The switch for the overhead lights was taped into the off position so that nobody blasted sleepers. Ballard used her phone to check the bunks and saw that the two middle beds were taken by sleepers, one of whom was lightly snoring. She took off her shoes and put them in a cubbyhole, then grabbed two sleep packs and tossed them up onto one of the top bunks. She climbed the ladder and flipped the thin mattress over before crawling into the sleeping space. It took her five minutes to spread the sheets and get under a blanket. Clasping the two pillows around her head to ward off the sound of snoring, she tried to go to sleep.

As she tailed off into darkness, she thought about the two warnings to stand down that she had gotten during the day. She knew she had somehow triggered them with her actions the day before. She reviewed her steps, trying to remember every detail of every move she had made and still could not locate the land mine she had apparently stepped on.

Fighting sleep, she backed things up further into Friday night and then moved forward again, using her memory like a battering ram. This time she hit on

23

A loud round of raucous laughter from the roll-call room penetrated the Honeymoon Suite and woke Ballard. She felt disoriented and almost banged her head on the ceiling as she started to get up. She pulled her phone and checked the time. She was shocked to learn that she had slept until ten a.m., and knew she would have gone longer if not for the mid-watch roll call being conducted across the hall.

She balled up her sheets, blankets, and pillows and carefully climbed down from the top bunk. She noticed she was the only one left in the room. Dumping everything in a hamper, she put on her shoes and made her way down the hall to the women's locker room.

Under the hot shower, she came to fully and tried to recall the events of the night before. She remembered that she had fallen asleep with a question: How did Rogers Carr know that she had been calling the missing Matthew Robison? Today was Monday, a day off, but she resolved to know the answer to that question before the day was through.

After dressing in fresh clothes from her locker, Ballard sat on a bench and composed a text to Carr.

Need to talk. Are you around?

She hesitated for a moment and then sent it. She knew that Carr might share it with others and discuss how to proceed. But she was banking on him not doing that. She knew a quick response to her text would indicate he had not shared it with anyone yet.

In person? Where? Not the PAB.

She thought about things and returned the text, setting up the meeting. Her choice for a location was the fourteenth floor of the Criminal Courts Building because it would be a perfectly natural place for police detectives to be seen. If anybody at Major Crimes or the PAB asked Carr where he was going, he could just say the courthouse, and it would not raise a question. The location would also put Ballard in close proximity to the County–USC Medical Center, where she hoped to find Ramona Ramone conscious and alert later in the day.

Before leaving the station, she knocked on Lieutenant McAdams's door in the detective bureau and updated him on the Ramona Ramone investigation. He was reserved about Trent's collection of brass knuckles and use of the phrase *upside-down house* to describe his home. McAdams cautioned that the evidence was circumstantial and reminded her that the basis of Ballard's excitement was an ex-wife's claims.

"You're going to need more than that," McAdams said.

"I know," said Ballard. "I'll get it."

After checking out the late-shift plain wrap, Ballard headed downtown on the 101 freeway. Battling the traffic going into downtown, finding parking, and then waiting for the elevator in the courthouse made her twenty minutes late for her meeting with Carr, but she found the detective from Major Crimes sitting on a bench outside a courtroom door, checking messages on his phone.

She slid onto the wooden bench next to him.

"Sorry I'm late. Everything went wrong. Traffic, parking, had to wait ten minutes for a fucking elevator."

"You could've texted, but never mind that. What's this about, Ballard?"

"Okay, yesterday I asked you a question, and you never answered it. We got distracted or you moved on, but I never got a full answer."

"What question?"

"You asked me why I had called Matthew Robison and I asked you how you knew that I had."

"I did answer that. I told you I was given the information that you were trying to reach him."

"I don't deny it. But who told you that I'd been calling him?"

"I don't get it. Why does this matter?"

"Think about it. Robison is missing, right?"

Carr didn't answer right away. He seemed to be very carefully weighing what information to share with her.

"We're looking for him, yeah," he finally said.

"I assume that wherever he's at, if he's alive, he's got his cell phone with him, right?" she asked quickly. "Or was it recovered at his home or elsewhere?"

"Not as far as I know."

"Then if he's out there in hiding, he has his phone. If he's dead, then whoever killed him has his phone.

Either way, how is it known that I called him? Are you going to tell me they pulled his call records that quick? I've never turned a phone company warrant around in less than a day before, let alone on a Saturday when nobody's working. On top of that, he's a witness, not a suspect. There is no probable cause for a warrant to pull his records in the first place."

Carr didn't respond.

"I guess the alternative is that they have my records or a tap on my phone, but that doesn't make sense unless you lied to me yesterday and I actually am a primary suspect. If that's the case, you wouldn't have let me tape our conversation. And you wouldn't have talked to me period without Mirandizing me."

"You're not a suspect, Ballard. I told you that."

"Okay, then it comes back to my question. How does anyone know I was calling Robison?"

Carr shook his head in frustration.

"Look, I don't know," he said. "Maybe it was a welfare warrant. He's gone and they got a warrant to pull his records because they're worried he might be in trouble or something."

"I already thought about that, but it doesn't work," Ballard said. "If they wanted to find him to see if he was okay, they would have pinged his phone to find his location and check on him. There's something else. Somebody knows I called him. Who told you?"

"Listen to me. All I know is that my lieutenant came out of the meeting and told me you had been calling Robison and I needed to find out why and shut you down. That's it."

"Who's your lieutenant?"

"Blackwelder."

"Okay, what meeting was Blackwelder in?"

"What?"

"You just said he came out of a meeting and gave you instructions about me. Don't play dumb. What meeting?"

"He was in the meeting with Olivas and a couple other RHD guys. Major Crimes got called in after Chastain got hit, and it was the meeting where Olivas brought Blackwelder up to speed."

"So Olivas is the source. Somehow he knew that I had been calling Robison."

Carr looked around the busy hallway to make sure no one was overtly watching them. People were going by in all directions, but none seemed to be interested in the two detectives.

"Maybe," he said. "He wasn't the only guy in the room."

"More than maybe," Ballard said. "Think about it. How did Olivas know I was calling Robison if he doesn't have his phone?"

Ballard waited but Carr said nothing.

"Something doesn't add up," she said.

"This is part of your cop theory, isn't it?" Carr finally said. "You want to put this on a cop."

"I want to put it on the person responsible. That's it."

"Well, then, what's the next move here?"

"I don't know. But I think you need to proceed with caution."

"Listen, Ballard, I get it. Olivas fucked you over big time. But suggesting without a shred of evidence that he knows about this, or has information about—"

"That's not what I am doing."

"Seems like it to me."

Frustrated, Ballard looked around the hallway while she decided what to do.

"I have to go," she finally said.

"Where?" Carr asked. "You still need to steer clear of this, Ballard."

"I have my own case to work. So don't worry."

She stood up and looked down at Carr.

"Don't look at me like that," he said. "You have zero evidence of anything. You have a theory. But even if you are right about it being a cop, trying to put it on the guy everyone knows is your antagonist in the department doesn't sell, Ballard."

"At least not yet," Ballard said.

She started to walk off.

"Ballard, would you come back here?" Carr said.

She turned back and looked down at him again.

"Why?" she said. "You're not going to do anything and I got a case that I need to work."

"Just sit down a minute, will you?" Carr pleaded.

She reluctantly sat.

"You did this yesterday," Carr said. "'I have a case to work. Good-bye.' What's so important about this other case?"

"There's a guy out there hurting people because he likes it," Ballard said. "He's big evil and I'm going to stop him."

"Thomas Trent?"

"How the fuck do you know that?"

But then she shook her head. She didn't need the answer, though Carr gave it.

"You know that every access to NCIC is logged," he said. "I saw that you ran down the three stiffs in the booth and this Thomas Trent. I was wondering who this guy was and what the connection was."

"Now you know," Ballard said. "No connection. You people . . . That case has nothing to do with Chastain or the Dancers or anything else."

"Good to know."

"Look, are you going to do anything with what I just gave you or not?"

"I will, Ballard, but think about what you're suggesting. A police lieutenant kills five people in a bar, then takes out one of his own people? For what? Because he's got—what? Gambling debts? It's a big fucking stretch."

"There's no explanation for why people kill. You know that. And if you cross that line, what's to stop you from going from one to six?"

She looked off and down the hallway. In that moment, she saw a man avert his eyes from her. He was across the hall and one courtroom down. He was wearing a suit but he looked more cop than lawyer.

Ballard looked casually back at Carr.

"There's somebody watching us," she said. "Black male, stocky, brown suit, across the hall and down one."

"Relax," Carr said. "That's Quick, my partner."

"You brought your partner?"

"You're a wild card, Ballard. I wanted to make sure things were cool."

"Was he there yesterday when we had our 'dinner date' too?"

"He was nearby, yeah."

Ballard looked back over at Carr's partner.

"He doesn't look that quick to me," she said.

Carr laughed.

"His name is Quinton Kennedy," he said. "We call him Quick."

Ballard nodded.

"So look," Carr said. "I'm taking all of this under advisement, okay? I'm going to go back and talk to my lieutenant and finesse out the thing about Robison's phone. I'll find out how we knew you called him. If it's there like you think, I'll get back to you, and then we have to talk about the next step. Where we take it."

"We take it to the D.A.," Ballard said. "We take it to J-SID."

"Well, let's not get ahead of ourselves here. We need a lot more than knowledge about your phone calls. There still could be a reasonable explanation."

"You keep thinking that, Carr. And keep Quick on your six. You don't want to end up like my former partner."

Ballard stood up again. Without another word she walked off toward the elevator alcove. She threw a mock salute toward Quick and he squinted his eyes at her as though he didn't know who she was. But it was too late for that.

24

Ballard got good and bad news when she arrived at the acute-care nursing station on the third floor at County-USC. The good news came when she was informed that Ramona Ramone was conscious and alert and that she had been upgraded to fair condition. The bad news was that she was still intubated, unable to talk, and through hand signals appeared not to know why she was hospitalized or what had happened to her.

Ballard was allowed to visit, and as she entered the room, Ramona opened her still-swollen eyes a sliver and they looked at each other for the first time. Something about seeing this victim awake and coming to understand her dire circumstances was gut-wrenching. There was utter fear in her eyes. Fear of the unknown.

"Ramona," Ballard began. "I'm Renée. I'm a detective with the Los Angeles Police Department and I'm going to find the man who did this to you."

Ballard put the file she was carrying down on the side table and stood at the side of the bed. Ramona's eyes were nervous and moving rapidly. Her face was still heavily swollen on the right, giving it an asymmetrical shape. Ballard reached over and held her hand, putting her thumb into the palm.

"You're safe now," she said. "Nobody will hurt you anymore. What I want you to do now is squeeze my thumb if you understand what I'm telling you."

Ballard waited and soon she felt the squeeze.

"Okay, good. That's good, Ramona. Let's do this: I will ask you yes and no questions, okay? If your answer is yes, then you squeeze my thumb one time. If your answer is no, then squeeze twice. Okay?"

She waited and got one squeeze.

"Good. The nurse told me that you're having trouble remembering what happened to you. Is it a total blank?"

Two squeezes.

"So there is some that you remember?"

One squeeze.

"Okay, let me tell you what we know and then we will go from there. Today is Monday. Late Thursday night you were found in a parking lot on Santa Monica Boulevard near Highland Avenue. It was an anonymous call, and the officers who responded at first thought you were dead. That's how bad you looked to them."

Ramona closed her eyes and kept them shut. Ballard continued.

"You were momentarily conscious as the officers waited for a rescue ambulance. You said something about an upsidedown house and then you lost consciousness. That was all we had to go on. Since then I have been to the RV where you lived, and the people there said you had been gone for five days. I think someone held you all that time, Ramona. And he hurt you very badly."

Ballard saw a tear form in the corner of one of Ramona's eyes. She blinked it away and then looked at Ballard. It was time to start asking questions.

"Ramona, do you remember the upside-down house?"

Two squeezes.

"Okay. What about the man who hurt you? Do you remember him?"

Ballard waited but there was no reaction from Ramona.

"Does that mean it's kind of fuzzy?"

One squeeze.

"Okay, that's all right. That's fine. Let's start with some basics, then. Do you remember what race the man was?"

One squeeze.

Ballard had to be careful not to lead her. A defense attorney could tear her apart on the stand for any false move.

"Okay, I'm going to go through some choices and you keep squeezing once or twice depending on your answer. Okay?"

One squeeze.

"Was he Hispanic?"

Two squeezes.

"Okay, how about African-American?"

Two squeezes.

"Was he a white man?"

One long squeeze.

"Okay, he was a white man. Thank you. Let's try to work on a description. Did he have any physical aspect that stood out?"

Two squeezes.

"Did he wear glasses?"

Two squeezes.

"Did he have a mustache or a beard?"

Two squeezes.

"Was he tall?"

One squeeze.

"Over six feet?"

Ramona shook her hand, adding a third signal to the conversation.

"Does that mean you're not sure?"

One squeeze.

"Okay, got it. Good. You shake your hand like that whenever you're not sure. I have some photos here that I would like to show you. It's called a photo lineup, and I want to see if one of these men looks like the man who hurt you. Is it all right to show you?"

One squeeze.

"I'm going to show you six at once, and you take your time and look and then I'll ask you if you recognize any of the photos. Okay?"

One squeeze.

Ballard let go of Ramona's hand and turned to the side table to pick up the file. She folded the cover back. Six mug shots were displayed in six individual windows cut into a second file. Beneath each photo was a number. She held it over the bed and a foot from Ramona's eyes. She watched as the victim's eyes moved across the photos, fear and apprehension clear in them. Ballard held the file without speaking for almost a minute.

"Okay," she said.

She put her thumb back into Ramona's palm.

"Do any of the men in the photo lineup look like the man who hurt you, Ramona?"

Ballard waited and finally Ramona shook her hand.

"You're not sure?"

One squeeze.

"Okay, let's just go through them. Does the man in the photo marked number one look like the man who hurt you?"

Two squeezes.

"Does the man in the photo marked number two look like the man?"

Two squeezes.

"Okay, what about number three? Does that look like the man who hurt you?"

This time Ramona shook her hand.

"You are not sure but there is some familiarity there."

One squeeze.

"Okay. Let's take the next one. The man in the photo marked number four."

Another handshake.

"Number four also looks familiar."

One squeeze.

"How about number five, Ramona? Could that be the man who hurt you?"

A soft handshake, almost hesitant.

"Number five is a maybe too. Let's look at six now. Could he be the man who hurt you?"

Two strong squeezes.

"Okay, definitely not."

Ballard folded the file over and put it back down on the table. Ramona had registered familiarity with three of the six photos but no direct identification of any. Trent's photo had been in the five spot. The other two photos that had drawn recognition belonged to two men who were currently in state prison and could not have been the man who abducted and assaulted the victim.

It was not a good response and Ballard had to shake off her disappointment. Ramona had a brain injury and was still recovering. Ballard knew that such injuries took varying amounts of time to heal and that something not remembered now might be recalled in vivid detail later. The memory might also never return. It would be a waiting game, but she didn't want to wait. Whether it was Trent or not, whoever had hurt Ramona could strike again while Ballard waited for her brain to heal.

Ballard put on a bright face when she turned back to the victim.

"You did good, Ramona. The important thing is that you continue to heal and we'll see if more of your memory comes back."

Ballard reached over and squeezed her hand.

"I'll be back tomorrow to check on you."

Ramona squeezed back.

On her way to the stairs Ballard noticed a uniformed security guard loitering near the nursing station. She had not seen him before. Ballard walked over to talk to him, flashing her badge as she approached.

"Ballard, LAPD. Are you always on this floor?"

"No, the nursing supervisor requested extra security because of the crime victims up here."

"Good. Was that authorized by Roosevelt?"

"Nah, Roosevelt is the night supe."

Ballard produced a business card and handed it to the guard.

"Keep a watch on the patient in three-oh-seven. Anything happens, let me know, okay?"

The guard studied the card for a moment.

"You got it."

Outside the front doors of the hospital Ballard stopped and took stock of where things stood. She was facing the depressing realization that her investigations were stalling on all fronts. With Ramona Ramone unable to identify her attacker, there was no evidence and no case against Trent, no matter how sure in her gut Ballard was that he was the abductor.

As for the Chastain/Dancers investigation, it wasn't her case, and Carr, her connection to it, seemed unwilling to vigorously pursue the major leads she had provided.

It all left her feeling out of sorts, like she was powerless. She reached into her pocket and ran her thumb along the teeth of the key Beatrice Beaupre had sent out to her the night before. She tried to control an urge to go to the upsidedown house and see what was inside. It was a big line to cross and she knew it was her frustrations that were pushing her into considering it.

She left the key in her pocket and pulled out her phone. She called the Acura dealership in the Valley and asked for Thomas Trent. Making sure he was in a verifiable location was the first step in crossing that line.

"I'm sorry, Tom is off today," the operator said. "Would you like to leave a message?"

"No, no message," Ballard said.

She disconnected and felt a slight sense of relief that she needed to stand down the urge to ghost Trent's house. With him off work it would be too dangerous. Even if he wasn't in the house, he could show up at any time. An idea that had seemed like a possibility was now a nonstarter.

"Fuck it," Ballard said.

It was only two p.m. and it was her day off. She wasn't back on duty until near midnight the following day. She decided to do the only thing that would allow her to clear her head and chase away the feeling of consternation.

She decided to go north.

25

By four p.m. Ballard had turned in the city-ride and picked up her van, grabbed lunch, and then driven out to Venice for her dog. She was now on the Pacific Coast Highway heading north toward Ventura. She had the windows down and the sea air was blowing in. Thoughts of the cases were floating in her wake. Lola sat in the front passenger seat with her snout out the window and in the wind.

All of that changed about an hour into the ride and just past Point Mugu when she received a call from a number with an 818 area code. The Valley. She didn't recognize it but took the call.

It was Trent.

"Hi there!" he began cheerfully. "Tom Trent here. And guess what I am looking at."

"I have no idea," Ballard said hesitantly.

"An Arctic white 2017 RDX, fully loaded and ready to go. When do you want to come by the dealership?"

"Uh, you're there now?"

"Sure am."

Ballard didn't understand, since she had called a few hours earlier and been told that he was off. Trent seemed to sense her confusion.

"I'm supposed to be off today," he said, "but vehicle intake called and said we got the white RDX in,

273

so I came in pronto. I want to make sure nobody else grabs this out from under us. What time works for you tonight?"

Ballard knew she could set up an appointment and then go to his house while he was at the dealership, waiting. But in the hours since she had left the hospital, she had retreated from that line and now was unsure she could cross it. She had also already called her grandmother and said she was coming up for dinner.

"Tonight's not good," she said. "I can't come in."

"Stella, I brought this in here for you," Trent said. "It's beautiful. It's got the rearview camera, everything. How about you stop by on your way home from work again?"

"I'm not going home tonight, Tom. I'm out of town."

"Really? You go off surfing in that surf truck of yours?"

Ballard froze but then remembered that she had driven her van into the lot when she had taken the test-drive, and her board had been on the roof.

"No, Tom, I'm not surfing. I'm out of town on business and I'll get back to you when I return. I'm sorry for any misunderstanding."

She disconnected before he could respond. There was something about the call that creeped her out—his sense of familiarity based on a test-drive.

"Fuck," she said.

Lola turned from the window and looked at her.

Her phone buzzed again and immediately a sense of rage built inside. She thought Trent was calling her back.

But it wasn't Trent. It was Rogers Carr.

"Okay, it was a warrant," he said. "RHD pulled it from his phone records."

He was talking about Robison's phone and Ballard's calls to it. She was skeptical.

"How'd they get around probable cause? He's a witness, not a suspect."

"They didn't say he was a suspect. They cited exigent circumstances and that the holder of the phone was in possible danger. That's it."

"Did you get anything else? Like who else called him and who he called?"

"No, Ballard, I didn't. I didn't even ask, because that was not the part of the investigation I was given."

"Of course not. I mean why go the extra mile when it's easier to keep your head buried in the sand?"

"Ballard—"

She disconnected and rode the rest of the way to Ventura in silence, barely able to contain her frustration with being on the outside, looking in.

That night at dinner, Ballard's grandmother tried to cheer her up by making her a childhood favorite: black beans and rice with guacamole and fried plantains. Ballard loved the food but still had little to say other than to compliment the cook. It was the cook who did most of the talking and asked the questions.

Tutu was a small woman and seemed to be shrinking with age. Her skin was nut-brown and hard from years in the sun, first teaching her only son to surf and then traveling to beaches around the world to watch him compete. Still, her eyes were sharp and she knew her granddaughter better than anyone.

"Are you working on a case?" she asked.

"I was," Ballard said. "It kind of stalled out on me."

"But you're working on something. I can tell. You're so quiet."

"I guess so. I'm sorry."

"You have an important job. It's okay."

"No, it's not. I need to forget about things for a little while. If you don't mind, after dinner I'm going to go out to the garage and do some laundry and wax a shorty to use tomorrow."

"You're not going to paddle?"

"I think I need a change of pace."

"Do what you need to do, darling. After the dishes, I'm going to go up to bed."

"Okay, Tutu."

"But tell me, have you heard anything lately from Makani?"

"No, not since Christmas."

"That's a shame."

"Not really. It is what it is. She finds a phone on Christmas and when she needs something. That's fine."

Makani was Ballard's mother. As far as Renée knew, she was alive and well and living on remote ranchland in Kaupo, Maui. She had no phone and no Internet. And she had no inclination to be in regular contact with the daughter she had let go to the mainland twenty years ago to live in the home where her dead father had grown up. Even when Ballard had returned to her native Hawaii to go to the university, there was no connection. Ballard always believed it was because she was too strong a reminder of the man Makani had lost to the waves.

Ballard stayed in the kitchen to help with the dishes as she always did, working side by side with her grandmother at the sink. She then hugged her and said good night. She took Lola out to the front yard and looked up at a clear night sky while the dog did her business. Afterward, she walked Lola to her dog bed, then went to her room to retrieve the drawstring laundry bag she had brought in earlier from the van.

In the garage Ballard dumped her dirty clothes into the washing machine and started the cycle. She went over to the board rack that ran along the rear wall of the garage. There were eight boards arranged in slots according to size: her life's collection so far. She never traded in boards. There were too many memories attached to them.

She pulled a short board out of the first slot and took it over to an upside-down ironing board she used as a waxing and cleaning stand. The board was a six-foot Biscuit by Slick Sled with pink rails and a purple paisley deck. It was her first board, bought for her by her father when she was thirteen, and chosen for the vibrant colors rather than the surfing design. The colors were faded now by years in sun and salt but it still made tight turns and could pound down the face of a wave as well as a newer model. As she got older, more and more it seemed to be the board she pulled from the rack.

From day one with it, Ballard had always liked the process of cleaning and waxing the board and preparing for the next day's outing. Her father had taught her that a good day of surfing started the night before. She knew detectives at Hollywood Division who spent hours shining their shoes and oiling their leather holsters and belts. It demanded a certain focus and concentration and took them away from the burden of cases. It cleared their minds and renewed them. For Ballard, waxing a surfboard did the same trick. She could leave everything behind.

First she took a wax comb out of the toolbox on the nearby workbench and started stripping the old wax off the deck. She let it all flake to the concrete floor to pick up later. The last step of the process was the cleanup.

Once she got most of the old wax peeled off, she grabbed the gallon jug of Firewater off a shelf over the workbench. She poured the cleaning solvent onto a rag and wiped down the board's deck until it held a shining reflection of the overhead light. She stepped over and hit the wall button that opened the garage door so the chemical smell of the cleaner would dissipate.

She came back to the board, dried it with an old terry-cloth robe, and then grabbed an unopened cake of Sex Wax off the shelf. She carefully applied a base and then a thick top coat to the deck. She had always surfed goofy foot—right foot forward—and was sure to double down on wax on the tail section, where she would plant her left heel.

Every surfer was particular about how they combed their wax. Ballard always followed her father's lead and combed front to back, leaving grooves that followed the waterlines.

"Go with the flow," he would say.

When she was finished, she flipped the board over on the stand to finish the job with the most important part of the whole process: cleaning and slicking the surface of the board that would meet the water.

She first leaned down and studied the integrity of an old fiberglass patch near the nose. The board had gotten dinged in a surf bag on a trip to Tavarua Island in Fiji. In twenty years it had been all over the world, and her father's patchwork was the only blemish. She saw that fibers from the patch were beginning to fray and she knew she needed to take the board into a glass shop soon. But it would be good for at least one more day at the beach.

She next grabbed a surf key out of a can on the bench and tightened the keel fin. Finally, she poured more Firewater onto the board and cleaned the entire surface. She dried it, and it was good to go. It was so slick and shiny, she could see herself in it when she tilted the board up to move it to her van.

She also saw sudden movement coming from behind her. Before she could react, a black plastic bag came down over her head and was pulled tight around her neck. She dropped the board and started to struggle. She grabbed at the plastic and the hands that held it tight behind her head. Then a thickly muscled arm came around and formed a vise on either side of her neck. A forearm was driven into the back of her neck, pushing her further into the V hold. Locked in the vise, she felt her feet come off the ground as her attacker leaned back and used his chest as the fulcrum upon which to lift her.

26

Ballard opened her eyes and tried to raise her head. There was dim light coming from behind her. She tried to get her bearings and instinctively knew she had been drugged. When she turned her head, her vision sloshed like water in a bucket and then caught up and steadied. She squeezed her eyes shut and then reopened them. Things didn't change.

She realized she was naked, and there were several points of pain across her body. A gag was drawn tightly across her mouth and pulled back between her teeth. And she couldn't move. She was sitting in a wooden straight-backed chair. Her wrists were down by her hips, bound to the back posts of the chair. She had been bound so tightly and for so long that all feeling was gone from her fingers. A belt wrapped her torso and held her securely to the seat back. Her ankles were attached to the front legs of the chair.

She tried to remember what had happened. Had she been beaten? Had she been raped? She found it hard to control her anxiety, and the harder she tried to breathe through the gag, the more her chest expanded against the belt that cut into her ribs just beneath her breasts.

She raised her head again and took in the space. To her left she saw her blurred reflection in a full-length wall mirror. The bindings on her wrists and ankles were black plastic zip ties.

There was also a small table to the left, with nothing on it but a key. At the far end of the room, the floor-to-ceiling curtains were closed and she could see light leaking in around the edges but could not tell if it was sunlight, moonlight, or artificial light. She saw her clothes in a pile on the floor near the curtains. It looked like they had been torn or cut from her body.

She knew where she was. The lower room of Thomas Trent's upside-down house. She was now seeing it from the other side of the glass. The grim realization of that and of the situation she was in punched an awful dread into her chest. She flexed against her bindings but couldn't move.

She started breathing through her nose. The passage was unobstructed and she took in long, deep pulls of air. She knew that the more oxygen she got into her blood, the sooner the poison—whatever she had been drugged with—would be gone. Her mind raced as she tried to remember what had happened. She brought up images of the surfboard and the garage. She had been grabbed from behind. She remembered being choked and felt a physical revulsion at the memory.

Tutu. Had her grandmother been taken or hurt? How did Trent even know about Ventura?

She remembered talking to Trent about the car while she was driving out. He had called and she had turned down the invitation to the dealership. Was the call a hoax? Had he been following her? How did he find out that she was a cop?

There seemed to be only one answer to these questions and it was like a second punch of dread to the chest.

Beatrice.

Ballard realized she had read the ex-wife wrong. Beatrice had told Trent about her.

But that still didn't account for Ventura, for the jump from the customer named Stella to Ballard. Ballard had said nothing to Beatrice about going to the dealership and actually speaking to Trent.

She then recalled the call on the PCH and remembered telling Trent that she was out of town. He mentioned the surf truck. Had he tracked her through her van? She flexed against the bindings once more and still couldn't move.

She then heard his voice, and it chilled her.

"Don't bother, Renée. You can't break those."

Ballard looked into the mirror but could not see him anywhere in the room. Then he stepped out from an alcove and came up alongside her. He walked past and then turned to look down at her. With two hands he roughly pulled the gag down over her chin and left it hanging around her neck.

"Where's my grandmother?" Ballard asked, her voice tight with fear. "What did you do to her?"

Trent stared at her for a long moment, seemingly savoring her fear.

"I assume she's still sleeping in her bed at home," he finally said. "You should be more worried about yourself."

"What did you give me? You drugged me."

"Just a little shot of ketamine. I keep it for special

occasions. I had to make sure you were manageable during the ride in."

Ballard immediately computed a piece of positive news. She knew about ketamine. Over the years she had dutifully read and studied all departmental bulletins regarding the spectrum of date-rape drugs that had come into vogue and then turned up in sexual assault cases. Ketamine's primary and intended use was as an anesthetic. But she also knew that its effects didn't linger long. She could already feel herself shaking off the trancelike lethargy she had awoken with just minutes ago. She would soon be fully alert. She had to count it as a mistake on Trent's part, and where there was a mistake, there was hope.

"Fuck you, Trent," she said. "You think you're going to get away with this? No chance. There are people who know about you, people I've talked to. Reports written. I have a partner. I have a lieutenant. This is over. You are over—no matter what you do to me."

He frowned and shook his head.

"I don't think so, Renée," he said. "They're going to find your surf truck parked at a beach far up the coast from here, and there will be no sign of you anywhere. They'll know that you've been unhappy, and even your grandmother will have to say you seemed distant and a little depressed."

Ballard wondered if he had been in her grandmother's house the whole time she was there. Had he listened to her conversation—what there was of it—with Tutu at dinner?

"Meanwhile, they may come talk to me, but what will they have, Renée? Nothing. They'll have nothing.

And I'll have witnesses who heard me call you and tell you the car you ordered was in. They'll say I begged you to come to the dealership but that you said no, you no longer wanted it."

He paused there for effect.

"You're the detective," he finally said. "How does that play? No body, no evidence, no case."

She didn't answer and he came forward then and leaned down, putting one hand on the chair post next to her left ear for balance. He then reached down and dragged his other hand across her thighs and then down between them. She went rigid.

"You're mine now," he whispered.

She turned her face and tried to pull back in the seat, but there was nowhere to go. He brought his hand up and squeezed the muscle of her right biceps as if to check her strength.

"I like a good fight," he said. "I knew when I first saw you that you could fight. You're going to be fun."

He then caressed her right nipple as he straightened up with a smile.

"Another thing I like?" he said. "No tan lines. I had you down for tan lines when I saw you at the dealership. That smooth brown skin—what are you? Are you Poly? Maybe half white, half Polynesian? Maybe a little Mexican too?"

"Fuck you," she said. "What I am is the one who will take you down."

He laughed at that.

"We'll see, Renée," he said. "And we can talk about all of that later. But right now, I have an important question for you."

He then reached over to the table and picked up the key. He held it out in front of her face. Ballard recognized it—the key Beatrice had given her. She'd had it in the pocket of her jeans.

"Where did you get this?" Trent asked.

"I don't know what you're talking about," Ballard said. "It's not mine."

"Well, I know it's not yours, because it's a key to my house. I tried it on the front door. But it was in your pocket and I want to know how you got it."

"I told you, it—"

Suddenly Trent's left arm shot outward and he grabbed Ballard by the throat. He moved in and used his leverage to slam her head against the back of the chair and hold it there. He leaned down and she could feel his hot breath on her face.

"Don't lie to me."

She couldn't respond. His grip was crushing her airway. She could feel darkness closing in again before Trent finally let go.

She tried her voice but her throat felt damaged.

"I'm telling you, it's not my key."

"I found it in your clothes! I go through your clothes and find a key to my own—"

He stopped abruptly. He looked at the key, and Ballard saw a dark realization cloud his face.

"That bitch," he said. "She gave you this. You talked to that cunt ex-wife of mine, didn't you?"

"No, Trent," Ballard said. "I don't even know who you're talking about."

Trent waved the key six inches from her face.

"Liar," he said. "She gave you this. She kept it and

286

she gave it to you. So you could come into my home. That fucking bitch!"

He stepped away and raised his hands in fists next to his temples. Ballard could see the rage in his eyes. He then abruptly turned back to her.

"Well, you know what?" he said. "What I'm going to do is set up a little reunion with her and me and you, Renée. This is going to be fun."

"Trent, wait," Ballard said. "You don't want to do that. You do anything to her, and it will bring the police right here to your door. You know that an ex-husband is at the very top of the list whenever a woman is murdered. With me, you might have a shot at getting away. Not her. Leave her out of this."

Trent tossed the key onto the table and took a position directly in front of Ballard. He leaned down and put his balled fists on his thighs.

"Isn't that all noble of you to try to save her like that? But what happens if, like the surfer girl, the wife just disappears without a trace?"

"Same thing, Trent. They come right here."

"I don't think so. Not when the wife is a sadomasochistic porno queen. You know what I think? I think they'll say, 'Good riddance to her.'"

"Trent, don't do this. She has nothing—"

She didn't get to finish. Trent reached forward and with both hands roughly pulled the gag up and back into place across her mouth. He then reached back to a rear pocket and produced a black eyeglass case. He opened it to reveal a syringe and small amber vial with a label on it. Ballard knew it was ketamine and he was going to drug her again.

"Just need to put you out for a little while," Trent said. "And when I come back, we'll have a party with my beautiful bride."

Ballard struggled against her bindings, but it was a lost cause. She tried to talk against the gag but couldn't form words. He stuck the syringe through the rubber top of the vial and drew a quantity of clear liquid.

"They use this stuff on cats and dogs," he said. "It works pretty good on humans too."

He put the vial and eyeglass case on the table and went through the process of holding the needle up and flicking it with his finger.

"Don't want any bubbles now, do we?"

Ballard felt tears forming in her eyes. All she could do was watch him. He then leaned down, putting one hand on the chair post again. He harshly stabbed the needle into her left thigh. Ballard jerked, but that was all she could do. Trent slowly pushed down the plunger with his thumb and she felt the needle's contents course into her body.

"Hits pretty fast," Trent said. "Two minutes tops."

He stepped back and started putting the syringe and vial back into the case.

"Might need this with the bitch," he said. "She knows how to put up a fight."

Ballard watched him from a distance, as if through a tunnel. She could already feel the ketamine moving into her system, doing its job. She tried to flex her muscles against her bindings and couldn't do even that. She was helpless. Trent noticed and looked over at her after snapping the eyeglass case closed. He smiled.

"Feels good, doesn't it?"

Ballard stared at him as she felt herself slipping away. Soon the tunnel collapsed and became a pinhole of light. And then even that was gone.

27

Ballard tasted blood. She opened her eyes but was disoriented. Then it all came back. The upside-down house. The chair. The bindings. Trent. The gag had torn both corners of her mouth when he had pulled it back into place. Her neck felt stiff and hard to move. Once again, her vision wobbled as she brought her chin up.

The room was dark. Trent had turned the light off when he left. She could see only the dim outline of light around the curtains across the room. She had no idea how long she had been unconscious or how long it would be before Trent came back.

She looked around and saw a dark image of herself in the mirror, still bound. She tensed her body and found the bindings as strong and unyielding as before. She tried to calm her thinking and lower the sense of panic she felt.

She started with Beatrice. Trent had gone to get her. She knew where the upside-down house was and where Beatrice lived and worked. It was a minimum twenty-five-minute drive each way in routine traffic. If it was the middle of the night, he would be much faster. If it was the middle of the day, much longer. Trent would also have to find a way to abduct and control Beatrice. If she was alone at the warehouse, that would be one thing. If she was in the midst of video production, there would be people around, and that would complicate matters considerably and cost Trent time.

There were too many variables and none mattered, because Ballard did not have the starting point of knowing how long she had been unconscious. The one thing she did know gave her an adrenaline shot of hope. She was now alone and Trent had made a mistake. Earlier, when she had looked at herself in the mirror, she had seen that her wrists and ankles were bound to the chair posts with black plastic zip ties. They looked like the kind bought at a hardware store. Thin and designed to bundle cables or for other industrial and household needs, not the kind carried by police and used for binding human beings.

Regardless of their purpose or strength, Ballard knew that all zip ties had one thing in common; they were totally susceptible to the laws of physics.

In law enforcement, zip ties, or flex cuffs, were officially considered temporary restraining devices. They were not in the same league as handcuffs for the simple reason that one was made of plastic and the other was made of steel. There were plenty of stories and warnings passed in official memoranda, roll-call rooms, and the back hallway chatter of station houses. The message was simple: always keep your eye on an arrestee in flex cuffs. It didn't matter how strong they were. Plastic is subject to the laws of physics. Friction creates heat. Heat expands plastic.

Ballard tried to move her wrists, this time not pushing against the restraints but rather moving her hands up and down along the vertical chair posts. The bindings were so tight that she could not move them more than a half inch either way. But one half inch up and one half inch down was enough. She started moving her arms like pistons, up and down, up and down, as quickly as she could, creating friction between the plastic and the wood. The hard plastic straps almost immediately started cutting painfully into her skin. But soon she could also feel the heat she was creating, and that pressed her to move her arms faster and harder.

The pain grew almost intolerable and soon she could feel blood starting to drip from her wrists down across her hands. But Ballard didn't stop. And soon the half inch of movement became an inch and then two inches as she felt the plastic start to loosen.

She bit down on the gag and tears streamed down her face, but she kept going, stopping every two minutes by her count to quickly check the circumference of the binding. She was giving the same effort on both sides but soon it became clear that the binding on her left wrist was reacting to the friction and heat more quickly. She stopped the effort on the right side and doubled down on the left, sending all her strength into the piston action of her arm.

Her arm ached all the way up to her shoulder and neck but she pressed on. Soon blood and sweat on her wrist and hand made them slick, and suddenly, on an upward pull, her hand came all the way through the binding, its edge scraping skin off the side of her palm.

She had one hand free and she screamed into the gag, a primordial cry of release. She brought her bloody hand up, her fingers still numb, and managed to pull the gag down over her chin.

"Motherfucker!" she yelled to the room.

She moved quickly after that. Trent had left the key on the table. Ballard could see it glinting in the light from the sliding door. She reached for the table but was a foot short. Using her free arm as a pendulum, she rocked the chair forward until it tipped. As it toppled, she made a grab for the key, but she missed and fell face forward in the chair.

But now on the floor she could easily reach the leg of the table. She pulled it over and tipped it forward. The key slid onto the floor within reach. She grabbed it but her thumb and finger were too numb to get a secure grip.

She tried to shake life back into her left hand while she went to work with her right, once again moving her arm up and down the chair post. Soon she had enough feeling in her left hand to grip the key, and she used its teeth like a saw on the softening plastic binding her right. In moments the second binding snapped and both of her hands were free.

Still lying sideways on the floor, she unbuckled the belt that was around her torso. Her ankles were still bound to the chair. She turned onto her left side and, bending sideways, was able to grab one of the cross struts between the front and back legs of the chair. She tried to jerk it loose from the legs but it was solidly in place. Using the heel of her already bleeding hand, she swung a blow down on the strut and again it was unmoved. She hit again and then again with similar result.

She put everything into the next swing and wasn't sure if the crack she heard was the strut or a bone in her hand.

"Goddammit!"

She paused a moment, until the pain eased some, then grabbed the strut and pulled. The wood had split and by pulling it in the middle, she broke it loose. She then slid her plastic binding down along the leg and free of the chair.

With all but one limb free, Ballard was able to manipulate the chair and brace it against the room's wall. She then kicked through the remaining strut with the heel of her free foot, not feeling much pain from the impact because her foot was completely numb.

Finally free, Ballard sat on the floor and tried to rub feeling back into her ankles and feet. As sensation returned, they began to pulse with a stabbing, burning pain. She tried to stand and walk but was unsteady and she pitched forward onto the floor. She crawled the rest of the way across the room to the pile of her clothes.

Her clothes had been cut in so many places, they were completely unusable. Her hope that her cell phone would be in the pile was dashed as she remembered leaving it charging in her bedroom when she had gone out to the garage.

She knew she would need to look elsewhere in the house for a phone and for clothes. She tried to get up again, putting her hand out and using the mirrored wall for support. She left a bloody handprint.

With her other hand she yanked back the curtain and saw that the light that leaked around the edges came from an overhead porch light. It was dark outside. It looked like the middle of the night.

Just as she realized this meant Trent's travel time across the empty streets of the Valley would be considerably less than she'd hoped, the house seemed to shake with a loud vibration from above.

The garage door was opening.

Adrenaline flooded Ballard's body. She moved across the floor, still unsteady on her feet. She opened the door to the room and stepped into a small hallway. She saw stairs going up and a trapdoor opening on the floor. She hesitated, then stepped back into the room with the mirror and closed the door. She knew where she was in the house but didn't know the layout beyond the room she was in. She knew she could go through the sliding door and up the exterior stairs. That would put her naked and free on the street. She could knock on doors until she got to a phone and a 911 call.

But what about Beatrice? It was Ballard's duty to protect and serve. If Trent had abducted his ex-wife, could Ballard get help to the house in time to save her?

She heard a door closing sharply up above. Trent was now inside.

Ballard looked around, and her eyes fell on one of the broken cross supports from the legs of the chair. It had splintered lengthwise to a sharp point. She quickly reached down and grabbed it, then tested the point against her thumb. It was sharp and it could break skin. It would be a matter of grip and thrust.

She moved behind the room's door with her new-found weapon. And almost immediately she knew it was a bad plan. Her hands and feet were still partially numb and painful. The weapon she held required a close-in assault, and Trent was far bigger and far more powerful. She had the element of surprise but even if she moved in and stabbed Trent in the back, she would be unlikely to bring him down, and then she would be engaged in hand-to-hand combat with a much stronger foe.

She heard heavy footsteps coming downstairs. She guessed that there were two flights of stairs from the garage to the bottom level.

Ballard pulled herself back against the wall and got ready to follow the only course of action she had. But then she remembered something and lurched across the room toward the curtains. She slapped them aside and grabbed the wooden broomstick out of the sliding-door channel. She then turned back toward the door and grabbed what was left of her bra out of the pile of destroyed clothes as she went.

She leaned the broomstick against the wall next to the door's hinges and quickly went to work. Trent's steps on the stairs had stopped and she heard him moving on the floor directly above her. His steps were labored and she guessed he was carrying Beatrice.

The bra had been cut between the silk cups and shoulder straps and then apparently yanked off Ballard's body. The back clasp was still linked. Ballard quickly tied the garment tightly around her right thigh and slid the makeshift wooden dagger from the chair in against her skin.

She now heard Trent's steps on the stairway leading down to the bottom level. He would soon be entering the room. She grabbed the broomstick and stepped away from the wall, taking a position on the blind side of the door that still gave her space to swing.

The door opened. The first thing Ballard saw was a pair of bare feet as Trent carried an unconscious Beatrice in.

"Honey, I'm—"

Trent stopped when he saw the bloody handprint on the mirrored wall. He then started to scan the room and came to the empty chair and table overturned on the floor. Without so much as a thought for Beatrice, he dropped her like deadweight to the floor and made a move to turn back to the door.

Ballard took him by surprise, as he didn't think to check his blind side. He seemed to think she had already fled. As he turned, her first swing with the broomstick caught him flush across the right side of his face. It made a snapping sound and she thought it was the sound of his cheekbone breaking.

She didn't wait to see what the impact of the blow was. She pulled the broomstick back and went lower with the second swing, striking Trent across the torso, connecting with his ribs. This time the sound was heavier, like the sound of a punching bag. Trent made a painful noise and doubled over. Ballard then swung again, putting all her strength into a shot across the crown of his head.

The broomstick snapped in half on impact, the free end flying across the room and hitting the mirror. But somehow Trent stayed up. He brought both hands to his head and stutter-stepped backward unsteadily. He was like a dazed fighter about to go down, but then he rallied and started to straighten up.

"You fucking bitch!" he yelled.

Ballard dropped the broken broomstick and threw her body into Trent's, knocking him back against the wall. She drove her shoulder into him, pinning him. He closed his arms around her as she reached down and yanked the dagger from the improvised holster.

She gripped it tightly and drove the point into Trent's gut. She then pulled back and followed it with three quick stabs across his gut like a prison shanking. Trent yelled in pain and let go of her. Ballard stepped back, her arm up and ready to go at him with the dagger again.

Trent stared at her, his mouth open in a look of surprise. He then slid down the wall into a sitting position, trying to hold his gut together. Blood was flowing out between his fingers.

"Help me," he whispered.

"Help you?" Ballard said. "Fuck you."

Moving sideways so she could keep Trent in sight, Ballard went to Beatrice and squatted down. She reached to her neck to check for a pulse. Beatrice was alive but not conscious, most likely drugged with ketamine too, she thought. Ballard stole a glance down and saw that her face was swelling on the right side and that she had a split lip. She had not gone easily with Trent.

Trent was now listing to his left side. He'd lost strength in his hands and had dropped them to his lap. Blood now flowed unstopped from every puncture. His eyes were fixed and he was bleeding out. Still holding the improvised dagger ready, Ballard moved in and patted the blood-soaked pockets of his pants, looking for a phone. There was none.

She pushed Trent all the way over and turned him facedown. He made a gasping noise but no other sound. She untied the bra from around her thigh and then used it to tie Trent's hands behind his back. She assumed he was dead or close to it, but she wasn't going to take any chances.

Ballard left the room and went up the stairs to search for a phone and clothes she could put on. Getting help for Beatrice was the priority. She went all the way to the top floor in hopes of finding a phone in the kitchen.

There was a wall-mounted landline. Ballard dialed 911.

"This is Detective Ballard, Hollywood Division. Officer needs help. One-thousand-two Wrightwood Drive. Repeat, officer needs help. I've got one suspect down, one victim down, and one officer injured."

Ballard kept the line open and dropped the phone to the floor. She looked down at her naked body. Her arms, legs, and left hip were heavily splattered with blood. Most of it was her own, but some had come from Trent. She moved out of the kitchen and was going to go down to the next level, where there would be clothing in Trent's bedroom. But as she moved through the hallway, she saw an open door to the garage. Her van was parked in the bay.

She realized that Trent had taken her from Ventura in her own van. It had been part of his plan to take her body somewhere to be hidden and then dump the van far up the coast. She assumed that his own car was somewhere in the vicinity of her grandmother's house and that he had planned to pick it up before his return to Los Angeles.

Ballard entered the garage and found the van unlocked. She opened the side door and reached in for the beach clothes she left on hooks next to the spare tire. She pulled on sweatpants and a black tank. Over that she wore a nylon jacket with the Slick Sled logo on it. Next she opened the lockbox and grabbed her gun and badge. She was putting them into the pockets of the jacket when she heard the first siren approaching.

Then she heard Beatrice scream from the room below.

Ballard moved quickly down the stairs.

"Beatrice!" she called. "It's okay! It's okay!"

She got to the room. Beatrice was still on the floor, sitting up. She held her hands to her mouth and stared wide-eyed across the room at her ex-husband's body. Ballard held her hands up in a calming motion.

"You're all right, Beatrice. You're safe now. You're safe."

Ballard moved to Trent and reached down to his neck to check for a pulse. Behind her, Beatrice spoke hysterically.

"Oh my god, oh my god, this isn't happening."

There was no pulse. Ballard turned back to Beatrice and knelt down.

"He's dead," she said. "He's never going to hurt you or anybody else again."

Beatrice grabbed her tightly.

"He was going to kill me," she said. "He told me."

Ballard hugged her back.

"Not anymore," she said.

28

Patrol units from North Hollywood Division arrived first, followed by a fire truck and two rescue ambulances. The paramedics checked Trent's pulse and pupils and found no indications of life. They decided not to transport him and left his body in place for the investigators who would follow from the Coroner's Office and the LAPD.

The other team treated Beatrice Beaupre for superficial injuries to her face and ribs and determined that there were no residual effects from the ketamine Trent had dosed her with. They then treated Ballard for the wounds on her wrists and mouth. They wrapped her wrists in gauze and tape, which left her looking like someone who had attempted suicide. They checked the bruising on her neck from when she was choked out by her abductor but found no additional injury.

Ballard asked the female paramedic to take photos of her injuries on her phone and then e-mail them to her. She also pulled down the side of her sweatpants for a photo of the blood on her hip. She was disgusted by it but knew that she should not clean herself of Trent's blood. It was evidence. Not of Trent's guilt, because there would never be a trial now, but in support of the story she would tell.

The first detectives to arrive were from North

Hollywood Division, even though it was clear that the case would be handed off to the Force Investigation Division, since it involved a death at the hands of an officer. Following protocol, one of the locals called FID with the initial report and received instructions to sequester Ballard and send Beaupre in a car downtown to the PAB, where she would be interviewed by an FID base team.

Ballard was taken out of the house and also placed in a car, where she waited over an hour for the FID field team to assemble after being rousted from sleep. During that wait she saw dawn break over the Valley. She also borrowed a phone from one of the North Hollywood detectives and called the Ventura Police Department to ask for a welfare check on her grandmother. A half hour later, while she was still waiting in the backseat, the detective opened the door and told her that VPD had called back and reported that her grandmother was safe.

The FID team consisted of four detectives, a lieutenant, and a mobile command post, which was essentially a trailer that had work spaces, computers, printers, television screens, and Wi-Fi, as well as a camera-ready interrogation room.

The lieutenant's name was Joseph Feltzer. Ballard knew him from what she called the Spago case, the tangle she and Jenkins had had with the burglar in the HVC house off Doheny Drive. He had been fair during that investigation, though in no way a homer automatically looking to clear cops of wrongdoing. But that had largely been an investigation of Jenkins and his clobbering of the burglar who attacked Ballard. This time the focus would be exclusively on Ballard and she knew that her history of making a complaint against Olivas made her a target for elimination from the department. She had to be very careful here until she knew whether Feltzer was a straight shooter.

While his four detectives put on booties and gloves before entering the house, Feltzer opened the door of the plain wrap and invited Ballard into the MCP. They didn't speak until they were sitting on either side of a table in the interrogation room.

"How are you feeling, Detective?" Feltzer began.

"Pretty numb," Ballard said.

It was an accurate assessment. All of Ballard's systems had gone from overdrive during her captivity to cruise control upon her escape and later determination that her grandmother and Beaupre were safe. She felt dazed. Like she was watching someone else go through the investigation.

Feltzer nodded.

"Understandable," he said. "I have to ask, are you wearing your sidearm?"

"Actually, it's in my pocket," Ballard said. "You can't put a holster on these sweatpants."

"I need to collect that from you before we start."

"Really? I didn't shoot the guy. I stabbed him."

"Protocol. Can I have the weapon, please?"

Ballard pulled her Kimber from her jacket and handed it across the table. Feltzer checked the thumb safety and put it in a plastic evidence bag, then wrote something on it and placed it in a brown paper bag he put on the floor.

"Are you carrying a backup?" he asked

"No, no backup," she said.

"Okay, so let's start. I'm sure you know how this goes, Detective Ballard, but I'll tell you anyway before we turn on the tape. I will give you the Miranda advisement and you will refuse to waive your right to remain silent. I will then give you the Lybarger admonishment and you'll tell me what happened. After we have your story on tape, we'll go into the house and you'll walk me and my team through it all over again. You okay with all of that?"

Ballard nodded. The Lybarger admonishment was used to compel an officer to answer questions without an attorney present. It was named after an officer who was fired for refusing to do so. It compelled an officer to talk but had an exclusion that disallowed these statements from being used in a criminal proceeding against the officer.

Feltzer turned the video equipment on, went through both legal advisements, and then got down to business.

"Let's start at the top," he said. "Detective Ballard, tell me what happened and what led to the death of Thomas Trent by your hand."

"Trent was a primary suspect in the abduction and assault of Ramón Gutierrez, a male prostitute, in Hollywood," Ballard said. "Trent somehow found out where I live in Ventura and came there last night without my knowing. While I was prepping a surfboard in the garage with the door open, he came up behind me and pulled a plastic bag over my head. He abducted and drugged me and took me to this location—his home. He may have sexually assaulted me while I was unconscious, but I don't know. I woke up naked and tied to a chair. He then told me he was going to abduct another victim

304

and he drugged me again before apparently leaving the premises. I regained consciousness before he returned and managed to free myself. Before I could escape from the house, he returned with the second victim. Fearing for her safety, I stayed in the room where he had left me. I armed myself with a broomstick from the sliding-door track and a sharp piece of wood I had broken off the legs of a chair. When he entered with the second victim, I engaged him in a physical altercation, striking him several times with the broomstick until it broke. He then managed to get his arms around me and grab me. Knowing he was much bigger than me and fearing for my life, I stabbed him multiple times with the splinter of wood. He eventually let go of me, collapsed on the floor, and died shortly afterward."

Feltzer was silent for a long time, possibly stunned by the complexity of the story, even in short form.

"Okay," he finally said. "We're going to go through this in greater detail now. Let's start with the Gutierrez case. Tell me about that."

It took Ballard ninety minutes to go through everything under Feltzer's detailed but nonaccusatory questioning. At times he brought up seeming inconsistencies and at others questioned her decision-making, but Ballard knew that any good investigator asked some questions that were designed to incite upset and even outrage in their subject. It was called trying to get a reaction. But she maintained her cool and spoke calmly during the entire interview. Her goal was to keep it together through this phase, no matter how long it took, knowing that eventually she would be left alone and would be able to let herself go. Over the years she had read several primers in the police union newsletter and knew to repeatedly use key words and phrases like "fearing for the safety of myself and the other victim" that she knew would make it difficult for FID to find Trent's killing other than justified and within the department's use-of-force policy. FID would then recommend to the District Attorney's Office that no action be taken against Ballard.

She also knew that it would come down to whether her words matched the physical evidence collected in Trent's house, her van, and the garage up in Ventura. After not straying during the interview from what she knew had happened, she left the interrogation room, confident that there would be no contradictions for Feltzer and his team to grab on to.

When she emerged from the trailer, she saw that the crime scene had become a three-ring circus. Several police vehicles as well as forensic and coroner's vans were clustered in the street. Three TV vans lined up outside the yellow tape on Wrightwood, and up above, news choppers circled. She also saw her partner, Jenkins, standing on the periphery. He nodded and held up a fist. She did as well and they mimed bumping from twenty feet apart.

By ten a.m. Ballard had completed the walk-through with the FID team. Most of the time had been spent in the bottom-level room, where Trent's body remained, hands still tied behind his back with her bra. Ballard felt fatigue crushing her. Other than the minutes when she had been drugged into unconsciousness, she had been going for over twenty-four hours straight. She told Feltzer she was not feeling well and needed to crash. He said that before she could go home, she needed to go to a Rape Treatment Center to find out whether Trent had raped her while she was unconscious and for evidence to be collected. He was arranging for one of his detectives to drive her when Ballard asked if her own partner could be the escort.

Feltzer agreed. They made an appointment for a follow-up interview the following morning and then the FID lieutenant let her go.

As she was leaving, Ballard asked about her van and was told it was going to be impounded and examined by the forensics team. She knew that meant it would likely be a week or more before she got it back. She asked if she could take any belongings out of it and was again told no.

When she stepped outside the house, she saw Jenkins waiting for her. He gave her a sympathetic smile.

"Hey, partner," he said. "You doing okay?"

"Never better," she said, meaning the opposite. "I need a ride."

"Absolutely. Where to?"

"Santa Monica. Where are our wheels?"

"Down behind the news vans. I couldn't find any parking."

"I don't want to walk by the reporters. How 'bout you go get it and come back to pick me up?"

"You got it, Renée."

Jenkins walked off down the street, and Ballard waited in front of the upside-down house. Two of Feltzer's detectives came out the front door behind her and climbed into the MCP. They didn't say a word as they passed Ballard.

Jenkins took Mulholland all the way to the 405 freeway before heading south. Once they were out of the hills and Ballard knew she'd get a clear signal, she asked to borrow her partner's phone. She knew she would have to sit through a psychological exam before being allowed to return to duty. She wanted to get it over with. She called the Behavioral Science Unit and made an appointment for the next day, fitting it in after her follow-up appointment with Feltzer.

After giving Jenkins his phone back, Ballard collapsed against the car door and slept. It wasn't until Jenkins was exiting the westbound 10 that he reached over and gently tapped her shoulder. Ballard awoke with a startle.

"Almost there," he said.

"I just want you to drop me off and then go," she said.

"You sure?"

"Yes, I'm sure. Don't worry about me. Go home to your wife."

"I don't feel good about that. I want to wait for you."

"John, no. I want to be by myself with this. I'm not even sure it happened, and if it did, I was out and I'll never remember it. Right now I just want to do this by myself, okay?"

"Okay, okay. We don't have to talk about it. But if you ever do, I'm here. Okay?"

"Okay, partner. But I probably won't."

"That's okay, too."

The RTC was part of the Santa Monica–UCLA Medical Center on 16th Street. There were other hospitals where Ballard could have gone to get a rape examination and evidence kit but the RTC had a reputation as one of the premier facilities in the country. Ballard had ferried enough rape victims there during the late show to know that she would be met with full compassion and professional integrity.

Jenkins pulled to a stop in front of the intake doors.

"You don't have to talk about this, but at some point you need to tell me about Trent," he said.

"Don't worry, I will," Ballard said. "Let's see how FID goes, then we'll talk. You thought Feltzer was fair on the Spago case, right?"

"Yeah, pretty much down the middle."

"Let's hope he doesn't have anybody on the tenth floor whispering in his ear."

The Office of the Chief of Police, or OCP as it was known, was on the tenth floor of the PAB.

Ballard opened her door and got out. She looked back in at Jenkins.

"Thanks, partner," she said.

"Take care, Renée," he said. "Call me if you want."

She waved him off and he drove away. Ballard entered the facility, pulled her badge from her jacket, and asked to see a supervisor. A nurse named Marion Tuttle came out from the treatment section and they talked. Forty minutes later Ballard was in a treatment room. The blood had been cleaned off her hip, and cotton-swabbed samples had been placed in evidence jars.

Swabs had also been taken during a humiliating and intrusive examination of her body. Tuttle then conducted a presumptive test for semen on the swabs using a chemical that would identify the presence of a protein found in sperm. This was followed by an even more intrusive anal and vaginal examination. When it was finally over, Tuttle let Ballard cover herself with a smock while the nurse dropped her surgical gloves in the examination room's medical waste container. She then checked off a form on a clipboard and was ready to report her findings.

Ballard closed her eyes. She felt humiliated. She felt sticky. She wanted to take a shower. She had spent hours bound and sweating, had been adrenalized by fight-or-flight panic, and had fought a man twice her weight, and all that after possibly being raped. She wanted to know, yes, but she also wanted this all to be over with.

"Well . . ." Tuttle said. "No swimmers."

Ballard knew she meant no semen.

"We'll test the swabs for silicone and other indications of condom use," Tuttle said. "There is some bruising. When was the last time you had sexual relations before this incident?"

Ballard thought about Rob Compton and the not-gentle encounter they had shared.

"Saturday morning," she said.

"Was he big?" Tuttle asked. "Was it rough?"

She asked the questions matter-of-factly and without a hint of judgment.

"Uh, both," Ballard said. "Sort of."

"Okay, and when was the last time before that?" Tuttle asked.

Aaron, the lifeguard.

"A while," Ballard said. "At least a month."

Tuttle nodded. Ballard averted her eyes. When would this be over?

"Okay, so the bruising could be from Saturday

morning," Tuttle said. "You hadn't had sex in a while, your tissues were tender, and you say he was big and not too gentle."

"Bottom line is, you can't tell if I've been raped," Ballard concluded.

"No definitive indication internally or externally. Nothing came up on the pubic comb, because you don't have a lot down there to comb. Bottom line, I couldn't go into court and say under oath one way or the other, but I know in this case, that doesn't matter. It's just you. You need to know."

"I do."

"I'm sorry, Renée. I can't tell you for sure. But I can introduce you to someone here you can talk to and she may be able to help you come to terms with not having an answer. She may be able to help you move on from the question."

Ballard nodded. She knew that the same territory would likely be covered in the psych exam she would undergo the next day at BSU.

"I appreciate that," she said. "I really do and I'll think about it. But right now what I think I need most is a ride. Can you call a car service and vouch for me? My wallet and phone are up in Ventura. I need to get up there and I don't have a car."

Tuttle reached out and patted Ballard on the shoulder.

"Of course," she said. "We can do that."

29

Ballard got to Ventura and her grandmother's house by four p.m. She retrieved her wallet from her bedroom and used a credit card to pay the driver who had taken her up the coast. She tipped him well for not talking during the journey and for letting her rest her head against the window and fall into a dreamless sleep. Back inside the house, she locked the door and hugged Tutu in a long embrace, reassuring her that she was fine and that everything was going to be all right. As promised the night before, Tutu had gone to bed after doing the dishes. She had slept through Ballard's abduction from the garage and only learned of it when the police arrived to make sure she was okay.

Ballard then hugged her dog and this time it was she who was reassured, by Lola's calm and stoic presence. She finally went into the hallway bathroom. She sat on the floor of the shower and let the spray come down on her until she emptied the house's hot-water tank.

As the water stung her shoulders and penetrated her scalp, she tried to come to terms with what had happened in the past twenty-four hours and the fact that she would never know exactly what had been done to her. More than that, she also examined for the first time the fact that she was a killer. It didn't matter whether it was justified, she was now a part of the population that knew what it was to take a life. She had known from day one at the academy that she might one day use her weapon to kill someone, but this was somehow different. This was something that could never have been anticipated. No matter what she had repeatedly told the investigators, she had killed as a victim, not as a cop. Her mind kept flashing back to those moments during the struggle with Trent when she had gone at him like a prison assassin with a shank.

There was something inside her she didn't know she had. Something dark. Something scary.

She had not one micron of sympathy for Trent, and yet she was beset by conflicting emotions. She had survived what no doubt was a kill-or-be-killed situation, and that thought brought a life-affirming euphoria. But the exhilaration was short-lived as questions intruded and she was left wondering if she had gone too far. In the internal courtroom, legal thresholds like *I feared for the safety of myself and others* held no meaning. They were not evidence of anything. The jury delivered its verdict based on evidence never shared outside the confines of the guilty mind. Inside, Ballard knew that Thomas Trent, no matter the size and content of his evil, should still be alive.

The thought of Trent's death gave way to the unanswered questions: How did he know she was a cop? How did he find her in Ventura? The fact that he had turned against Beatrice Beaupre in the end told Ballard that she was not the source. She once again reviewed, as well as she could remember, her conversations with Trent at the car dealership, during the test-drive, and while she was driving to Ventura. She recalled nothing that could have revealed her as a law enforcement officer. She wondered if it had been the firm handshake she had used to elicit a response of pain in him. Was that the tell? Or was it her questions about the bruises that followed?

She then thought about the van. Trent had seen the van when she pulled into the dealership. Had he somehow been able to run the plate and get her true identity and the address of the house in Ventura? He worked at a car dealership, where DMV transactions were carried out dozens of times every day. Perhaps Trent had a source, a friendly DMV clerk who registered new plates and had access to the registrations on existing ones. During the abduction Trent spoke about her tan lines and her ethnic origins, revealing a fascination with her that was established during the dealership visit. Maybe, Ballard realized, Trent began stalking her because she was an intended target, not because she was a cop targeting him.

Again, the bottom line was that Trent was dead. Ballard might never get an answer to her questions.

She didn't notice that the water had gradually turned cold until her body began to shake with chills. Only then did she get up and get out.

Lola sat dutifully at the door of the bathroom.

"Come on, girl."

Ballard padded down the hallway to her room in bare feet, a large white towel wrapped around her body. She closed the door to her bedroom and noticed that Tutu had finished the laundry she had started the night before in the garage. Her clothes were neatly folded on the bed, and Ballard was overjoyed at the prospect of putting on fresh and clean things.

She put on a bra and underwear. But before getting dressed further, she checked her phone, which was charging on the bedside table, where she had left it. The screen said she had eleven new voice-mail messages. She sat on the bed and started playing them one by one.

The first two messages were from Jenkins and had been left before they had connected at the crime scene. He had gotten word about the investigation into an officer-involved death on Wrightwood Drive and wanted to know if she was okay. The second message was to let her know he was going to the crime scene to find her.

The next message was from an academy classmate Ballard maintained ties with. Rose Boccio had heard on the blue pipeline that Ballard was at the center of an officer-involved death being investigated in Studio City.

"Balls!" she said, using Ballard's academy nickname. "Thank god you're all right. Call me. We need to talk."

The fourth message was similar. It was from Corey Stead-man of RHD. Another friend hoping Ballard was okay.

The fifth caller was Rob Compton, parole agent and sometime lover. He evidently was not aware of what was going on with Ballard and was not calling about her abduction or killing of Thomas Trent.

"Hey, Renée, it's Robby. Listen, we got a hot one. An ATF agent called me about the stolen Glock we recovered from our boy Nettles. Pretty interesting stuff. Hit me back, okay?"

It took Ballard a moment to place what Compton was talking about. The events of the past day had been so acute that they had completely crowded other cases and memories from her mind. Then she remembered. Christopher Nettles, the one-man crime wave. Compton had put in an ATF request on the three presumed stolen weapons recovered from Nettles and his room at the Siesta Village motel.

Ballard made a mental note to call Compton as soon as she got into the proper mental state to work cases. She thought that diving back into the Nettles caper would be a welcome diversion from her current situation.

The next message was from her direct supervisor, Lieutenant McAdams. He opened by telling Ballard he was relieved to hear that she was reasonably okay after the ordeal. That said, he began reading an order that had come to him from on high that put Ballard on light duty while the investigation of the officer-involved death proceeded.

"So I'm working on the schedule and I'll get somebody paired up with Jenkins," McAdams concluded after reading the order. "You're riding the pine on dayside until FID finishes up and you get the all clear from BSU. It's all pretty routine. Give me a call back or shoot me an e-mail to let me know you received and understand this order. Thanks, Renée."

The next couple messages were from well-wishers within the department. One of these was Rogers Carr of Major Crimes.

"This is Carr and, wow, I just heard. Glad you're okay, glad you're good, and glad you took that big evil out of the picture. I'm around if you need anything."

Ballard had been deleting the messages as she heard them but she saved the recording from Carr. She thought she might want to listen to it again, especially the part about taking big evil out of the picture. She thought that the message might be reassuring to listen to the next time her internal jury started deliberating the case and leaning toward a guilty verdict.

The next message was also a keeper. It was from Beatrice Beaupre. She was crying, as she had left it just an hour earlier.

"They finally let me go. They asked a lot of questions and then they asked them all over again. Anyway, Detective Ballard, I told them the truth. You saved my life. You saved both our lives. He was going to kill me, I know it. He told me so when he injected me. I thought that was it. Then you were there to save me. You were so good. You fought him and got the upper hand. I told them. I told them what I saw. Thank you, Detective Ballard. Thank you so much."

Her voice trailed off into a sob as Beatrice hung up. The message, though heartfelt, gave Ballard pause. She knew Beatrice had not seen the fight with Trent. She was unconscious. The message indicated she had told the FID investigators she had seen what she hadn't. Had Beatrice perceived that the FID was trying to fault Ballard in some way and turn it into a bad killing? She had to be careful here. She couldn't call Beaupre back to inquire about these concerns. That might be viewed by the FID as witness tampering. It was a firing offense to try to manipulate an internal investigation. Ballard had to bide her time and be cautious. The call from Beatrice was a good heads-up.

Her feelings of concern seemed more than justified when she got to the last two messages. The first of these was from Lieutenant Feltzer of FID. He was requesting that they move up the hour of their appointment for a follow-up interview. He said that the crime scene investigation had been completed and all initial interviews conducted.

"We need to sit down with you and iron out the inconsistencies," he said. "Please come to the FID office tomorrow morning at, let's say eight o'clock. We'll try to get you out of here as soon as possible."

The first thing Ballard thought about was whether she should bring a union defense rep with her to FID. She had picked up an adversarial tone in Feltzer's voice and given the message from Beatrice, she was growing more concerned the more she thought about what Feltzer had said about inconsistencies. Then it struck her. Her choice for a defense rep would have been Ken Chastain. He was smart. His analytical mind could have helped her decipher the moves being made against her. He would have been perfect in helping her form her answers to their questions.

But he had betrayed her and now he was dead. She had no one she felt comfortable asking to sit next to her. No one close, no one smart and cunning enough. Not Jenkins. Not Steadman. She was alone against this.

If that conclusion wasn't depressing enough, the last message on her phone was the true chiller. It had come in less than thirty minutes ago while she had been in the shower. The caller was a reporter from the *Times* named Jerry Castor. Ballard had never spoken to him but he was known to her. She had seen him at various crime scenes and press conferences, especially during her time with RHD.

Reading the *Times* coverage of the department over

time gave insight into the allegiances of different re-porters. The angles the stories took often revealed the sources, even if unnamed, behind them. Castor was considered a Level 8 reporter by those in the depart-ment who monitored such things. This was a reference to the makeup of the PAB. The building was ten floors, with command staff and administration largely housed on floors eight through ten, with the chief on top.

It was believed that Castor was a reporter more plugged in on the three upper floors than on the seven below. It made dealing with him more career dangerous for the rank and file than with other reporters. That was one reason Ballard had always steered clear of him.

"Detective Ballard, Jerry Castor over at the *Times*," his message began. "We haven't met but I cover the cop shop and I'm working on a story over here about the death of Thomas Trent. I really need to talk to you about it today. My main question is about the fatal injuries Mr. Trent sustained. As I understand it, this man was unarmed and not charged with any crime but he ended up getting stabbed multiple times, and I'm curious to know if you'd care to comment on how that figures in with justifiable use of deadly force. My first deadline is at eight o'clock tonight, so I am hoping to hear from you by then. If not, the story will reflect our unsuccessful efforts to reach you for your side of things."

Castor thanked her, left his direct number in the newsroom, and hung up.

What felt like a punch to Ballard's gut wasn't the re-porter calling her out in terms of the deadly force. At the academy, they don't teach you to shoot once when you need to fire your weapon. If deadly force is warranted, you use deadly force in whatever quantity is necessary to get the job done. Legally and departmentally, whether she stabbed Trent four times or only once didn't matter. What got to Ballard was that someone inside the department had told the reporter the details of the killing and pushed them out into the uninformed public space. Someone had called Castor, knowing that the details provided would be cause for debate and vilification.

She felt like she had been cut loose from the department and was on her own.

There was a knock on the bedroom door.

"Renée?"

"I'm getting dressed. I'll be out in a minute."

"Honey, I'm making fish tonight. I got some barramundi fresh from Australia. I hope you can stay."

"Tutu, I told you, just because they call it fresh doesn't mean it's fresh. How can anything be fresh if it's packed in dry ice and flown or shipped all the way from Australia? Stick with stuff you know is fresh. Halibut from the bay."

There was silence and Ballard felt like shit for taking out the frustrations of the moment on her grandmother. She started dressing quickly.

"Does that mean you don't want to stay?" Tutu asked through the door.

"I'm really sorry but it's a work night and they're calling me in early," Ballard said. "I need to pick up a rental car and go soon."

"Oh, sweetie, you've been through so much. Can't you take the night off?" Tutu asked. "I'll cook something else."

Ballard finished buttoning her blouse.

"It's not about the fish," she said. "Cook your fish, Tutu. But I can't stay. I'm sorry. Are you okay with Lola here for a couple more days?"

She opened the door. Her tiny grandmother stood there, worry clearly on her face.

"Lola is always welcome here," she said. "She's my buddy. But I want her owner here too."

Ballard reached out and hugged her, holding her in a fragile embrace.

"Soon," she said. "I promise."

Ballard didn't like lying to her grandmother but the full and honest explanation was too complicated. She had to get back to the city. Not only did she have the session with Feltzer the next morning and the psych exam to follow, but she knew that she couldn't fight this battle from up in Ventura. She had to get to ground zero to make her stand.

30

Most people were trying to get out of L.A. Ballard was trying to get in. She steadily goosed her rented Ford Taurus through heavy rush-hour traffic on the 101 freeway toward downtown. The miles went by so slowly, she feared she would miss the eight-o'clock deadline at the *Times*. She had devised a plan that she believed might give her the upper hand against those working against her in the department.

She knew a couple things about how the murky lines between the media and law enforcement were negotiated. She knew there was little cooperation and even less trust. Those who chose to cross those murky lines guarded against risks. It was that practice she was going to use to her own purposes.

The PAB and the Times Building sat side by side on First Street, with only Spring Street separating them. The two giant bureaucracies cast jaundiced eyes at each other, yet at times they certainly needed each other. Ballard finally got to the area at 7:20 and parked in an overpriced pay lot behind the newspaper building. She took a shoulder bag containing some of her clean clothes with her and walked to a coffee shop on Spring Street that offered a clear view from its corner window of the block-long stretch of road that separated the newspaper and police buildings.

Once situated with a cup of coffee at the counter behind the corner window, Ballard pulled her phone and called Jerry Castor on his direct newsroom line.

"This is Renée Ballard."

"Oh! Uh, hi, I'm glad you called. I wasn't—there's still time for me to get your comments into the story."

"I'm not giving you any comments. This conversation is off the record."

"Well, I was hoping to get some reaction to what I'm saying in my story, which is—"

"I'm not giving reaction, I'm not giving comments, and I don't care what you say in your story. I'm hanging up now unless you agree that this conversation is off the record."

There was a long silence.

"Uh, okay, we're off the record," Castor finally said. "For now, at least. I just don't understand why you wouldn't want to get your side of it into the story."

"Are you recording this?" Ballard asked.

"No, I'm not recording."

"Well, just so you know, I am. I've been recording since the start of the call. Are you okay with that?"

"I guess so. But I don't see why you—"

"You'll understand in a few minutes. So that is a yes on recording?"

"Uh, yes."

"Okay, good. Mr. Castor, I'm calling to tell you that your information is wrong. That you are being manipulated by your LAPD sources to put out a story that is not only wrong but designed to inflict harm upon me and others."

"Harm? How is that?"

323

"If you tell a lie in your paper, that harms me. You need to go back to your sources and take a look at their motives and then ask them for the truth."

"Are you saying you didn't stab Thomas Trent multiple times? That your statement wasn't contradicted by another victim's statement?"

That second part was new information and it would be helpful to Ballard.

"I'm saying you have been lied to and I have this conversation on tape," Ballard said. "If you proceed with that story and its lies and out-of-context statements, then this recording with its direct warning will go to your editor and other media outlets so it will become clear to the community and in your workplace what kind of reporter you are and what kind of newspaper the *Time*s is. Good night, Mr. Castor."

"Wait!" Castor cried.

Ballard disconnected and waited, keeping her eyes on the Spring Street employee entrance of the Times.

She was working off of a fact, a supposition, and an assumption. The fact was that it was against the law and the policy of the LAPD to publicly disclose the details of a personnel investigation. Ballard had killed a man that morning in the line of duty. That was news and the department was duty bound to inform the public. That came in the form of a press release all parties had agreed upon. Ballard and Feltzer had written the three-paragraph statement while they had been in the command post that morning. But Ballard had not agreed to releasing any more details of the killing or the subsequent investigation. Castor obviously had details that went beyond the press release. It meant he had a source who was feeding him those details in violation of the law and department policy.

Ballard's supposition was that Castor's source would be smart and cagey and would be sure not to place himself in a position where he could be compromised. He would certainly not reveal the details of a personnel investigation in a phone call that could be recorded or heard by others without his knowledge. Whatever motivated a source to spill to the newspaper, the actual leaking would be clandestine and not take place on the phone, in the newspaper office, or at the LAPD.

That led to the assumption. Ballard had just thrown a fastball at Castor and she guessed that he would run, figuratively, in a panic to his source in order to salvage the story. He needed to tell his source what Ballard had just said. If there were ground rules about not talking on a phone, then Castor would be walking out of the Times Building at any moment to head to a meeting with his source.

Ballard's only worry was that the reporter's secret spot for meeting his source might be the very coffee shop where she was now sitting. It would be perfectly reasonable for a reporter from the Times Building and an LAPD employee from the PAB to cross paths in a coffee shop equidistant from both their work locations. Words and documents could be exchanged in the line to order, at the waiting counter after ordering, or at the sugar and cream stand.

Ballard visually tracked one man for half a block after he stepped through the Times door and headed north and away from her. After finally deciding he was a bogey, her eyes returned to the building's doors just in time to see the real Jerry Castor emerge. He turned south, passing by the coffee shop from the other side of Spring Street. Ballard dumped the coffee she had bought but hadn't even tasted. She stepped out onto the sidewalk and headed south, tracking Castor from the other side of the street.

There was a time when following someone on foot at night in downtown L.A. would have been impossible to pull off because of the scarcity of pedestrians after the nine-to-five workday ended. But the district had begun to thrive in recent years, with many young professionals deciding to avoid the angst of killer traffic and live in the area where they worked. Restaurants and nightlife soon followed. On this night near eight p.m. Ballard had no problem keeping other pedestrians between herself and Castor, though it did not appear that the reporter was thinking about the possibility of a tail. He never looked behind himself once. He never cleverly glanced into the reflection of a shop's plate-glass window. He walked swiftly and with purpose, like a man on a mission, or a deadline.

Castor led Ballard south for four blocks, until he got to the corner of 5th Street, then took a right and disappeared through an open door. Ballard wondered if it was a move designed to lose a tail, but as she caught up, she saw a neon sign that announced the business as THE LAST BOOKSTORE.

Ballard entered cautiously and found a giant bookstore in a space that appeared to have formerly been the grand lobby of a bank. There were rows of freestanding bookshelves angled between Corinthian columns rising two stories to an ornate coffered ceiling. On one wall hung a sculpture of books forming a wave. Balconies fronting small art-and used-record shops offered a view down onto the main floor, which was crowded with customers. Ballard had no idea of the place's existence and the excitement of the find almost made her forget her quarry.

Using a set of shelves dedicated to the classics as a partial blind, Ballard scanned the lower level of the bookstore, looking for Castor. The reporter was nowhere to be seen, and it was impossible to cover every corner of the space because of the shelves, columns, and other obstacles to her vision.

Ballard saw a man with a name tag pinned to his shirt walking toward the checkout counter near the door.

"Excuse me," she said. "How do I get upstairs?"

"I'll show you real quick," the man said.

He walked Ballard over to an alcove that had been hidden from her sight and pointed to a set of stairs. She thanked him and quickly started up.

The upper-level balconies afforded Ballard a fuller view of the bookstore below. There were several reading alcoves created by shelf stands positioned at right angles and complete with old leather chairs or couches in the privacy spots. It was the perfect place for a clandestine meeting.

Ballard scanned the whole place twice before finally spotting Castor in an alcove almost directly below her. He was sitting on the edge of a couch, leaning forward and in animated but quiet conversation with another man. It took a moment for the other man to turn his face so that Ballard could clearly see it.

It was Lieutenant Feltzer.

Ballard didn't know whether to be more outraged by Feltzer's treachery or jubilant that she now knew who the leak was and could do something about it.

She pulled her phone and surreptitiously took several photos of the meeting below. At one point she switched to video, when Castor stood up like he was in a hurry and looked down at Feltzer. He waved his hands in a dismissive way and then walked out of the alcove and crossed the main floor of the store. Ballard kept the camera going, tracking the reporter until he left the store through the door he had used to enter.

When Ballard brought the camera back across the floor to the alcove where Feltzer had been sitting, he was gone. She lowered the phone and scanned the store as best as she could. There was no sign of Feltzer.

Ballard suddenly became concerned that Feltzer had seen her and that he was on his way up to the second level. She turned to the steps but she saw nobody coming up. She was safe. Feltzer must have left the store, taking a different route through the maze of shelves and then out the door.

Ballard went down to the main floor, watching for Feltzer but catching no glimpse of him. She exited the store onto 5th and looked about. No sign of Feltzer.

Ballard guessed that Feltzer, like Castor, had walked to the meeting but that he had passed the same four blocks via Main Street instead of Spring. Main was more convenient from the PAB's exit and it put space between the reporter and his source. She saw the light at the intersection change and crossed, then followed 5th to Main Street. At the intersection, she casually looked around the corner and north on Main. There, about two blocks away in the direction of the PAB, she saw a man walking with a fast pace that she recognized as Feltzer's hard-charging gait.

Concerned that Feltzer would be more alert than Castor to the possibility of a tail, Ballard waited another ten minutes before heading up Main herself. When she got to First, she turned right and walked down into Little Tokyo.

At the Miyako Hotel she checked into a room after being assured by the desk clerk that there were several sushi choices on the room-service menu.

She got to the room and ordered dinner first thing. Then she opened her shoulder bag and laid out the clothes she planned to wear in the morning. The meeting with Feltzer was going to be pivotal.

While she waited for her food, she pulled out her phone and Googled the business number for defense attorney Dean Towson. She expected Towson wouldn't be in his office this late but he would most likely get her message. Defense attorneys were used to getting late-night calls from clients. And judging by how fearful Towson had grown by the end of Ballard's interview with him Sunday morning, he would return the call promptly.

The call went through to an answering service, and Ballard spoke to a live individual instead of a computer.

"My name is Detective Renée Ballard with the LAPD. I spoke to Mr. Towson Sunday morning about a murder investigation. Please get a message to Mr. Towson tonight. I need him to call me back as soon as possible, no matter how late. This is urgent."

She disconnected and began the wait.

To pass the time, she put on the room's television and was soon distracted by the political infighting and name-calling presented every night on cable TV.

Towson's callback came faster than the sushi.

31

At 8:25 a.m. Wednesday morning, Ballard walked into the FID offices at PAB with Dean Towson. It had been Towson's idea to arrive late and to ignore Lieutenant Feltzer's two calls and messages to Ballard, asking where she was. It put Feltzer on edge before they even got there.

As head of one of the unit's two squads, Feltzer had a private office. It was small and they had to wheel a chair in to accommodate Towson. He and Ballard sat across a desk from the visibly annoyed lieutenant, who had closed the door.

"Detective Ballard, I'm not sure why you see the need to have an attorney present," Feltzer said. "You are still subject to Lybarger and are compelled to answer questions. If anything criminal arises out of this investigation, then of course all statements from you will be disallowed."

He raised his hands off his desk in a gesture that suggested this was simple stuff and they did not need a lawyer to complicate it.

"I intend to fully cooperate and answer all questions," Ballard said. "But only if I have my attorney present. You said in your message that we needed to clear up some inconsistencies. Why don't we do that and not worry about my having representation?"

Feltzer considered it, clearly looking like a man worried about walking into a legal trap of some kind.

"We're going to record this," he finally said. "As with the first interview."

He opened a desk drawer and got out a digital recorder. As he was setting it to record, Towson removed his phone from the inside pocket of his suit coat and put it on the desk.

"We'll be recording the session as well," he said.

"Whatever floats your boat," Feltzer said.

"Thank you," Towson said.

"Let's start with the other victim, Beatrice Beaupre," Feltzer said. "In your statement yesterday, you said that she was unconscious when she was brought into the room by Trent."

"I believe I said she 'appeared' to be unconscious," Ballard said. "My focus was on Trent, not her."

"Ms. Beaupre has told us that she was in fact conscious at the time and was pretending not to be so that she might have a chance of escaping from Trent."

"Okay. That's entirely possible."

"She goes on to say that she saw you and Trent engage in the struggle that resulted in his fatal injuries. And her description of what happened differs markedly from yours."

"Well, she would definitely have had a different view of it."

"I'm giving you the chance to correct the record if you wish."

"I would just defer to Ms. Beaupre's account. I was engaged at the time in a life-and-death struggle with a man nearly twice my weight and size. I wasn't stopping to take notes or commit my moves to memory. I was trying to stay alive and to keep Ms. Beaupre alive as well."

It was an answer Ballard and Towson had rehearsed because they assumed that the discrepancies Feltzer alluded to in his phone message were the contradictions between her and Beaupre's statements. Ballard and Towson had met at six-thirty that morning in the breakfast room at the Miyako Hotel to prepare for the FID appointment. The rehearsed response covered all contradictions with the threshold factor in justified homicide. Fear of death or great bodily harm to the officer or citizenry.

"I think that covers it, Lieutenant," Towson said. "Do you have anything else for my client?"

Feltzer looked at Towson.

"Yes, I do," he said.

There was a confidence in Feltzer's voice that put Ballard on high alert.

"Have you had any communication with Ms. Beaupre since the incident occurred and you two were separated for questioning?" Feltzer asked.

"Nothing direct," Ballard said. "She called my cell phone yesterday and I didn't take the call. She left a message thanking me for saving her life. I haven't responded to the call yet, because I thought it would be inappropriate to speak with her before your investigation is concluded."

Another carefully crafted and rehearsed answer.

"I still have the message," Ballard said. "I could put it on speaker and play it for the recording if you wish."

"We'll get to that later if we need to," Feltzer said.

"Your late arrival has backed me into other appointments, so let's move on. Yesterday you said that when you managed to free yourself while Trent was gone, you did not immediately leave the house because you were not sure where you were and whether you could escape. Is that fair to say?"

"We are talking about a very brief moment," Ballard said. "Those were my thoughts initially, but then I heard the garage door and knew that Trent was back and that he most likely had another victim with him, because he had told me he was going to abduct his ex-wife."

"But your initial answer indicates you had no idea where you were."

"Well, I certainly assumed I was in Trent's house, and I knew where he lived because I had backgrounded him when he became a person of interest in my investigation."

"Had you ever previously been in that house?"

There it was. Feltzer had information he hadn't had when he'd questioned her the day before.

"No, I had never been inside that house," Ballard said.

She had to assume that the two North Hollywood patrol officers she had met on Wrightwood on Friday night had come forward.

"Had you ever been on the premises of Thomas Trent's home?" Feltzer asked.

"Yes, I had been on the premises," Ballard answered without hesitation.

Towson leaned slightly forward. He was now flying blind. Ballard had not discussed at breakfast her attempt to ghost Trent's house, because she'd had no idea

334

it would come up. Towson now had to trust that Ballard knew how to navigate this set of questions.

"How so, Detective Ballard?" Feltzer asked.

"On Friday evening I confirmed that Trent was at his job at the car dealership and I went to his house to look around," Ballard said. "My victim had described being taken to an upside-down house. I felt it was important to see if Trent's home matched that description."

"Detective, did you call in a false report of a prowler on Wrightwood Drive in order to facilitate this 'look around'?"

Towson put his hand on Ballard's arm to stop her from responding.

"She's not going to answer that," he said. "This is a use-of-force investigation. We are not going to discuss unrelated matters."

"It is related," Feltzer said. "My information is that Detective Ballard on Friday night was on the porch outside the room where she was later allegedly held captive and where she killed Thomas Trent. She said in her statement that she didn't know where she was and couldn't escape. That is in conflict with the facts I've accumulated."

"Being outside a room and being inside a room are completely different," Towson countered. "My client had been assaulted, drugged, and possibly raped—all of which affected her perceptions."

"The curtains were closed," Ballard added. "I didn't know I was in the room off that porch."

Towson waved a hand in a dismissive manner.

"This doesn't fly, Lieutenant," he said. "You are wasting our time. There is clearly an agenda here. You are attempting to build a case to dismiss Detective Ballard for reasons that don't exist. She didn't escape. She stayed back and risked her life to save another. Are you seriously trying to make this count against her? Where does this come from?"

"There is no agenda here," Feltzer said. "And I strenuously object to your characterization of this investigation. You are completely out of line."

"You want to talk about what's out of line?" Towson said. "This is what's out of line."

The lawyer opened his briefcase, took out the folded A section of that morning's *Los Angeles Times*, and dropped it on the desk. The story on the Trent killing had caught the bottom corner of the front page. The story was bylined with Jerry Castor's name.

"I have nothing to do with what the media reports," Feltzer said. "I have no say in how complete or incomplete the story is."

"Bullshit," Ballard said.

"This story includes details that go far beyond the official press release put out yesterday by the department," Towson said. "Not only that, but the release of selective details and the omission of others puts my client in an unfavorable light. It's a hit piece."

"We will look into how the *Times* came to have their information," Feltzer said.

"That's hardly reassuring when the investigator is probably the one who leaked it," Towson said.

"I warn you, sir," Feltzer said angrily. "I will put up with a lot from you, but I'm not going to allow you to assault my reputation. I play by the rules here."

Feltzer's face grew red with anger. He was putting

on a credible show. He was also playing directly into Ballard and Towson's hands.

"Your anger indicates that you would agree that the leaking of details outside the agreed-upon press release is a violation of Detective Ballard's privacy rights under the law and the policy of this department," Towson said.

"I told you, we are going to look into the leak," Feltzer said.

"Why?" Towson asked. "Was it illegal or just not fair?"

"It was against the law, okay?" Feltzer said. "We will investigate."

Towson pointed toward Feltzer's computer screen.

"Well, Lieutenant, we'd like to help with that investigation," he said. "Let me give you a link to pull up."

"What are you talking about?" Feltzer said. "What link?"

"It's a website that we will be directing LAPD command staff and local media to at a press conference later today," Towson said. "It's Jerry and Joe dot com. Pull up your server and check it out."

Feltzer's computer screen was on a side extension to his desk so that it would not be a visible barrier between him and anyone sitting across the main desk from him. He turned now and activated the screen. He pulled up his server and started typing in the website address.

"Jerry with a J," Ballard said. "As in Jerry Castor."

Feltzer paused for a moment, his fingers hovering over the keyboard.

"It's okay, Lieutenant," Towson said. "It's just a website."

Feltzer typed. The website opened on his screen. It was a single page with a nine-second video playing in a loop: a downward view of Feltzer meeting with Jerry Castor at the Last Bookstore the night before. Towson had hatched the idea for the site at breakfast and had bought the domain and set it up while he and Ballard were eating.

Feltzer watched the video in stunned silence. After the third loop, he killed the screen. He was turned away from Ballard and Towson, so neither one of them could fully see the look on his face. But his head bowed as he obviously considered his predicament. In seconds he determined that the time-stamped video spoke for itself and that his situation was untenable. Like the political animal the video revealed him to be, he slowly turned back to Ballard and Towson, a look on his face that was somewhere between panic and acceptance of dire consequences.

"So what do you want?" he said.

Ballard was elated. Their plan to corner Feltzer had worked flawlessly.

"We want this obvious effort to drive Detective Ballard from the department to stop right here," Towson said.

He waited and Feltzer nodded once, almost unnoticeably.

"And we want another story on the *Times* website by six p.m. tonight and in the hard copy tomorrow morning," Towson continued. "We want fuller details leaked to your friend Jerry Castor, details that put Detective Ballard in the positive light she deserves. I want to see words like *hero* and *in policy* and *justified* in the story."

"I can't control how they write," Feltzer protested. "You know that."

"Try, Lieutenant," Towson said. "Your friend Castor has just as much reason as you to set the record straight. He won't look good if this comes out in some of the media around town. He'll look like the shill for LAPD management that he is, and I don't think the editors across the street will like that."

"Okay, okay," Feltzer said. "That it?"

"No, not even close," Ballard said. "I want access to Trent's house and access to all evidence your team took out of there. There's still an investigation to conduct and close. I want to see if there is any indication that Trent did this to other victims."

Feltzer nodded.

"Done," he said.

"And another thing," Ballard said. "I go from here to BSU to get my psych exam. I want my return-to-duty slip expedited."

"You can't expect me to reach into BSU and—"

"Actually, we do expect it," Towson said, cutting Feltzer off. "You tell them you are under pressure from the chief's office to wrap this up and get Ballard back on the job because the chief wants hero cops back on the street."

"Okay, okay," Feltzer said. "I'll make it all happen. But I'll need you to take that link down. Somebody could stumble across it."

"It will go down when you make good on this agreement," Towson said. "Only then."

Towson looked at Ballard.

"We good?" he asked. "We covered everything?"

"I think so," she said.

"Then let's get out of here," he said.

Towson said it in a tone that made his disgust clear. He stood up and looked down at Feltzer. The detective lieutenant was pale, like he had just seen his life flash in front of his eyes. Or his career, at least.

"In a previous life, I worked J-SID cases at the D.A.'s Office," Towson said. "I've still got friends over there, and they're always looking to take down guys like you, guys who let ego and power go to their heads. Don't give me a reason to pick up a phone and get reacquainted."

Feltzer simply nodded. Towson and Ballard left the office and closed the door.

32

In the courtyard in front of the PAB, Ballard thanked Towson for saving her career. He said she had done that herself.

"You following the reporter last night—that was genius," he said. "That's all we needed, and the beauty of it is, it will keep Feltzer in line. As long as you have that, you're in good shape."

Ballard turned back to look up at the PAB. The tower of City Hall was reflected in the glass facade.

"My partner on the late show, he says PAB stands for Politics and Bullshit," she said. "This is one of the days I think he's right."

"You take care, Renée," Towson said. "Call if you need anything."

"You're going to invoice me, right?"

"I'll think about that. This is a situation where the accomplishment is its own reward. The look on Feltzer's face after he saw the loop? That was worth a million dollars."

"I'm not a pro bono case, Counselor. Send me a bill—just not for a million dollars."

"All right. I will."

The mention of money reminded Ballard of something.

"By the way, do you have a business card?" she asked.

"I'm going to recommend you to someone."

"Sure do," Towson replied.

He dug into his suit coat pocket and gave her a short stack of cards.

"Take a few," he said. "They're free."

She smiled and thanked him.

"You know, I forgot to ask: Has anyone from the Dancers case come to talk to you about Fabian?"

"I assume I have you to thank for that. Yes, I was interviewed."

"Who came?"

"A detective named Carr."

Ballard nodded.

"You tell him anything you didn't already tell me?" she asked.

"I don't think so," Towson said. "As I recall, you were quite thorough."

Ballard smiled again and they headed their separate ways, Towson across the courtyard toward the federal courthouse a block away, and Ballard to the steps that were to the east side of the PAB. She was pleased to hear that Carr had followed up with Towson. Maybe that meant he also was finally buying into her suggestion that a cop was involved in the shooting.

At the top of the stairs, Ballard turned right and went to the Memorial for Fallen Officers. It was a contemporary sculpture in which the names of officers killed in the line of duty were etched on brass plates and attached to a cagelike wooden edifice. Most of the brass plates had weathered over time, leaving those marking recent deaths brighter than the others. It was easy for her to pick out the brightest and shiniest plate. She stepped up and saw that it had the name Ken Chastain on it.

She stood there somberly for a few moments, until her phone buzzed, and she pulled it out of her back pocket. It was Rob Compton.

"Renée, I just heard! What the fuck! Are you okay?"

"I'm good."

"Why didn't you call me, baby? I just read about this in the fricking paper."

"Well, don't believe everything you read. That's not the whole story, and it's going to get fixed. I didn't call you yesterday because I didn't have my phone most of the day. I finally got to it last night. What's the story with the ATF?"

"Never mind, that can wait. I just want to make sure you're okay. When can we get together?"

"I don't want the ATF to wait, Robby. I need to stay busy. What've you got?"

She started walking down the steps and back to the courtyard. Her rental car was still in a lot behind the Times Building and she headed that way.

"Well, an agent from over there called me on the weapon search we put in," Compton said. "His name is John Welborne. You know him?"

"I can count on one finger the number of ATF agents I know," Ballard said. "I don't know him."

"Do you know it's now called the ATFE? They added Explosives."

"Nobody calls it that. Are you going to tell me or not?"

"Okay, well, this guy Welborne called about the stolen Glock that Nettles had. It's got a big-time flag on it. It was taken off a Brinks guard during an armored-car takedown two years ago in Dallas. I don't remember the case, but the guard it was taken from? He was executed with it. Same with his partner."

"Holy shit."

"Yeah, that's what I said. So at first they were thinking we had the guy—you know, Nettles. But Nettles was in prison at the time of this thing in Dallas. So the gun had to have been stolen a second time in one of the burglaries he committed."

"And probably a caper that went unreported. Because if you had a gun stolen that was used in a double murder armored-car job, you wouldn't call the cops and report a burglary. You'd lie low and hope that gun disappeared."

"Right. So here's the thing. These feds, they wouldn't normally stop to ask a parole agent shit. They'd just blow on by me. But we put these guns into the computer before we knew what was what—you know, like which house they were stolen from. So Welborne's calling me up, chomping at the bit, wanting to move on this."

"But he can't."

"Nope, he's stuck, waiting on me."

"Where is Nettles? Did he get sent back up yet?"

"Not yet. He's still in County and scheduled to go in front of the judge tomorrow."

Ballard was quiet as she thought through the situation. She was technically relieved of duty pending the psych exam and the FID case. She wondered if she could move her BSU appointment up and get it out of the way. She would really be counting on Feltzer to come through with the forced agreement to streamline everything.

"I'm supposed to be riding the pine because of this

other thing," she said. "But I'm hoping it clears today."

"No way they clear you that quick," he said. "Not with what's in the paper today."

"I've got somebody working on that. We'll see."

"So then, what do you want to do?"

"How much discretion do you have with Nettles?"

"Some, yeah. It's the weapons: felon with a firearm. That's the play."

"Well, I'm downtown right now. I have an appointment with Behavioral and then I could clear. We could go see Nettles at County and find out if he wants to help himself by telling us where he got the Glock. When he finds out it was used in a two-bagger, he'll probably be more than happy to disown it and tell us where it came from."

"Okay, I need a couple hours myself. I have something unrelated going and I need to clear a move like this. I don't think it will be a problem, but I just have to follow protocol and talk to the boss about trading with Nettles. How about we meet at Men's Central at twelve? That'll be lunch and they should be able to grab him up for us."

"See you then."

As Ballard headed to her car, she called Lieutenant McAdams at Hollywood Detectives.

"L-T, I'm not sure when or if I'll make it in today," she said.

"Ballard, you're supposed to be on the bench till this FID thing clears," McAdams said.

"I know. I'm down here at FID right now."

"What's going on?"

"I got called in for more questions. And after this, I

345

go to BSU for the psych exam. I don't know how long this will take."

"Did you see the *Times* today? More importantly, did FID see it?"

"Yeah, everybody's seen the *Times* and it's bullshit."

"Then where the fuck did it come from?"

"Good question, L-T."

"Ballard, a word to the wise, watch your ass."

"Roger that."

The Behavioral Science Unit was located in Chinatown. Ballard's appointment wasn't until 10:30, so she called to see if she could get it bumped up by a half hour or more. The phone receptionist almost laughed before telling her the request could not be accommodated.

With time to kill, Ballard got her car out of the pay lot and drove over to County-USC. She found that Ramona was no longer in the acute-care ward. She had been upgraded to fair condition, and with that came a change of rooms. She was now sharing a room with another patient. She was conscious and alert. The swelling around her eyes was way down and the bruising had moved to the yellow-green stage. The stitches had been removed from her lower lip as well. Ballard entered the room and smiled at her, but there didn't seem to be any recognition.

"Ramona, I'm Detective Ballard. I'm assigned to your case. I came by on Monday. Do you remember?"

"Not really."

The voice was unmistakably male.

"I showed you photos? To see if one was of the man who hurt you."

"I'm sorry."

346

"No, it's okay. In fact, it doesn't really matter now. That's why I came by. To tell you that the man who hurt you is dead. So you don't have to be afraid or worry about him anymore. He's gone."

"You're sure it was him?"

"Very sure, Ramona."

"Okay."

She looked down as though she might be about to cry at the news. Ballard knew Ramona was safe now, but only from one predator. She was leading a life that was sure to bring more. Ballard pulled one of the cards she got from Towson out of her pocket and held it up.

"I wanted to give you this. This is a lawyer I've worked with, and I think he's pretty good."

"Why do I need a lawyer? What do they say I did?"

"Oh, no, nothing like that. I'm not supposed to give out legal advice, but if I was, I would tell you that you should sue the estate of the man who did this to you. I am pretty sure he had a large amount of money invested in his house. I think you should get a lawyer and go after some of that money. He victimized you, and you should collect from his estate before anybody else does."

"Okay."

But Ramona did not reach out for the business card. Ballard put it down on the table next to her bed.

"It's right there when you need it."

"Okay, thanks."

"I'm going to leave my own card too. Later on, you will probably have questions. You can give me a call."

"Okay."

It was an awkward exit, because with the case concluded by Trent's death, there was no need for Ballard to

347

spend more time with Ramona. As she left the hospital, Ballard wondered if she would ever see her again. Perhaps, she thought, she had suggested the lawsuit against Trent's estate because she knew she would be called in to testify about the case.

She wondered if it was a subconscious move to seek the kind of fulfillment that came from taking a case from beginning to end. Trent was dead but Ballard might still be able to take him to trial and get a guilty verdict.

33

Ballard sat in an office with Dr. Carmen Hinojos, the director of the Behavioral Science Unit. The room was decorated in blond wood, cream-colored walls, and pale curtains. The window looked across the roofs of Chinatown toward the spire of City Hall. They sat facing each other in comfortably cushioned chairs that contradicted the uncomfortable situation for Ballard.

"Have you ever killed anyone before?" Hinojos asked.

"No," Ballard said. "First time."

"How are you feeling about it today?"

"To be honest, I feel fine about it. If I hadn't killed him, he would have killed me. I have no doubt."

She immediately regretted starting her answer with "to be honest." Usually when people said that, they were being anything but honest.

The session continued down avenues of questioning Ballard had fully expected. As with almost every situation an officer faced regarding internal investigations and procedures, she was well versed in what would be asked and how it should best be answered. The union newsletters carried case examples all the time that were analyzed in depth. Ballard knew that the important thing to say and project with Hinojos was that there was no second-guessing of her actions up to and including

349

the killing of Trent. Showing regret or remorse would be wrong moves. The department needed to be assured that if returned to duty, she would not have any hesitation in doing her job, that she would not hesitate if placed in a kill-or-be-killed situation.

Ballard was calm and forthright during the interview and showed discomfort only when Hinojos veered away from questions about the Trent killing to asking about her childhood and the path she took to law enforcement.

Ballard began to feel like she was trapped. She had to reveal herself to a stranger or risk that her return to duty would be delayed by further analysis or treatment. Ballard didn't want that. She didn't want to ride the pine. She tried to put a positive spin on things in terms of the good things she had learned from bad experiences. But even she knew that finding the positive in things like her father's untimely death, her mother's abandonment of her as a teenager, and the year she spent homeless was a difficult task.

"Maui has the prettiest beaches in the world," Ballard said at one point. "I surfed every morning before going to school."

"Yes, but you had no home to go to and a mother who didn't care," Hinojos said. "No one should face that at that age."

"It wasn't that long. Tutu came for me."

"Tutu?"

"Hawaiian for *grandmother*. She brought me back here. To Ventura."

Hinojos was an older woman with white hair and golden-brown skin. She had been with the department for more than thirty years. On her lap was an open file that contained the psychological report drawn from the examination conducted when Ballard had first applied to the LAPD fifteen years earlier. Much of the history was there. Ballard hadn't known enough at the time to keep her past to herself.

Ballard had not been back to BSU since that initial exam.

"Dr. Richardson has an interesting workup here," Hinojos said, referring to the initial examiner. "He says disorder in your young life drew you to law enforcement. A job where you enforce laws and enforce order. What do you think about that?"

"Well," Ballard said, stalling. "I think we need to have rules. They are what makes society civilized."

"And Thomas Trent broke the rules, didn't he?"

"Yes, big-time."

"If you had the chance to relive the past seventy-two hours and make smarter choices, do you think Thomas Trent would still be alive?"

"I don't know about smarter choices. I think I made the right choice in the moment. I would prefer answering questions about what did happen and why. Not speculation about what could have happened or what could have been."

"So no regrets, then?"

"Sure, I have regrets but not for what you probably think."

"Try me. What regrets?"

"Don't get me wrong, I had no choice. It was him or me. In that situation I have zero regrets, and if faced with the same circumstances, I would do what I did again. But I do wish he were still alive so I could arrest him and we could take him to trial and he would rot in prison for what he did."

"You believe that by being stabbed and losing his life he got off easy."

Ballard thought for a moment and then nodded.

"Yeah, I do."

Hinojos closed the file.

"Okay, Detective Ballard, thank you for your candor," she said.

"Wait, that's it?" Ballard asked.

"That's it."

"Well, do I get the RTD?"

"That will be forthcoming, but I am going to suggest that you take some time off to recuperate mentally. You have been through a trauma, and there are unanswered questions about what happened to you when you were drugged. Your mind is bruised as well as your body. Like the body, the mind needs time to heal. It needs time to settle from this."

"I appreciate that, Doctor. I really do. But I have active cases. I need to wrap them up and then I can take time off."

Hinojos smiled in a tired sort of way, as if she had heard what Ballard said a thousand times before.

"I guess all cops come in here and say the same thing," Ballard said.

"I can't blame them," Hinojos said. "They are worried about losing their jobs and identities, not worried about the consequence both have on them. What would you do if you were not a police officer?"

Ballard thought for a moment.

"I don't know," she said. "I haven't thought about it."

Hinojos nodded.

"I've done this a long time," she said. "I've seen long careers and careers cut short. The difference is in how you handle the darkness."

"The darkness?" Ballard said. "I work the late show. There is nothing but—"

"I'm talking about the darkness within. You have a job, Detective, that takes you into the bleakest side of the human soul. Into the darkness of people like Trent. To me it's like the laws of physics—for every action, there is an opposite and equal reaction. If you go into darkness, the darkness goes into you. You then have to decide what to do with it. How to keep yourself safe from it. How to keep it from hollowing you out."

She paused there and Ballard knew not to speak.

"Find something that protects you, Detective Ballard."

Hinojos got up from her chair then and the session was over. She walked Ballard to the room's door. Ballard nodded a good-bye.

"Thank you, Doctor."

"Stay safe, Detective Ballard."

34

Ballard was twenty minutes late getting to Men's Central Jail, but Compton was there, waiting for her. They signed in and Ballard stowed her backup gun in a locker before they were placed in an interview room to wait while Christopher Nettles was located and brought to them.

"How are we going to do this?" Ballard asked.

"Let me do the talking," Compton said. "He knows I'm the one with the power. I filed on him with the gun. That's our currency."

"Sounds like a plan."

While they waited, Compton reached over and lifted Ballard's hands and somberly studied the bandages on her wrists.

"I know, it looks like I tried to end it all," she said. "I'll only need the bandages for a week."

"The bastard," Compton said. "I'm just glad you put him down."

Ballard told Compton the short version of what had happened with Trent and how an illegal leak to the *Time*s had bent the story against her. Compton shook his head. Ballard decided not to tell him about how the rough sex they had had Saturday morning had hindered the ability of the RTC nurse to determine if she had been raped. That discussion could keep for another time.

354

The conversation as it was ended when the door opened and Nettles was escorted in by two jail deputies. He immediately objected to the presence of Ballard, claiming that she had mistreated him during his arrest.

"Sit down and shut up," Compton said sternly. "You don't get to decide things like that."

The deputies put him in a chair and locked one of his wrists to a steel ring at the center of the table.

"So what do you want?" Nettles said.

Compton waited until the deputies stepped out.

"Do you have any idea about your situation, Christopher?" he asked. "You're going up in front of a judge tomorrow. Has a lawyer been by to talk to you?"

"Not yet," Nettles said.

He flicked his cuffed hand in a gesture that suggested he wasn't worried.

"Well, the reason you haven't seen a lawyer is that a lawyer isn't going to be able to help you," Compton said. "Your parole has been revoked and you're going back up to Corcoran, and there isn't a damn thing a lawyer can do about it."

"I only had a bullet left," Nettles said. "I can do that, no sweat off my balls."

He looked at Ballard as he said it. Ballard knew that a bullet was a year in the pen.

"And what? You think the D.A.'s going to just let all those burglaries slide?" Compton asked.

"What I hear people saying in here is that all the D.A.'ll do is stack 'em right next to my current situation, and I won't do an extra day on account of overcrowding," Nettles said. "How 'bout that?"

"Then how about the felon with a gun charge I just added to your résumé? That's five years stacked on top of the bullet. You can do that, no sweat off your balls?"

"The fuck you talking about, man?"

"I'm talking about a plus-five."

"That's bullshit!"

Nettles shook the handcuff violently. He pointed his free hand at Ballard.

"This is because of you, bitch!" he yelled.

"Don't blame me for your crimes," Ballard threw back at him. "Blame yourself."

Ballard kept her hands on her lap and below the table. She was wearing a long-sleeved blouse, but she didn't want to risk Nettles seeing the bandages around her wrists and asking questions.

"Look, Christopher, why do you think we're here?" Compton said. "You think we get off on giving you the bad news?"

"Probably," Nettles said. "She does."

"Actually, you're wrong," Compton said. "We're not here to bring bad news. We're the light at the end of your tunnel. We came to help you help yourself."

Nettles settled down. He knew there was a deal to be made now. He looked suspiciously at Compton.

"What do you want?" he asked.

"I want to know about the guns," Compton said. "I want to know where you stole them from. I want addresses, details. You give me that, and we start subtracting from the total. You see?"

Ballard appreciated that Compton was not directly asking about the Glock. It was better not to reveal their

356

specific intention to Nettles. The ex-con might then attempt to manipulate the interview.

"I don't know, man," Nettles whined. "How am I supposed to remember addresses?"

"Think," Compton said. "You must have some idea what houses you hit. Start with the gun you were carrying. The Glock model seventeen. You must've liked it, because you didn't pawn it. Where'd that come from?"

Nettles leaned forward and put the elbow of his free arm down on the table. He used his free hand to work his jaw like *The Thinker* as he considered the question.

"Well first of all, all three of those guns came from the same house," he finally said. "I just don't remember the fucking address. Don't you people get burglary reports for these things?"

Compton ignored the question.

"What about the street?" he asked. "Do you remember the street name?"

"No, I don't remember any street name," Nettles said.

Ballard had connected six of the credit cards found in Nettles's room at the Siesta Village with burglary reports where no firearms were reported as taken. This meant those victims had either lied about the guns or there was at least one burglary committed by Nettles that was not reported—most likely because a murder weapon had been stolen. The six known cases had all been located on streets a few blocks from the Siesta Village, creating a pattern extending north, east, and west from the motel.

There was no freeway or other impediment to accessing the neighborhood south of the motel, and yet none of the known burglaries had occurred there. This told Ballard that the house they were looking for might be south.

"Did you ever hit any houses south of the motel where you were staying?" Ballard asked.

"South?" Nettles responded. "Uh, yeah, I hit south."

Compton threw her a look. She wasn't supposed to ask the questions. But she continued the line of inquiry.

"Okay, how many times did you go south?"

"Once or twice. The houses that way weren't as nice. People had junk."

"When did you hit down there?"

"When I first started."

"Okay, according to the motel, you had been there nine days before your arrest. So in the first couple days, you went south?"

"I guess so."

"How long have you had the guns?"

"It was one of the first ones."

"From south of the motel?"

"Yeah, I guess. I think it was the second. Yeah, the second. The guy thought he was real fucking clever hiding the guns behind the books on his shelves, but I always knock the books off the shelves. Right to the floor. People hide all kinds of good shit behind the books. That's how I found the guns."

Ballard took out her phone and went to the GPS app. She pulled up a map centered on Santa Monica Boulevard and Wilton Place, where the Siesta Village motel was located. She started reading off the names of streets to the south. Saint Andrews, Western, Ridgewood,

Romaine—Nettles kept shaking his head until she came to Sierra Vista.

"Wait," he said. "Sierra Vista. That sounds familiar. I think that's it."

"What did the house look like?" Ballard asked.

"I don't know, it looked like a house."

"Did it have a garage?"

"Yeah, a garage in the back. Separate."

"One floor, two floors?"

"One. I don't fuck around with two-story jobs."

"Okay, was it brick, wood structure, what?"

"Not brick."

"How'd you get in?"

"I went in the backyard, and popped a slider by the pool."

"Okay, so there was a pool."

"Yeah, next to the garage."

"So there was a gate, then? Like a fence around the pool?"

"The whole backyard. It was locked and I climbed over."

"Was it a wall or a fence?"

"Fence."

"What color was the fence?"

"It was like gray. Stained gray."

"How'd you know nobody was home?"

"I was parked on the street and I saw the guy leave."

"In a car?"

"Yeah."

"What kind of car? What color?"

"It was a Camaro. Yellow. I remember the car. Cool car. I wanted that car."

"How'd you know the place was empty? Just because the guy drove off didn't mean the house wasn't full with a wife and kids."

"I know, I always knock on the front door. I have a work shirt with my name on the pocket. I act like I'm a gas inspector looking for a leak. If somebody answers, I just go through the motions and go to the next one."

"So, what did the front door look like?" she asked.

"Uh, it was yellow," Nettles said. "Yeah, yellow. I remember because it was like the car. The dude liked yellow."

Ballard and Compton exchanged a look, though they said nothing. They had what they needed for now. A yellow door and yellow car on Sierra Vista. It wouldn't be hard to find.

35

There was no yellow door on Sierra Vista. Ballard and Compton drove up and down its four-block stretch four times in the Taurus but saw no door painted yellow.

"You think Nettles intentionally fucked us?" Ballard asked.

"If he did, he only fucked himself," Compton said. "The deal is based on results."

Compton turned and looked out the side window, a sign to Ballard that he was holding something back.

"What?" she said.

"Nothing," he said.

"Come on, what's wrong?"

"I don't know, maybe you should have stuck with the plan and let me handle the questions."

"You were taking too long and I got him describing the house. Don't pout."

"I'm not pouting, Renée. But here we are, Sierra Vista. Where's the yellow door?"

He gestured through the windshield. Ballard ignored the complaint. It was unfounded. If he hadn't believed Nettles, he would have said something in the interview room. He didn't, and now he was blaming Ballard for the seeming failure of the move.

She came to a point where Sierra Vista dead-ended into a T and she pulled over. She looked at the map on her phone screen to see if the street continued elsewhere. She found nothing and used her thumb and finger to expand the map. She checked other streets in the neighborhood to see if there was another Sierra. There wasn't, but there was a Serrano Place two blocks south. She put the phone down and pulled the car away from the curb.

"Where are we going?" Compton asked.

"I want to check out another street over here," Ballard said. "Serrano, Sierra—maybe Nettles got it wrong."

"They don't even sound close."

"Yes they do. You're just pouting."

Serrano Place was only one block long. They covered it quickly, Ballard checking the houses on the left and Compton the right.

"Wait a minute," Compton said.

Ballard stopped. She looked out his window at a house with a French door with a yellow frame. The house had tongue-and-groove wood siding. No bricks.

She inched the car forward past the driveway and saw that there was a single-car garage detached from the house at the back of the property. A wooden fence, grayed by exposure to the elements, enclosed the backyard.

"The fence is weathered, not stained," she said. "Think there's a pool back there?"

"If I wasn't pouting, I'd say yes," Compton said.

She punched him in the shoulder and kept driving. Two houses down the street, she pulled to the curb.

"Take off your belt," Ballard said.

"What?" Compton said.

"Take off your belt. It will look like a leash. I'm going to see if there's a pool. If I had my van, I'd have a real leash, but your belt will have to do."

Compton got it. He slipped off his belt and handed it to her.

"Be right back," she said.

"Be careful," he said. "Fire a shot if you need me."

She got out and walked down the sidewalk back to the house with the yellow French door. She dangled the belt from one hand and called the name Lola out repeatedly. She walked up the driveway that ran next to the house.

"Lola! Here, girl."

She smelled the pool before she saw it. The sharp odor of chlorine pervaded the rear of the house. She got to the weathered fence and had to stand on her toes to catch a glimpse of what was on the other side. She confirmed the pool and was making a turn to go back out to the street when her eyes caught on the row of windows that ran along the top of the garage door. She hesitated because she wasn't tall enough to look through the glass. Then she saw the handle on the door, situated about a foot off the driveway surface.

Ballard stepped over. She put one foot on the handle and tested some of her weight against it. It felt sturdy enough. She put her full weight on the handle, and her fingers gripped the thin sill below the windows. She pushed herself up the garage door and looked in.

Parked in the garage was a yellow Camaro.

She dropped to her heels and turned to get back to her car. A man was standing in the driveway, looking at her.

"Oh, hey, have you seen a dog?" Ballard said quickly. "A brindle boxer mix?"

"You mean in my garage?" the man said.

"Sorry about that, but when she gets loose, she likes to hide. It's a real pain in the butt."

He was Latino and wearing workout pants, running shoes, and a hoodie, like he was heading out for a jog. She kept her arm in motion so the dangling belt would not be still enough for him to see that it wasn't a leash. She headed past him toward the street, hoping to not forget the plate number she had read off the Camaro.

"Do you live around here?" the man asked.

"Over on Sierra Vista," Ballard said. "Have a nice day."

She kept moving down the driveway. When she got to the street, she called her dog's name out a few more times but walked on. She got to the Taurus and jumped back in.

"Fuck, fuck, fuck, I blew it," she said.

She wanted to run the Camaro's plate before she forgot the number, but she realized she didn't have a rover, and of course the rental car had no police radio.

"What happened?" Compton asked.

She was watching her side mirror, expecting to see the man step out of the driveway to track her.

"A guy came out," she said. "I think he made me."

"How?" Compton asked.

"I don't know. Something about his eyes. He made me."

"Then let's blow."

There was no sign of the man in the mirror. She started the car. Just then, she saw the Camaro come out of the driveway and turn the opposite way down Serrano.

"There he goes," she said. "Yellow Camaro."

She waited until the Camaro turned right at the end of the block and was out of sight. She U-turned away from the curb and headed in the same direction. She pulled her phone and called the communications center on speed dial. She then recited the license plate and requested a computer run.

"I'll hold," she said.

At the corner, she turned right. There was no sign of the Camaro. She gunned the Taurus, and they headed north, block by block, checking right and left for the Camaro. They didn't see it.

"You think you spooked him?" Compton asked.

"I don't know," Ballard said. "He saw me looking through the window of the garage at the car."

"Shit."

"Well, what would you have—"

The dispatcher came back with the information and Ballard repeated it so Compton could get it.

"Eugenio Santana Perez, seven fourteen 'seventy-five. No record. Thank you."

She disconnected.

"The guy's clean," Compton said. "Maybe we're barking up the wrong tree."

"Yellow door, yellow Camaro—it's him," Ballard said. "He matches Nettles's story. Maybe the guy just bought the gun off somebody, but it's not the wrong tree."

They made their way up to Santa Monica, and there was still no sign of the Camaro.

"Right or left?" Ballard said.

"Fuck it," Compton said. "He blew right out of there after seeing you. Now I have to call Welborne and tell him we may have fucked this up."

"Not yet."

"What are we going to do?"

"Just chill. I'm not finished looking. Besides, there's still the house. You can give ATF-*E* that."

She saw an opening in the traffic and went straight, crossing Santa Monica and staying north. They continued to check streets until they got to Sunset. She then took a right toward the 101 freeway.

"I'll take you back downtown," Ballard said, defeat in her voice.

"This is fucked up," Compton said.

But as they approached the southbound freeway ramp, Ballard saw a glimpse of yellow two blocks ahead. A yellow car had turned into a lot and disappeared.

"Wait, did you see that?" she said. "It was yellow."

"I didn't see shit," Compton said. "Where?"

Ballard drove past the freeway ramp and kept east on Sunset. When she got to the turn-in the yellow car had taken, she saw it was to a Home Depot with a massive parking lot. The entrance was clear and she remembered how it always used to be lined with men looking for day work. That had changed when Immigration and Customs Enforcement started routine immigration roundups.

Ballard pulled in and started cruising the lot. They came upon the yellow Camaro in a spot in the far corner. There were plenty of spaces closer to the entrance to Home Depot, so it appeared abandoned there. Ballard checked the plate. It was the car they were looking for.

"Shit," she said.

"He's gone," Compton said. "Fuck, another guy who watched *Heat* too many times."

"What?"

"The movie *Heat*. From the nineties? Inspired the North Hollywood bank shoot-out?"

"I was on a surfboard in Hawaii most of the nineties."

"This guy played by De Niro was a robber. He had one rule: first sign of heat, you have to be able to leave everything behind. Just like that."

Ballard kept cruising, looking at the faces of men on foot in the parking lot, hoping to see the man from the driveway.

She had no luck. Finally, she turned the car into the corner of the lot and came to a stop. Through the windshield they could see the Camaro fifty yards away.

"This is so fucked," Compton said. "We should've just called Welborne. Instead, I listened to you about doing it ourselves."

"Are you fucking kidding me?" Ballard said. "You're blaming *me*? You wanted this just as much as I did."

"You're the one who always has to win. To show the guys up."

"Holy shit, I can't believe you. If you're so worried about the feds, why don't you just Uber your ass out of here. I'll call Welborne and give him what we've got and put it all on me. I mean, why not, right? Everybody else wants to blame me for everything. Just get the fuck out of the car."

Compton looked at her.

"You're serious?" he asked.

"Deadly," Ballard said. "Get the fuck out."

With his eyes still on her, Compton opened his door like he was threatening to leave if she didn't stop him.

She didn't.

Compton got out and looked back in at her. She said nothing and kept her gaze on the Camaro. He slammed the door. She refused to turn to watch him walk away.

"And another one bites the dust," she said to herself.

36

Ballard didn't get to Hollywood Division until almost five o'clock. She had spent most of the afternoon dealing with ATFE and FBI agents, explaining her moves that morning after the interview with Nettles. She left Compton out of it, telling the agents she had acted on her own after leaving Men's Central. The upset of the feds was mollified to a small degree when she looked at a set of photos they had and identified the man she had seen in the driveway. They said Eugenio Santana Perez was an alias but refused to tell her what his real name was. It was clearly a we'll-take-it-from-here situation with a heavy tone of you-fucked-this-up-and-now-we-have-to-unfuck-it to top it off.

The feds impounded the Camaro and were waiting on a warrant to enter the house on Serrano Place when Ballard was dismissed with a sarcastic thank-you from Agent Welborne. Back at the station, she pulled a gray interoffice envelope out of her mailbox and went to the lieutenant's office to get her new desk assignment. McAdams was standing at his desk, taking his gun out of the drawer and clipping it to his belt, a sign that he was heading home. Things were winding down across the entire bureau.

"Ballard, you decided to show up," he said.

"Sorry, I got tied up downtown, and while I was

there, I went to check on my victim from the Trent case," she said. "Is there a specific desk you want me to take?"

McAdams pointed out the window of his office to the desk on the other side of the glass. It was the worst desk in the house because it was right outside his office and the computer was positioned so that the lieutenant could see its screen at any time. It was known in the squad as the sitting-duck desk.

"I was going to put you there, but now it looks like I don't even have to find somebody for the late show," he said.

"What do you mean?" Ballard asked.

"Well, you must've talked a good game of it down there today, because, the *L.A. Times* be damned, I just got the word that FID is calling the Trent killing within policy. And not only that, you got your RTD too. Congratulations."

Ballard felt a great weight lift off her shoulders.

"I hadn't heard," she said. "That seems quick."

"Whoever your defense rep was, he's going to be in high demand, I'll tell you that," McAdams said. "The picture the *Times* drew up this morning wasn't pretty."

"I didn't use one."

"Then that makes this one even more worth celebrating. But if there's a K party, I don't want to know about it."

McAdams seemed to be giving a tacit nod of approval to a kill party. It had once been a secret tradition for officers to gather and drink after one of them had killed someone. It was a way of releasing the tension of a life-and-death encounter. Once the department formed the

FID to seriously investigate all officer-involved killings, the parties were pushed back until after an FID recommendation was released. Either way, the K party was anachronistic, and if they occurred at all now, it was only under deep secrecy. The last thing Ballard was interested in doing was celebrating her killing of Thomas Trent.

"Don't worry, no K party," she said.

"Good," McAdams said. "Anyway, I'm outta here. Since you've been at it all day, I'll leave Jenkins solo tonight, and you go back on shift starting tomorrow. All good?"

"Yeah, all good. Thanks, L-T."

Ballard looked around and saw an empty desk with a reasonably new computer monitor on it. It was far away from the lieutenant's office and the sitting-duck desk. But when she got there, she noticed a mug of coffee and paperwork spread across the work space. She then did a pivot and spotted another desk nearby in the burglary row that looked empty and unused and had a decent monitor.

She sat down and the first thing she did was go online to see if the *Times* had anything on the FID investigation that corrected the morning's story. There wasn't anything yet. She pulled out one of the business cards she had gotten from Towson and started writing him an e-mail, detailing what she had heard from her lieutenant and reporting that there was no action on it so far from the *Times*. Her cell phone buzzed just as she hit the send button. It was Rogers Carr of Major Crimes.

"Hey, did you get my message?"

"I got it, thanks."

"So how are you doing?"

"I'm doing all right. My L-T just told me I'm off the pine because FID is calling it within policy."

"Of course it was within policy, are you kidding me? It was totally justified."

"Well, you never know. This may come as a surprise to you but I've pissed some people off in the department."

"You? I find that hard to believe."

That was enough sarcastic banter for Ballard.

"So I heard you checked out my lead with the lawyer," she said. "Towson."

"Who told you that?" Carr asked.

"I have sources."

"You were talking to the lawyer, weren't you?"

"Maybe. So what's the story?"

Carr didn't say anything.

"Holy shit," Ballard said. "You take my lead and run with it and now you won't even tell me what you got from it? I think we're having our last conversation, Detective Carr."

"It's not that," Carr said. "It's just that I don't think you're going to like what I tell you."

Then it was Ballard who was silent, but not for too long.

"Tell me," she said.

"Well, yeah, your lead has panned out," Carr said. "Towson said Fabian told him he could deliver a bent cop. Then we got the ballistics back today and that sort of pivoted things around here."

"'Pivoted'? Why is that?"

"They didn't match. The weapon used to kill Ken Chastain was not the same one used in the booth at

372

the Dancers. The theory at the moment is two different shooters."

"They're saying the cases aren't connected?"

"No, they aren't saying that. Just two weapons, two different shooters."

Ballard knew she didn't have the full picture. If the two cases weren't linked by a weapon, then there was something else.

"So what am I missing?" she asked.

"Well, that wasn't the full ballistics report," Carr said.

"Carr, come on, stop dicking around."

"They identified the weapons off the slugs and brass. The gun in the booth was a ninety-two F. And in the garage, it was a Ruger three-eighty."

Ballard knew that bullet casings collected at the crime scenes and the slugs from the bodies revealed markings identifiable to specific models of firearms. Firing pins and gun-barrel rifling left proprietary indentations and striations.

She also knew the significance of the weapons identified. The 92F was a 9-millimeter Beretta, and it was on the list of firearms approved by the department for carry by detectives. The Ruger was a small popper that was easily concealed and used for close-in work. It, too, was on the department's approved list for backup weapons.

It also was a hitter's gun.

Ballard was silent while she considered this information. The one piece she reluctantly added to it was her knowledge that Chastain carried a Beretta 92F, or at least he had when they were partners. It drew a question she hated to ask.

"Chastain carried a ninety-two F. Did they run his gun against the slugs from the Dancers?"

"They would have if they had his gun."

That was new information.

"You're saying whoever shot him then reached inside his jacket and took his gun?"

"Apparently. His weapon has not been recovered."

"So what are they thinking?"

"I was redirected today. I was told to take a deep dive into Chastain. Dig up everything."

"That is bullshit. He's not the Dancers shooter."

"How do you know that?"

"I just do. I knew him and this isn't him."

"Well, tell that to Lieutenant Olivas."

"What exactly is he saying?"

"He's not saying anything. At least to me. But one of those guys that got killed in the booth was mobbed up."

"Yeah, Gino Santangelo. Out of Vegas."

"Well, you can take it from there."

Ballard thought for a moment.

"Take it where?" she said. "I totally don't get this."

"You're the one who first said it was a cop. You were just looking at the wrong cop."

"So Chastain is the booth shooter. He kills a mob guy and then the mob hits him back. That's the working theory? Well, I don't buy it. Why would Kenny do it?"

"That's why we're doing the deep dive. And actually, that's why I called you."

"Forget it. I'm not going to help you pin this on Chastain."

"Listen to me, we're not going to pin this on anyone. If it's not there, it's not there, but we have to look."

"What do you want from me?"

"Four years ago you two were partners."

"Yes."

"He was in financial trouble then. Did he talk to you about it?"

The news was surprising to Ballard.

"He never said a word. What kind of trouble and how do you know?"

"Deep dive, remember? I pulled his credit history. He missed nine payments on the house and was in foreclosure. He was going to lose the house and then, all of a sudden, it all went away. The bank was paid off and he got solvent—like overnight. Any idea how?"

"I told you I didn't even know about the problem. He never told me. Have you talked to Shelby? Maybe somebody in the family helped them out."

"Not yet. We want to know more before we go to her. That's not going to be pretty."

Ballard was silent. She couldn't remember a time when Chastain seemed to be under any sort of pressure from outside the job, financially or otherwise. He was always steady-going.

She thought of something Carr hadn't covered.

"What about Metro?" she asked.

"Metro?" Carr said. "What do you mean?"

"The kid. The witness. Matthew Robison."

"Oh, him. He calls himself Metro? We still haven't found him. And frankly, we're not expecting to."

"But how does he fit into the theory?"

"Well, we know he called Chastain on Friday about

five and Chastain went to find him. We think he thought Robison was a threat."

"So he takes out Robison, hides or buries the body somewhere, and then goes home. Only there's a mob hit man waiting there and he pops Chastain in the head before he can even get out of the car."

"And takes his gun."

"Right, and takes his gun."

They were both silent for a long time after that. Until Ballard addressed the elephant in the room.

"Olivas is still steering all of this?"

"He's in charge. But don't go down that road, Renée. The ballistics are the ballistics. That's not something you can steer. And the financials are what they are as well."

"But why take the gun? The shooter in the garage. Why did he take the thing that would prove or disprove all of this? Without having that gun for comparison, this is all circumstantial. It's theory."

"There could be a hundred reasons why the gun was taken. And speaking of circumstantial, there is one other thing."

"What?"

"We checked with Internal Affairs on Chastain, and there wasn't an open file on him. But they had a string file, where they put the anonymous stuff that comes in. It runs from complaints about 'some cop was rude to me' to 'some cop keeps coming into my store and taking orange juice without paying'—ticky-tacky stuff like that."

"Okay."

"Well, like I said, they had no open file on Chastain,

but there were two anonymous reports in the string file about an unnamed cop getting into card games and then not being able to cover his losses."

"What card games?"

"Didn't say, but you know if a guy wants to get into a high-stakes game in this town, then he can find a game. If you move in that world."

Ballard shook her head, even though she knew Carr could not see this. She looked around to make sure her conversation wasn't being heard. The squad room was almost empty now, as most detectives began to shut things down by four every day. Still, she leaned into the shelter of her cubicle and spoke quietly to Carr.

"I'm still not buying it," she said. "You guys have nothing but a missing gun, and like you said, there could be a hundred reasons why it's gone. It's like you're more interested in pinning this on Chastain than in finding out who killed him."

"There you go with that word again," Carr said. "We aren't 'pinning' anything on anybody. And you know what, I really don't understand you, Renée. Everybody knows that two years ago Chastain hung you out to dry, you lost the upward trajectory of your career and ended up working the late show. And here you are, defending him in a situation where there is clearly a lot of smoke. I mean, a *lot* of smoke."

"Well, that's the thing, right? A lot of *smoke*. Back when I worked downtown, before I supposedly 'lost my upward trajectory,' we needed more than smoke. We needed a lot more."

"If there is fire, we're going to find it."

"Good luck with that, Carr. I'll talk to you later."

Ballard disconnected and sat frozen at the desk. She had started the theory that the Dancers shooter was a cop. Now that theory was a monster and had Chastain in its sights.

She wondered how long it would be before Carr found out that the backup gun on her ankle was a Ruger 380.

37

Ballard calmed herself. The Ruger on her ankle was on the department's short list of approved backups. She and probably a thousand other cops owned one.

She then started overthinking it, wondering if Carr already knew she had one and the purpose of the phone call was to see if she'd bring it up voluntarily. Her keeping quiet may have landed her on the suspect list.

"They are really thinking a cop did the Dancers thing?"

Ballard swiveled in her chair and saw a detective named Rick Tigert sitting at the desk directly behind hers. She had not realized that he could have overheard her half of the conversation with Carr.

"Look, don't repeat that anywhere, Rick," she said quickly. "I thought you had left."

"I won't, but if it's true, the department's going to be dragged through the shit once again," Tigert said.

"Yeah, well, some things can't be helped. Look, I don't know if it's true, but just keep it to yourself."

"Yeah, no problem."

Ballard turned back to her temporary desk and started opening the interoffice envelope that she had found in her mail slot. The previous recipient had his name crossed out on the address line, just above Ballard's name. It said Feltzer/ FID. The envelope contained copies of the search warrant return executed at Thomas Trent's house the day before. Feltzer had made good on his coerced promise to share. The return was the document submitted to the court that had authorized the warrant. The law required law enforcement to report back to the judge so that there was an outside authority standing vigilant against unlawful search and seizure. The returns were usually very detailed about every item taken during a search. Feltzer had also supplemented this with a stack of crime scene photos of each item seized in the place where it was found.

Ballard tried to put the Chastain matter out of her mind for the time being by jumping back onto the Trent case. She studied the list of items taken from the house on Wrightwood. Most were common items that served a purpose in a household or workshop but could take on sinister qualities when in the possession of a suspected serial sex offender. Things like duct tape, zip ties, pliers, a ski mask. The zinger was the collection of brass knuckles from a drawer in a bedside table in the master bedroom. There was no further description of them, so Ballard immediately flipped to the photos and found the shot of four pairs of brass knuckles in the drawer. Each set was of unique design and materials, but all carried the same words on the impact plates. *GOOD* and *EVIL*. Ballard assumed that one of the sets was the weapon that Ramona Ramone had been tortured with.

While she didn't need the brass knuckles to solidify the case against Trent, especially since no case would be moving forward, there was still a silent moment of clarity, fulfillment, and knowledge that she had followed the correct trail in her investigation. Her only regret was that she had no one to share the moment with. Jenkins wasn't coming in for another six hours and he had never been invested in the case anyway. Only Ballard had been committed to it.

She noticed that Feltzer had included copies of all the crime scene photographs, so she slowly leafed through the stack of 8 × 10s. It was a photo tour of the house, and Ballard was reminded that she had never seen the entire place. She was struck by the normalcy of it. Spare and out-of-date furnishings were in every room. The only piece that allowed her to date the photos as reasonably contemporary was the flat-screen television on the living room wall.

The last photos in the stack were of the lowest room in the upside-down house. And these included shots of Trent in situ—as he had been found. There was more blood on him and the floor than Ballard had remembered. His eyes were half-lidded. She spent a long time studying the photos of the man she had killed. She only pulled her eyes away when her cell phone started to buzz. She looked at the screen. It was Towson.

"Have you checked the website?" he said. "It's up. It's good."

"Hold on," she said.

She pulled up the *Times* website on her screen. The story wasn't the main selection on the home page but it was the third story listed. She opened it, noted that it had Jerry Castor's byline, and quickly read it. She was pleased with what she saw. Especially the money paragraph.

Sources within the department said early reports that questioned Ballard's actions did not include the entire raft of evidence and circumstances reviewed. It is expected that the department's Force Investigation Division will make a determination that Ballard acted bravely and used justifiable force when she stabbed Trent with a splintered piece of wood in an effort to save her life and that of another victim abducted by the suspect. The FID's findings will go to the Los Angeles County District Attorney's Office, which will make a final determination on the detective's actions.

"Yeah, it's good," Ballard said. "What do you think?"

"I think we made a mistake," he said. "We should have told Feltzer you wanted a promotion to captain too. He gave us everything we wanted! In fact, I checked on your van and they said you can pick it up tomorrow. They're finished with it."

She hadn't known he was going to do that. His taking that initiative suggested to Ballard that things were maybe going to get awkward with Towson.

"Thank you very much, Dean," she said. "For all of it. You really turned this around."

"Wasn't me," he said. "You made this about the easiest case I've ever handled."

"Well, good. And by the way, I gave your card to Trent's victim—the one who brought me into the case. I told her she should go after the equity in that house and to call you."

"Well, I'm much obliged. And you know, Renée, this is now a closed matter, as far as my involvement. That means it would not be a conflict if we were to stay in touch—you know, socially."

There it was. The awkward overture. It was routine to get hit on by men in the department as well as the larger field of the justice system. That was how she and Compton had hooked up—a shared experience leading to something more. She had been feeling Towson's interest growing since the interview at his town house Sunday morning. The problem was, she did not return his interest, especially after the ordeal she had just been through.

"I think I want to keep this on a professional level, Dean," she said. "I may need your legal services in the future and I like how you handled this—a lot."

She hoped that puffing him up on a professional level would allow the personal rejection to go down easier.

"Well, of course," he said. "Whatever you need, Renée. I'm here for you. But think about it. We could always have both."

"Thank you, Dean," she said.

After ending the call, Ballard went back to the photos, studying once again the shots of Trent's body and the room on the bottom floor of the upside-down house. Seeing the body and the blood allowed her to go back to it and go over it in her mind's eye. She relived the steps she took, the escape from her bindings, and then the attack. She cupped her right hand around her left wrist. It was the one she had first freed, and it had suffered the deepest laceration from the zip tie. The photos made her feel the pain again. But it was earned. It was sacrifice. She could not articulate it even to herself, but going through it again in her head and not second-guessing anything was therapeutic. It was needed.

She almost didn't hear her name being called from the other side of the squad room. She looked up and saw Danitra Lewis waving a clipboard at her from just outside McAdams's office. Lewis was the division's records and property clerk. Ballard knew that at the end of each day, Lewis dropped off evidence logs in the lieutenant's in-box so that he would be apprised of the comings and goings on different cases.

Ballard got up and went over to see what she wanted.

"What's up, Danitra?"

"What's up is I need a disposition on the property you got in my locker. You can't just leave it there forever."

"What do you mean?"

"I'm saying you've got that bag sittin' in one of my boxes since last week."

"The one going to Chastain at RHD? He was supposed to take it Friday."

"Well, like I'm saying, it's still in that locker, and it's got a hold for you on it, not him. I need you to come get it. I need the space."

Ballard was confused. The evidence bag contained the belongings of Cynthia Haddel, the waitress gunned down in the Dancers massacre. Ballard knew that she was an ancillary victim but it didn't make a lot of sense to her that Chastain had not taken the property bag early Friday morning when he had been at the station. She had told him about it. But even if Chastain hadn't taken the bag because his hands were full with the witness Zander Speights, it should have been transported by courier Monday morning to Property Division downtown and held for him there.

That was the procedure. But Lewis was saying that none of that had happened. That the bag was on hold for her.

"I don't know what's going on with that, but I'll go check it in a few minutes," Ballard said.

Lewis thanked her and left the squad room.

Ballard went back to the desk she was using, stacked the photos and the search warrant return together, and put them back into the interoffice mailer so that they would not be lying around on display. She then locked the envelope in her file cabinet and headed back to the property room.

Lewis was gone and the room was empty. Ballard opened the locker in which she had put the brown paper bag that contained Cynthia Haddel's personal effects. She took the bag out and carried it over to the counter. The first thing she noticed was that the bag was double taped. A second layer of red evidence tape had been applied over the first, meaning the bag had been opened and resealed since Ballard had placed it in the locker early Friday morning. She assumed that Chastain had done this. She next checked the property transfer label and saw that this, too, was new. Handwritten instructions on the label said to hold the property for Detective Ballard at Hollywood Division. Ballard recognized the handwriting as Chastain's.

Ballard grabbed a box cutter off the counter, cut through the tape, and opened the bag. From it she pulled the plastic evidence bags she had placed inside the paper bag the morning after Haddel's murder. She noticed that one of these was also double taped. It had been opened and resealed.

Without breaking the new seal on the bag, she spread it out on the counter so she could see its contents through the plastic. There was an inventory list inside and she was able to check everything against it, from Haddel's phone to her tip apron to the cigarette box containing the vial of Molly.

Based on what Rogers Carr had said about Chastain now being the focus of the investigation, Ballard wondered what Chastain had been up to. Was there something in the bag that he wanted to keep hidden from RHD? Was it something on Haddel's phone? Or had he taken something?

There was no easy answer. Ballard grabbed the top corners of the bag and flipped it over on the counter so that she could examine its contents from the other side. Right away she noticed a business card that hadn't been there before slipped down into the cellophane wrap of the cigarette box. It was Chastain's LAPD business card.

Ballard went over to a latex glove dispenser on the wall and grabbed a pair. She snapped the gloves on and went back to the evidence bag. She cut the seal and reached in for the cigarettes. She removed the box and examined it closely before slipping the business card out. There was a name written on the side of the card, not visible when it had been behind the cigarette box cellophane.

Eric Higgs
VMD

Ballard didn't recognize the name or know the meaning of the initials *VMD*. She put the card aside and opened the cigarette box. The vial was still there and it appeared to be half full—as it was when Ballard had discovered it.

She decided to look through everything to see if anything else stood out to her as having been tampered with. The phone was now useless. It had long since used up its charge. She opened the tip apron next and saw what appeared to be the same contents as before, a fold of currency, more cigarettes, a lighter, and a small notebook. She took out the money and counted it. Not a dollar was missing, and there was no clue as to what Chastain had been up to.

Ballard pulled out her phone. She took off a glove, typed in Eric Higgs, and fired the name into her search engine. She got a variety of responses. There was an artist, a college football player, a chemistry professor at the University of California, Irvine, and several others. But none of the people with the name connected to Ballard on any level of significance.

She next typed VMD into the search engine and got numerous results, including references to Visual Molecular Dynamics, Veterinary Medicines Directorate, and Vector Meson Dominance. Far down the list, she saw the words Vacuum Metal Deposition, and the explanatory line beneath it grabbed her attention with one word.

The physical process of coating evidence with very thin metal film . . .

Ballard remembered reading something about this process. She clicked on the link to an article and started reading. VMD was a forensic technique in which applications of gold and zinc to evidence in a low-pressure environment revealed latent fingerprints on objects and materials usually deemed too porous to produce prints. The process had been successful in applications on plastics, patterned metals, and some woven fabrics.

The article was two years old and from a website called *Forensic Times*. It said the technique was complicated and required a sizable pressure chamber and other equipment, not to mention the expensive metals gold and zinc. Therefore, its study and application were primarily carried out on the university level and in private forensic labs. At the time of the article, it said neither the FBI nor any major metropolitan police department in the United States had a VMD chamber and that this was hindering law enforcement use of the technique in criminal cases.

The article listed a handful of private labs and universities where the application of VMD was either offered or being studied. Among these was UC Irvine, where Ballard had just determined that an Eric Higgs was a chemistry professor.

Ballard quickly repackaged all of Cynthia Haddel's property back into the brown paper bag and resealed it with tape from a dispenser on the counter. She then carried the bag back to the detective bureau, where she went to work tracking down Professor Higgs.

Twenty minutes later, and thanks to the University Police Department, she placed a call to a lab assigned to the professor. Ballard judged the voice that answered as being too young to be a professor.

"I'm looking for Professor Higgs."

"He's gone."

"For the day?"

"Yeah, for the day."

"Who is this?"

"Well, who is this?"

"Detective Renée Ballard, Los Angeles Police Department. It's very important that I reach Professor Higgs. Can you help me?"

"Well, I . . ."

"Who is this?"

"Uh, Steve Stilwell. I'm the grad assistant in the lab."

"Is this the VMD lab?"

"Well, it's not exactly a VMD lab, but we have the setup here, yeah."

Ballard grew more excited with the confirmation.

"Do you have a cell phone for Professor Higgs or any way I could reach him?"

"I have his cell. I guess I could . . . I'm not sure it's allowed."

"Mr. Stilwell, I'm calling about a murder investigation. Do you understand? Either give me that number or call Professor Higgs yourself and ask permission to give it to me. I need you to do one or the other right now."

"Okay, okay, let me get the number. I have to look it up on this phone so I won't hear you if you say anything."

"Just hurry, Mr. Stilwell."

Ballard couldn't contain herself while waiting. She got up and started pacing one of the aisles in the detective bureau while Stilwell got the number out of his phone. Finally, he started to call it out as he read it off his phone screen. Ballard raced back to her workstation and wrote the number down. She disconnected the call with Stilwell just as he brought the phone back to his mouth and said, "Got it?"

She dialed the number and a man answered after only one ring.

"Professor Higgs?"

"Yes."

"My name is Ballard. I'm a detective with the Los Angeles Police Department."

There was a long moment before he responded.

"You worked with Ken Chastain, didn't you?"

Ballard felt a bolt of pure energy go through her chest.

"Yes, I did."

"I thought you might call. He told me that if anything happened to him, I could trust you."

38

It was a brutal drive in heavy traffic down to Irvine in Orange County. Professor Higgs had agreed to come back to the school and meet Ballard at his lab. Along the way, she thought about the lead she was chasing. Ken Chastain had very clearly left it for her to find. He knew he was on dangerous ground and he had a backup plan that would kick in if something happened to him. Ballard was that plan. By redirecting the Haddel property back to her, Chastain guaranteed that she would get it after the weekend and would find the clue leading to Professor Higgs.

When she finally got to UC Irvine, she had to call Higgs twice on his cell to get directions to the Natural Sciences Building, where he was on the fourth floor.

The building seemed empty as Ballard entered, and she found Higgs alone in his lab. He was tall and gangly and younger than Ballard had expected. He greeted her warmly and seemed relieved of some weight or concern.

"I didn't know," he said. "I'm so damn busy I don't have time to read a newspaper or watch TV. I didn't know what happened until yesterday, when I called the number he gave me and his wife told me. It's an awful thing and I hope to god this had nothing to do with it."

He gestured toward the back of the lab, where there

was a steel pressure tank about the size of a washer-and-dryer stack.

"I'm here to try to find that out," Ballard said. "You spoke to his wife?"

"Yes, she answered the phone," Higgs said. "She told me what had happened and I was completely stunned."

It meant that Chastain had given Higgs his home number, not his office line or his cell number. This was significant to Ballard because it was another indication—along with his actions at the crime scene and his handling of the Haddel evidence—that Chastain was trying to keep at least some of his moves on the Dancers case below the surface and untraceable through normal measures.

"Is there a place where we could sit down and talk?" Ballard asked.

"Sure, I've got an office," Higgs said. "Follow me."

Higgs led the way through a series of interconnecting labs within the general lab and into a small and cluttered office big enough for a desk and single visitor's chair. They sat down and Ballard asked him to tell the story of his interaction with Chastain from the start.

"You mean, go back to the first case?" he asked.

"I guess so," Ballard said. "What was the first case?"

"Well, the first time I ever spoke to Detective Chastain was when he called me up about two years ago. He said he had read about VMD in the *Journal of Forensic Sciences* or some other journal—I can't remember which one—and he wanted to know if the process could raise fingerprints on a basketball."

Higgs's story was already ringing true for Ballard.

She knew from her years as Chastain's partner that he prided himself on staying up on advances and techniques in forensics, interrogation, and legal protocol. Some of the other detectives even nicknamed him "The Scholar" because of his extracurricular reading. It would not have been unusual for Chastain to pick up the phone and call a scientist directly when he had a question about evidence.

"Did he say what the case was?" Ballard asked.

"Yeah, it was a shooting on a playground," Higgs said. "A kid got into an argument during a one-on-one game, and the other kid grabbed a gun out of his backpack at the side of the court and shot him. So Detective Chastain thought the shooter had to have left prints on the ball because he had been playing with it, you know? But the police lab said they couldn't do it because the ball was rubber and had a dimpled and porous surface. He asked me to give it a try."

"And what happened?"

"I like a challenge. I told him to bring it down here, and we tried but we couldn't pull anything up that was usable. I mean, we got some ridges here and there but nothing that he could take back and put through the latent print archives."

"So, then what?"

"Well, that was sort of it. Until he called me last week and asked if he could send me something he wanted to try to get a print off of."

"What was it?"

"He called it a thumb button."

"When exactly was this call?"

"Early Friday. I was in the car, heading here, and he

called my cell. I can check my phone log if you want the exact time."

"If you don't mind."

"Sure."

Higgs pulled the phone out of his pocket and went into the call list. He scrolled through the listing of calls going back to early Friday morning.

"This is it," he said. "Came in at seven-forty-one a.m. Friday."

"Can I see the number?" Ballard asked.

Higgs held the phone out across the desk, and Ballard leaned forward to read the screen. The number was 213-972-2971, and Ballard knew it wasn't Chastain's cell. It was the general number at Hollywood Station. Chastain had used a landline in the property room to call Higgs at the same time he was going through the evidence bag containing Cynthia Haddel's property.

"What exactly did he ask you when he called?" Ballard asked.

"He said he was dealing with emergency circumstances on a big case," Higgs said. "And he wanted to know if I could VMD something as small as a dime and get a print off it."

"And what did you tell him?"

"Well, I first asked what material we were talking about, and he said it was a metal button that had an uneven surface because of an imprint. I told him all I could do was try. I told him that once, I actually got a print off a dime, right off of Roosevelt's jaw. So he said he would send it down and that I should only talk to him about it."

It was clear to Ballard that by 7:41 a.m. Friday

394

morning, less than eight hours after the massacre at the Dancers, Chastain already knew or was at least suspicious that there was police involvement. He took measures to hide his suspicions and protect himself—using the station's phone instead of his own to call Higgs and leaving behind the evidence bag containing his business card with Higgs's name written on the back.

"So he mailed it to you or delivered it?" she asked.

"Mailed it. It came Saturday by certified mail," Higgs said.

"Do you by any chance still have that packaging?"

Ballard was thinking in terms of being able to document the chain of custody of the evidence. It could become important if there was a trial. Higgs thought for a moment and then shook his head.

"No, it's trashed. The cleaners come through here on Saturday night."

"And where is the button?"

"Let me go get it. I'll be right back."

Higgs got up and left the office. Ballard waited. She heard a drawer in the lab open and close and then the professor came back. He handed her a small plastic evidence bag containing what looked like a small black cap that was threaded on the inside of its edges.

Ballard was sure it was the bag and object that she had glimpsed Chastain with at the crime scene early Friday morning. Chastain had obviously recognized what it was and knew its significance.

She turned the bag to study the object. It was actually slightly smaller than a dime, with a flat head and a word stamped across it.

It was a word familiar to Ballard but she couldn't immediately place it. She pulled her phone so she could plug the word into a search engine.

"It came with a note," Higgs said. "In the package. It said, if something happens, trust Renée Ballard. So when you called—"

"Do you still have that note?" Ballard asked.

"Uh, I believe I do. Somewhere around here. I'll have to find it but I know I didn't toss it."

"If you could, I'd like to see it."

Ballard pressed the search button and got two hits on the word. *Lawmaster* was the name of a motorcycle used by Judge Dredd in a series of comic books and movies. It was also a company that made leather equipment belts and holsters geared toward the law enforcement community.

Ballard clicked on the link to the company's website as she remembered the brand. Lawmaster specialized in leather holsters, particularly the kind of shoulder holsters favored by the gunslingers in the department—the testosterone-enhanced hard chargers who put form over function and were willing to take the discomfort of having leather straps crisscross their backs over the simple ease and comfort of a far less macho hip holster.

Most of these gunslingers were the young up-and-comers who never missed a chance to check their looks in a mirror or take their jackets off at a crime scene to impress onlookers as well as themselves. Still, there were also some old-school cowboys who preferred the gunslinger look. And Ballard knew Lieutenant Robert Olivas was among them.

The website showed a variety of shoulder holsters, and Ballard clicked on one that counterbalanced the gun under one arm with double ammo clips under the other. She enlarged the accompanying photo and studied the workmanship of the holster. She saw several adjustment points for giving the holster a custom fit and positioning the weapon at an angle offering easy access to its wearer. These adjustment points were held in place by shallow screws and threaded black caps with the Lawmaster logo stamped on them.

It was a cascade moment, when all the details of the investigation came together. Ballard now knew what Chastain knew and understood his moves in surreptitiously taking evidence from the crime scene and attempting to analyze and safeguard it from afar.

Ballard held up the plastic bag containing the Lawmaster cap.

"Professor Higgs, were you able to get a print off this?"

"Yes, I was. I got one good solid print."

39

Ballard stayed in the Miyako again Wednesday night, taking sushi for dinner in her room once more before going to sleep. She had enough clothes in her bag for another day without replacement and in the morning made the quick drive over to the Piper Technical Center, which was home to the Latent Print Unit as well as the department's aero squadron.

Every detective with more than a few years on the job has procured a tech in each of the forensic disciplines who can be counted on for an occasional favor or a jump in the waiting line when needed. Some of the disciplines are more important than others because they are more common to crimes. Fingerprints are found at just about every crime scene and therefore the Latent Print Unit was the most important place to have a connection in the entire forensic sandbox. Ballard's go-to was a supervisor named Polly Stanfield.

Five years earlier, Ballard and Stanfield had worked a difficult case where fingerprints were the link between three separate sex-assault murders, but while the prints from each scene matched, Stanfield could find no match in the various databases that housed print records around the world. Only the relentless efforts of both women finally resulted in an arrest when Stanfield surreptitiously accessed a database of rental applications for a massive apartment complex in the Valley that was geographically central to the murders. Renters at the complex were required to give fingerprints with their applications, but nothing was ever done with them. It was just a way of discouraging applicants who might lie about having criminal records. Once Stanfield's work identified the suspect, Ballard and her then-partner, Chastain, had to find another way to come up with his name so as not to reveal Stanfield's hack of the apartment complex's rental applications. They resorted to the tried-and-true anonymous call from a burner cell revealing the suspect's identity to a department crime-tip line. And no one ever knew the difference.

Ballard got Stanfield in the divorce. That is, when she and Chastain split as partners, most people in the department and ancillary agencies chose a side to stand with. Stanfield, who, in a long career in law enforcement, had encountered her share of overly aggressive men and sexual harassment, sided with Ballard.

Ballard knew Stanfield worked seven to four, and she was there at the door of the LPU with two lattes at 6:55 a.m. An earlier phone call between the two women had covered the basics of what needed to be done, so Stanfield was not surprised by Ballard's appearance or by the high sugar content of her latte. It had been special-ordered.

"Let's see what you've got," Stanfield said by way of a greeting.

As a supervisor, Stanfield had a small cubbyhole office but it was still better than the open work pod most of the other print techs got. Stanfield was well versed in how to deal with what Ballard was bringing in. The VMD process resulted in a fingerprint being temporarily identifiable on a surface of the holster cap. It had then been photographed under oblique lighting conditions by Professor Higgs.

What Ballard had for Stanfield was a photograph of a thumbprint.

Stanfield began her work with a magnifying glass, looking closely at the photo to confirm there was a usable print.

"This thumb is really good," she finally said. "Good, clear ridges. But it's going to take a while. It's a scan-and-trace job."

That was more than a hint from Stanfield that she would prefer not to have Ballard looking over her shoulder the whole time. She needed to scan the photo into her computer, then go through a tedious process of using a program to trace the lines and swirls of the thumbprint so that a clean print could be run through the Automated Fingerprint Index System. There were more than seventy million prints in the AFIS data bank. Sending a print through did not bring instantaneous results. And often the results, when they came, were not singular. A search often kicked out several similar prints, and that required the print tech to make the final comparison under a microscope to determine if there was a match.

"You want me to leave and come back?" Ballard asked. "How long?"

"Give me at least a couple hours," Stanfield said. "If I get through it quicker, I'll call."

Ballard stood up.

"Okay, but remember," she said. "Keep this under

the table. Don't tell anyone what case it is or what you're doing. And if you get a match, tell only me."

Stanfield put the magnifying glass down on the lab table and looked at her.

"Are you trying to scare me?" she asked.

"No, but I want you to be cautious. If you get a name and it's the name I'm thinking it will be, then you'll understand what I'm saying."

Ballard didn't want to share her investigative theory with Stanfield prior to the work. She didn't want to infect her conclusions with any preconceived ideas of who the print would match.

"Holy shit," Stanfield said. "Well, thanks a lot, Renée. You know I really liked working here."

"Don't be so dramatic," Ballard said. "Just see what you get and I'll be back."

40

Ballard used the time to walk over to the print shed that was located behind Piper Tech. Knowing how citizens were often treated when they attempted to pick up their impounded and printed vehicles, she half expected a delay in the paperwork from FID releasing her van. But it was ready to go. She wasn't wrong about her expectations about its condition, however.

The first clue was the driver's door handle, which was still dusted with black fingerprint powder. She opened the door and found the driver's compartment bombed with powder as well. She knew from crime scene experience that the black powder could ruin clothes and be impossible to get out with home car-washing. She went back to the garage's office and angrily demanded that the van be returned in drivable condition. This resulted in a stare-down with the garage manager, but he changed his demeanor when Ballard produced her badge. He dispatched two of his garage greasers with a high-powered vacuum, a roll of paper towels, and a bottle of industrial-strength cleaner to the van.

Ballard stood by, watched the work, and pointed out every spot they missed. After an hour she thought about calling Polly Stanfield but she knew that would only annoy her. She decided to check in at Hollywood

Detectives instead and called Lieutenant McAdams's direct line.

"Ballard, what are you doing awake?" he asked. "I have you back on the schedule tonight."

"I'll be there, L-T, don't worry," she said. "Just checking in. What's happening in the Six?"

"Only thing I got going is an assist with the feds. They got a takedown team surrounding some fool holed up in the Bat-cave."

That was a reference to a cave up in Bronson Canyon that had been used during the filming of the 1960s *Batman* television show.

"What do they want him for?"

"A double-bagger in Texas. Killed two armored-car guards a couple years ago and lammed it over here."

"What are we doing?"

"Crowd and traffic control."

Ballard knew it was the guy she had spooked with Compton. She wondered if she would escape with no blowback from the feds if they successfully brought him down at the Bat-cave. Just then, she got a call-waiting buzz on her phone. She checked and saw it was Stanfield.

"Hey L-T, I have a call coming in. I gotta go."

"Okay, Ballard, go."

She disconnected and switched over.

"Polly?"

"I got a hit on that thumb. It's a cop. What did you get me into, Renée?"

41

Ballard stepped out of an interrogation room at the Metropolitan Detention Center, crossed the wide hallway, and entered the control center. She looked at the monitor for the interrogation room. Lieutenant Olivas sat in the chair facing the overhead camera, his arms pulled into a locked position behind his back. He knew she was looking at him and had his head tilted back. He scowled at the camera.

Ballard raised her phone and took a photo of the monitor. She then texted the shot to Rogers Carr with a message.

I need help. He won't talk to me.

As she expected, it didn't take long for Carr to respond.

WTF?!!! Where are you?

Her reply was terse. She wasn't interested in a text debate. She needed Carr to come to the jail.

MDC. You coming? I want to flip him.

There was no response. Minutes dragged by and she

404

knew Carr was debating with himself whether to come over, whether to risk his career and the enmity of the department by getting involved in the attempted take-down of a prized lieutenant. Ballard tried one more time to coax him.

I have the evidence.

Another minute went by. It felt like an hour. Then Carr returned.

On my way.

Ballard realized she had been holding her breath. She released it in relief and turning to the two officers monitoring the screens told them that Carr was on his way.

She was still in the control center when Carr was announced and he entered the hallway fifteen minutes later. Ballard stepped out to meet him. His forehead was slick with a film of sweat. That told her that he had covered the three blocks on foot and must have left the PAB without hesitation after their text conversation. He glanced through the square window on the door to interrogation room A and looked at Olivas. He then quickly turned away as though he couldn't take what he saw. He focused on Ballard and spoke in a low, con-trolled voice.

"What the fuck, Ballard? How the hell did you get him in here?"

"I lured him out of the PAB. I told him I had someone here who was ready to confess."

"And then you fucking arrest him? On what *evidence?*"

He said the last word too loud, almost as a shriek. He brought his hand to his mouth and checked the officers in the control center, then dropped back down to a whisper.

"Listen to me, you are moving too fast," he said. "Everything I have? It points to Chastain, not Olivas. Not a fucking RHD lieutenant. Do you know what you're doing here? You are committing career suicide. You need to stop this right now."

"I can't," Ballard said. "I know it wasn't Chastain. He took measures because he knew it was a cop. That's why Olivas killed him."

"What measures? Ballard, what evidence do you have? You are letting your issue with Olivas take this over and—"

"Kenny took evidence from the crime scene at the Dancers. Evidence that it was a cop."

"What are you talking about? What did he take?"

"A piece of a holster that came loose when the shooter pulled his gun. I was there. I saw him take it. That and the wire—he knew it was a cop."

Carr looked off for a moment as he composed his thoughts. He then leaned down and in close to Ballard.

"Listen to me. What you saw was Chastain covering his own tracks. He was the shooter and you have fucked this up beyond belief. Now I'm going to go in there and talk to Olivas. And I'm going to try to salvage this and save your job."

Carr signaled to one of the officers in the control

center to unlock the door. He then looked back at Ballard.

"If you're lucky, you'll end up riding a bike on the boardwalk," he said. "But at least you'll still have a badge."

"You don't understand," Ballard protested. "There's evidence. I have—"

"I don't want to hear it," Carr said, cutting her off. "I'm going in."

The jail officer walked over to a wall unit of small lockers. He opened one and removed the key from its lock.

"Okay, you need to put your weapons in here," he said. "Sidearm, backup, knife, everything."

Carr walked over and put one of each into the locker, pulling his holstered sidearm off his belt, then a folding knife from his back pocket. He leaned one hand against the wall so he could raise his right leg, pull up the cuff of his pants, and detach an ankle holster containing his backup. The jail officer closed and locked the wall compartment and handed Carr the key. It was on an elastic band that Carr snapped around his wrist. He then looked at Ballard.

"I hope to fuck this doesn't bring me down with you."

The officer opened the door to the interrogation room and stepped back to allow Carr in. Carr walked across the threshold and toward the table, where Olivas sat.

Ballard followed Carr, and the jail officer closed the door, locking them in.

Carr started to turn when he realized that Ballard had come in behind him.

"I thought you—"

Ballard grabbed Carr by the right arm and, in a move taught to her at the academy and long practiced since, yanked it behind his back while throwing her left shoulder into him. Carr pitched forward across the empty chair and table. At the same moment, Olivas rose from his chair, revealing that his hands were not cuffed, and slammed Carr chest-down on the table.

Olivas put his full weight down on Carr as Ballard pulled the handcuffs off her belt and worked them around Carr's wrists.

"Good," she yelled.

Olivas then dragged Carr completely across the table and flung him onto the seat where he had just been. He grabbed him with two hands by the jacket collar and pulled him up into a sitting position. He then hiked a thumb over his shoulder toward the upper corner of the room.

"Smile for the camera, Carr," he said.

"What the fuck is this?" Carr demanded.

"Had to separate you from your weapons," Ballard said.

Everything seemed to dawn on Carr. He shook his head.

"I get it, I get it," he said. "But you've got it wrong. You can't do this."

"Yeah, we can," Olivas said. "We have a warrant for your weapons."

"He had a hip holster on today," Ballard said.

Olivas nodded.

"Of course he did," he said. "His shoulder rig was falling apart without that screw cap he lost."

"Listen to me," Carr said. "I don't know what you

408

people think you have, but you've got no probable cause. You are totally—"

"What we have is your thumbprint on that cap from your rig," Olivas said. "How's that end up at the crime scene when you were nowhere near that crime scene?"

"Bullshit," Carr said. "You don't have shit."

"We have enough to run ballistics on your guns," Olivas said. "We match them up and we'll have a six-pack to run across the street to the D.A."

"And it will be *adios*, motherfucker, to you," Ballard added.

"Funny how being a cop worked against you," Olivas said. "Most guys would get rid of the weapons. Hard to do that when they're registered with the job. Tough to go in to the boss and say you lost both your guns. So my bet is that you kept them and thought you were going to skate."

Carr looked stunned by the turnabout of events. Olivas leaned down, put his palms on the table, and recited the Miranda warning. He asked Carr if he understood his rights, and the detective ignored the question.

"This is wrong," Carr said. "This is fucked up."

"You killed Chastain," Ballard said. "You killed them all."

She had stepped close to the table, her body tense. Olivas put his arm out as if to block her from launching herself at Carr.

"You knew you had lost that button off your holster," she said. "You had access to the task force room and you checked the evidence report. It wasn't on there and that's when you knew somebody was working it off book, somebody who knew it was a cop."

"You're crazy, Ballard," Carr said. "And soon the whole world will know."

"How'd you know it was Kenny?" she asked. "Because he was the lieutenant's golden boy, the only one who'd risk going off book on this? Or didn't it matter? Was Chastain just the fall guy because you found out he carried a ninety-two F and owed money? You just figured you could pin the whole thing on him?"

Carr didn't answer.

"We're going to find out," Ballard said. "*I'm* going to find out."

She stepped back and watched as a cold and instant reality seemed to fall on Carr, covering him like a thick black blanket.

Ballard could read it in his face as he went from confidence to crisis, from thinking he had a shot at talking his way out of the room to visions of never seeing daylight again.

"I want a lawyer," he said.

"I'm sure you do," Ballard said.

42

For the second time in the day Ballard was walking evidence through analysis. She didn't need a go-to in the firearms and ballistics unit. It was a case involving the murder of an LAPD officer, which automatically moved it to the front of any line. And to be sure, Olivas had called ahead and put his considerable weight behind the need for urgency. A ballistics expert named C. P. Medore would be waiting for her upon arrival.

The cold truth that Ballard was carrying with her, along with the guns seized from Carr, was that the D.A.'s package they had used to batter Carr with was not as strong as they had boasted. Since the VMD processing was a rarely used forensic procedure and it was handled in this case wholly outside of the police lab, it would be open to heavy attack by any defense attorney worth his weight in objections. *Detective, are you telling this jury that this critical examination of evidence was carried out by college students in a chemistry lab? Are you expecting us to believe that this so-called evidence was literally stolen from the crime scene and then FedExed to this college lab?*

What was additionally troublesome was the chain-of-evidence issue. The key piece of evidence with the suspect's fingerprint was spirited away from the crime scene without documentation. Chastain was now dead, and Ballard was the sole witness who could place the holster button at the scene. Her own personal history with the department and her credibility would come under withering assault as well.

The bottom line was that they needed more. If either of the guns taken from Carr was matched to the Dancers shooting or the Chastain hit, then that case would be as solid as the Santa Monica Mountains and Carr would be crushed under its weight.

The cases were fraught with sentencing enhancements known as special circumstances: murder of a law enforcement officer; home invasion; lying in wait. Any one of these could put Carr on death row, and all three would practically guarantee it. While the state of California hadn't executed an inmate in a decade and there was no indication that things would change in the future, it was still known to both cops and convicts alike that a death sentence was a ticket to insanity when the years of isolation—one hour per week out of the solo cell—began to take their toll. Facing that, Carr might be willing to plead out to get a deal that took death row off the table. He'd then have to admit his crimes and their motivations. He'd have to tell all.

Medore was there and waiting with another tech at the entrance to the gun unit. Each man took one of the separately packaged weapons from Ballard. Their first stop was the tank room, where they fired shots from the guns into the water, thus producing spent and un-damaged bullets suitable for comparison to the slugs removed from the victims in the two cases. They then entered the ballistics lab and set up at a comparison microscope and went to work.

"Can you do the Ruger first?" Ballard asked.

She wanted the answer on the Chastain murder as soon as possible.

"No problem," Medore said.

Ballard stood back and observed. She had seen the exacting process done dozens of times before, and her mind shifted to what had happened back at the city jail after Carr had been arrested and Olivas had set assignments for the investigation's new direction. Ballard was given the ballistic assignment, while three other detectives were assigned to Carr and ordered to take his life down to the studs in an attempt to link him to the men murdered in the booth at the Dancers and to learn the motivation behind the massacre. Olivas gave himself the assignment of apprising command staff of what was happening and of the need to alert the department's media managers. It was unlikely that Carr's arrest would stay under wraps for long, and the department needed to get out in front of the story.

When it was all said and done and people started going separate ways, Olivas told Ballard to hang back for a moment. When they were alone, he put out his hand. The gesture was so unexpected that she shook it without thinking. Then he wouldn't let go of hers.

"Detective, I want to bury the hatchet," he said. "This thing shows what kind of investigator you are. You're smart and you're fierce. I could use you back on my team, and I could make sure it happens. You'd be back working days, unlimited OT. A lot of good reasons to come back."

Ballard stood there speechless at first. She was holding the evidence bags containing Carr's weapons.

"I need to get these to firearms," she said.

Olivas nodded and finally released her.

"Think about it," he said. "You're a good detective, Ballard. And I can turn the other cheek for the good of the department."

Ballard had turned then to leave the jail. She walked out, thankful that she had held back from swinging the evidence bags and raking Carr's guns across Olivas's face.

As she watched Medore at the microscope, she tried to move her thoughts back to the case.

There were still many questions and loose ends. Chief among them was the missing Matthew Robison. Once Ballard learned that it was Carr's thumbprint on the holster cap, she started running the facts of the case through the new angle of Carr as killer. She saw the connection that had eluded her before. Carr had been part of the Major Crimes task force that had taken down the human-trafficking cabal at the port on Friday morning. She had seen him herself on the five-o'clock news. She realized now that Robison, last seen by his girlfriend on the couch watching TV, could have seen the report and recognized Carr from the night before at the Dancers. He then could have picked up the phone at 5:10 p.m. and called Ken Chastain to tell him.

It was that call that set several things in motion. Chastain now had further confirmation that the Dancers shooter was a cop. He had to go out and wrangle Robison to lock down his information and make sure he was safe. The question was, who got to Robison first, Chastain or Carr?

As a Major Crimes detective, Carr had routine access

to RHD computers as well as to the division's war room. If he was back-reading the Dancers case reports as they were coming in Friday, he could have picked up on Robison and been suspicious of Chastain's dismissal of him as a witness. In trying to cover the fact that Robison had apparently gotten a good look at the shooter, Chastain had labeled him as DSS—didn't see shit. The effort may have had a completely opposite effect in that Carr might have thought Chastain was trying to camouflage a solid witness. Carr was the shooter, so he knew that the chances were good that someone in the club had gotten a look at him. He very likely would have been checking witness reports to see if that was so.

Ballard came out of these thoughts when she saw Medore step back from the microscope and ask the other tech to take a look. She knew he was soliciting a second opinion because a lot was on the line with this case.

Ballard's phone buzzed. It was a blocked number and she took it.

"Ballard, anything yet?"

It was Olivas.

"Your man C.P.'s on the scope. Shouldn't be long. You want to hold? It looks like he's just getting a second opinion."

"Sure, I'll hold a minute."

"Can I ask you something?"

"What is it?"

"Carr knew I had been calling Matthew Robison to try to find him. When I asked him how he knew, he said that after Chastain got hit, RHD pulled a warrant

415

for Robison's phone records in an effort to find him. Was that true, or was Carr trying to cover that he had Robison's phone because he had killed him?"

"No, we did do that. We first tried to ping his phone but it was turned off. So we pulled call records to see if there was anything there that would help. Why, Ballard? What's it mean?"

"It means he might still be alive out there somewhere. Chastain may have gotten to him and hidden him before Carr even knew about him."

"Then we have to find him."

Ballard thought about that. She had an idea but wasn't up to sharing it yet—especially with Olivas.

Just then, Medore turned to her from his lab bench. He gave her a thumbs-up.

"Lieutenant, we've got the first match. Chastain was killed with Carr's backup. We've got Carr cold."

"Excellent. We'll start putting a package together for the D.A. Let me know on the other weapon as soon as you know."

"You want me on the package?"

"No, my guys will handle it. Have you thought about my offer to come back to the team?"

Ballard hesitated before answering.

"Ballard?" Olivas prompted.

"Yes," she finally said. "I thought about it. And I like the late show."

"You're telling me you're going to pass?" Olivas said, surprise clearly in his voice.

"I pass," Ballard said. "I went to you this morning with the Carr print because it was your team's case and there was nowhere else to go with it. And I knew I could use you to draw Carr to MDC. But that's it. I'll never work for you again."

"You're making a big mistake."

"Lieutenant, you tell the world what you did to me and you own it, then I'll come back to work for you."

"Ballard, you—"

She disconnected the call.

43

The second ballistics comparison was a match between Carr's service weapon and the slug taken from Gino Santangelo's brain. Late in the day, Carr was charged with six counts of murder, with special circumstances added on the Chastain kill.

That night, Ballard returned to the late show. After roll call, she and Jenkins took the plain wrap and drove up Wilcox to the Mark Twain hotel. They parked out front and pushed the button on the front door to gain admittance.

When they had been partners, Ballard and Chastain had worked a murder-for-hire case in which they needed to stash the intended victim for a couple days so that her husband would think she had disappeared, as he had paid an undercover officer to make happen. They had put her in the Mark Twain. The following year, they had another case where they used the hotel to stash two witnesses brought in from New Orleans to testify at a murder trial. They needed to make sure the defense could not find them and attempt to intimidate them and dissuade them from giving their testimony.

It was Chastain who had picked the place both times. The Twain, as he called it, was his go-to stash house.

Ballard told Jenkins her theory about Robison being alive and he agreed to take a ride with her to the Twain.

After she held up her badge to a camera over the hotel door, Ballard and Jenkins were buzzed in. When they got to the desk, Ballard showed her phone to the night man. On the screen she had Robison's driver's license photo.

"William Parker, what room's he in?" she asked.

William Parker was a legendary LAPD police chief in the 1950s and '60s. Chastain had used the name for one of the witnesses from New Orleans.

The night man didn't look like he wanted any part of the trouble the police could cause in the middle of the night at a hotel where most customers paid in cash. He turned to a computer, typed a command, and then read the answer out loud.

"Seventeen."

Ballard and Jenkins moved down the first-floor hallway until they stood on either side of room 17. Ballard knocked.

"Matthew Robison," Jenkins said. "LAPD, open the door."

Nothing.

"Metro," Ballard said. "My name is Detective Ballard. I worked with Detective Chastain, who brought you here. We're here to tell you it's over. You're safe and you can go home to Alicia now."

They waited. After thirty seconds, Ballard heard the lock flip. The door opened six inches and a young man looked out. Ballard was holding her badge up.

"It's safe?" he asked.

"Are you Matthew?" Ballard asked.

"Uh, yes."

"Detective Chastain brought you here?"

"That's right."

"It's safe, Matthew. We'll take you home now."

"Where's Detective Chastain?"

Ballard paused and looked at Robison for a long moment.

"He didn't make it," she finally said.

Robison looked down at the floor.

"You called him Friday and said you just saw the shooter on TV," Ballard said. "Didn't you?"

Robison nodded.

"Okay, well, we're going to take you by the station first to look at some photos," Ballard said. "After that, we'll take you back to your apartment and Alicia. You'll be safe now, and she's worried about you."

Robison finally looked up at her. Ballard knew he was trying to decide if he could trust her. He must have seen something in her eyes.

"Okay," he said. "Give me a minute to get my stuff."

44

Ballard got to the water late that morning because of the drive up the coast to collect her dog. By the time she had pitched her tent on Venice Beach and was walking toward the surf with her board under her arm, the morning layer had completely choked off the sun and visibility was low. She stepped in undaunted. It had been too long since she had been on the water.

She spread her feet to the edge of the board's rails and bent her knees. She started digging deeply into the water and shocking her muscles with the workout.

Dig . . . dig . . . dig . . . glide . . . . Dig . . . dig . . . dig . . . glide . . .

She headed straight out into the fog and soon she was lost in it. The heavy air insulated her from any sound from the land. She was alone.

She thought about Chastain and the moves he had made. He had acted nobly on the case. She thought maybe it was his redemption. For his father. For Ballard. It left her bereft and still haunted by their last encounter. She wished in some way they had settled things.

Soon her shoulders began to burn and the muscles of her back cramped. She eased up and stood tall. She used the paddle blade as a rudder and turned the board. She realized there was no horizon in sight, and the tide was in that short moment of stasis before it shifted. It was not going in or out, and she wasn't sure which direction to point the board.

She kept her momentum with languid paddle strokes, all the while looking and listening for a sign of land. But there was no sound of waves crashing or of people's voices. The fog was too dense.

She pulled the paddle from the water and twirled it upside down. She rapped the handle end hard on the board's deck. The fiberglass produced a solid sound that Ballard knew would cut sharply through the fog.

Soon afterward she heard Lola start to bark and she had her direction. She paddled hard again and started to glide across the black water, heading toward the sound of her dog.

As she came through the mist and caught sight of the shore, she saw Lola at the waterline, panicked and frantically moving north and then south, unsure, her bark now a howl of fear at what she could not understand or control. She reminded Ballard of a fourteen-year-old girl who had done the same thing on a beach a long time ago.

Ballard paddled harder. She wanted to get off the board, drop to her knees in the sand, and hug Lola close.

ACKNOWLEDGMENTS

The author wishes to thank many people for their help with the creation of Renée Ballard and this novel. First, a great debt of thanks goes to LAPD detective Mitzi Roberts, who served in many ways as the inspiration for Renée. The author hopes that Renée has done Detective Roberts proud.

Also of immeasurable help were Detective Tim Marcia and his former colleagues Rick Jackson and David Lambkin.

Many thanks to Linda Connelly, Jane Davis, Terrill Lee Lankford, John Houghton, Dennis Wojciechowski, and Henrik Bastin for early and insightful reads of the work in progress.

Asya Muchnick deserves much credit and gratitude for editing an unwieldy story and coordinating responses from a cast of different editors, including Bill Massey, Harriet Bourton, and Emad Akhtar. Lastly, the author's deep appreciation goes to Pamela Marshall for another great job of copy-editing.

Many thanks to all who helped.

MICHAEL CONNELLY

interviews

Detective Renée Ballard

Michael Connelly

I was expecting someone who works the night shift to be as pale as a vampire.

Renée Ballard

Well, I actually spend a lot of my off hours at the beach. I get my Zen from paddling. It's a great work out, giving me upper body strength which you need in this job, and it's what I call a mind sweeper at the same time. You get out there on the water, sometimes surrounded by the fog, and everything else slips away. It keeps me sane.

MC

Do you actually like working through the night?

RB

I have to admit that I didn't like it at first – who would? It was a demotion and any demotion that comes when you haven't done anything to deserve it is a tough pill to swallow. But then I got into it and realized it's a great place to be. First of all, when you're working the late show, you're far away from the politics of the department. Your day begins when everybody else's ends, and that includes the department brass. Then take the night; there are less people out and about, and this city is very beautiful at night. There is a certain stillness out on the streets that I like. On Hollywood Boulevard most of the shops have roll down security doors that they drop at night and many of these have murals on them. Hollywood stars and scenes from movies. You only see that if you are out on the streets at night. It's one of the secrets of the city you only learn if you're working the late show.

MC

I guess you get a good variety of crimes to investigate too.

RB

You really do. A lot goes on when ninety per cent of the populace is in bed sleeping. Because crime doesn't sleep. And on this job you are not stuck in one discipline, like only investigating robberies for example. You handle everything that comes up. If patrol needs a detective to roll on something then that's you. The downside is I don't get to carry through on a lot of these cases. I do the crime scene work and I interview witnesses, but if I haven't made an arrest by dawn then I'm supposed to turn the case over to the appropriate dayside detectives.

MC

Supposed to? Don't you have a problem with that? I mean, isn't the reason you were investigated recently by your own department because you wouldn't give up a few of your cases? I'm talking about the Dancer's nightclub shooting for one, then there was the investigation the media dubbed the 'Upside Down House' case.

RB

All I can say is sometimes you can't let a case go. It means too much to you and any good detective will tell you that there are some cases that are keepers and damn the rules and regs.

MC

I think I get that. So, you've spoken here about what you like about the late show, what's the part you don't like?

RB

Oh man, that's easy. It's the suicides. I sign off on a lot of suicides. The patrol sergeant always calls me in to take a look to make sure it's not a set-up of some kind. So I encounter a lot of suicides, a lot of stories about people who lost hope or were in very desperate situations because of money or love. It's depressing. I think that's maybe why I hit the beach and go out on my board at the end of watch. I need to see sunshine at the end of my day.

MC

Have you ever turned the focus of the detective inside you toward the woman you see in the mirror? I guess what I'm asking is why do you do this? It takes a certain kind of personality to want to be a detective. It's dangerous on a multitude of levels. Why not leave it for somebody else? A man, for example.

RB

Careful where you're treading there, buddy. Gender doesn't matter when it comes to good detective work. Most of the time it's about getting people to open up and tell you stories, whether they're a witness or a victim or a suspect. I think in some ways women have better skills than men in drawing stories out of people, getting them to converse. If I had to name a skill I have, I would say it is getting people to talk to me.

MC

And sometimes they talk themselves right into prison.

TWO KINDS OF TRUTH

THE BRAND NEW BOSCH THRILLER
BY
MICHAEL CONNELLY

TURN THE PAGE FOR AN EXTRACT NOW.

Harry Bosch works cold cases, helping out the under-funded
San Fernando police department. When a double murder at
a local pharmacy is called in, Bosch is the most seasoned
detective on the scene.

But with experience come the ghosts of long-forgotten
crimes. A death row inmate claims Bosch framed him, and
that new DNA evidence proves it.

The LAPD investigators say the case is watertight, leaving
Bosch out in the wilderness to clear his name and keep a
sadistic killer behind bars.

There's only one person he can trust to help prove his
innocence: Mickey Haller, the Lincoln Lawyer . . .

As both cases tangle around him, Bosch learns that there
are two kinds of truth: the kind that won't die and the kind
that kills.

1

Bosch was in cell 3 of the old San Fernando jail, looking through files from one of the Esme Tavares boxes, when a heads-up text came in from Bella Lourdes over in the detective bureau.

LAPD and DA heading your way. Trevino told them where you are.

Bosch was sitting at the makeshift desk, a wooden door he had borrowed from the Public Works yard and placed across two stacks of file boxes. After sending Lourdes a thank-you text, he opened the memo app on his phone and turned on the recorder. He put the phone screen-down on the desk and partially covered it with a file from the Tavares box. It was a just-in-case move. He had no idea why people from the District Attorney's Office and his old police department were coming to see him. They had not called ahead, and he knew that could be a tactical move on their part. Bosch's relationship with the LAPD since his forced retirement two years earlier had been strained at best and his attorney had urged him to protect himself by documenting all interactions with the department.

While he waited for them, he went back to the file at hand. He was looking through statements taken in the weeks after Tavares had disappeared. He had read them before but he believed that the case files often contained the secret to cracking a cold case. It was all there if you could find it. A logic discrepancy, a hidden clue, a contradicting statement, an investigator's handwritten note in the margin of a report—all of these things had helped Bosch clear cases in a career four decades long and counting.

There were three file boxes on the Tavares case. Officially it was a missing-persons case but it had gathered three feet of stacked files over fifteen years because it was classified as such only because a body had never been found.

When Bosch came to the San Fernando Police Department two years before to volunteer his skills looking at cold case files, he had asked Chief Anthony Valdez where to start. The chief, who had been with the department twenty-five years, told him to start with Esmerelda Tavares. It was the case that haunted Valdez as an investigator, but as police chief he could not give adequate time to it.

In two years working in San Fernando part-time, Bosch had reopened several cases and closed nearly a dozen—multiple rapes and murders among them. But he came back to Esme Tavares whenever he had an hour here and there to look through the file boxes. She was beginning to haunt him too. A young mother who vanished, leaving a sleeping baby in a crib. It might be classified as a missing-persons case but Bosch didn't have to read through even the first box to know what the chief and every investigator before him knew. Esme Tavares was more than missing. She was dead.

Bosch heard the metal door to the jail wing open and then footsteps on the concrete floor that ran in front of the three group cells. He looked up through the iron bars and was surprised by who he saw.

"Hello, Harry."

It was his former partner, Lucia Soto, along with two men in suits whom Bosch didn't recognize. The fact that Soto had not let him know they were coming put Bosch on alert. It was a forty-minute drive from both the LAPD's headquarters and the D.A.'s office downtown to San Fernando. That left plenty of time to type out a text or call him up and say, "Harry, we are heading your way." But that hadn't happened, so he knew that the two men he didn't know had put the clamps on Soto.

"Lucia, long time," Bosch said. "How are you, partner?"

He stood up, deftly grabbing his phone from beneath the files on the desk and transferring it to his shirt pocket, placing the screen against his chest. He walked to the bars and stuck his hand through. He squeezed Soto's hand rather than shaking it. Her grip was tight and he took that as a message: be careful here.

It was easy for Bosch to figure out who was who between the two men. Both were in their early forties and dressed in suits that most likely came off the rack at Men's Wearhouse. But the man on the left's pin-stripes were showing wear from the inside out. Bosch knew that meant he was wearing a shoulder rig beneath the jacket and the hard edge of his weapon's slide was wearing through the fabric. Bosch guessed that the silk lining had already been chewed up. In six months the suit would be toast.

"Bob Tapscott," he said. "Lucky Lucy's partner now."

Bosch wondered if he was related to Horace Tapscott, the late South L.A. musician who had been vital in preserving the community's jazz identity.

"And I'm Alex Kennedy, deputy district attorney," said the second man. "We'd like to talk to you if you have a few minutes."

"Uh, sure," Bosch said. "Step into my office."

He gestured toward the confines of the former cell now fitted with steel shelves containing case files. There was a long communal bench left over from the cell's previous existence as a drunk tank. Bosch had files from different cases lined up to review on the bench. He started stacking them to make room for his visitors to sit.

"Actually, we talked to Captain Trevino, and he says we can use the war room over in the detective bureau," Tapscott said. "It will be more comfortable. Do you mind?"

"I don't mind if the captain doesn't mind," Bosch said. "What's this about anyway?"

"Preston Borders," Soto said.

Bosch was walking toward the open door of the cell. The name put a slight pause in his step.

"Let's wait until we're in the war room," Kennedy said quickly. "Then we can talk."

Soto gave Bosch a look that seemed to impart the message that she was under the D.A.'s thumb on this case. He stepped out of the cell, closed the metal door, and locked it with a long jail guard's key that he put in his pocket.

They left the old jail and walked through the Public Works equipment yard out to First Street. While waiting for traffic to pass, Soto spoke again, but not about the case that had brought them up to San Fernando.

"Is that really your office, Harry?" she asked. "I mean, really, a jail cell?"

"Yep," Bosch said. "That was the drunk tank and sometimes I think I can still smell the puke when I open it up in the morning. But it's where they keep the cold case files, so it's where I do my work. They store the old evidence boxes in the other two cells. Easy access all around. And usually nobody to bother me."

He hoped the implication of the last line was clear to his visitors.

"So they have no jail?" Soto asked. "They have to run bodies down to Van Nuys?"

"No, we've got a jail," Bosch said. "It's part of the station. State-of-the-art, single-man cells. I've even stayed over a few times. Beats the bunk room at the PAB, with everybody snoring."

She threw him a look as if to say he had changed if he was willing to sleep in a jail cell. He winked at her.

"I can sleep anywhere," he said.

When the traffic cleared, they crossed over to the police station and entered through the side door. The detective bureau was through the first door on the right. Bosch opened it with a key card and held the door as the others stepped in.

The bureau was no bigger than a single-car garage. At center were three workstations tightly positioned in a single module. These belonged to the unit's three full-time detectives, Danny Sisto, a recently promoted

439

detective named Oscar Luzon, and Bella Lourdes, just a month back from a lengthy injury leave. The walls of the unit were lined with file cabinets, radio chargers, and a coffee-and-printing station below bulletin boards covered in Wanted posters, work schedules, and departmental bulletins. Up high on one wall was a poster depicting the iconic Disney ducks Huey, Dewey, and Louie, which were the proud nicknames of the three detectives who worked in the module below. Captain Trevino's office was to the right and the war room was on the left. A third room was subleased to the Medical Examiner's Office and used by two coroner's investigators who covered the entire San Fernando Valley.

Bosch saw Lourdes peeking over a partition from her desk. He gave her a nod of thanks for the heads-up. It was also a sign that so far things were okay. He then led the visitors into the war room. It was a soundproof room with walls lined with white boards and flat-screen monitors. At center was a boardroom-style table with eight leather chairs around it. The room was designed to be the command post for major crime investigations, task force operations, and coordinating responses to public emergencies such as earthquakes and riots. The reality was that such incidents were rare and the room was used primarily as a lunchroom, the broad table and comfortable chairs perfect for group lunches. The room carried the distinct odor of Mexican food. The owner of Magaly's Tamales up on Maclay Avenue routinely dropped off free food for the troops and it was usually devoured in the war room.

"Have a seat," Bosch said.

Tapscott and Soto sat on one side of the table, while

Kennedy went around and sat across from them. Bosch took a chair at one end of the table so he would have angles on all three visitors.

"So, what's going on?" he said.

"Well, let's introduce ourselves," Kennedy began. "You, of course, know Detective Soto from your work together in the Open-Unsolved Unit. And now you've met Detective Tapscott. They have been working with me on a review of a homicide case you handled almost thirty years ago."

"Preston Borders," Bosch said. "How is Preston? Still on death row at Q last time I checked."

"He's still there."

"So why are you looking at the case?"

Kennedy had pulled his chair close and had his arms folded and his elbows on the table. He drum-rolled the fingers of his left hand as if deciding how to answer Bosch's question, even though it was clear that everything about this surprise visit was rehearsed.

"I am assigned to the Conviction Integrity Unit," Kennedy said. "I'm sure you've heard of it. I have used Detectives Tapscott and Soto on some of the cases I've handled because of their skill in working cold cases."

Bosch knew that the CIU was new and had been put into place after he had left the LAPD. Its forma-tion was the fulfillment of a campaign promise made during a heated election in which the policing of the police was a hot-ticket debate issue. The newly elected D.A.—Tak Kobayashi—had promised to create a unit that would respond to the seeming groundswell of cases where new forensic technologies had led to hundreds of exonerations of people imprisoned across the country.

Not only was new science leading the way, but old science once thought to be unassailable as evidence was being debunked and swinging open prison doors for the innocent.

As soon as Kennedy mentioned his assignment, Bosch put everything together and knew what was going on. Borders, the man thought to have killed three women but convicted of only one murder, was making a final grab at freedom after thirty years on death row.

"You've gotta be kidding me," Bosch said. "Borders? Really? You are seriously looking at that case?"

He looked from Kennedy to his old partner Soto.

He felt totally betrayed.

"Lucia?" he said.

"Harry," she said. "You need to listen."

2

Bosch felt like the walls of the war room were closing in on him. In his mind and in reality, he had put Borders away for good. He didn't count on the sadistic sex murderer ever getting the needle, but death row was its own particular hell, one that was still harsher than any sentence that put a man in general population. The isolation of it was what Borders deserved. He went up to San Quentin as a twenty-six-year-old man. That meant fifty-plus years of solitary confinement. Less if he got lucky. More inmates died of suicide than the needle on death row in California.

"It's not as simple as you think," Kennedy said.

"Really?" Bosch said. "Tell me why."

"The obligation of the Conviction Integrity Unit is to consider all legitimate petitions that come to it. Our review process is the first stage, and that happens in-house before they go to the LAPD or other law enforcement. When a case meets a certain threshold of concern, we go to the next step and call in law enforcement to carry out a due diligence investigation."

"And of course everyone is sworn to secrecy at that point."

Bosch looked at Soto as he said it. She looked away.

"Absolutely," Kennedy said.

"I don't know what evidence Borders or his lawyer

brought to you, but it's bullshit," Bosch said. "He murdered Danielle Skyler and everything else is a scam."

Kennedy didn't respond but from his look Bosch could tell he was surprised he still remembered the victim's name.

"Yeah, thirty years later I remember her name," Bosch said. "I also remember Donna Timmons and Vicki Novotney, the two victims we couldn't make cases on. Were they part of this due diligence you conducted?"

"Harry," Soto said, trying to calm him.

"Borders didn't bring any new evidence," Kennedy said. "It was already there."

That hit Bosch like a punch. He knew Kennedy was talking about the physical evidence from the case. The implication was that there was evidence from the crime scene or that had been collected elsewhere by Bosch that cleared Borders of the crime. The greater implication was incompetence or, worse, malfeasance—that he had missed the evidence or intentionally withheld it.

"What are we talking about here?" he asked.

"DNA," Kennedy said. "It wasn't part of the original case in 'eighty-eight. The case was prosecuted before DNA was allowed into use in criminal cases in California. It wasn't introduced and accepted by a court up in Ventura for another year. In L.A. County it was a year after that."

Kennedy nodded to Soto.

"We went to property and pulled the box," she said. "You know the routine. We took clothing collected from the victim to the lab and they put it through the serology protocol."

"They did a protocol twenty-nine years ago," Bosch

said. "But back then, they looked for ABO markers instead of DNA. And they found nothing. You're going to tell me that—"

"They found semen," Kennedy said. "It was a minute amount, but this time they found it. The process has obviously gotten more sophisticated in thirty years. And it didn't come from Borders."

Bosch shook his head.

"Okay, I'll bite," he said. "Whose was it?"

"A rapist named Lucas John Olmer," Soto said.

Bosch had never heard of Olmer. His mind went to work, looking for the scam, the fix, but not considering that he had been wrong when he closed the cuffs around Borders's wrists.

"Olmer's in San Quentin, right?" he said. "This whole thing is a—"

"No, he's not," Tapscott said. "He's dead."

"Give us a little credit, Harry," Soto added. "It's not like we went looking for it to be this way. Olmer was never in San Quentin. He died in Corcoran four years ago and he never knew Borders."

"Big surprise there," Tapscott said. "Those prisons are only three hundred miles apart."

His misplaced sarcasm gave Bosch the urge to backhand him across the mouth. Soto knew her old partner's triggers and reached over to put a hand on Bosch's arm.

"Harry, this is not your fault," she said. "This is on the lab. The reports are all there. You are right—they found nothing. They missed it back then."

Bosch looked at her and pulled his arm back.

"You really believe that?" he said. "Because I don't. This is Borders. He's behind this—somehow. I know it."

"How, Harry? We've looked for the fix in this."

"Who's been in the box since then?"

"The last person to pull the box was you. Eleven years ago, when you were working with Allingwood on Borders's final appeal. Show him the video."

She nodded to Tapscott, who pulled his phone and opened up a video. He turned the screen to Bosch.

"This is at Piper Tech," he said.

Piper Tech was where the LAPD's records and evidence property archives were located, along with the fingerprint unit. The aero squadron had the roof. Bosch knew that the integrity protocol in the archival unit was high. Sworn officers had to provide departmental ID and fingerprints to pull a case. The boxes were opened in an examination area under twenty-four-hour video surveillance. But this was Tapscott's own video, recorded on his phone.

"This was not our first go-round with CIU, so we have our own protocol," Tapscott said. "This is us opening the box. We video the whole thing. Doesn't matter that they have their own cameras down there. And as you can see, no seal is broken, no tampering."

The video showed Soto displaying the box to the camera, turning it over so that all sides and seams could be seen as intact, as well as the red tape that sealed it and was wrapped twice around it for good measure—a habit Bosch had employed for decades when archiving evidence. Soto manipulated the box in a bored manner and Bosch read that as her thinking they were wasting their time on this one. At least up until that point, Bosch still had her in his court.

Soto then used a box cutter attached by a wire to

an examination table to slice through the evidence tape and open the box. As she started removing items from the box, including the victim's clothing and an envelope containing her fingernail clippings, she called each piece of property out so it would be duly recorded.

Before the video was over, Tapscott pulled the phone back and killed the playback. He then put the phone away.

"On and on like that," he said. "Nobody fucked with the box. What was in it had been there from day one."

Bosch was silent for a long moment as he considered for the first time that his thirty-year belief that he had put a sadistic killer away for good was bogus.

"Where'd they find it?" he finally asked.

"Find what?" Kennedy asked.

"The DNA," Bosch said.

"One microdot on the victim's underwear," Kennedy said.

"Easy to have missed back in 'eighty-eight," Soto said. "They were probably just using black lights then."

Bosch nodded.

"So what happens now?" he asked.

Soto looked at Kennedy. The question was his to answer.

"There's a hearing scheduled in department one-sixteen next Wednesday," the prosecutor said. "We'll be asking Judge Houghton to vacate the sentence and release Borders from death row."

"Jesus Christ," Bosch said.

"He has a lawyer and he'll be filing a claim against the city," Kennedy continued. "We've been in contact with the City Attorney's Office. We're probably talking

447

about a settlement well into seven figures."

Bosch looked down at the table. He couldn't hold anyone's eyes.

"And I have to warn you," Kennedy said. "If a settlement is not reached and he files a claim in federal court, he can go after you personally."

Bosch nodded. He knew that already. A civil rights claim filed by Borders would leave Bosch personally responsible for damages if the city chose not to cover him. Since two years ago Bosch had sued the city to reinstate his full pension, it was unlikely that he would find a single soul in the City Attorney's Office interested in indemnifying him against damages collected by Borders. The one thought that pushed through this reality to him was of his daughter. He could have nothing but an insurance policy to leave her.

"I'm sorry," Soto said. "If there were any other . . ."

She didn't finish and he slowly brought his eyes up to hers.

"Nine days," he said.

"What do you mean?" she said.

"The hearing's in nine days. I have until then to figure out how he did it."

"Harry, we've been working this for five weeks. There's nothing. This was before Olmer was on anybody's radar. All we know is he wasn't in jail at the time and he was in L.A.—we found work records. But the DNA is the DNA. On her clothing, DNA from a man later convicted of multiple abduction-rapes. Similar to Skyler without the death. I mean, no D.A. in the world would touch this or go any other way with it."

Kennedy cleared his throat.

"We came here today out of respect for you, Detective, and all the cases you've cleared over time. We don't want to get into an adversarial position on this."

"And you don't think those cases are affected by this?" Bosch said. "You open the door to this guy and you might as well open it for every one of the people I sent away. If you put it on the lab—same thing. It taints everything."

Bosch leaned back and stared at his old partner. He had at one time been her mentor. She had to know what this was doing to him.

"It is what it is," Kennedy said. "We have an obligation. 'Better that one hundred guilty men go free than one innocent man be imprisoned.'"

"Spare me your bastardized Ben Franklin bullshit," Bosch said. "I put Borders in the vicinity of all three of those women's disappearances and your office passed on two of them, some snot-nosed prosecutor saying there was not enough. This doesn't fucking make sense. I want the nine days and I want access to everything you have and everything you've done."

He looked at Soto as he said it but Kennedy responded.

"Not going to happen, Detective," he said. "As I said, we're here as a courtesy. But you're not on this case anymore."

Before Bosch could counter, there was a sharp knock on the door and it was cracked open. Bella Lourdes stood there. She waved him out.

"Harry," she said. "We need to talk right now."

There was an urgency in her voice that Bosch could

not ignore. He looked back at the others seated at the table and started to get up.

"Hold on a second," he said. "We're not done."

He stood up and went to the door. Lourdes signaled him all the way out with her fingers. She closed the door behind him. He noticed that the squad room was empty—no one in the module, the captain's door open and his desk chair empty.

"Harry, we've got two down in a robbery at a *farmacia* on the mall."

"Two what? Officers?"

"No, people there. Behind the counter. Two one-eighty-sevens. The chief wants all hands on this. Are you okay? You want to ride with me?"

The California Penal Code designation for murder was 187. Bosch looked back at the closed door of the war room and thought about what had been said in there. What was he going to do about it? How was he going to handle it?

"Harry, come on, I gotta go. You in or out?"

Bosch looked at her.

"Okay, let's go."

They moved quickly toward the door to the lobby and the side entrance of the station. He pulled his phone out of his shirt pocket and turned off the recording app.

"What about them?" Lourdes said.

"Fuck them," Bosch said. "They'll figure it out."

3

San Fernando was a municipality barely two and a half square miles and surrounded on all sides by the city of Los Angeles. To Harry Bosch it was the proverbial needle in the haystack, the tiny place he had found when his time with the LAPD ended with him still believing he had more to give and a mission unfulfilled. Racked by budgetary shortfalls in the years that followed the 2008 recession, and having laid off a quarter of its forty officers, the Police Department actively pursued the creation of a voluntary corps of retired law officers to work in every section of the department, from patrol to communications to detectives.

When Chief Valdez reached out to Bosch and said he had an old jail cell full of cold cases and no one to work them, it was like a lifeline had been thrown to a drowning man. Bosch was alone and certainly adrift, having unceremoniously left the department he had served for almost forty years at the same time that his daughter left home for college. Most of all, the offer came at a time he felt unfinished. After all the years he had put in, he never expected to walk out the door one day at the LAPD and not be allowed back in.

At a period in their lives when most men took up golf or bought a boat, Bosch felt resolutely incomplete. He was a closer. He needed to work cases, and setting up shop as a private eye or a defense investigator wasn't going to suit him. He took the offer from the chief and soon was proving he was a closer at the SFPD. And he quickly went from part-time hours working cold cases to mentoring the entire detective bureau. Huey, Dewey, and Louie were dedicated investigators but together they had a total of less than ten years' experience as detectives. Captain Trevino was only part-time in the unit himself, responsible for supervising both the communications unit and the jail. It fell to Bosch to teach Lourdes, Sisto, and Luzon the mission.

The mall was a two-block stretch of San Fernando Road that went through the middle of town and was lined with small shops, businesses, bars, and restaurants. It was in a historic part of town and was anchored on one end by a large department store that had been closed and vacant for several years, the JC Penney sign still on the front facade. Most of the other signs were in Spanish and the businesses catered to the city's Latino majority.

It was a three-minute drive from the police station to the scene of the shooting. Lourdes drove her unmarked city car. Bosch tried his best to put the Borders case and what had been discussed in the war room behind him so that he could concentrate on the task at hand.

"So what do we know?" he asked.

"Two dead at La Farmacia Familia," Lourdes said. "Called in by a customer who went in and saw one of the victims. Patrol found the second in the back. Both employees. Looks like a father and son."

"The son an adult?"

"Yes."

"Gang affiliation?"

"No word."

"What else?"

"That's it. Gooden and Sanders headed out when we got the call. Sheriff's forensics have been called."

Gooden and Sanders were the two coroner's investigators who worked out of the sub-leased office in the detective bureau. It was a lucky break having them so close, since they would have to examine the bodies before the detectives and forensics techs could take over the scene. While Bosch had solved three cold case murders since coming to work for San Fernando, this would be the first live murder investigation, so to speak, since his arrival. The protocol and pace would be quite different.

As Lourdes turned in to the mall, Bosch looked ahead and saw that the investigation was already starting off wrong. Three patrol cars were parked directly in front of the *farmacia*, and that was too close. Traffic through the two-lane mall had not been stopped and drivers were going slowly by the business, hoping to catch a glimpse of the horrors that were inside.

"Pull in here," he said. "Those cars are too close and I'm going to move them back and shut down the street."

Lourdes did as he instructed and parked the car in front of a bar called the Tres Reyes and well behind a growing crowd of onlookers gathering near the drugstore.

Bosch and Lourdes were soon out of the car and weaving through the crowd. Yellow crime scene tape had been strung between the patrol cars, and two officers stood conferring by the trunk of one car while another stood with his hands on his belt buckle, watching the front door of the *farmacia*.

Bosch saw Chief Valdez standing near the open front door of the store with Sisto and Luzon. It appeared that they were waiting for the all-clear from the coroner's investigators before entering the crime scene. That was the only good thing Bosch had seen so far. He gave a short, low whistle that drew their attention and then spun a finger in the air to signal he wanted to group everybody into a meeting.

Everyone gathered between two of the patrol cars. Bosch looked at Valdez and waited for the chief to give him the nod to take charge.

"Okay, we need to protect the crime scene a lot better than this," he began. "Patrol, I want you guys to move your cars out and to shut down this block on either end. Tape it up. Nobody comes in without authorization. I then want clipboards on either end, and you write down the name of every cop or lab rat that comes into the crime scene. You write down the license-plate number of every car you let out too."

Nobody moved.

"You heard him," Valdez said. "Let's move it, people. We've got two citizens on the floor in there. We need to do right by them."

The patrol officers moved quickly to their cars to carry out Bosch's orders. That left him with the chief and the three detectives as the black-and-whites backed out on either side of them. Bosch once more looked at Valdez for confirmation of his authority, because he didn't expect his next moves to go over well.

"I still have this, Chief?" he asked.

"All yours, Harry," Valdez said. "How do you want to do it?"

"Okay, we want to limit people inside," Bosch said. "That's going to be Lourdes and me. Sisto and Luzon, I want you going down the street in both directions. We're looking for witnesses and cameras. We—"

"We got here first," Luzon said. "It should be our case."

At about forty, Luzon was the oldest of the three investigators, but he had the least experience as a detective. He was moved into the unit six months ago after twelve years in patrol. He had gotten the promotion to fill the void left by Lourdes's leave of absence and then Valdez found the money in the budget to keep him on board at a time when there was a spike in property crimes attributed to a local gang called the SanFers.

"That's not how it works," Bosch said. "Lourdes is going to be lead. I need you two to go two blocks in both directions. We're looking for the getaway vehicle. We need video and I need you guys to go find it."

Bosch could see Luzon fighting back the urge to again argue Bosch's orders. But he looked at the chief and saw no indication that the man ultimately in charge disagreed with Bosch.

"You got it," he said.

He headed in one direction while Sisto headed off in the other. Sisto did not complain.

"Take down plates and phone numbers," Bosch called to them.

"Harry," Valdez said. "Let's talk for a second."

He stepped away from Lourdes and Bosch followed. The chief spoke quietly.

"Look, I get what you're doing with those two. But I want you on lead. Bella's good but this is what you do."

"I get that, Chief. But you don't want me. We have to think about when this gets into court. You don't want a part-timer on lead. You want Bella. They try character assassination on her, and she'll eat their lunch after what happened last year and then her coming back to the job. On top of that, she's good and she's ready for this. And besides, I may have some problems coming up soon from downtown. You don't want me on lead."

Valdez looked at him. He knew that "downtown" meant from outside the SFPD, from Bosch's past.

"We'll have to talk about that later," he said. "So where do you want me?"

"Media relations," Bosch said. "They'll get wind of this soon enough and will start showing up. 'The little town with a murder problem'—it'll be a story. You need to set up a command post and corral them. That and see if you can get more bodies from patrol to come in and help with the canvass. There were people in all of these shops. Somebody saw something."

"You got it. What if I can get Penney's to open up and we use that as the CP? I know the guy who owns the building."

Bosch looked across the street and down half a block at the facade of the long-closed department store.

"If you can get lights on in there, go for it. What about Captain Trevino? Is he around?"

"I have him covering the shop while I was here. You need him?"

"No, I can fill him in on things later."

The chief headed off and Lourdes came up to Bosch.

"Let me guess, he didn't want me as lead," she said.

"He wanted me," Bosch said. "But it was no reflection on you. I said no. I said it was your case."

"Does that have something to do with the three visitors you had this morning?"

"Maybe. Why don't you stick your head inside and see how Gooden and Sanders are doing? I want to know when we're going to get in there. I'll call the sheriff's lab and get an ETA."

"Roger that."

Lourdes headed toward the door of the *farmacia* and Bosch pulled his phone. The SFPD was so small, it did not have its own forensics team. It used the Sheriff's Department unit and that often put it in second position for services. Bosch called the liaison at the lab and was told a team was on the road to San Fernando as they spoke. Bosch reminded the liaison that they were working a double murder and asked for a second team, but he was denied that request. He was told there wasn't a second team to spare.

As he hung up, he noticed one of the patrol officers he had given orders to earlier standing at the new crime scene perimeter at the end of the block. Yellow tape had been strung completely across, closing the road through the mall. The patrol officer had his hands on his belt buckle and was watching Bosch.

Bosch put his phone away and walked up the street to the yellow tape and the officer manning it.

"Don't look in," Bosch said. "Look out."

"What?" the officer asked.

"You're watching the detectives. You should be watching the street."

Bosch put his hand on the officer's shoulder and turned him toward the tape.

"Look outward from a crime scene. Look for people watching, people who don't fit. You'd be surprised how many times the doer comes back to watch the investigation. Anyway, you're protecting the crime scene, not watching like one of these looky-loos. Got it?"

"Got it."

"Good."

The forensic team of two evidence technicians arrived shortly after that, and it was another thirty minutes before Bosch, Lourdes, and the team entered the farmacia to go to work. They wore gloves and paper booties. As he entered behind Lourdes, Bosch leaned forward and whispered.

"Make sure you take time just to observe."

"Okay."

When Bosch was a young homicide detective, he worked with a partner named Frankie Sheehan, who always kept an old milk crate in the trunk of their unmarked car. He'd carry it into every scene, find a good vantage point, and put the crate down. Then he'd sit on it and just observe the scene, studying its nuances and trying to take the measure and motive of the violence that had occurred there. Sheehan had worked the Danielle Skyler case with Bosch and had sat on his crate in the corner of the room where the body was strewn nude and viciously violated on the floor. But Sheehan was long dead now and would not be taking the free fall awaiting Bosch.

4

La Farmacia Familia was a small operation that appeared to Bosch to rely mostly on the business of filling prescriptions. In the front section of the store, there were three short aisles of shelved retail items relating to home remedies and care, almost all of it in Spanish-language boxes imported from Mexico. There were no racks of greeting cards or point-ofpurchase candy displays. There was no cold case stocked with sodas and water. The business was nothing like the chain pharmacies scattered across the city.

The entire back wall of the store was the actual pharmacy, where there was a counter that fronted the storage area of medicines and a work area for filling prescriptions. The front section of the store seemed completely untouched by the crime that had occurred here. Bosch moved down an aisle to the left, which brought him to a half door leading to the rear of the pharmacy counter. Immediately he saw blood spatter on the white plastic drawers behind the counter. He then saw Gooden squatting behind the counter next to the first body. It was a man on his back, his hands up and palms out by his shoulders. He was wearing a white pharmacist's jacket with a name embroidered on it.

"Harry, meet José," Gooden said. "At least he's José

until we confirm it with fingerprints. Through and through gunshot to the chest."

He formed a gun with his thumb and finger as he gave the report and pointed the barrel against his chest.

"We're talking point-blank," he added. "Maybe six to twelve inches. Guy probably had his hands up and they still shot him."

Bosch didn't say anything. He was in observation mode. He would form his own impressions about the scene and determine if the victim's hands were up or down when he was shot. He didn't need that information from Gooden.

He moved into a hallway to the left and came up behind Lourdes. The passageway led to the work and storage areas and a restroom. There was a door marked Exit that presumably led to a back alley. In the hallway, Sanders, the second coroner's tech, was on his knees next to a second body, also a male. He wore a pale blue pharmacist's coat. He was facedown, one arm reaching out toward the door. There were blood smears on the floor, leading to the body. Lourdes walked down the side edge of the hallway, careful not to step in the blood.

"And here we have José Jr.," Sanders said. "We have three points of impact: the back, the rectum, the head—most likely in that order."

Bosch stepped away from Lourdes and crossed over the blood smears to the other side of the hallway so he could get an unobstructed view of the body. José Jr. was lying with his right cheek against the floor. He looked like he was in his midtwenties, a meager growth of whiskers on his chin.

The blood and bullet wounds told the tale. At the first sign of trouble, José Jr. had made a break for the rear door, running for his life down the hallway. He was knocked down with the first shot to the upper back. On the floor, he turned to look behind him, spilling his blood on the floor. He saw the shooter coming and turned to try to crawl toward the door. The shooter had come up and shot him again, this time in the rectum, then stepped up and ended it with the shot to the back of the head.

Bosch had seen the rectum shot in prior cases, and it drew his attention.

"The shot up the pipe—how close?" he asked.

Sanders reached over and used one gloved hand to pull the seat of the victim's pants out and taut so the bullet entry could be clearly seen. With the other hand he pointed to where the cloth had been burned.

"He got up in there," Sanders said. "Point-blank."

Bosch nodded. His eyes tracked up to the wounds on the back and head. It appeared to him that the two entrance wounds he could see were neater and smaller than the one shot to José Sr.'s chest.

"You thinking two different weapons?" he asked.

Sanders nodded.

"If I were betting," he said.

Bosch nodded in reply.

"Okay, do what you have to do," he said.

He carefully stepped back down the hallway and moved into the pharmacy's work and drug-storage area. He started by looking up and immediately saw the camera mounted in the corner of the ceiling over the door.

Lourdes entered the room behind him. He pointed up and she saw the camera.

"Need the feed," he said. "Hopefully off-site or to a web-site."

"I can check that," she said.

Bosch surveyed the room. Several of the drawers where stores of pills were kept were pulled out and dropped to the floor, and loose pills were scattered across it. He knew the difficult task of inventorying what had been in the pharmacy and what was taken lay ahead. Some of the drawers on the floor were larger than others and he guessed that they had contained more commonly prescribed drugs.

On the worktable, there was a computer. There were also tools for measuring out and bottling pills in plastic vials as well as a label printer.

"Let's get the photographer in here before we start stepping on pills and crunching them," he said.

"I'll go get him," Lourdes said.

After Lourdes went out, Bosch moved into the hallway again. He knew they would be here until late into the night. The whole place needed to be photographed and videoed, and then the forensics team would gather and document every pill and piece of evidence in the place. A homicide case moved slowly from the center out.

In the old days he would have stepped out at this point to smoke a cigarette and contemplate things. This time he went out through the front door to just think. Almost immediately his phone vibrated in his pocket. The caller ID was blocked.

"That wasn't cool, Harry," Lucia Soto said when he answered.

"Sorry, we had an emergency," he said. "Had to go."

"You could have told us. I'm not your enemy on this. I'm trying to run interference for you."

"Are they with you right now?"

"No, of course not. This is just you and me."

"Can you get me a copy of the report you turned in to Kennedy?"

"Harry . . ."

"I thought so. Lucia, don't say you're on my side, running interference for me if you're not. You know what I mean?"

"That's not fair and you know it."

"Look, I'm in the middle of things here. Give me a call back if you change your mind. I remember there was a case that meant a lot to you once. We were partners and I was right there for you. I guess things are different now."

He disconnected. He felt a pang of guilt. He was being heavy-handed with Soto but felt he needed to push her toward giving him what he needed. He dropped the thought when he saw Lourdes walking up with a troubled look on her face.

"What's wrong?"

"I came out and Garrison signaled me over to the tape. He had the wife and mother there and she was hysterical. I just put her in a car and they're taking her to the station."

Bosch nodded. It was a good move.

"You up for talking with her?" he asked. "We can't leave her over there too long."

"I don't know," Lourdes said. "I just ruined her life. Everything that's important to her is suddenly gone."

"I know, but you have to establish rapport. You never know, this case could go on for years. She's going to need to trust the person carrying it and it shouldn't be me."

"Okay, I can do it."

"Focus on the son. His friends, what he did when he wasn't working, enemies, all of that stuff. Find out where he lived, whether he had a girlfriend. And ask her if José Sr. was having any problems with him at work. The son is going to be the key to this."

"You get all that from a shot up the ass?"

Bosch nodded.

"I've seen it before. On a case where we talked to a profiler. It's an angry shot. It has payback written all over it."

"He knew the shooters?"

"No doubt. Either he knew them or they knew him."